BREAKING THE RULES

"While it may not appear so, someone in Washington is quite concerned about this little scenario over here. Enough so that they've taken two submarines off nuclear deterrence patrol and assigned them to this area of the world." The admiral's face looked grim. "This *will* work, I assure you."

"And if it doesn't?" Bailey asked.

The admiral's face took on a hard sheen. "That option is not acceptable. Another very bloody conflict on land will touch every nation in the world. If politics prevents our leaders from confronting this threat openly, then we do what we can."

"Regardless of orders."

RITES OF WAR

C.A. MOBLEY

JOVE BOOKS, NEW YORK

RITES OF WAR

A Jove Book / published by arrangement with
the author

PRINTING HISTORY
Jove edition / February 1998

The Putnam Berkley World Wide Web site address is
http://www.berkley.com

ISBN: 0-515-12225-4

A JOVE BOOK®
Jove Books are published by The Berkley Publishing Group,
a member of Penguin Putnam Inc.,
200 Madison Avenue, New York, New York 10016.
JOVE and the "J" design are trademarks belonging to
Jove Publications, Inc.

PRINTED IN THE UNITED STATES OF AMERICA

10 9 8 7 6 5 4 3 2 1

RITES
OF
WAR

PART

I

WARS AND RUMORS OF WARS

Fundamentally, the part of the submarine in naval tactics is to operate alone, in accordance with its character and its principal task of carrying out, unseen, its annihilating attack on an adversary of considerably superior fighting strength.

—*THE U-BOAT COMMANDER'S HANDBOOK*
Section I.A.12 (1943)
(translated by U.S. Navy)

1

---

17 NOVEMBER 2001:
THE YELLOW SEA

DPRK SUBMARINE 12

Captain Kanko had no reason to suspect his submarine was in danger. The Korean Romeo-class diesel boat lurched from crest to trough like a drunken pig, sucking down air through her snorkel mast, running her engines at high rpm, and recharging her massive bank of batteries. Uncomfortable, running on the surface in rough seas, but hardly dangerous.

The twenty-year-old submarine had only rudimentary sensors and fire-control systems, but she was sturdy and seaworthy. Five hours out of port, thirty miles west of Korea, she was in the familiar waters of the Yellow Sea. She was returning to port for resupply after two weeks of surveillance on the American battle group conducting amphibious operations off the coast of South Korea.

Forty minutes earlier, Captain Kanko had yielded to the inevitable. A winter storm had made recharging the batteries at snorkel depth impractical. Each time the sea washed over the buoyant flotation ball in the snorkel mast, the diesel sucked air from the interior of the boat, creating an ear-popping pressure drop inside the boat and stalling the engine. He'd finally surfaced the boat, given up on staying on course and settled simply for keeping her bow pointed into the rough seas and the snorkel mast above the waves.

The batteries were now fully charged. And none too soon. Half of the control room crew was already retching from seasickness. He grimaced, trying to ignore the sounds and smells.

The Romeo barreled headlong down into the depths without so much as a worried look at the water below her. One minute after submerging, as she passed the fifty-meter mark, the first active sonar pulse rang her hull like a bell. That was her first hint that she was not alone in the sea. The spiraling acoustic signature of a torpedo followed seconds later.

With all of her kinetic energy committed to her oblivious dive, the Romeo didn't have a chance to maneuver. The torpedo caught her on the forward quarter, killing the control room crew instantly, then blazing a trail through the ship for tons of foaming ocean. Frigid seawater filled the forward half of the boat, dragging her bow down.

Two engineers in the battery compartment had time to dog down the hatch before the water reached them. One of them was crushed as the metal battery frame broke loose from the deck and slid forward. The other scrambled back against the far bulkhead for something solid to hold on to, screaming, knowing already it was too late.

As the forward part of the submarine twisted and warped, the battery room hatch sprung loose from its waterproofing gasket. Seawater followed, forming chlorine gas as it churned the battery acid spilling across the deck. The second man died.

Farther aft, cold water on hot engines finished what the torpedo's warhead started. The diesel engines splintered and cracked, shredding the rest of the crew members before they could drown.

U-504

The sea was rarely silent and never entirely safe. *Kapitan* Karl Merker kept his palm pressed flat against the submarine's sonar speaker. The thin-gauge metal quivered under his skin. The broad spectrum noise of the Romeo's diesel engines was gone, replaced by short, fat blips of transient noise, hard pops, and groans of old metal taking the men inside it below the surface of the ocean for the last time.

Four thousand meters south and one hundred meters below the Romeo, *U-504* slipped quietly through the ocean. Shock-mounted, closed-cycle engineering allowed the German boat to run her diesel engines while submerged, freeing her from the need to come shallow and snorkel. Running on battery power as she was now, the Type 215 submarine was a ghost.

Ancient metal cracking, another explosion. The last sounds of the Romeo breaking up, then the normal sounds of the sea. Then rasps from merchant ship propeller shafts, *chirrs* of shrimp, and the dark counterpoint of distant sound-suppressed military vessels. A drilling rig hammered away in the background, adding noise across the entire spectrum. The chattering complex waveform of sound flooded the submarine's small control center.

Touching the speaker was Merker's own daily ritual, a private reminder of what was outside their thin hull. On long deployments, men caught up in the endless cycle of watches, meals, and sleep began to see the U-boat's narrow passageways and equipment-packed compartments as a self-contained, invulnerable world. It wasn't, and would never be. The Romeo's captain had known that in his last moments.

Even if the Korean diesel boat had possessed advanced passive and active sensors, noise suppression and counter-detection equipment, her self-noise would have blinded her.

Not that the Romeo could have detected this U-boat on her best day.

No one could.

Merker glanced over at his executive officer, Frederick Kraeken, who was poised at the bottom of the ladder that led to the conning tower, an automatic weapon cradled in his arms. Three enlisted men similarly armed clustered around him, crowding the cramped command center. "You heard it—she had no warning. No one could have made it out alive."

"Our orders say no survivors." A dark flush spread up under Kraeken's skin from his throat to broad, flat cheekbones, almost black under the red lights of the control room. The XO's eyes seemed to catch shards of the ambient light, concentrating them into blue sparks.

"No. Stow your gear and return to your stations," Merker said.

"But the—"

"*No*. It is *not* operationally necessary." Merker turned back to the officer of the deck, the OOD. "Find the Americans."

Merker turned back to the plotting table and stared down at the track lightly penciled on the tracing paper. On the opposite side of the chart, the navigator, *Leutnant dur See* Ehrlich, was meticulously inking in a red *X* to mark the Korean submarine's grave.

"Sunset?" Merker asked.

"In ten minutes, *Kapitan*."

"Good." He straightened and stretched, hearing the small bones in his spine crack and complain. A long day, and one that wasn't over yet. Years from now, he'd probably forget the seeping weariness that was creeping into his mind, the result of too many hours without sleep. All that would remain would be the memory of his first kill. He grimaced. It was different from what he'd anticipated.

Earlier that morning, he'd studied his face carefully in the small mirror in his cabin, wondering if the next twenty-four hours would mark him in some way. His hair, almost colorless under the fluorescent lightbulbs, had grown slightly too long and curled uncomfortably under his collar, and his eyes were unexpectedly dark and thoughtful in an otherwise classic Aryan face. His beard was full and thick, a shade darker than his hair.

He rubbed one cheek thoughtfully, considered shaving the beard as a rite of passage. From what he could see of his ghostly green reflection in the sonar screen, there was no magic to first blood, no visible tattoo of a warrior.

He understood now what the old World War II U-boat captains had left unsaid in their diaries. The fear, the urgent compulsion to get away from the scene of the attack overrode everything else. The final emotion was not triumph, but sickening relief that nothing had gone wrong and gratitude that the hours of waiting to attack were over. It was not a reaction that could have been explained—or justified—in the company of other warriors. Nor a trait that any man wanted to show on his face.

Merker measured off the space between the coast and their position with his fingers, looked across at the navigator, and pointed at the overhead. The young *Leutnant dur See,* already inculcated into the traditions of silence that marked the routines of a submarine, nodded enthusiastically instead of speaking.

Merker sighed. The navigator was still too inexperienced to anticipate what was to come. A mild winter storm was a sickening roller coaster for a submarine at periscope depth. In the close confines of a submarine, queasiness and headaches would bloom into a virulent seasickness far more contagious than the milder strains suffered by deep-draft surface ships. One stifled retch, and in seconds the entire crew would be puking.

There was no help for it, though. According to the last message they'd received, they should be within hunting distance of the American forces.

"Periscope depth," he ordered quietly. He reached for a package of dry crackers as insurance against the rough weather.

Thirty minutes later, Merker's palms were rubbed raw from rasping on the line-wrapped stabilizer bar running overhead. Barely submerged, *U-504* rolled and lurched in the heavy seas. Her rounded hull was built for fast, silent running out of reach of the surface, not stability at the alien boundary between air and water. He felt a fleeting surge of sympathy for the Korean submarine commander who'd had to endure this in his final hours.

Still, along with the darkness, foul weather provided some measure of safety for the submarine and her nearly retching crew. The wind-lashed waves hid her periscope from any casual observers wandering the rain-soaked decks of the warship and generated enough ambient noise to hide the U-boat from the passive sonars on board the ships. It would have been better had the night been moonless, but the operation couldn't be delayed until the lunar cycle.

The angle to port on the deck decreased slightly. He waited for a moment, timing his command to coincide with the point in the roll at which the deck was almost level.

"Up periscope."

The silver column slid up from the deck noiselessly. In one fluid motion, Merker released the overhead bar, crouched, and pulled the black plastic handles down from their recessed slots in the rising cylinder. As soon as the periscope cleared the waves, he spun it around quickly, surveying 360 degrees. Two video monitors, one in the control center and one in sonar, were slaved to the periscope.

One second: The American amphibious ship USS *Wasp* filled the scope, nailed to the monitor by the crosshairs and silhouetted by the sun setting behind her.

Two seconds: A frigate, the USS *Lewis B. Puller,* followed 40 degrees later by the boxy profile of an Aegis cruiser. He envied their fore-and-aft pitch in the waves, a sharp contrast to the sickening yaw and roll of the submarine's round hull.

"Down scope!" Merker reached for the overhead bar again and glanced at the figures in the lower right-hand corner of the monitor. Total exposure, three seconds. A good time—not an excellent one, but still acceptable under these conditions.

Wasp was only five thousand meters away, well within torpedo range. He concentrated on the details of the attack, trying to ignore his churning stomach. To be ill now—no, unacceptable. Too much depended on the next ten minutes, not the least of which was the survival of this boat and its crew.

This time it would be different. The Romeo—well, what had there been to see except green lines and blots on the sonar screen? This time he would watch the ship shiver as the torpedo plowed into her, see flames burst suddenly from one small spot to run up the superstructure and down the sides of the ship. The crew would drop into the cold ocean like ants into beer, desperate to escape before the sea claimed their ship. There would be time—a few seconds, perhaps, but enough—to enjoy the final exultation of the kill.

The amphibious ship was so large that tactical elegance was hardly required for the attack approach. Nor was a killing shot necessary.

Indeed, it made little difference whether the *Wasp* was hit at all.

USS *WASP*

On board *Wasp,* most of the crew was lined up for the evening meal. While all combat systems and watch stations were manned, the ship was secured from daily routine. On the bridge, duty section three was waiting impatiently for section one to finish chow and relieve them.

Petty Officer Pratt traded a look of disgust with the boatswain's mate of the watch (BMOW), then looked down at the chart spread across the quartermaster's table. He picked up a pencil and pretended to work on the dead reckoning course laid out for the ship. Of all the watch sections on the ship, Pratt hated this one the most.

Suddenly the bridge seemed confining. He picked up a pad of forms and strolled over to the starboard hatch that let out onto the bridge wing.

"Time for your coffee break?" the OOD asked.

"Weather observations, sir." He held up the pad, fairly confident that the officer wouldn't remember when he'd last been out on the bridge wing.

"Very well," the OOD said perfunctorily. "Go ahead."

"Aye, aye, sir," Pratt said. A little too loudly, the tiniest bit over the line. His tone earned him a sharp look from the junior officer of the deck, the JOOD, but the OOD appeared not to notice.

Pratt swung the long lever that dogged the hatch down and shoved the heavy metal door out. He kept one hand on the metal bracket door handle to prevent the wind from slamming it back against the skin of the ship.

The wind tore at the pad, ruffling the sheets back over his hand. He leaned back against the steel hatch, holding it in place while he dogged it shut.

He peered out at the sea, estimating the height and direction of the waves, thanking his luck that he wasn't assigned to the frigate or the cruiser. Both plowed through the waves, taking green water across their weatherdecks, their bridges obscured occasionally by flumes of spray.

Sea state four, Pratt decided, cumulus clouds with tops at least forty thousand feet. Forty knots of wind. He'd get the barometer readings and the exact wind speed when he went back inside. Converting the readings from the anemometer mounted high on the ship's mast from relative readings to true wind would kill another ten seconds of the watch.

Pratt muttered a quiet oath at the sea and sailors in general, and the bridge crew of the *Wasp* in particular.

U-504

The last digit on the clock over the navigator's plotting table flickered, then rearranged itself into the next higher number. "Two minutes," the navigator murmured, his voice carrying throughout the silent compartment. Half an hour earlier, the weapons stations had opened the outer doors to the torpedo tubes and flooded the chambers.

"One thousand meters," sonar announced quietly.

"Very well," Merker acknowledged. The ship pinned in the crosshairs of his periscope was partially obscured by mist and rain, although her size and flat deck made the identification easy. He tweaked the handle, sharpening the image, and waited impatiently for the feeling of anticipation. But moments from firing, his mind insisted on noticing the pain in his hands and a cramp creeping into his left foot.

"Fire one. Fire two," he ordered. The submarine shivered as high-pressure compressed air blew the torpedoes out of the tubes. He heard one sonarman mutter an oath at the noise the air bubbles made.

"On straight run," sonar reported.

At fifty knots, the torpedo could cover the distance to the *Wasp* in a little less than five minutes, but *U-504* had less time than that. Sound traveled faster than any undersea weapon could, almost fifty miles every minute. Within seconds, the high-pitched whine of the torpedo propeller would reach the sonarmen on the other ships. *U-504* had just ripped off her own cloak of invisibility as surely as if she'd surfaced in front of the battle group.

"Make your depth fifty meters, speed twenty knots," Merker ordered.

USS *WASP*

Pratt pressed his back against the superstructure. The wind was coming from the other side of *Wasp*, and the metal shell that contained the bridge carved a dry spot out of the storm on the leeward side of the bridge.

Even with nasty weather, the natural climate was preferable to the squalls inside the bridge. He stared out at the churning water and wondered why he'd ever left Tennessee.

The rain stopped for a moment, and something caught his attention. A narrow streak of disturbed water, the foamed wake barely visible against the thrashing sea. He stared at it, trying to decide what peculiar combination of wind and weather could have produced a trail that looked so much like—oh, *Jesus.*

He yanked the heavy hatch open and shouted, "Torpedo! I saw a torpedo wake, starboard—" The blare of the sonar warning buzzer cut him off.

"Torpedo starboard side, three thousand yards!" a sonarman screamed over the circuit.

The OOD stared at Pratt for a second, as though he'd seen a ghost. "No," he said softly. Remembering his duty, he snapped, "Hard left rudder, all ahead flank! Boats, the collision alarm! No time for general quarters."

The massive amphibious ship responded slowly to maximum rudder and heeled slightly into the driving wind and rain. Pratt saw *Puller* start to turn toward them.

He heard a small noise. The ship shuddered slightly, as though taking a rogue wave at a bad angle. For a moment, he was convinced the torpedo had missed.

The deck shot up from under his feet and the ship rolled

hard to port. The motion catapulted Pratt fifteen feet across the bridge and pinned him against the glass window four feet above the deck. Loose pencils, plotting tools, and books pelted his back. Pratt stared down at black water, closer to the bridge than it had any right to be.

A body slammed into the glass beside him, then slid down, held against the bulkhead by the roll of the ship. Suspended between air and water, Pratt saw the OOD crumpled beside him, blood streaming down his face.

The ship hung at an angle, hesitating, as though deciding whether her metacentric height would permit her to do anything besides continue her arc down toward the sea. Pratt started praying, aware that the deck behind him was slanted too much for him to clamber away from the ocean.

The angle on the deck decreased almost imperceptibly at first. *Wasp* rocked first to starboard, then back to port. Every time she started to settle back down into her natural orientation to the water, a secondary explosion shook the ship.

Pratt slid down to the deck and started crawling toward his plotting table. The OOD lay motionless on the deck, and the boatswain's mate was struggling to his feet and reaching for the 1MC mike. The JOOD—Pratt finally spotted him draped over the SPA-25 radar repeater, his forehead and cheeks slicked with blood from a gash on his forehead but still conscious.

"General quarters, general quarters," the JOOD rasped before he slid off the repeater and onto the deck.

Pratt heard *Puller* order off a torpedo before his vision faded away. He crumpled unconscious on the deck moments later.

U-504

The submarine dove steeply through the thermocline. Even though her deck was pitched downward, the three-axis motion died out within moments of submerging. Merker breathed a sigh of relief when he was finally able to release the overhead support bar. His nausea faded to a background sensation of discomfort. All that remained was to escape.

"Torpedo inbound!" the sonarman said.

The frigate, it had to be. He'd thought he'd be more afraid at this moment than any other, but the strength of adrenaline and his survival instinct blanked out everything except the need to escape. His training overrode his emotions, and he assessed the incoming torpedo for what it was—a desperate blind shot down the line of bearing of U-504's torpedo. It was intended to panic the submarine—him—into making a mistake.

"Classification?" he said, the question cut off by the answer from sonar.

"Acoustic! Speed, thirty knots!"

"Decoys. Make your depth one hundred meters. Hard left rudder," he ordered automatically. A hard turn coupled with a speed and depth change would create a churning mass of bubbles in the water, what submariners called a knuckle. He glanced at the equipment status board, checking to make sure the sophisticated noise cancellation electronics were still on-line. Sea trials in their home waters had consistently proved that a torpedo would either home in on the decoys, specially crafted devices that mimicked the acoustic sounds of a submarine, or fail to acquire any target at all.

Four months ago, when they'd left German waters, he would have been reluctant to bet his life on those systems. Now he had no choice.

Merker heard Ehrlich mutter a frightened prayer. He spared an instant to glare at the younger officer, then fixed his gaze back on the instrument board. Green lights, green lights, green—he kept up his scan, trying to keep his attention on every single indicator at once.

U-504's deck pitched down thirty-eight degrees, as steep a descent angle as she dared. The narrow boundary beneath the ocean's acoustic layers was her safe haven. Deeper, and her sound would radiate farther to sonobuoys or a ship's array dangling below the layer. Shallow was equally dangerous. The region between acoustic layers provided the best chance of masking her high-speed dash away from the American ships.

The acoustic counterdetection equipment should be de-

tecting the active sonar signals assaulting the hull and generating a signal exactly out of phase with the sonar. If it
worked as advertised, it would cancel out the acoustic energy that should have been reflected off the submarine back
to the searching surface ship.

"Torpedo has acquired the decoy," sonar reported.

Close, too close! "Flank speed," he ordered. If the torpedo exploded on the decoy at this range, the resulting pressure wave could do serious damage to the submarine.

"Cavitating," sonar warned. Shallow depth and high
speed created areas of low pressure behind each blade of
the propeller. Air dissolved in the seawater leeched out and
formed bubbles that streamed out behind each blade. As
the propeller turned, the area of low pressure moved, and
the bubbles collapsed, generating detectable noise.

"Explosion!" the sonarman screamed. Seconds later, the
deck careened down and the submarine shook violently as
her stern shot upward on the leading edge of the pressure
wave. Merker hung on to the overhead bar and waited,
dangling from his bleeding palms. Just as abruptly, the bow
moved up. A few minutes later, the shaken planesman had
the bow tipped down again, executing the last order given.

"Still cavitating," sonar reported.

Merker shook his head. Cavitation was the least of his
worries during depth changes. The thin hull popped and
groaned like a tin roof in a hailstorm from the changing
pressure gradient on the hull. Water rushing over the limber
holes on the hull also caused highly detectable flow tones,
as did the hydraulic systems operating the diving controls.

"All stations, report status," he ordered. Terse replies
crowded the sound-powered phone circuit. A small leak
around the main shaft bearing, a few bruises, and one broken arm. *U-504* had suffered no major damage, although
the leak on the bearing would need close watching.

Three minutes later, the deck leveled off and the transient
mechanical noises stopped. "Fifty meters, sir," the planesman announced.

He acknowledged the report. Even at depth, they were
far from safe yet. He debated briefly decreasing his speed
to eliminate the final acoustic beacons to a passive sonar,

the churning propeller and the electric motor that drove it, and decided against it. Since the earliest days of German submarine operations, speed had always proved to be the most effective tactic in escaping, and the propeller design they'd pirated from the British Swiftsure-class submarine was far quieter than a standard propeller, more like a small jet engine. Twenty-four blades instead of the standard four to seven, with thirty stators guiding the flow of water over them, produced an exceptionally low turns-per-knot ratio. Fewer rotations of the central shaft per knot of speed meant less noise.

Once they'd cleared the area, they'd drop down to five knots and become a virtual black hole in the ocean. He looked at the clock over Ehrlich's table, then snapped his fingers at the chart and pointed at the navigator. Ehrlich started, then picked up his pencil, his face still pale and his fingers shaking slightly. Merker ignored him.

Six minutes since the attack, a little less than thirteen hundred meters from their firing location. With any luck, it would take the helicopters at least ten minutes to launch. In another twelve minutes, *U-504* would be almost four thousand meters from the ships.

USS *PULLER*

The frigate snapped off another torpedo down the line of attack and then hesitated, torn between chasing the sub and standing by to rescue the *Wasp*'s crew. Her active sonar was holding solid contact on both the decoy and the submarine. The decoy grew louder and closer, and the submarine faded off the scope. After a hurried conversation with the one officer still conscious in *Wasp*'s combat direction center, the frigate turned into the wind to launch her SH-60F helicopter.

"Chip light," the tactical action officer announced.

Puller's captain groaned. The small magnetic detector in the helicopter's compressor casing thought it had found slivers of metal in the oil sump. "How long?"

"Five minutes, the pilot says," the TAO replied.

The captain nodded, stifling his next question. It usually

took the helicopter at least twenty minutes to check the
sensing probe, drain the oil, and inspect for internal damage
to clear a chip light gripe. Shortcuts—he didn't want to
know.

"Tail depth?" he asked instead.

"Sixty feet. We'd like to slow down, get it below the
layer." The frigate controlled the deployed depth of its passive sonar array by varying its own ship's speed.

"Do it. That's where I'd be, if I were her. Or in the
layer."

The TAO murmured into his headset. Almost immediately, the captain felt the deck shift slightly as the frigate
dropped her speed. The small ship was superbly responsive
to the two aircraft jet engines that drove her propeller.

"Status on the helo?" he asked.

"Requesting we put some speed back on to get some
more wind over the deck, and asking for a green deck,"
the TAO responded.

"Get them their wind and get 'em airborne."

Two minutes later, he heard the roar of the helicopter
crescendo, then deepen. He glanced at the closed-circuit TV
next to the blue tactical screen. The Seahawk lifted off the
deck, wobbled, then gained altitude and veered away from
the ship.

U-504

"Elapsed time, twenty-five minutes," the navigator announced.

"Sonar, report all contacts," Merker demanded.

"Active sonar, bearing two-five-zero, range seven thousand meters, probable Perry-class frigate. Omnidirectional—
she doesn't have us, sir."

"Is she maneuvering?"

"She made one turn fifteen minutes ago, probably to
launch aircraft. We picked up a helicopter right after that."

Merker nodded. Every minute that went by increased the
area the helicopter would have to search.

"Five knots," he ordered.

Two hours later, Merker finally drew in a deep breath.

There was no indication that they'd been detected, and every minute that passed increased the margin of safety. He let himself relax, and took a sip from a cup of cold coffee.

He knew the moment he swallowed it that it was his first mistake of the day. The few minutes spent at periscope depth had taken their toll on his inner ear. Seasickness could be delayed indefinitely by the judicious consumption of crackers and antiemetics, but the slightest deviation from preventive measures brings immediate and disastrous results.

Merker left the command center abruptly and sought the relative privacy of his cabin immediately aft of the spaces. He slammed the sliding door shut, grabbed a pillow, and bolted for the toilet. Cupping the pillow around the back of his head and pulling the edges down to touch the sides of the toilet to muffle the sounds, he gave in to the only sure and certain cure.

USS *WASP*

The senior quartermaster took the pencil out of Pratt's hand and gently shoved him back into the corner behind the plotting table. The BMOW had slapped a piece of gauze and a strip of tape over the cut above Pratt's eye—for now, that would do. Pratt stared at the chart, wishing that the lines and position marks would come into focus.

"Captain's on the bridge," the boatswain announced. Pratt squirmed until he got his back against the starboard bulkhead and squinted at the hatch. His neck was starting to hurt too much to turn his head. A chill water pipe bit into his back. The people darting around the bridge were no more than dark shadows, one indistinguishable from the next, giving the conversations he overhead a sense of unreality.

"How bad?" he heard the captain say. He focused on a blur that looked to be the right size and shape.

"Last count, fifteen dead, twenty in serious condition, maybe forty with minor injuries. Like Pratt there," the XO answered, gesturing toward the quartermaster's plotting table. "About the twenty—maybe five of them won't make it. Doc says that's only a guess, though."

The captain frowned. "Mostly engineers?"

"All the casualties, yes. And most of the seriously wounded, too. It hit main control."

"Damage?"

"They've got the fire out, but we've still got a hell of a hole in our side. Might be some damage to the shaft, too. Two seals are leaking. I think they can handle the flooding," the XO said. "Maybe."

"Maybe," the captain echoed. "*Puller*'s CO claims he got the bastard. They lost contact shortly after they took a shot at him."

The XO shook his head. "Hell proving it one way or the other. You're not going to find much debris in this sea state. The waves will churn up any oil, too."

Pratt watched the shadows flit around the bridge, executing preplanned responses that they'd practiced and prayed that they'd never use. For the Koreans to do this— Jesus, they had to be insane! Didn't they realize that every American military asset would be on their soil or off their coast in a matter of months, especially with fifteen dead sailors? There was no *way* the Koreans could win, none. Why in the hell would they start a war they couldn't win?

Hours later, Pratt's vision started to return. As soon as he could see the chart clearly, someone slid a pencil into his hand and fled to join a damage control team. Acrid smoke from below drifted up onto the bridge. From the reports streaming into the bridge, Pratt could tell that *Wasp* had reflash watches set on the fires and the flooding under control. *Wasp* was in no danger of sinking, but in no shape to fight.

He listened to the voice reports volleying back and forth over the radio circuits. Finally, two hours later, he plotted the course change. The final OPREP-3 reports sent, *Wasp* started limping back to the United States, escorted only by a rabidly paranoid frigate.

Fourteen sailors and one marine were dead. Two more died the next day from smoke inhalation. Thirty-two others were injured seriously enough to be evacuated back to the United States, and another fifty-six were classified as walking wounded and retained on board *Wasp*. One of the MEDEVAC injured died thirty-one thousand feet over the Atlantic Ocean, twelve minutes before the flight started its final approach to Washington, D.C., and Bethesda Naval Hospital, bringing the body count up to seventeen.

Four days later, the first amphibious group left San Diego for Korea. Across the United States, battalions and squadrons scrambled to mobilize. Reserve army units flooded the National Training Center at Fort Irwin, California, alternately swearing at the blasted landscape of the Mojave Desert and praying that the brief refresher training would be enough to keep them alive. The USS *Nimitz* and USS *Lincoln* battle groups got under way two weeks after the *Wasp* was hit, fully loaded with sufficient weapons, spare parts, and provisions for a deployment of indefinite length. Tucked deep within both aircraft carriers were tactical nuclear weapons. Their cruiser escorts carried the nuclear version of long-range Tomahawk land attack missiles. Except for a few ships and battalions assigned to NATO exercises or peacekeeping operations, every American military force was either en route to Korea or preparing to join the second wave of forces deploying.

Most of the American public supported the mobilization, albeit with some degree of anguish by a generation who'd already spilled enough blood on that peninsula. The political and national security interests prayed the conflict would be a repeat of Desert Storm, already knowing it wouldn't be. Christmas came and went quietly as families were torn apart by the mobilization.

By January, a massive amphibious invasion force was massed off the eastern coast of Korea. Two regular army divisions were poised along the border, and sun-charred army reserve sustaining, resupply, and reinforcement assets were chivvying for priority at docks and airfields. Prepositioned war reserve stocks around the peninsula were staged for issue to the arriving forces.

The North Korean forces continued to mobilize to the border.

The international press reported both the United States' righteous claims to vengeance for the attack on the *Wasp* as well as the North Koreans' angry denunciations of the United States' attack on their submarine. Amnesty International laid a wreath of roses at the last known location of the Korean submarine and demanded that the United States admit its wrongdoing.

During the entire buildup phase of the conflict, no one— not even the National Security Agency—ever answered Petty Officer Pratt's question.

2

22 FEBRUARY 2002:
WASHINGTON, D.C.

THE NATIONAL SECURITY AGENCY

"Say that again." Jerusha Bailey leaned back in her chair and looked at Jim Atchinson with astonishment.

Atchinson sighed. "All I'm asking for is a little cooperation. Your reserve active duty is coming at an inconvient time. Reschedule it—just push it back a couple of months. We need you here."

"Jim, I can't. I would if I could, but it's just not possible. This NATO exercise has been in the works for seven months. I've been to every planning conference, every briefing—if I pull out, it would leave my unit in a bad spot, not to mention affect the navy's training. It's only for two weeks."

NSA, along with every other government organization, had eyes and assets riveted on Korea. Atchinson, director of operations and Bailey's immediate superior, had already pulled three people off her team to try to keep up with the frantic demands for intelligence and threat assessments. Her own division, Western European Issues, was barely keeping pace with Allied demands for information.

And now Jim wanted more. No matter that her navy reserve unit was due for a two-week deployment to participate in a NATO exercise. Or that she'd given Jim four months of advance notice that she'd be deploying. Evidently none of that mattered, since he hung on the door frame, gazing at her with sorrowful, pleading eyes.

More and more, she'd come to resent the peculiarly inconsistent combination of pleading and patronizing that represented Jim Atchinson's style of leadership. It was a gender thing—she was certain of that after talking to the other senior female analysts in operations. Atchinson seemed unable to see a female in terms other than as his mother or his daughter. He'd never managed to treat her just as an analyst at the world's most elite national intelligence agency.

Or as a senior officer in the naval reserve. If anything, that role seemed even more incomprehensible to him than her working at NSA.

As a commanding officer of Mobile Inshore Undersea Warfare Unit 106, Bailey had to go with her unit when it deployed. *Had to*. Even as she tried once again to reassure him, she knew it was useless.

"NSA's own reserve unit will be here next week to pick up the slack," she said calmly. "I know these people— hell, Jim, *you* know them. They're entirely capable of picking up the slack while I'm gone."

"If you worked Eastern Issues, you wouldn't be going." His pleading tone was gone, replaced with the paternal voice she detested.

Bailey tapped the rolled-up cylinder of her orders against the side of his desk. "Legally, you can't stop me. I've given you plenty of notice that my two weeks of reserve duty were scheduled. You *have* to let me go."

Atchinson snorted. "Having your orders canceled could happen. Faster than you think. Your work at NSA should be your priority."

Bailey stood, planted her palms on his desk, and leaned across it to glare down at him. "You've got no reason to lean on me like this."

Atchinson straightened up, toyed with the stark white collar protruding from his dark blue suit. "It's nothing personal, Bailey. Not this time. But I see no point in the navy sending you to England for a NATO exercise when the only theater the United States has any legitimate concern over at this time is Korea."

"For now."

"That's all we deal with." Atchinson tossed his pencil on the desk. "Look, maybe someday there'll be another European conflict. The odds are it won't be in our lifetime. So frankly, other than serving as a training ground for new analysts, Europe is a dead issue. As soon as you have enough field experience, I'm going to suggest that you be moved to a more productive area."

"That sounds like an excellent topic for discussion— when I get back."

After Atchinson finally left, Jerusha felt her anger wilt. Six months at NSA and she still hadn't mastered the intricacies of working at a civilian organization that ran like the military. It should have been familiar, comforting. After all, she'd spent almost ten years in the navy, mostly on ships and in threat analysis units. Terry Intanglio, Atchinson's boss, had been interested in her expertise in submarines and ocean surveillance systems.

Interested enough to offer her a position at NSA. Interested enough to follow her career thereafter. If she told him about her difficulties, Bailey had no doubt that Terry Intanglio would do something.

It might even help. In the short run.

"Civilians don't frown like that." She looked up and saw Pete Carlisle standing in the doorway. "Save it for active duty."

"Why, have you got something special planned for me?" She pointed at the chair Atchinson had just vacated. "Come on—make my day."

Pete settled into the chair and hooked one leg over the armrest. "From the sound of it, Jim's just pegged your fun meter."

"Practicing the tricks of the trade?" she asked.

"My original offer still stands. You remember."

She did. Pete headed up a section of the electronic support division, an esoteric collection of acoustic and computer experts who specialized in extracting discrete signals embedded in noise. After her first two weeks at NSA, once it became clear that Atchinson was not going to be leading her fan club, Pete had offered to have Jim's office wired for sound. At the time, she'd thought he was joking. After six months at NSA, watching and being the target in several sophisticated electronic practical jokes, she was no longer sure he had been.

Apart from a warped sense of humor, she and Pete shared one other common interest: the naval reserve. Pete had spent five years on active duty as a sonar technician on board a ballistic missile submarine. When she'd learned he'd maintained his reserve affiliation, she'd promptly recruited him to fill a vacant billet in her own unit. While Pete had more seniority that she did at NSA, he filled a senior enlisted billet in the unit Bailey commanded.

"Let's get this active duty over with first. Atchinson's ready to try to get my orders canceled. I'll go to Terry before I'll let him get away with that," she said.

Pete shook his head. "Think this through first. Chain of command and sheer brute force—there are better ways to get what you want out of Atchinson. It's not enough just to be in the right."

"What are you saying?"

"Just this. Political power works in strange ways around here. Learn to use it—or it will use you. In some ways it's not that different from the navy."

"It shouldn't be like that. There are laws about reserve duty. If anyone ought to obey the laws, it should be a government organization like NSA."

Pete stood, stretching lazily to his full height. "God save me from idealists. Would you rather be right or get what you want? Think about *that*."

Bailey watched him leave, felt her anger subside into frustration. It was so clear-cut this time—Atchinson had to let her go. *Had to.*

But maybe there's something to what he's saying. Remember why you left the navy? Sound familiar?

Unfortunately, it did.

On her last ship, the executive officer had pressured her relentlessly to gundeck the readiness figures for the engineering department. She'd resisted, reported their maintenance status accurately, and been slammed in her fitness reports. As a junior lieutenant commander, she'd felt the prospect of spending another twelve years compromising her own integrity unpalatable, and at the time she'd thought that was what staying on active duty would require.

She leaned back in her chair and stared at the calendar. In less than a week, she'd be Commander Bailey again. Not Jer, not Jerusha, not even Miss Bailey. And, at least in her unit, she'd make sure that no junior officer ever went through what she had on active duty. Duty, honor, and commitment meant something to her—and she'd make sure her sailors understood that.

3

23 FEBRUARY 2002:
THE NORTH SEA

U-504

U-504 slipped silently across the invisible line dividing the North Sea from the rest of the Atlantic Ocean. The grueling, high-speed dash across the Pacific, refueling on moonless nights at sea from *Spessart,* a German Navy tanker, had exhausted the entire crew.

"There it is." Merker left the periscope exposed a second longer than he should have, letting the hazy outline of England's west coast linger on the monitor bolted into the forward corner of the control room. The thought of walking on land felt oddly daring and slightly unsettling, just as returning to port did.

It was always disorienting, those first few moments after mooring when he stared out at the pier from the conning tower, blinking in natural sunlight, his movements still careful and awkward from months of living in confined quarters. The U-boat would feel awkward and lumbering, her normal gentle motions stilled by heavy mooring lines, and the silence from the submarine's engineering plant seemed to demand immediate emergency action. By the time they returned to Germany, the first signs of spring would be in the air, compounding the confusion since they'd left during late autumn.

Their two days in port at the Piel submarine base had been barely enough time to let them reprovision and rearm. Seeing their families had been out of the question, both from a security standpoint and from sheer lack of time.

Now at periscope depth, rocking gently in the unexpect-edly calm water twenty miles east of the United Kingdom, it seemed to each man that he'd spent a lifetime at sea. Their lives ashore were distant memories, the familiar cycle of watchstanding, eating, and sleeping in the cramped con-fines of the seventy-five-meter-long boat more normal and comfortable than their two days tied up to a pier.

"If they knew, they'd kill us," Merker said. He pointed at the American ship caught in the crosshaired sight of the periscope monitor. "Ironic, isn't it? The first ship we see in our own waters—and the first close enough to run an attack simulation since Korea—is American. We're going to pass within seven thousand meters of her, and she doesn't even know we're here."

Kraeken grunted. "We could surface and still not be at-tacked. There's no indication that they suspect anything. At least not from the message traffic from the General Staff."

Merker turned to Ehrlich. "How much longer?" The U-boat had been ordered to lay a barrier of moored mines across the entrance to two British naval ports. The weapons consisted of a warhead in a neutral buoyancy shell tethered to a weight. The length of cable connecting the two was intended to keep the mine concealed beneath the surface and deep enough to keep small surface craft from detonat-ing it. The planned line of mines was equally divided be-tween magnetic-influence and acoustic-triggering devices.

While minelaying was a normal operation for a subma-rine, the General Staff had again complicated matters by ordering *U-504* to follow a particular transit route to and from the harbors. Not unexpected, given the degree of con-trol they'd exercised over *U-504*'s departure from the North Sea. But this route specified multiple interception points, a circuitous trek down to the northern edge of the English Channel, then back up to British ports.

The plan puzzled him. He understood the overriding ne-cessity for blockading the British forces in their ports. Ashore, German land forces were moving to consolidate their power in the ravaged, fragmented countries that com-prised Eastern Europe. After a decade of unsuccessful U.N.

peacekeeping efforts, the rest of the world had finally declared the problems resolved and pulled out. The exhausted civilian populations, equally decimated by war and foreign assistance, were in no position to resist Germany's insistent offers of help.

European wars might be fought on land, but they were won at sea.

Merker pulled the friendly force locator message off the boards and studied the position of the other naval forces crowding into the North Sea. The British ships and submarines were still in port, waiting for the other NATO assets to move into position before sortiling. Two French submarines were well to the north, playing warm-up detection games with a Dutch frigate. The American destroyer and frigate—well, there was no uncertainty as to their position. The only other U.S. asset in the theater was a small coastal surveillance unit on the northern tip of Scotland, and *U-504* was well capable of neutralizing its capabilities.

After studying the operational schedule for evolutions in *Northern Lights,* he thought he'd divined the logic underlying the plan. The General Staff must be using the exercise to mask *U-504*'s presence and to provide an alternative explanation for any unexplained events. Certainly the exercise played a major factor in every step of Germany's real plan—which was hardly an exercise. Just as Korea had.

"Two minutes until the first release position, *Kapitan,*" the navigator said immediately.

"Very well."

Ehrlich looked older, Merker thought. They all did. Three months in transit to Korea, two weeks on station, three months back—that long encased in steel, living, breathing, and sweating in close quarters below the ocean changed men. Korea had tempered Ehrlich's eager exuberance into a hard aggressiveness, soured Kraeken's drive into reflexive hostility.

And what has it done to me? He stared down at the planned line of mine positions arcing across the entrance to the British harbor, still no closer to an answer than he'd been off the coast of Korea.

"Not that the mines would be of much use as a self-defense weapon," the XO continued as though Merker hadn't spoken. "You shouldn't have let us sail with so few torpedoes. It makes no tactical sense."

Merker sighed. At least the man had the sense to lower his voice. In the past four months, Merker had gone from irritation to anger to rage over Kraeken's persistent insubordination. Finally, some two thousand miles ago, he'd settled for indifference.

"How do we close the gate behind us, then?" Merker asked, more from habit than from any real desire to discuss the issue yet again. "We have two torpedoes, enough for self-defense. The rest of the space was needed for the mines. The General Staff thought this out carefully. We seal the British into their harbors, then lock the rest of the world out. The other submarines are needed to keep the NATO battle group distracted with the exercise—for now. The wolf pack forms the moment we have the entire fleet locked in the North Sea."

"Another U-boat—"

"The mutual interference problems—"

"Submarines in packs—"

"Fifteen seconds," Ehrlich said, interrupting the argument that now took place in telegraphic phrases instead of complete sentences.

"Leave it be," Merker said to the XO. "I have work to do."

"*We* have—"

"*SILENCE.*" Merker caught himself, took a deep breath. "Give the order, navigator."

"Aye, aye, sir." Ehrlich was staring at the sweep hand on his watch. "Five, four, three—weapons, navigator. Fire one."

The submarine shivered as compressed air shot the mine out of the tube. Merker grimaced. Not as much noise as a torpedo, but still—he looked over at sonar, reassuring himself that there was no telltale spiral of a torpedo's propellers singing across the spectrum.

"Good shot, sir," the weapons officer said. "Permission to flood tube two?"

"Flood tube two." Merker watched Ehrlich ink in the penciled projected mine position.

"Fifteen minutes, steady on this course," Ehrlich said without prompting.

"Six more mines to pen up twenty warships, gentlemen." Merker tried to sound confident and calm. The crew—they'd heard him at the edge of anger too often in the past eight months. "Get these off right, and I will buy the first round when we get into port." A ragged, forced cheer answered him.

"If," Kraeken said. "If, not when."

Her mission would have been unthinkable—if not impossible—during the decades when Germany had been an occupied country, severed by the powers that invaded her during World War II. In the post–Cold War, postreunification years, Germany surged ahead of her weaker European neighbors. By the year 2000, Germany politically and economically dominated the European continent. It was time to finish what history began.

Merker's fingers felt a deep hammering sound grow stronger. A North Sea oil rig, one of the many dotting the seascape. Had he been given a choice, he would have planned a more southerly transit out of their home waters, steering clear of the noise the drilling produced. The General Staff had been adamant, insisting on this route and no deviation.

The Prussian passion for precision. With his free hand, Merker touched the schedule folded into a tight square in his breast pocket. If everything worked according to plan, the Continent would be theirs again by late spring.

Merker stared at the sonar speaker, trying to decide what had caught his attention. Not a surface ship sound, no—the sonarman was still slouched in his bolted-down chair, eyes closed, listening intently. It had been an inaudible quiver of noise under his hand, even lower in frequency than the oil rig dominating the spectrum. He arched his palm away from the speaker and concentrated on his fingertips.

"Surface contact," Sonar announced. "Bearing three-ten, range five thousand yards."

Merker nodded. He'd already felt the new vibrations, the

high-pitched winch squeal, the shimmery pings from fish-finder sonar. "Probably a fishing boat. Come right to avoid her. Stay at least two thousand yards away from her stern to avoid the nets. We'll resume ordered course and speed when we're clear of her."

SS *ANNA LEONA*

Anna Leona was one hundred fifty feet long, drawing almost forty-five feet of water. She was returning to Bristol after three weeks fishing along the Rockalls north of Scotland. Her holds were packed with cold-water fish, in high demand now from health enthusiasts and restaurants throughout Britain and continental Europe. It had been a profitable six weeks at sea, although the weather had been as foul as it normally was in October. There had been no major equipment failures, and the two eight-cylinder diesel engines deep in her hull were running smoothly.

Large steel bolts held the engines in place, dogged down to the metal deck in the engineering spaces. The rapid-fire cycle of noise—fuel injection, ignition, cylinders firing, crankshaft turning—had a clean, unobstructed path to the hull. The sounds carried for miles in the deep, cold water of the North Sea.

"Be dark before we get in." *Anna Leona*'s master pointed at the horizon. Red and gold bands were already edging along the boundary between sea and sky. "Anna's not expecting me for another three days."

The first mate shot him a sly glance. "Too late to be going home. You don't know what you might find there, coming in like this with no warning. The ship's named *Anna Lion* for a reason, you said."

The master grinned. "That's what I been thinking. Might be best for all if I stay in town tonight, maybe walk the trouser snake a bit. See the better half tomorrow, perhaps."

"A gentleman you are, Danny. I've always said so."

The first mate took his hand off the helm long enough to reach for the cold mug of tea sitting on the ledge in front of him. He took a swig of it, then grimaced.

"Fancy a few pints before you go home?" the master asked.

"Hell, yes. Wash the taste of this bleeding lousy tea out of my mouth. Cheap bastard, aren't you, buying this crap?"

The master smacked him lightly on the back. "With what you'll make off this trip, you can buy your *own* bloody tea next cruise."

FOUR HUNDRED FEET BELOW SS *ANNA LEONA*

Buried under two feet of mud, slime, and debris, the mine felt the magnetic pull of a large mass of metal, as it had at least fifty times each day since it had been seeded here in 1944. The force waned, then increased again. The pressure piston moved slightly in response to each change in the electromagnetic flux, generating another small trickle of electricity as its armature cut through the magnetic lines of force. Another ship, another few more microvolts of charge. Even buried under two feet of mud and debris as it was now, the mine fed.

The nations bordering the North Sea charted the magnetic anomalies on the seabed regularly, insurance against a day when they might have to clear the heavily traveled trade routes. Decades ago, a Frenchman had pinpointed the location of this particular chunk of metal, and it was noted on all the minesweepers' charts as wreckage from a World War II German U-boat kill.

Like many early naval mines, this one was shaped like a torpedo. The titanium casing, produced during the last years of World War II, when Germany had finally cracked the secret of shaping the capricious metal, still protected its contents from the corrosive seawater. The small magnetic generator and primitive signal transducer still worked. A high-pressure gas canister tucked into the midsection of a stripped-down torpedo contained a toxin outlawed from the armories of most civilized nations.

In the submarine's conning tower, a small transmitter siphoned off data from the submarine's inertial navigation system. At a precise point in the ocean, one that had been predetermined by the Third Reich decades before, the transmitter pulsed once.

The mine heard it. The frequency and duration—all parameters exactly as they should be. Deep inside the titanium shell, a relay in the spectrum analyzer clicked over. Electrons trickled out of the capacitor and into the firing circuits. The mine armed.

Using World War II techniques for determining an acoustic contact's depth in the water, the mine's analog circuits reached a decision. Not this one. Too deep. Acceptable targets ran shallow. The firing circuit switched into standby, still armed—but waiting.

This one. The mine shot a small spark into the propellant. A small explosion broke the torpedo free of the mine casing and spewed a cloud of silt into the water. The torpedo warhead, designed to penetrate deep into the hull of its target before detonating, raced toward the surface.

Two generations before, a Jewish prisoner had been caught in one of the torpedo factories sabotaging weapons. It had been subtle work, minor inaccuracies in machining and sloppy welding that he'd hoped would slip by the Nazi inspectors. It hadn't. The worker had been executed on the floor of the machine shop as an example to the other prisoners. Almost all of his work had been reinspected and the faulty weapons removed from the inventory. The inspectors missed one.

The sudden movement after decades of inaction was too much for the faulty weld near the torpedo's propeller. It split open, spewing the remaining fuel into the ocean. The torpedo's acceleration bled off, but its momentum carried it on toward the surface.

Two meters below the surface, the torpedo's warhead ruptured. Instead of detonating inside the hull of its target, its payload spewed out of the cracked welds. Gas bubbled up through the water, foaming the sea into a pale pink patch just forward of the fishing boat. It drifted up into the air, forming a fetid pool at sea level in front of the fishing boat.

The empty torpedo casing filled quickly with seawater. Now slightly heavier than the water around it, it sank back down to the seabed. It came to rest in thick ooze five hundred meters away from its original position.

SS ANNA LEONA

"And I ain't spending *my* pay on tea," the first mate answered. "*Your* expense, it is. Part of the contract, it being your boat and all. Not the crews or officers."

"Then wot you complaining about? It's free for you, so you can drink what I buy." The master was irritated now, wondering whether he might be better off just steaming alone that evening. Or even going on home, surprising the lass for a change.

He felt his pulse pound unexpectedly hard, and had a momentary thought that perhaps his doctor had been right. Avoid getting all lathered up, eat better, lose ten pounds. Get the blood pressure down and you'll be fishing for another two decades, the doc had said.

Suddenly his gut tightened into a hard knot, jerking him over doubled up. The master gasped, tried to yell for help, now convinced in his terror that he was having a heart attack.

The deck smacked him on the side of the head, and he dimly realized that he'd fallen over. His throat felt frozen, spasmed into rigidity. The first mate—where the hell was he? The master tried to roll over, to call out, even to swear, but he'd lost all voluntary control of his body. He felt a warm flood down around his groin, searing heat tracing a path from his throat down to his abdomen as though he'd swallowed caustic lye.

Something hard dug deep into his loose stomach muscles, then the suffocating pressure of a heavy body lying on top of him. A face rolled into view in front of him, the tongue protruding and swollen, the flesh mottling red and purple. The eyes were half shut and staring. Just before the master's vision faded completely, he realized it was the first mate.

The gas drifted down the passageways of the *Anna Leona,* flooding the ship. A dogged-down hatch into engineering slowed its progress, but there was a small rupture in the watertight gasket.

Five minutes after the torpedo detonated, the entire crew was dead.

U-504

"Fishing boat's stopped, *Kapitan*." The sonarman pointed to a set of lines that abruptly ended on his passive acoustic display. "I'd say she's let her nets out and is waiting for them to fill. We'll hear the winches again any moment."

"Did you hear something else?" Merker asked. "Just before she stopped—a noise like a small explosion?" He tapped the speaker grate. "I felt it here. A bit earlier, too, something similar."

"No, *Kapitan*. Here, though—a small noise spike on the printout, very-low-frequency. It could have been a minor seaquake."

"Perhaps." Merker studied the jagged black shape on the paper. He shrugged and handed the printout back to the sonarman. "It's not important."

Nothing was. Not after Korea.

4

25 FEBRUARY 2002:
THE NORTH SEA

The research ship cruised east from England at a stately fifteen knots. The ship was ostensibly funded by a joint NATO operating budget, but that money barely covered the cost of its fuel. The black, off-budget funds that its passengers provided were necessary to keep it from rusting. In reality, it was little more than a spy boat for rent.

"Who the hell is the bitch?" Mike Peal, NSA's European special teams coordinator, pointed at the tall woman standing at the bow of the ship. He kept his voice low.

Washington hadn't bothered to tell him who his passenger would be, just that he should afford her every cooperation possible, including full biochemical warfare protective gear. They'd given him one day to prepare for her embarkation. Given the resources stashed in his warehouse, it had been more than enough time.

Peal knew better than to ask questions, and there was no telling who the woman really was and how much power she wielded in the organizational labyrinth of U.S. intelligence and security agencies. While the biochem requirements bothered him, it certainly wasn't the first time. Nor would it be the last, he suspected.

"A looker, isn't she? Most of those Stateside honchos are butt-ugly." Derrick Garner, one of Peal's three team leaders, grinned knowingly. Like his boss, he spoke quietly.

Peal grimaced. Black hair, blue eyes—hell, she had to be almost six feet tall. Built like a swimmer, too, just the way he liked his women. Not that it would ever be safe to make a play for her. "I'd take ugly and friendly over Aphrodite out there. Make small talk with her, count your balls when you're done."

"What's this all *about*?" Garner looked peeved. "Come on, Mike—didn't they tell you anything?"

The coordinator shrugged. "You know how it is. They tell me to show up in a biochem suit, I do it. All I know is we bag the bodies and deliver them to the air force. The chick's going to check out the boat. You and me—we're just the muscle on this one."

"All this just to check out a derelict fishing boat?"

Peal pointed at the hull, now visible through the fog and the steam inside his helmet. The bow was tied up to a bright orange buoy, and a yellow-orange flag flew from its mast. "A *quarantined* fishing boat."

Bailey swiped a rag across the outside of her visor. It didn't help. Between the natural fog off England's coast and the mist clouding the inside of her visor, visibility was atrocious.

"Lady, we'll take over now. You go on back inside. You can take the helmet off once you're through the decontamination airlock." The coordinator's words were muffled by his suit, but the patronizing tone was not. He reached out one hand as though to touch her. Something in her expression froze his movement.

"Tie up next to her. And follow me," she ordered.

She vaulted over the railing to the fishing boat, catching herself as she slipped on the damp deck. One knee slammed into the deck. She groaned as she stood up, then checked the suit for tears.

Bailey took a moment and looked around the deck, avoiding the bodies she'd have to look at sooner or later. A typical deep-water fishing boat, broad-beamed with a deep draft. The deck and railing were scarred, evidence of hard use and careful preservation maintenance.

The bodies. She walked over to them and stared down. Just what the hell was she doing here? She was an analyst, not a field technician.

The first two bodies lay crumbled together, an older man sprawled over a younger one. The faces were bloated, distorted, colored green from advanced decomposition. The features seemed to have slid around on the faces, odd bumps and bulges instead of noses and ears. The mouths were twisted open, with the lips peeled back from the teeth as though they were trying to speak. The eyes were missing, and deep, pitted wounds on the rest of the face were evidence of the reason. She glanced overhead at the flock of seagulls circling the boat, waiting.

All right, I've seen them. Underneath her markedly queasy stomach, she felt the anger uncurl again.

It took her thirty minutes to tour all the spaces on the fishing boat, starting with the cramped bridge with its outdated navigation gear and ending up in the stinking holds filled with rotting fish. Peal and Garner followed her, immediately responsive to her gestured commands to collect the bodies. She took videos of the entire boat, concentrating on the bodies and the evidence of sudden death—a charred pot of stew in the galley, the abandoned navigational chart with a heavy stroke of pencil scarring the otherwise orderly plot. Peal waited with her on the weatherdecks as Garner finished bagging the crews' remains.

The body bags were stored in an airtight connex box on the aft weatherdeck of Peal's boat. Once they were safely in there and the vessel was five miles away from the quarantined fishing boat, Peal removed his protective gear.

He watched Bailey follow suit and heard her drawing in a deep breath of sea air as soon as she removed the heavy biochem ensemble headgear. Her face was pale, the delicate skin around her eyes blanched.

"Ugly," Peal remarked, on the off chance that she'd give him some clue as to what had happened on this boat in his area of responsibility. "How'd they know we'd need the biochem suits?" An involuntary shiver ran up his spine.

Bailey's face was drawn into a hard mask. "I don't know. But I intend to find out as soon as I get back to D.C."

"If it looks like I'll be needing them often. . . ." Peal let the remark trail off, stopping short of asking for a back brief on the entire mission. Biochem sabotage—the possibilities for disaster were limitless.

"I don't know," Bailey repeated. "But I should."

26 FEBRUARY 2002:
WASHINGTON, D.C.

THE NATIONAL SECURITY AGENCY

"I simply took you at your word." Atchinson leaned back in his high-backed black leatherette chair and laced his fingers together over his stomach. Innocent, slightly questioning—it was a look he'd mastered years ago. "You've mentioned several times that NSA is concentrating on Korea to the exclusion of the rest of the world, most particularly your areas of responsibility. This fishing boat—I thought you'd want to see it for yourself."

"And this has nothing to do with my upcoming reserve duty, correct?" Bailey stared at him, seething.

"Of course not. Terry explained NSA's policy to me again. At your request, I believe. I must thank you for that—I hadn't realized I was treading on such protected legal duties." Atchinson's words were smooth and congenial. "But this incident in the North Sea—any thoughts on it?"

"I just got back this morning. I haven't had a chance to type up my report, but there's nothing I can add to my original message until the toxicology reports come back."

Atchinson sighed. "Well, I suppose it can wait until you return from your reserve duties. Frankly, I suspect it's just a virulent case of food poisoning."

Come off it. You're playing payback. Terry snapped you up short for trying to screw with my reserve duty, so you're going to make it as difficult for me as you can. Admit it— sending me to the North Sea three days before I leave was supposed to teach me to toe the line, wasn't it?

She felt the waves of exhaustion ripple over her, shorting her temper and blunting her senses. Jet lag—Atchinson had given her just enough time to get home, start to reacclimate to this time zone before she'd head back across the pond for *Northern Lights.*

"At least it gave you the opportunity to gain some additional field experience," Atchinson continued. "Even Terry agrees that that's your one shortcoming."

"Looking at dead fishermen is supposed to cure that? Just what exactly was I supposed to learn from that? I need lab reports, chemical analyses, not firsthand looks at dead bodies." The image of the two men coiled together came back unbidden.

Atchinson leaned back in his chair and interlaced his hands over his belly. He stared up at her, seemingly unfazed. "I didn't object when you were promoted over several more qualified candidates, you will recall."

"Men, you mean."

He continued as though she hadn't spoken. "Director Intanglio assured me you were quite capable of getting up to speed. In fact, I was told you'd welcome the opportunity for additional training missions. Are you telling me otherwise now?"

She shook her head. There was clearly no way out of this one. Terry Intanglio might be one of the good guys, but she couldn't go running to him over every minor conflict with Atchinson. Use the silver bullet too often and it became useless.

"No. Of course not. Now, unless there's anything else, I've got a few things to take care of before I leave tomorrow morning," she said finally.

Atchinson nodded. "Have an enjoyable two weeks. This time away will give me a chance to plan out the rest of your training schedule. The lab reports should be back by then."

5

1 MARCH 2002:
SCOTLAND

MIUWU 106

Three days later, the memories of the dead fishermen receded to nightmares instead of constant companions. The airlift of her unit to Britain, the constant demands of command, and slipping back into the military lifestyle all helped her compartmentalize it. In two weeks, after *Northern Lights*, she'd deal with the question of the derelict fishing vessel. That, and Jim Atchinson.

Deploying with the MIUWU always restored her self-confidence. After ten years in the community, this tour as commanding officer had proved more demanding and fulfilling than she'd ever thought possible. She might be a rookie at NSA, but within the perimeter of the MIUWU camp she had complete responsibility for everything from the quality of the food to tactical prosecution of the submarines participating in the exercise.

The Mobile Inshore Undersea Warfare special operations van perched on the edge of the bluff on the northernmost tip of Scotland. To the south, the rest of the U.S. and NATO forces were arrayed in an extended formation, completing the final preparations for the exercise. According to the OPORD, the MIUWU would monitor the northern entrance to the English Channel, serving as a tripwire for the forces designated as aggressors for the war game.

Bailey walked from the tents that housed her people to the large green trailer set up near the edge of the cliff. The security guard stationed at the steel hatch saluted, then spoke into his headset. The door opened. Bailey stepped into the van.

Immediately to her left, a complete communications suite took up one quarter of the van, with racks of transmitters and encryption gear mounted against the long sides of the van. Just to the left of the door was a small ledge for the watch officer's log, and across the van from that an SPS-64 radar and a plotting table protruded two feet from the wall. Sonar owned the far end of the van. An SQR-17 sonar set with its associated tape recorders and CD-ROM training systems sat perpendicular to the radar. Speakers and secure radio sets took up most of the available wall space. The six people on watch were crowded between the equipment.

Trailing down the cliff was the shore termination stretch of their fiber-optic acoustic array. Earlier that day, two sonarmen and a boat crew had launched the RHIB—rigid hull inflatable boat—to deploy it. The array was one of the new generation of detection devices designed specifically for the MIUWU, and *Northern Lights* was to be its first full operational test.

"What the hell was that?" Bailey stared up at the speaker hardwired to the SQR-17(A) sonar. "It sounded like a toilet flushing."

"Not biologic, skipper." Sonarman First Class Carlisle frowned. "Maybe a small seaquake?" He shook his head, dismissing his own suggestion. "No. The frequency was too high."

"Best guess?"

"Something underwater that wasn't born there."

"Thanks. Could I trouble you for a bit more refined classification?"

"I don't know, ma'am. It sounded like air bubbles."

"Go active," she ordered. The sonarman reached out and toggled the transmit switch, ordering the buoy to ping.

"Nothing. No, wait—it's dissipating, whatever it was. One of the exercise submarines, on station early maybe." He shrugged. "I can't give you an exact source, but that's what I'd call it."

"It takes one to know one. Or to find one." Bailey

turned to the watch officer. "Make a contact report to HMS *Oberon*. Call it a low-confidence submarine detection, and see if they've seen anything interesting in the area."

HMS OBERON

Royal Navy Petty Officer Benjamin Tartley yanked the sheet out of the printer and held it out to the officer of the deck. "Contact report from the Americans."

Lieutenant Colin Fielding frowned. "A bit eager, aren't they?" He turned to sonar. The curtain that normally separated sonar from the rest of the British diesel submarine's control room was pulled back. "Did you hold anything along that bearing?"

The sonarman shook his head. "Too far away, maybe."

"That can be corrected," Fielding said. "Tartley, fetch the captain. And smartly." He grinned.

RNPO Tartley headed aft, already sick of the word play on his name after only two weeks at sea.

"Come right, steady on course one two seven," Fielding ordered. Why did it always have to happen in the last fifteen minutes of *his* watch? The Germans and their damned Teutonic efficiency—couldn't they be *on time* for an exercise for a change, instead of two hours early?

Oberon's captain appeared at the hatch leading into the control room. His hair was rumpled, his eyes still bleary from the brief nap he'd been trying to catch between evolutions. He snagged his teacup from the pegboard on the aft bulkhead and listened to the officer of the deck's explanation.

"Always wake me if you have a question," he said, waving away the Fielding's pro forma apology. "Damned Krauts. You'd think they could read a fucking schedule."

"Treat it as real?"

"Bloody right. It's the only way to train." The captain drained his cup of tea, then motioned for the mess cook hovering behind him. "More. Fresh this time, not boiled to tar. Tartley." The RNPO sighed as he took the cup and headed aft toward the wardroom.

The captain turned back to Fielding. "Get the fucking bastard. We'll teach her to show up early."

U-504

"Oberon-class diesel." The German sonarman swore quietly. "She wasn't there before. I swear it, *Kapitan*."

"Does she have us?" Merker asked.

"No—maybe. I don't know."

Merker stood, crossed the compartment in three steps, and stationed himself behind the sonarman. He motioned to the XO to join him. "Tell me what you see."

"A reason to have more torpedoes. I told you—"

"She's turning toward us," the German sonarman reported.

Merker swore quietly. Had the British boat heard the small noises the U-boat had made planting the bottom-moored mines? Would they believe it, even if they had? Or would they decide that it was simply an elaboration on the scheduled *Operation Northern Lights* exercise?

He touched the schedule, nestled in his front breast pocket. Torpedo exercises in this area were supposed to provide a cover story for any inadvertent noise the mine-laying operation generated, but being shadowed or harried by a British submarine would prevent them from proceeding with the mine blockade operation. Worst-case scenario: The stupid Brit would come shallow and blunder into it, detonating it.

"No survivors," Kraeken said, interrupting his train of thought. "And no premature disclosures. The General Staff was quite clear on that as well. Even though they—"

"I know my orders." Merker turned to sonar. "Take her."

MIUWU 106

The torpedo's high-pitched squeal cut through the speaker noise for a few seconds, then faded away. A dull, muffled thud followed it.

"What the—shit, that was an explosion!" Carlisle turned pale and swore softly.

"Excercise load?" Bailey asked.

"No. That was a war shot—it had to be. They're supposed to be shooting exercise loads, and not for another two hours. They didn't schedule a *live* torpedo shot without telling us, did they?"

Bailey stared down at the evidence printing in wavering lines across the stylus, ending abruptly with a spike of noise. "Maybe."

Had there been a change in the schedule? To shoot a torpedo at a target, even at a wrecked hulk, without notifying ASW assets in the area was criminally negligent. And if that's what'd just happened, it was the last straw in the series of screw-ups, miscommunications, and general disregard of the MIUW's contribution to the NATO exercise. If she'd had a choice, they'd have pulled out three days ago, after the first cheap joke about naval reserve units.

Then again . . .

"I think we'd better find out," she said finally.

HMS OBERON

RNPO Tartley clung to a fire pump and watched the water rise. When the explosion shook the ship, he'd been passing by one of the many small machinery compartments that honeycombed the ship. The violent, twisting turn of the boat had thrown him against the hatch. By reflex as much as anything, he'd darted into the compartment and dogged the door down immediately.

The water was up to his waist now, a foot higher than it had been five minutes ago. The remaining air was getting foul, and taking on the distinctive bite of chlorine. Was it his imagination?

The surface of the water eddied and bubbled. Seawater on the batteries—chlorine gas. He took a shallow breath, felt the air sear delicate tissue. A deep coughing fit seized him, each gasp drawing the gas deeper into his lungs.

The water inched up, now covering the second-from-the-bottom button on his blue chambray shirt. He flexed his foot, standing on tiptoes now on the fire pump, straining to get away from it.

He heard noise above him. Outside the hull, a droning *thrum-thrum*. A propeller.

The sound faded, then died out completely. Even knowing that it was probably the boat that had attacked them, he felt the last vestige of hope die. Against all reason, he'd hoped—he glanced over at the other sailor trapped in the compartment. The body was floating facedown in the water, his back already bumping gently against the overhead as the water eddied and surged around him.

Even with his skin numbed to ice by the frigid North Sea waters, RNPO Tartley felt the rising flood lap at his chin. He tilted his neck back, moving his mouth and nose as close to the ceiling as possible. A cold wavelet lapped at his lips.

The EEBD—emergency escape breathing device! RNPO Tartley fumbled with the container bolted to the wall, managed to jerk out one of the thin plastic hoods. He pulled it over his head, his fingers clumsy from the cold. An involuntary shiver shook him, and he felt an odd sense of peace flood his body. Curious, the water that had been so achingly cold now seemed warmer and—familiar, in a strange way.

The water plastered the mask to his face, sealing itself over his mouth and nose and pinning his eyes open. The canister—something about a cord he needed to pull and—no, never mind. He could breathe now, he was certain of it. Feel the cool oxygen washing down his throat, filling his lungs. Odd that it tasted so salty, but perhaps . . .

Just before consciousness faded completely, he took a deep breath of seawater.

U-504

Merker leaned on the plotting table. Across from him Ehrlich was once again marking the grave of an enemy submarine.

The captain measured off the space between the coast and their position with his fingers, looked across at the navigator, and pointed at the overhead. The young *Leutnant dur See* nodded enthusiastically.

"Get us to the first intercept point, then come to periscope depth." Merker reached for a package of dry crackers as insurance against the rough weather.

Merker jammed his tongue against the back of his throat and tensed his stomach muscles, willing himself not to vomit. The uneasy roiling in his stomach abated for a moment, and he reached for a few more crackers to cut the incessant sloshing of digestive juices back and forth in his gut. He popped two crackers in his mouth just as the submarine took a particularly vicious roll to port, and felt his feet start to skid on the damp tiles.

The damned dehumidifier again. Even German engineers occasionally suffered from machinery gremlins that defied their best efforts to isolate and repair, and two days in port hadn't been long enough to chase this one to ground. Months deployed without shipyard maintenance were taking their toll. Repair crews had patched two minor leaks and stripped down two fuel pumps to replace shot bearings. Faced with mounting potential series equipment casualties, crew comfort and environmentals had to wait.

The scrubbers were still removing most of the diesel fumes, galley smells, and miscellaneous unpleasant human odors that accumulated in the U-boat, but the rising humidity had started to affect their performance as well. They could live with the stench—the human nose quickly ceased to notice persistent smells—but the moisture in the air was a problem. It coated every flat surface with a slippery patina of water and oil, even reducing the crackers to limp, glutinous squares. He abandoned the idea of another cracker and reached for the overhead bar with his free hand, wincing as his raw palms rasped across the line-covered stabilizer.

According to the last message they'd received, they should be within hunting distance of the British forces. As wolf pack leader, Merker was responsible for guiding the other submarines into position and coordinating the phased plan of attack and misdirection.

And this time, the targets were ships that could fight back.

FIVE HUNDRED METERS BELOW U-504

In *U-504*'s conning tower, a transmitter coupled to a tumbling gyroscope recognized its position. The equipment had been installed inside the hollow bulkhead of the tower, thinly disguised as a normal black-box piece of gear. It wasn't. The plans and codes for its operation had been rediscovered only recently.

Using the entire hull of the submarine as an antenna, the transmitter softly pulsed out a very-low-frequency—VLF—acoustic signal.

The VLF signal cut through the mud and bounced off the upper portion of the mine. A fiber-impregnated acoustic diaphragm flexed, transmitting the signal energy through a thick oil reservoir to the rudimentary spectrum analyzer swathed in layers of waterproofing and metal. Seconds later, a relay snapped shut.

The mine, laid over fifty years ago, armed.

For twenty-four hours, the British and NATO chains of command chuckled over the MIUWU contact report. The senior British commander added a short note regarding the report to the daily submarine broadcast from the dedicated satellite, thinking it might amuse the submariners now at sea preparing for *Northern Lights*. That the Americans had obviously mistaken a prefire test for an actual attack and explosion would be superb ammunition at the Officers' Club celebrations after the NATO exercise.

The next day, the report was no longer amusing.

6

2 MARCH 2002:
SCOTLAND

MIUWU 106

Bailey and Carlisle stood at the edge of the bluff, leaning into twenty knots of wind to keep their balance, and staring at the faint gray outlines of the ship. Its port running light was barely visible through the fog. "It's USS *Ramage*." Carlisle passed his binoculars to Bailey.

"I'm surprised she's in this close," Bailey said, tweaking the picture into sharper focus. The oddly angled superstructure of the Aegis-class destroyer was just visible above the horizon. "Did you tell them we're holding contact on the German sub they're supposed to be prosecuting?"

"I did." Carlisle shrugged. "You know the regular navy. Guess *Ramage*'s TAO—tactical action officer—doesn't think a bunch of reservists could find a submarine that the mighty destroyer missed."

"Blew you off, did he?"

"It was a *she*—Lieutenant Commander Collins, I believe the name was. And yes, she did."

"How rude of us. Holding acoustic contact on the one target *Ramage* can't seem to locate," Bailey said.

"*Torpedoes* are rude. So are green flares. We're merely—well informed." Carlisle looked smug.

"Captain—flash traffic for you in the van," the lookout called. "Lieutenant Boston wants to know if you'd like to see it now."

Bailey looked at Carlisle and shrugged. "Duty calls.

Come on back in with me. Might be something you'll need to know.''

Back inside the special operations van, Bailey scanned the text of the message for details. HMS *Oberon* had missed her last two regular communications breaks, and had now been unlocated for thirty-six hours. The message mentioned the low-confidence torpedo detection by the MIUWU unit the day before, managing to convey the distinct impression that the contact was considered a spurious anomaly.

All participating units in *Operation Northern Lights* were asked to maintain a continuous watch on Gertrude, the underwater telephone system, and to advise the British commander immediately if even the slightest indication of transmission occurred. The last paragraph tersely requested reports on any new oil slicks or sightings of debris.

Bailey ripped the message in half. The Brits hadn't terminated the exercise and put every asset they had on the search. Ergo, the torpedo shot and the missing submarine were probably no cause for alarm. Some submariner screwed up and forgot to change the code of the day. Or maybe it was all an exercise insertion by the British command to see how the forces would react to a report of a missing friendly. Stranger things than no-notice SUB MISS drills happened during NATO exercises.

Bailey glanced at the black-cased standard navy-issue clock. ''Those idiots on *Ramage* are going to take a green flare up their ass if they don't start listening to us. Or a torpedo, if we're right about what we saw two days ago.''

''In about two minutes. Maybe three.'' Carlisle indicated the jagged line tracing from top to bottom on the sonar screen. ''That U-boat's three thousand yards off her port bow. And *Ramage* doesn't have a clue. Why the hell are we even here? They don't listen when we report a torpedo shot followed by an explosion, and they're sure as hell not talking to us now. This was supposed to be a *coordinated* subtracking exercise.''

''Damned if I know what they're thinking. Even if it's only an exercise, you'd think they'd sound a little more concerned. Especially after *Wasp*.''

   Carlisle shot her a sly, sideways glance. "You think we ought to tell *Ramage* who we are? In real life, I mean?"

   She shook her head. "For the next two weeks, we check our collars and name tags to find out who we are."

   "Whatever you say, boss," Carlisle said. "But when we get off active duty and back to the National Security Agency, you can forget about me making coffee."

USS *RAMAGE* (DDG 82)

Captain Robert Daistrom, commanding officer of USS *Ramage*, raised his binoculars and tried to find HMS *Victory*. According to the SPS-10 surface search radar, the British cruiser was five thousand yards off *Ramage*'s starboard bow, supposedly supporting the search pattern *Ramage* was executing. It might as well have been five hundred miles. With visibility fewer than five hundred feet in the fog, *Ramage* seemed to be alone in the North Sea.

   He heard a footstep on the steel deck behind him and stifled a sigh. Not all of the British forces were so far away.

   Admiral Ian Richardson, commander of the exercise Blue forces, joined Daistrom on the bridge wing railing. The United States had almost absentmindedly acceded to Britain's request to put *Ramage* under Richardson's direct command, a radical deviation from simply chopping OPCON—operational control—to the NATO commander. Admiral Richardson had immediately shifted his flag to *Ramage* and taken up residence in the flag quarters. His aide was berthed in with the chief engineer. So far, other than politely enduring the two British officers' complaints about American food, the arrangement had been working.

   "Any sign of my submarine, Captain? Or of the bloody Prussians?"

   He turned in reluctant courtesy. "I'm afraid not, Admiral. I'm ready to swear they never even got a copy of the measles." The MSEL—Master Sequence of Events List, the "measles"—was the schedule of exercises and evolutions that comprised the heart of the exercise. "I'll be damned if I see much of a training opportunity in this."

"Especially not when you'd rather be somewhere else, I suppose."

"How would you have felt about missing the Falklands, Admiral?"

The admiral regarded him sardonically. "Getting shot at is vastly overrated as a career path, Captain. And if this were actual combat, you and I would already be dead, since your chaps don't seem to be able to maintain contact on the Orange adversary submarine."

"If we don't hold her, then she's not there. Between the lousy fuel *Spessart* passed us yesterday and their lackadaisical attitude toward OPORD, the Germans are wasting our time. I don't see much point in being here instead of in Korea."

The admiral turned away to study the white-capped ocean.

Was it genetic? That cold, chiseled profile, beakish nose, slightly receding chin? A prerequisite for advancing rapidly in the British Navy, or just natural selection? However the United Kingdom had managed it, looking at Admiral Richardson, one could almost see the generations of seafaring experience that Britain had earned in every tiny corner of the world.

"The past is prologue to the present," the admiral said finally. "The Germans today are the Prussians of yesterday. They do not normally make mistakes of this kind. Ergo, I conclude there were no mistakes."

"But for what possible purpose? We get submarine detection practice, they get to run attack approaches to their hearts' content. No point in screwing themselves out of the training, not with the United States footing the operating costs."

"Oh, come on, Daistrom," the admiral said harshly. "Think about today's events critically, working on the assumption that the Pru—the Germans, if you will—had a purpose for acting as they did. I'm willing to bet that the submarine is exactly where it is supposed to be, and is the reason that I've got one submarine gone missing. All you've done is demonstrate that we can't detect and track her, and that your destroyer is none too picky about what she burns in her turbines. Not a bad intelligence-gathering day for the Prussians, is it?''

"Sir, with all due respect. Surely you're not suggesting the Germans *sank Oberon*? That's beyond probable. A screwed-up schedule or broken communications gear is more likely.''

"I don't require your agreement, Captain. We've been at this business a bit longer than you Yanks have. *Oberon* is missing, and neither you nor my own ships can tell me a deuced thing about it. Yes, I think the Germans are responsible. But until we come up with some sort of evidence, there's no chance that I can convince the Admiralty. This sea is filthy with U-boats, but none of my colleagues is going to accuse the Krauts based solely on my beliefs.''

"Admiral, I—''

"Were it an American submarine missing, I suspect you'd be a bit more open to the possibility. Now, I suggest you get your arse back into CIC and see if you can't manage to locate this last one. Perhaps a little command attention will motivate your chaps.'' The admiral turned and stalked back into the relative warmth of the bridge.

Daistrom slammed his hand down on the wooden railing that topped the bridge wing. A thin layer of ice cracked, then shivered off down the side of the ship to disappear into the lick of sea foam streaming back from the bow. He allowed himself one last appreciative look aft at the sleek lines of the ship, then followed the admiral back into the skin of the ship and aft to combat.

"Sonar, where the hell is she? The MIUWU says she's within weapons release range.'' Daistrom's salty New England twang was unmistakable over the bitch box.

"Come on, come on,'' Petty Officer First Class Digger muttered. He snapped the range scale on the scope out to ten miles, watched the cursor sweep once around it, then returned the active sonar display to the shorter-range mode. "What're those damned reservists calling a submarine?'' According to the measles, a Type 215 U-boat was operating at a depth of sixty feet somewhere in the five-mile box his sonar was searching.

Digger sighed, and pushed the button on his mouthpiece. "Little bitch's maybe slipped down below the layer, and everything I've got's shallow, Captain. Hell of a negative gradient today, and I'm getting shit for returns on active." He glanced at STG1 Henning, the sonarman running the passive gear, and shrugged. The rounded, pudgy figure of his best friend on the ship hulked over the horizontal printer equipment. Between the two of them, there wasn't a submarine around that could evade detection for long.

"Sir, I'd like to get *Snoopy 1* to drop a couple more buoys," Digger continued. "Set deep this time, around six hundred feet." *Snoopy 1* was an SH-60B ASW helicopter that was part of *Ramage*'s inventory of weapons and sensors. The Aegis-class destroyer carried two of the versatile helicopters, and *Snoopy 2* was currently preflighting on the deck.

There was a pointed pause on the circuit. "Six hundred feet. Be right this time," Daistrom's voice said.

Moments later, the call for flight quarters blared over the 1MC. Digger stood up, hopped onto his chair, and turned the volume down until the voice faded away. They could still hear the speaker in CIC if they really needed to know what was happening. A few moments later, they heard the hard beat of a helicopter's rotors turning at full power.

"Not good, shipmate," Henning said. "What if we were over in Korea doing this for real?"

"We can't hear her, she can't hear us. And she's damned sure not looking at us through a periscope. If she were that shallow, we'd have her right now."

"I don't know, Digger. There's something that bothers the shit out of me about this boat. I had her solid during the last availability period—engine noises, turn count, everything, on aural. Then all at once, nothing. If she'd pulled the plug, I ought to have at least caught some transients. Some air blowing out of the ballast tanks, hull popping under the depth pressure—hell, even the periscope rattling around. If she went deep, then she's figured out a way to do it quieter than I've ever seen. I should have seen something. The MIUWU claims she's got it—maybe they're all on drugs."

"I didn't see anything on passive either. But what else could it be? Submarines don't just disappear, and she was close, real close. If she was just beating feet out of here, she ought to have just faded out. There are two possibilities: first, the MIUWU sonar techs are stupid and they're calling acoustic multipathed garbage off some fishing a U-boat. Second, they're not stupid. The MIUWU's got their sonobuoys laid deep and our tail's still shallow, so we might have missed her in the thermocline. I heard they've got a new beamformer, too." Digger patted the side of his console. "As good as the SQR-89 suite is on this boat, it was obsolete three months after they installed it."

"Green flare, green flare port side!" a voice suddenly broke in on the ASW circuit.

"Oh, shit," Digger said quietly.

"How the hell—Digger, can they fire those flares from depth? I thought they had to be shallow for that."

"They do. Periscope depth or surfaced."

The two sonarmen traded concerned looks. Not a damned thing about this exercise had made sense so far.

"Goddammit, where the hell is she?" Daistrom snapped.

"Captain, I . . . I . . ." Ensign Blackthorne, the ASW officer, took a deep breath and tried to find his voice.

"You're on watch until you find her, mister. Now get this ship back in the game before I relieve you."

"TAO, recommend we come left to two-six-five to close the green flare location and execute Search Plan Alpha," the ASWO said. Daistrom saw the officer's eyes flick over in his direction.

"Combat, bridge. Green flare, *starboard* side, range, two thousand yards!"

Every noise ceased. The enlisted men and women stared at their scopes and charts, not moving, barely breathing. The ASWO somehow found the courage to look up at his captain, then found himself unable to look away, mesmerized like a mouse about to be eaten by a snake.

"You *do* know what a green flare signifies, mister. Don't you?" The captain's voice was low and deadly.

The ASWO nodded, cleared his throat, then found his

voice. "A simulated torpedo shot from a submarine, sir," he answered, profoundly grateful that his voice sounded almost steady.

"And that's two we've just taken up the ass, isn't it? With the rest of the task force watching."

"Yes, sir." What the hell had gone wrong? The young officer had his best team on in sonar. If anybody could find the contact, it ought to be Digger and Henning. And the captain ought to know that, instead of trying . . . Suddenly an idea occurred to him. "Captain? This evolution has been way outside of what we know about the two-one-five. I'd like to get these tapes off to the intelligence folks as soon as we can. Requesting green deck in thirty minutes for helo launch to get this to the P-3 squadron in Lakenheath immediately."

Daistrom glared. The ASWO met his gaze steadily now. The captain *was* right. The Aegis destroyer *should* have been able to find the submarine before the flares were shot, particularly at those ranges. He knew in his heart he hadn't screwed the pooch on leading his ASW team. Therefore something was wrong with the scenario.

"TAO—do it," Daistrom said abruptly. "Ensign Blackthorne and I will be in sonar, seeing if we can find out what the hell happened out there." He turned abruptly and stalked back to the sonar shack.

Ensign Blackthorne followed, aware of the new respect radiating out from the CDC operators. Not many people faced the captain's annoyance and survived. And until that very moment, the young officer had not even been sure that the captain knew his name.

Two hours later, the German submarine surfaced two thousand yards off *Ramage*'s port bow. Her skipper appeared in the conning tower accompanied by an enlisted man with a floodlight. Forty-five seconds after slowly blinking a polite message of thanks for providing target practice, she slipped back beneath the waves and disappeared off *Ramage*'s sonar.

Petty Officer First Class Digger secured the special attack team, collected the acoustic printouts and records, then walked out of sonar onto the bridge wing and flipped a bird at her wake.

MIUWU 106

Bailey handed the binoculars back to the lookout. "Well, we warned them. Not our fault if they get incoming after we reported the sub. Let's look at the detection again." Carlisle followed her into the operations van and slipped back onto the high stool stationed in front of the sonar.

"You're still holding the German boat?" she asked.

He stared at the screen for a moment, then swiveled around on the stool to face her. "Intermittently, like before. She's still tracking north, Jer—sorry. *Skipper,* I mean. Out of range in about five minutes, I think," Carlisle said. He sighed.

"Then get some more sonobuoys in the water. What the hell's the use of having a helicopter on alert for us if we don't use him?" she snapped.

"I called them two hours ago," Lieutenant Boston, the watch officer, broke in. "They're tied up looking for HMS *Oberon.*"

"Can't be helped, then," Bailey said. "Their helicopter, their ocean, and their exercise. Run the two-one-five sub training tape for me. I want to see it side by side with our detection."

"You don't trust me on the classification?" Carlisle asked.

"What the hell do you think? But I have an odd feeling *Ramage*'s skipper is going to want to discuss our—ummm, tactical circuit discipline with me. Make me smart enough on this to embarrass him right off. It might avoid a public execution."

Carlisle punched the START button on the CD-ROM. "You want the printer on?"

"No. Not yet." Bailey studied the green waterfall display building on the computer screen. A wide, evenly spaced set of lines dominated the display. They jagged to the right and then settled down at a larger spacing. "Okay, check me on the classification clues. A diesel engine—

that's easy enough—but not U.S., and not British. Strange
dynamics on the signature.''

"It's not your eyes," the sonar tech answered. "It's the
effect of the air-independent propulsion system, and loading
from the propulsor. That's a damned quiet submarine, but
those are the giveaways. The intelligence says that it might
be the effect of the supply loading on the engines. The
liquid oxygen doesn't feed smoothly enough to keep the
engine completely stable. You wouldn't notice it, listening
to the engine itself, but it'll show up as a little instability
on passive sonar.''

"Nothing from the propeller, right?''

"We can't even really call it that. They have a pump-jet
propulsor on those boats, an advanced design based on the
British Swiftsure-class one. It makes the two-one-five quieter than our ballistic missile boats, but it's so slow and big
that it drags on the engines a little when they get started.
Here, I'll show you.''

Carlisle pulled the keyboard toward him and clicked on
a series of menus. The waterfall accumulation of frequency
versus time information froze. "I'll just back it up about
twenty minutes—that's when the engine comes on-line.''
He found the time frame he wanted and clicked on the
START button.

The screen wiped off the old information and began ac-
cumulating green dots across the top. "Earliest information
at the top, oldest at the bottom,'' Carlisle reminded her.
"Watch, it comes on in about one minute.''

She nodded. Specks of green noise drifted down the
screen as though shoved out of position by the new information appearing at the top.

"There.'' A jagged line of dots crossed the screen from
left to right, then jigged back to the left. "See, it overshoots
its operating rpm's, then the governor catches it. Now
watch—this is the cool part.''

Instead of settling down onto a stable frequency distribution, the lines wavered sinuously for a few minutes. The
perturbations gradually died out, and the new engine sta-
bilized into the pattern she'd seen earlier.

"Impressive," she said. "It's not hard to pick out once you've seen it."

"We already knew that. The problem's not classifying it—it's detecting it. Weren't you paying attention last month?"

"Cut it out," she said quietly. "Not everyone in the van is cleared for what we do at work."

"They ought to be. The stuff I got right before we left work last week was a reverse Walker. Noise-suppression, counterdetection gear—hell, I can't *wait* to get these tapes back to the lab. *Ramage* ought to be told what she's up against. Hell, the whole U.S. Navy ought to know."

She nodded, understanding the reference to the Walker spy case and appreciating the sentiment behind it. The warrant officer convicted of espionage had passed on massive amounts of information on the U.S. Navy's most sensitive submarine quieting programs. "For what it's worth, you know I fought for full disclosure to the navy. Atchinson overruled me."

"He's an asshole. Let him spend a few years in the navy and he'd think differently about it." Five years ago, before he'd joined NSA, Carlisle had been a submarine sailor. The results of Walker's treason could very well have gotten him killed, if the Cold War had ever progressed to the shooting stage. If the government could have left the punishment of the spy up to the navy—or even in the hands of the men who served on submarines—the taxpayers would have been spared considerable expense.

"We can hardly count on these U-boats coming up to snorkel," she observed. "No convenient periscope sightings."

"You got that right. She doesn't need to, carrying her own air like that. She runs on batteries most of the time, and I bet she's got some damned long-endurance ones. Get low on juice, just light off this little stealth engine of hers, recharge for a couple of hours, and she slips back into black-hole mode on battery again."

"Sooner or later, she's going to make a mistake," she answered. "Somebody will forget a tool, and ground the machinery out to the hull and bypass all that fancy shock

mounting. The cooks will drop a pan of sauerkraut or a
seaman will forget he's at quiet ship and flush a toilet. They
screw up, you'll nail them.''

"I hope you're right about that," he said quietly. "I sure
do hope you are, Jer. Because I'm wondering myself."

Twenty minutes later, after she'd reviewed the watch log,
she headed back to the tent. The wind had died down. With
any luck, she could get a couple of hours of sleep before
the watch came to wake her.

She paused outside the van to refill her coffee cup. The
wind had abated slightly, although gusts still flexed the
high-frequency communications antennas deployed around
the van.

Ten more days and they'd be back on the C-5 transport
heading for sunny San Diego. From there, they'd scatter
back to their home states. For Carlisle and Bailey, that
meant D.C. Unless the buildup in Korea necessitated their
presence there.

Most military tacticians agreed that the return to Korea
would entail a long and bloody conflict. The northern part
of the country was geared for war. Tunnels and firing em-
placements honeycombed the area. While many believed
that the nKoreans—the politically correct way to refer to
the former North Korean republic—was hardly among the
more sensible countries in the world, surely even the rabid
Communists would realize that there was no good ending
to this scenario.

So far there was no indication that the United States was
considering pulling MIUWU 106 out of *Northern Lights*
for Korean operations. Just as well. Although they had M-
16s, shotguns, and .45 pistols in their inventory, MIUWU
units were intended to be used in rear area support, to control and monitor access to harbors when most of the heavy
fighting was over. They'd done just that during Desert
Storm and Desert Shield, with several units remaining over
there for nine months during the conflict. Based on her last
experience in Korea, though, it would be some time before
the area was secure enough for the MIUWU.

There were twenty-eight MIUWU units in the United
States. While 106's recent experience in the theater would

make them a prime candidate for deployment, there were several other units who'd been over there almost as recently. It would be a hell of an airlift, she thought, as well as a logistical nightmare if the unit was ordered to go directly from Britain to Korea.

She shuddered, less from the wind than from her memories of Korea. Any battle there would be long and brutal. Lurking beneath the polite veneer of her Korean hosts she'd seen a potential for brutality and savagery that still made her wonder why the United States supported them. State-sponsored terrorists, most of them.

She put the thoughts out of her mind and headed back to her tent, ashamed to be grateful that they weren't going.

THE NORTH SEA FLOOR

So far, no magnetic signature had been strong enough to trigger the mine's firing sequence, although several had come close enough to enable it to recharge its battery. It was now fully recovered from the activation sequence drain, and any sufficiently large mass of metal within two thousand meters would satisfy the target selection criteria hardwired into its relays. The mine was no longer a passive chunk of metal on the seabed floor, but a part of Germany's growing arsenal.

7

3 MARCH 2002:
THE NORTH SEA

U-504

With the moored mines laid outside the entrance to the two British harbors, *U-504* resumed tracing out the pattern dictated by the General Staff. En route to the first point on the plan, the crew slipped back into the normal routine, catching up on sleep and bitching about the food. Merker himself caught an uninterrupted two-hour nap and woke feeling refreshed.

The transit plan. The brief nap had refreshed him sufficiently to be able to focus on something beyond the tedious demands of ejecting chunks of metal at exact intervals across the mouths of harbors. The requirement for crossing particular points in the ocean and specified times and speeds still puzzled him, now more so than before. Instead of avoiding exercise areas and surface ships, the route now took them directly through the middle of an antisubmarine warfare detection exercise—an odd choice of intecepts for a submarine that was intended to remain undetected.

Merker had just stepped into the hatchway separating the control center from the central passageway when he heard a high-pitched metallic *ping*. Before he could turn back to the control center, something slammed into the middle of his back.

He hit the deck and rolled. A thin, high-pressure stream of water batted at him around the deck. He curled into a ball, shielding his face from the blast, and shouted, "Surface the boat!"

His voice was barely audible, whether because of the water or because of the other noises. He could hear and feel feet pounding on the deck; the noise cut through by sharp, arcing snaps as water hit the sensitive electronics. Within a minute, a damage-control-clad man stepped over him, moving to the edge of the passageway to avoid the water. Seconds later, the background hiss from the leak ceased.

Merker stayed curled on the deck for a moment, smelling the salty water, feeling it already start to drip off him on the deck. *This* was outside, only ten feet away from where he stood every day, pressing against the hull and waiting for some subtle flaw or mistake to give it an entrance to the boat. For a submariner, it was as unsettling as if the air he breathed had suddenly become visible.

He forced himself to roll over, schooling his face into impassivity. The control room was silent, the men avoiding his eyes.

Ehrlich cleared his throat. "*Kapitan,* do you still want—"

Merker cut him off. "If that leak had been any more serious, we'd be dead now. By delaying following orders, you risked the life of every man on this crew."

Ehrlich dropped his eyes to the chart. "Yes, *Kapitan.*"

Merker bit back a harsh reply. He noticed his hands were trembling. The sea was no longer the saving cloak of invisibility that hid him from all the rest of the world, silent and impenetrable, but another enemy.

"I'll be in my stateroom," he said finally. "Get me a damage report and send the engineer to see me." He turned and stalked off, clamping down on his self-control with every resource at his disposal, the curious matter of the reason for the transit plan submerged once again in the details of staying alive undersea.

MIUWU 106

Nine more days. Bailey shrugged her shoulders down into the jacket, trying to hunch down into the broad collar. The wet cold still bit at the back of her neck.

"How far into the availability period are we?" she asked as she stepped inside the surveillance van.

"Two hours," Lieutenant Jeremy Boston answered. "According to the schedule, three diesel submarines should be at periscope depth five thousand yards off the coast."

Lieutenant Boston was acting executive officer for this exercise. He was a small, wiry man, a marathon runner. Any trace of a Napoleonic complex she'd found common in other short men was drowned out in the continual flow of running edorphins in his bloodstream. Sandy hair, green eyes, and sharp wit were his most notable characteristics. Next year, after he'd been promoted to lieutenant commander, he'd be in line for a permanent XO position. From what she'd seen of him so far, he was ready for it.

The Germans had agreed to provide training services on their way out of port to participate in the next round of the war games, a symbolic demonstration of their willingness to share details of their military capabilities. The Type 215 diesels were to come to snorkel depth for two hours in the vicinity of the unit's sonobuoys, then surface and transit within visual range. That evolution would provide the MIUWU with not only acoustic training on the submarine's diesel engine signatures but also give the lookouts a chance to cut their teeth on a real periscope mast.

She nodded. "The Germans know exactly where the sonobuoys are, too. I called the commodore and gave him the positions so they could come dead-on to them."

The acoustic sonobuoys were laid in a straight line perpendicular to the shortest route through the North Sea from Germany to the battle group. The MIUWU was camped on a high bluff, the elevation extending the operational range of the antenna that picked up the low-voltage transmissions from the sonobuoys as well as increasing the line-of-sight capabilities of the radar.

So far they'd accomplished nothing except to shove everyone over the edge into sleep deprivation. Every single technician wanted to see the live detection on the Germans' subs, so the off-duty watch sections had taken to hanging around the van or the mess tent, waiting for something to happen.

Somewhere out there was a German submarine.

USS RAMAGE

"XO, any word from the MIUWU yet?" Captain Daistrom asked.

Commander Brubecker shook his head. "I'm not holding my breath. They were supposed to give us a heads-up on the subs heading out this way for *our* detection exercises. For an antisubmarine warfare asset, they're not a lot of help. Damned boat's probably cutting donuts right on top of their buoys—naw, I take that back. Donuts they'd recognize. They're probably all out on liberty drunk. You know reservists overseas—always looking for a party."

"We aren't having a lot of luck either," Daistrom pointed out. "Call their captain. Let's get him out here, maybe send a couple of people over to their camp. See if getting to know each other a little better produces any bright ideas. Besides, we ought to know a little bit about them—how much equipment they've got, how many people. All that sort of stuff."

The XO glanced up sharply. "In case we have to evacuate them? Captain, is there anything I should know? Admiral Richardson's been telling anyone who'll listen that the Germans are on the move again on the Continent, and now you're bringing up sealift capabilities."

Daistrom found himself unwilling to admit he'd been mulling over Admiral Richardson's theories. "That torpedo shot they reported—it's probably nothing, but with *Oberon* missing I'd have thought the Brits would be a damned sight more interested in it. But Richardson hasn't said anything about it. It's not like him to miss an opportunity to obsess over the Germans."

"You think there's something to it?"

"Not really. *Oberon* was an old boat. Besides, what are the odds that there could be another continental conflict starting without our getting some intelligence on it?" Daistrom forced a relaxed look. "Admiral Richardson has a lot of ideas. I'm not certain how many of them I agree with, but it makes for some interesting discussions. The MIUWU—it's just a training opportunity, okay?"

"If you say so, Captain."

NATO exercises were more than just tactical exercises for weapons and sensors. The events provided a chance to peer into the minds of their Allied counterparts, a time to learn how other nations thought and operated, and to iron out differences before the real thing. What puzzled Daistrom more than losing *Oberon* was why the British commander wasn't talking about it.

U-504

"Slowly. One knot when you're this close." Merker laid one hand on Kraeken's shoulder and pointed at the sonar screen. A small spark of phosphorescence blinked into view. It twinkled for a moment, then faded out. "A contact this small, you'll lose it if you generate any self-noise at all."

"It's right where they said it'd be. I'm close enough—let's do it." Kraeken looked feverish.

"Make sure," Merker cautioned. "You'll lose it in the noise when you extend the cutters." The retractable mechanical arms mounted just above the sonar dome were merely one more of the improvements on this boat. They were controlled from a small workstation jammed in next to the weapons console, and had been mounted on *U-504* along with the high-frequency, high-resolution sonar now tracking the tiny contacts.

Merker watched as Kraeken cautiously extended the mechanical arm, manipulating it with the joystick. The submarine's speaker rasped as the external monitor showed the arm making contact.

"I've got it." Kraeken turned to the OOD. "Now."

MIUWU 106

"Ma'am! Wake up, Captain. *Jer.*"

Her eyes opened, and she looked into Carlisle's worried

face. She propped herself up on one elbow. Carlisle held a hot paper cup out to her, and she wrapped her fingers around it gratefully.

"What time is it?"

"Zero-three-hundred. They want you in the van. Something funny's happening."

"I'm awake," she decided. "Be there as soon as I get dressed."

She went through the familiar routine of slipping back on the rest of her uniform, drained the last bit of coffee, and crumpled the cup.

She walked to the van, and the security watch let her in immediately, evidently primed to expect her arrival. She stepped up into the van and ran into a solid phalanx of enlisted watchstanders and officers. All four sonar technicians were clustered around their equipment at the far end of the trailer, and two electronics technicians had the electrical distribution panel partially exposed immediately opposite the door.

"Trouble," Boston said immediately. He glanced at the clock. "Forty-five minutes ago, the buoys started going off-line."

"How long have they been in the water?"

"Two hours. They should have been good for at least another six hours."

"Any indication why?"

"We're troubleshooting right now, making sure it's not a problem with the gear. Frankly, that's a long shot. They went off-line one at a time. If they'd gone off all at once, I'd be certain it was on our end, but they didn't."

She nodded. "Could be a cascading failure of some sort, I suppose. A problem with one channel causes something else to go down." She knew it sounded lame even as she said it.

"That's what I was hoping," Boston replied, pointing at the cluster of technicians, "and the reason for having the A-team out here. Long shot, though. There's something else, too. Carlisle heard something interesting on aural."

"What?"

"Let me get him to show you," the lieutenant said. He motioned to the sonarman, who was already rewinding a tape.

"In two seconds, sir," Carlisle said over his shoulder.

Bailey squeezed past the technicians to stand behind Carlisle. "You caught it on tape?"

"I haven't played it back yet, so I don't know how well it came through. If it's not here, I'll have to just tell you, but I'd rather you listened to it yourself. Here it is." He punched the PLAY button on the RD240 recorder.

She shut her eyes and listened. *Normal buoy sounds, waves—God, I'm glad I'm not out there! It even sounds cold out there. Nothing, nothing, nothing—hold it.* She opened her eyes.

"You caught that?"

"I heard *something*. Run it again—I want to see it on passive."

He backed the tape up, cued up the video display, and started it again. A few exceptionally narrow lines cut through the display vertically. Artifacts, caused by the van's own electrical power affecting the sonar system. Not good. She kept her eyes glued on the display.

"We're trying to hunt down the ground that's causing them," Carlisle said, answering the question he knew would come to mind. "So far, no luck."

She nodded. The background noise of water moving around the sonobuoy was strangely hypnotic. She heard the noise source again, a hard-to-define thrumming, like the twanging of a guitar string grounded against a nonacoustic board. Simultaneously, a fat blob appeared on the display. Carlisle let it run a few more moments, then stopped the tape.

"I only heard it once," he said. "Played it back a couple of times, and it's just that one detection."

"What is it?"

"I'm not entirely sure," he admitted. "It could be a lot of things. Something brushing against the buoy tether, some sort of acoustic test going on somewhere, even equipment off that oil rig hitting us from a couple of convergence zones away."

"When did the buoy go off-line?" she asked.

He answered by flicking the tape recorder on again. Two minutes after the noise, the background ocean noise cut out abruptly.

She studied the paper printout carefully, looking for anything that might give her a clue as to the noise's source. There was nothing on it, other than the background static generated by the sonar itself and the artifact lines indicative of an American power source.

"It sounds a little like a hydraulic source of some sort," she said slowly. "I've heard something similar off submarines maneuvering."

"That's what I thought, too. And the fact that the buoy goes off-line right after that is damned suspicious."

"What happened with the other buoys? How long after that did they go out?"

"Two went out before this one," he said. "I thought it might be a faulty buoy with the first one, and then the second one went out. At that point, I got worried. I switched the tape recorder into high speed, just as I would have if we'd caught a real contact. Five minutes later, number three—the one I just played for you—went cold. Two more went dead in the next thirty minutes, but there was no noise before they went. Just on this one."

"Any buoys still up?"

"Two are still sweet and cold. I don't know for how much longer, though."

The cold from the outside seemed to seep into the van, although she knew it was just the air conditioner kicking into high gear to deal with the large number of bodies crammed into the space, generating heat. "I'm not liking this," she said slowly. "Not one little bit."

Carlisle shook his head, not disagreeing but in puzzlement over the situation. "I don't know what to tell you, Captain."

"Give me your best guess."

He stared at the printout for a moment, collecting his thoughts. "You want my best guess? I think we've got a submarine out there—cancel that, an underwater vehicle of some sort—that's got the coordinates for our buoys. It's trolling along and cutting the lines that run between the sonobuoy itself and the floating antenna that transmits data to us. I don't know how, I don't know why—hell, I don't even know how they manage to zero in on a tiny little cable in a big ocean. But that's what this is. Yep, that's it."

He looked up at her, and she saw certainty in his eyes. "There's only one thing that keeps me from having you locked up as a certified lunatic, you know," she remarked with more nonchalance that she actually felt. "You know what that is."

Carlisle nodded. "Yes, ma'am, I do." Something passed between then. Behind her, Lieutenant Boston cleared his throat.

"Just one reason," she said, keeping her eyes locked on Carlisle's. "An inconsequential little thing that I think may earn me a padded cell right next to yours."

"And what would that be?" Boston pressed.

"Tell him," she ordered, finally looking back at the printout.

"She agrees with me," he said softly. "That's all she's trying to say. That there's a submarine out there killing off our sonobuoys."

She nodded. "That's about it. Not the worst part of it, though."

"But we didn't detect a submarine," the lieutenant said, slightly puzzled.

"*That's* the worst part. We've just lost coverage over our entire assigned area, and we don't even know how or why."

USS RAMAGE

"They what?" Digger asked.

"The MIUWU lost sonobuoy coverage to the south of us. Don't know that it'll make much difference right now. Nothing's scheduled for another six hours." Henning shrugged and gave a cursory glance at his screen. "I sure don't care—the only thing moving around in the MIUWU area is a British frigate, and we damned well don't need sonar to find her.''

"Probably something stupid, like forgetting to reset the mode after maintenance.'' Digger went back to reading his book.

HMS BRILLIANT

HMS *Brilliant* continued on her southerly track, cutting through the MIUWU detection area at twenty knots. She was late rendezvousing with the oiler, and her tactical circuits chattered with changes to the underway replenishment plan. Coming up with alternative courses and speeds was easier than usual. The area set aside for UNREP had been closed to commercial traffic for six hours for the ASW exercise. Even though the German submarines hadn't cooperated, the Notice to Mariners restriction on the water space had helped.

Finally. The mine felt a surge of energy as the ship approached. The magnetic signature increased rapidly, topping off the last remaining capacity of the battery. Unlike the last three contacts it had sensed, this one did not veer away from the small area of ocean the mine claimed as its own. At a preset flux level, the mine took the steps preliminary to firing.

"Fog, fog, always the bleeding fog," *Brilliant*'s captain muttered. He'd been on the bridge for the past five hours, keeping a watchful eye on the OOD. "Might as well be a submarine, for all the visibility we have.'' He walked over to study the Furuno radar mounted in one corner of the bridge. The screen was scattered with pockets of noise, the only contact the oiler ten miles in front of them. They were too far from land for the coast of Britain to reflect the high-frequency X-band transmissions of the Furuno.

"How much longer?'' he asked the navigator.

"Twenty minutes, sir. The oiler is on one-eighty at twelve knots, waiting for us.''

"Good." The captain turned to the OOD. "A slow approach on her now, since we can't expect a visual until we're damned near up her arse."

With the preliminaries out of the way, the firing circuits buried in the center of the mine were ready. One more incremental increase in magnetic flux and the hair-triggered relay would trip.

Seconds later, it happened. Power surged into the base of the torpedo, igniting the small amount of propellant there. The casing collapsed as the torpedo broke loose and seawater shorted out the components that had survived so long within their housing. The torpedo was already halfway to the surface by then.

As it reached the surface, at a preset pressure reading, the internal pressure inside the torpedo blew it apart. The gas canister inside discharged a red haze that melted into the fog, giving a sickly light-pink tinge to the fog immediately around it.

"Sir?" the port lookout said uncertainly.

The captain's head snapped up. "What is it?" Fog always held more dangers that anyone could anticipate. Small fishing vessels that didn't show up on radar were the worst, and often the first clue of their presence was the warning given by an alert lookout.

"The fog, Captain, it—" The lookout gagged and fell against the alidade mounted on the bridge wing.

The captain had two seconds to notice the discoloration in the fog before the first molecules of the gas reached him. His hands went to his neck reflexively as he felt himself start to choke. His trachea was already swelling shut.

The radio. The captain's fingers closed around the ship-to-shore mike. His arm jerked upward and his fingers flexed. It slipped out of his hand and fell, swinging in arcs at the end of the cord. The captain, now prone on the deck and convulsing, didn't notice. His brain had already begun the chaotic process of shutting down due to lack of oxygen. Ten seconds later, the toxins crossed the delicate blood-brain membrane and killed the captain minutes before he could suffocate.

Four decks below the waterline, the engineering watch had no indication that anything was amiss on the bridge. The toxin circulated through the ship on the internal air currents and eventually settled into their space. Two boiler technicians had just started the intricate process of opening valves and aligning the system for taking on fuel. Their first spasms opened exactly the wrong sequence of valves, and raw diesel fuel streamed out into the space. It crept across the deck plates and filled the bilges, eventually reaching the outer casing of a hot fuel pump. The resulting explosion blew a massive hole in the side of *Brilliant* and broke her keel. Seawater rushed in, exploding into steam as it extinguished the fire. Five minutes later, *Brilliant*'s bow slipped under the waves.

Ten miles away, the oiler began troubleshooting her radar, trying to determine why she was no longer holding contact on HMS *Brilliant*.

PART
2

COMMAND

The authority to attack contained in the rules for taking up the different positions, means, at the same time, an order to attack. In cases of genuine doubt, the commander must decide in favor of attacking. A successful attack is always a gain—a neglected opportunity cannot be made good.

—*THE U-BOAT COMMANDER'S HANDBOOK,*
Section VIII.D.377 (1943)
(translated by U.S. Navy)

8

4 MARCH 2002:
THE NORTH SEA

MIUWU 106

"Okay, you've got it," Bailey said. She picked up her overnight bag and slung it over one shoulder. "The helo should be here any minute."

Since HMS *Brilliant* had vanished, *Ramage* had been more than mildly interested in the odd strumming noise the MIUWU had detected when their buoys went off-line, as well as the snippet of torpedo detection they'd laughed at earlier. The British search teams had found oil slicks and debris, along with evidence that the ship had experienced a massive engineering fire. Still, the coincidence was too convenient to ignore.

Ramage's executive officer had contacted her on tactical and requested that she come out to the ship and bring the tapes with her. *Ramage* seemed to believe that its sonar suite had to be infinitely more sophisticated than the MIUWU's gear. Commander Brubecker had pointed out that not only might the ship be able to pull more signals out of the noise, but the MIUWU sonarman could also provide some valuable training for the *Ramage* technicians.

Bailey wasn't particularly convinced. Given the detection records of the two commands, her money was on the MIUWU.

Lieutenant Boston smiled. "Don't worry about us. We'll be fine."

"I'm not worried," she answered. "If I were, I wouldn't

be going." She looked at him sharply, then smiled. "Funny, I just had the strangest sense of déjà vu. I remember my first OIC job, taking a detachment down to the Gulf Coast in Texas for an exercise. I remember sitting there with that same expression on my face that you've got now, wondering—well, Lieutenant, never mind."

USS *RAMAGE*

Less than an hour later, the helicopter skittered up sideways to the destroyer and wobbled down to the deck. *Ramage* was only eighty miles off the coast, patrolling a ten-by-ten box. The chaplain met her on the flight deck and escorted her to the captain's cabin.

"Welcome aboard," Captain Daistrom said, then motioned her to a chair at his work table. "How was your flight?"

"Routine. Any landing you can walk away from is a good one," she answered.

The captain's cabin was larger than any she'd seen before on a combatant. He had two rooms, one serving as his office and dining area. She surmised that the bedroom was through the closed door to her left, since the room they were in did not contain the standard navy couch that folded out into a rack. The lower part of the bulkheads were paneled, the upper half painted high-gloss white. A few plaques and mementos dotted the compartment, but the most striking feature was the number of books the captain had. All were securely stowed in metal-braced bookshelves with bungee cords across the front, or in steel-gray book cabinets with glass fronts. Even in the worst seas, there would be no danger of one of the tomes falling out. A stuffed boar's head was mounted high on one wall. A holster hung from one yellowed tusk.

The man sitting opposite her went with the room. His red hair was clipped short and smudged with silver at the temples, his face all angles and grooves, and a strong nose jutted out from the weathered face above thin lips. Even seated, he was clearly massive. She suspected he would be able to clear the hatches on the ship without ducking, but not by much.

He followed her eyes, and saw her looking at the boar. "Nasty bastard, isn't he? It's an Australian ridgeback, the most vicious wild pig around."

"Shoot it yourself, sir?"

"No, my CO gave it to me when I was weapons officer. For some reason, he felt it was appropriate."

She nodded. Why the boar? She was certain she'd find out in the next days.

"You've brought the tapes with you?"

"Tapes and gram cuts," she said, referring to the hard-copy printouts from the passive sonar's display.

"Good. I asked the chaplain to track down the operations officer. You'll like her—sharp gal. She's eager to get her hands on these and let her people take a whack at it."

"Be nice if you can find something other than the one detection." She felt his eyes boring into hers, then moving over her body carefully, studying the ribbons and surface warfare insignia, pausing on the dull steel-toed combat boots with muddied soles. His brown eyes were hard chips of light, reflecting more light than was coming from the overhead fluorescent bulbs.

Finally, he nodded. "I don't have to tell you this worries the shit out of me. I'm hoping my people come up with something that says you're dead wrong. The odds are that they will, you know. Your explanation for the buoys is just too damned strange."

"I've got some good people in the unit. We heard what we heard."

"I'm not doubting that. But it's a lot more likely that you got a bad set of buoys than a submarine deliberately sabotaged them. How many times had their service life been extended?"

"They originally expired five years ago, and were extended a year at a time. The current use authorization expires next month."

He nodded. "So you might have had some bad batteries in them. And if they were all from the same lot, not surprising that they'd all go out at once. Hell, the noise your people heard could have even been associated with the failure in some way.''

"A possibility. Under other circumstances, I might even call it a probability. But HMS *Oberon* is still unlocated. And *Brilliant*'s so-called engineering casualty—''

"You have a problem with the Brit's explanations, Commander?''

"Only when I'm at sea on a ship, Captain. When I'm ashore, I'm willing to let them put out whatever bullshit explanations they want to.''

Daistrom frowned. "I'm not sure I like your tone of voice, Miss Bailey.''

She stood up. "In the past eight months, there've been an increasing number of fatal incidents involving civilian vessels on the North Sea. I was on board one just two days before I deployed for this exercise. Something is going on out here, something I don't understand. That makes me suspicious of everything I can't explain, and less likely to buy easy explanations for disasters. And, with all due respect, sir, you took two green flares the last time your people blew us off.''

He studied her for a moment, an appraising look on his face. "Sit down. I'm not a complete idiot. You know something.''

A tight smile crossed her face. "They told me not to underestimate you.''

"Sit down, dammit! You better start remembering how to follow orders if you're going to be on board my ship.''

She sank back into the chair, leaned across, and planted her elbows on the green tablecloth. "Fifty weeks out of the year, I work for NSA. I'm an analyst in the Operation Directorate, in charge of the Division for Western European Issues. It's mostly statistical analysis, charting out the balance of forces, rates of military-industrial-complex production, that sort of thing. The political analysis is handled by a separate division. But I grew up there—an army brat. I speak the language, I know the people.''

"Okay, so you know Germans. What does that have to do with us?''

"Nothing—maybe. But since I'm in the naval reserve, I

keep tabs on what happens at sea. In the past eight months, there have been three fishing vessels found floating around the North Sea with the crews on board dead. And now *Brilliant* and *Oberon*."

Daistrom snorted. "As rickety as some of those fishing boats are, I'm not surprised."

"You're misunderstanding. These boats had no damage, no indication of anything going wrong. We were waiting on autopsies when I left." Unbidden, Atchinson's face and his offhand conclusion that it had been food poisoning came to mind.

"And you think that's related to *Brilliant* and *Oberon*?"

She shrugged. "Maybe. Maybe not. But it's enough to worry me, especially while I'm at sea. When I get back home, I'll turn the experts loose on it. While I'm out here—"

A soft tap on the door interrupted her. The door opened, and a female officer strode into the compartment. "The chaplain said you wanted to see me, Captain?"

"Lieutenant Commander June Collins, my operations officer." Daistrom completed the introductions while Bailey assessed the other officer.

Collins was a few inches shorter than she was herself, darkly tanned and trim. Short-cropped, straight blond hair, startlingly blue eyes, a full mouth twisted into a hard line. In different clothes, she could have been a surfer.

No, not a beach bunny at all, she thought, studying the other woman more closely. There was something in her eyes, a hard, cold intelligence at odds with the rest of her soft, feminine appearance.

"Welcome aboard." Collins held out her hand. "You're one of the reservists, right?"

"I'm CO of the MIUWU unit."

"Fascinating." Collins's tone of voice left no doubt that she had little interest in the operations of any unit connected with the reserves. "You brought the data?"

Bailey touched her briefcase. "Right here."

"Good." Collins turned to Daistrom. "With your permission, sir, I'd like to get my people on this. We should have an answer for you shortly."

Daistrom waved them off. "Go to it." He shot a sardonic look at Bailey. "I'm sure you two will have lots to talk about."

Collins led the way to the combat unit. The compartment was at least five times bigger than its counterpart on her last ship and ten times as large as the MIUWU van. Even so, it was packed tight with radarscopes, plotting tables, and closed-circuit TVs. A three-paneled large blue video screen dominated the forward end of the room. Only one of the consoles arrayed before it was in use.

"Sonar's got its own compartment right aft of combat." Collins led the way past two plotting tables. "Quick tour— we'll come back later. Just ask if there's anything you don't understand. There've been some real changes in ASW since you left active duty."

"It hasn't been *that* long since I've been on a ship." And if the other officer knew what occupied most of her time during her normal workday, she'd have known better. The sniping between regular navy and reserve units was a pain in the ass.

"Mmm," Collins said noncommittally. "But that was back when the only ships women were assigned to were tenders and oilers. A destroyer's a different game altogether." Collins's tone of voice left no doubt as to exactly how different she thought it was. She shoved open a watertight door and stepped over the kneeknocker combing. "Sonar. You might know most of this gear, at least."

Bailey caught a quick glimpse of the equipment as they entered the sonar compartment before the sonarmen mobbed them. Familiar scopes and displays crowded one wall. Moments later, she'd been divested of her briefcase, and three men were eagerly rummaging through it. A chief petty officer cross-examined her on the details of both the torpedo detection and the premature buoy terminations. The 1MC cut him off.

"Flight quarters? Expecting more visitors?" she asked Collins.

"Welcome to the real world," Collins answered. "Admiral Richardson's coming aboard. He wants to see your raw data himself. The Brits are no slouch on ASW, you know. Or maybe you don't. Take my word for it—I've spent enough time operating with them to know."

"Am I expected to give a formal capabilities briefing?"

"Nothing fancy. The printouts and the audio will be enough. We'll probably hold it up here in sonar instead of the wardroom anyway."

"Be nice if someone had told me ahead of time."

Collins smirked. "Like I said—duty on a destroyer is a different world. You get used to it. Captain likes to see how we perform under pressure and on short notice."

"Okay by me." Bailey bit back an angry reply. Collins could have told her—*should* have. What had happened to the *esprit de corps,* the sense of community that used to exist between female officers at sea? Was there a new dividing line between women? Serving on combatants versus serving on support ships? "Does the admiral know this is a no-notice brief?"

"I imagine he does. He and the captain seem to get along quite well. They'll be most impressed, I'm sure." Collins looked singularly unconvinced.

The admiral interrupted Bailey only once, to ask a question about her own background, both military and civilian. His mouth twitched as she recited the standard cover story for her position at NSA. He sat silent, impassive, during the remainder of her brief on MIUWU community capabilities and the summary of action from the day before. Captain Daistrom looked vaguely disappointed.

"That concludes my brief, Admiral. May I answer any questions?" she said finally.

The admiral stirred in his chair, and she only then became aware of how long it had been since he'd moved. He turned to Daistrom. "Disturbing. What have your own blokes learned about this contact?" he asked Daistrom.

"So far, nothing much more than Commander Bailey has briefed. We're trying out a couple of our fancier tricks as we speak. We may have a better answer a little later today," the captain replied. "Two interesting things, though. In addition to the source she mentioned, the chief thinks he's caught a sniff of a mechanical transient sound right before the sonobuoy went off-line, but he's not ready to swear to it. Secondly, one of our bright youngsters calculated the speed of advance that would be required for one unit to travel to each buoy. Allowing five minutes for each sonobuoy to be terminated, the submarine's speed would only have to be five knots. Well within the capabilities of any boat.''

"Just so. Then the culprit may be our missing German U-boats.''

"Maybe.'' Daistrom looked doubtful.

The admiral transferred his gaze back to the front of the room. "And you, madam? Your best guess?''

"Would be the same as yours, Admiral.''

"Well, then. We seem to be in agreement—since I find your reasoning sound—yet I confess I wish I could poke some bloody big hole in your logic. We do not need an undetectable German submarine with undiscerned intentions wandering around in this part of the ocean, do we?''

Daistrom shook his head. "It may be a ghost on active, but what about passive sonar?''

"After last week, I'm inclined to believe this submarine may have some tricks for that as well,'' the admiral said.

"How can he avoid detection by active sonar? It's not that much of a problem for us, but I'm curious,'' Bailey asked. "We use active DICASS buoys occasionally, but as a rule we stick to passive.''

"For the same reasons that we do, I'm sure. An active transmission tells him at least as much about your position as it tells you about his. Too bloody much. There are a number of counters against active sonar, as you well know. Antiechoic coating on the hull, using the layers of the ocean to hide, and even some advanced work I've seen on what the Yanks have been calling a cloaking device.''

Bailey kept silent. She was familiar with a number of frighteningly effective new noise cancellation programs, but there was simply no way to discuss them with the British admiral—not without violating a number of security regulations.

"The principle is relatively simple," the admiral continued. "The submarine simply analyzes the sonar signals bombarding it, determines the transmission frequency, and echoes back a sound that is phase-negative to the original transmission. That nullifies the returning sound signal. I've been told they're also working on a system that will create a false contact at some distance from the real submarine. You can see how well that would work. Every asset in the area would go dashing off, pinging like a madman, searching the false contact. Not only would they be drawn away from the real submarine's location, but they would also provide additional targeting location data to the bastard," the admiral answered.

"We don't need this," Daistrom murmured. "We *really* don't need this right now."

The admiral shot him a sharp look. "None of us does. I understand your preoccupation with Korea right now. No doubt you'd far rather be there than here."

"Admiral, if I might ask *you* a question?" Bailey said.

He nodded permission.

"From what you've said, I gather the Germans haven't exactly been cooperative players out here, either. So they're not team players, and not nearly as aggressive as we thought. Why does that concern you, other than they've demonstrated their willingness to knock out some sonobuoys? Frankly, I'm not nearly as impressed with them as I'd expected to be," she said.

Daistrom made a sound that might have been a forced chuckle, might have been a stifled sneeze. "Admiral, if you don't mind, I'd like to try my hand at playing your role last week."

"By all means. I'll be interested to hear your thoughts, now that the ideas have had a chance to germinate."

In fifteen minutes, Daistrom took Bailey back through the chain of events at sea and pointed out the same possibilities that Admiral Richardson had made the week before. As he made the Admiral's arguments, he became aware of something he hadn't realized: However skeptical he'd been six days before, his subconscious had been convinced.

PATHFINDER 601

The Lockheed P-3C Orion aircraft flew a scant one hundred feet above the North Sea, its Magnetic Anomaly Detector boom, or MAD, trailing some twenty feet behind it. Although its primary mission was antisubmarine warfare, the P-3C was capable of performing almost any mission except air warfare that required extended time on station. Armed with Harpoon antiship missiles and torpedoes, this particular aircraft was on a less familiar mission.

"Madman, Madman," the enlisted technician called out. The aircraft immediately broke into a hard turn and headed back toward the same spot from a different direction.

The Madman call indicated that the boom had detected a metal object below the surface of the water. A second Madman call refined the location of the metal object, and the P-3C banked again to get a third vector on the object.

"What'd'ya think, Grady?" the pilot asked. "Mine? There's nothing on the charts here about a wreck or anything else."

The enlisted technician stared for a moment at the numbers rolling by in front of him. "I don't think it's a mine, sir. Do you know if we have any submarines in the area?"

"It's a sub?" The tension in the pilot's voice was evident.

"It's the right size for one—awful high readings for a mine. Could we drop a couple of buoys?"

"You got it. TACCO, get me some fly-to points."

Minutes later, the naval flight officer had input buoy locations and punched the data up to the pilot. Six *chunks* echoed in the aircraft as the small explosive charge shot the sonobuoys out from the undercarriage of the Orion.

"All six sweet and cold," the enlisted man reported shortly thereafter, meaning that while all the sonobuoys had activated in the water and were transmitting data, none of them held contact on a submarine.

"Diesel?" the TACCO asked. "Maybe on battery—you might not get anything then."

"Could we do another MAD pass?" the enlisted man

asked instead of answering. A nasty suspicion had just dawned.

Five minutes later, the P-3C had swooped back and forth across the spot again. The metallic object was located in exactly the same spot.

"Oh, shit," the TACCO said softly. He glanced at the technician. "You thinking what I'm thinking?"

The man nodded. "Yes, sir. I think somebody ought to call up the admiral and tell him we just found that missing British submarine."

9

4 MARCH 2002:
THE NORTH SEA

USS RAMAGE

Admiral Richardson's face was gray and drawn, the lines there etched more deeply than when Bailey had seen him just hours before. Something vital had seeped out of him and was slowly being replaced by something harder, if not as human.

"My condolences on the loss of your submarine and crew," she said.

He nodded abruptly, almost dismissively. "We'll know more in the next few days. Perhaps. Determining what happens in a submarine event is not an easy task. The only decision more difficult is what we do next."

"Next?" Daistrom asked.

The admiral finally turned away from the chart he was studying. "I hadn't thought there'd be another war during my lifetime. Conflicts, perhaps, something on the order of the Falklands. Men die in the service of their country, even during those, but war—this is another thing entirely." A sigh broke loose from somewhere deep inside him.

Daistrom glanced at Bailey and shook her head slightly. She held back her questions. The admiral caught the exchange.

"Don't look at me like that," he snapped. "Believe what you choose, but the fact is that Germany is behind this. And the United States, as she always does, will try as hard as she can to ignore the unpleasantness until events force her to react.''

"Admiral, I—'' Daistrom began.

"Oh, don't bother,'' the admiral said. "We'll do the dying for years again, just as we always have. The casualties—Christ. You Americans sit over across the pond and wait until you're forced into it. Just as you always have.''

"Is there anything we can do for you, sir?'' Bailey asked, ignoring the warning look Daistrom gave her.

"If it wouldn't be terribly much trouble, you might start by finding the bleeding submarine that's behind this.''

"Your own forces—''

"Are putting to sea as we speak. Submarines, destroyers—everything. I'm transferring my flag to HMS *Audacious*. Her helo should be overhead in two hours. She's getting under way at this very moment. As far as I'm concerned, *Ramage* is detached from further duties at that point.'' He gave Daistrom a withering look. "Korea may be in your future sooner than you think. At least until the Americans decide that Europe is still worth fighting for.''

HMS AUDACIOUS

HMS *Audacious* pulled smartly away from the pier, ignoring the two tugs alongside her. The two auxiliary propulsion units extended down from her hull were essentially small outboard motors designed to work immersed, using seawater as their cooling medium. Mounted fore and aft just off the keel, the APUs could swivel through 360 degrees, generating a two-to-three-knot side force sufficient to move the ship away from the pier under her own power.

Fifteen feet away from the pier, the captain disengaged the APUs and gave the OOD permission to engage *Audacious*'s main propulsion. Working with an offsetting wind, the OOD pulled smartly away from the pier, pivoted the ship in a twist to put her bow out toward the channel, and ordered a one-third-ahead bell.

Five minutes later, the ship cleared the first buoy at the harbor's entrance and crossed the line of demarcation into the southern portion of the North Sea proper.

SIX HUNDRED FEET BELOW

The old mine buried in the mud listened carefully. The sound waves generated by *Audacious*'s propeller throbbed through the ocean, bending up and around areas of greater sound velocity. Most of the noise was refracted back up to the surface of the ocean by the increasing pressure of the seawater at greater depths, or reflected back up by the soft ocean floor. Some of the sonic energy was absorbed in the muck and goo littering the seabed or bounced harmlessly away from the mine, scattered by harder debris with acute angles. A small school of fish absorbed some of the sound, radiating it out back in random directions.

One small arc of sound waves leaving the hull at a steeper angle obeyed Snell's law and continued their path down to the ocean floor. The energy levels decayed as they traveled through the increasingly dense water, but enough remained to pulse the acoustic diaphragm located on the top of the mine. The diaphragm compressed infinitesimally the heavy oil reservoir located under it, moving a piston through a magnetic coil and generating an electrical current proportional to the strength of the sound.

Other circuits studied the frequencies of the energy, comparing the fundamental frequencies of the complex waveform to the discrimination standards hardwired into it. A match, it finally decided. Classification: ship of war. It bounced the decision back over to the signal strength detectors, which added the qualifier "and close enough."

A relay tripped as the two discriminator circuits agreed. Power dumped into the mine's firing circuit, first arming the torpedo-shaped charge attached to the mine, then activating the small electric motor that served as its propulsion. It shot away from the metal casing that housed the detection circuits, sniffed out the direction of the strongest sound source, and arrowed toward it.

HMS *AUDACIOUS*

"Bit of nasty out there," *Audacious*'s captain mused, staring out at the ocean from the shelter of the bridge. Rain pelted the windows, and the offsetting winds he'd appreciated while getting under way caught the superstructure and added to the wave motion. "She'll have plenty of squalls to choose from, should she want to snort. Bloody nasty weather for the helos, too."

"I expect they'll manage, sir," his number one replied. "Sir—this business about the Krauts. Is it really—"

"I shan't speculate," the captain said, cutting him off. "And neither shall you. Admiral Richardson's been known to come up with some barmy ideas in his time, but the old geezer damned well is right more often than he's wrong. We've got our search area and—"

Audacious heaved herself out of the water as though attempting to get airborne. The captain and his XO had a split second to wonder before their heads smashed into the overhead.

The impact snapped the captain's neck. The XO, who'd been leaning over slightly to listen to his much-shorter commanding officer, took most of the impact on his back. The shock broke his spine between the third and fourth vertebrae, paralyzing him but leaving him partially conscious. When he hit the deck, the now violently pitching ship rolled him back and forth across the bridge like a log.

The rest of the bridge watchstanders lay crumpled around him, some dead, some surviving with only broken ankles. The XO tried to speak, tried to give the order to set general quarters, but had difficulty remembering exactly where he was and why he should do it. It seemed that it must be important, but just exactly why, he wasn't sure.

Groans and screams filled the bridge as the ship rocked and the injured and dead slid from one side of the ship to the other. Finally, they ended up piled together on the port side of the ship as *Audacious* settled into a steep fifteen-degree list.

Down below, the remaining uninjured crew members made a valiant attempt to fight the damage, but there was no possibility of beating back the torrent of water now filling up the lower levels and spouting up the ladder wells. The ship started sinking, stern first. Two uninjured engineering technicians who'd escaped serious injury by virtue

of being asleep in their racks held a hurried, shouted conference. Quickly reaching agreement, they started picking
up the wounded, transporting them up to the weather decks,
going back down for another load. They had time to make
three trips before the water was washing waist-deep on the
damage control deck.

The ship's weather decks were only inches above the sea
when they finally admitted that it was hopeless. Sobbing,
shocked, already feeling the pangs of survival guilt that
would haunt them the rest of their days, they loaded the
wounded they could reach into survival rafts, the igloo-
looking life rafts that would provide some protection from
the cold water.

By the time the downdraft of the sinking ship started to
tug at their frail rescue craft, eight men were in the raft.
They paddled away, trying to put distance between them
and the ship.

Rescue came quickly that close to shore. Four men died
before the cutter could reach them.

U-504

"The mines?" Merker asked the sonar technician. *U-504*
was fifteen miles away from the harbor, but the sonar
speaker still shivered from the noise.

The sailor nodded. "The bearings are a little off, but
what else would it be? It had to be one of the ones we just
laid. Maybe the tether broke and it drifted a bit."

Merker straightened up, nodding. While he hadn't
doubted that the mines would work, it was reassuring to
have proof. Still, the bearings error concerned him. "Odd
that it wouldn't be floating on the surface if the mooring
line snapped. Let's take a closer look. If we've got a containment problem, we need to know about it now."

Ehrlich snapped out a new course order to the OOD, then
resumed laying out a dead reckoning position along the new
course.

"Blood chum in the water," Kraeken announced
smugly. "Not only do we prove to them that they're bottled
up, but we draw in every ship in the area to assist in rescue

operations. An excellent opportunity for targets of opportunity."

"Opportunity—a danger as well. If they're concentrating on that area, it will be harder to draw them south," Merker said, his tone a shade sharper than he would have liked. But the man's enjoyment—the sheer pleasure he seemed to take in each attack—annoyed him. "We'll take those targets that we can without endangering the mission of the ship."

"*Kapitan*, might I conduct the next attack myself?" the XO asked. "For practice."

"We'll see." Merker turned back to the noise-cancellation panel and pretended to study the digital displays. Kraeken might see it as chumming the waters, and indeed, the mine attack would have just that effect.

For just a moment, Merker wondered if there was something wrong with him, some fatal weakness that made him unfit for command and that somehow had escaped the notice of his superiors. Following orders—even attacking ships without warning—was the duty of every professional naval officer. But to enjoy the action as though it were a sporting event, to take personal pleasure in a tactical victory that resulted in killing several hundred other men, somehow made mockery of the notion of duty.

He glanced over at Kraeken, who was now leaning over the sonar console, waiting for a contact, and repressed a shudder. Eight months ago, Merker had thought he would react exactly as the XO was now behaving—indeed, had expected, relished that final vindication of duty.

Korea had changed all that. Now, watching the emotions he'd thought he'd feel himself on Kraeken's face, he felt sick.

We have to kill them—should kill them—but we don't have to like it. He wondered whether that really meant anything at all.

10

USS RAMAGE

Daistrom turned up the collar of his jacket to deflect the icy blasts from the overhead air ducts and stared at the North Sea chart spread before him. Small X's marked the location of the wreckage the P-3C had found, along with the disappearances of HMS *Brilliant* and HMS *Audacious.*

"There is no more than twenty miles between any of these incidents," Admiral Richardson said, pointing to each X in turn. "Well within the capabilities of one diesel submarine."

"If that's what caused them," Daistrom answered. "But I'm hesitant of reading too much into that. *Oberon* was an old submarine—anything could have happened. We've lost a couple ourselves from engineering casualties. *Thresher* and *Scorpion,* for starters. HMS *Brilliant* could very well have been a catastrophic engineering casualty."

"And *Audacious*?" Richardson asked. "Damn it, man, we have to reevaluate each one of these accidents in light of her. The survivors were very clear on the sequence of events. She struck a mine in a harbor that's been charted by minesweepers almost weekly."

Bailey studied the chart. "Eliminate the impossible and what remains, however improbable, is the answer. Three engineering casualties? Another country, perhaps, but not Britain. No matter how old that submarine was, it's not likely."

Richardson glanced sharply at her. "Had I said that, I would have been accused of a bit of braggadocio."

She shrugged. "It's fact, not flattery. The O-boat class is a well-engineered, superbly maintained boat. I spent a couple of days poking around one when I was attached to RAF Brawdy." She didn't mention the countless hours she'd spent in NSA's intelligence library, studying the engineering specifications.

"Commander, don't you find it just a little far-fetched to believe that a German submarine is stalking this battle group?" Daistrom asked sarcastically. He looked over at the admiral. "Britain has our deepest sympathies for this tragic series of mishaps, but I find engineering mishaps a good deal more believable than a hostile U-boat."

"And how do you account for *Audacious*?" Bailey asked. "The men who survived were engineering technicians—snipes, not twidgets. Don't you think they'd be able to tell the difference between an engineering casualty and a mine?" She shook her head. "I don't buy it. Especially not with my sonobuoys going off-line just before *Brilliant* was attacked. Someone didn't want us to see what was happening."

Collins snorted. "Do you really think the Germans would be worried about what one reserve unit might detect? If that's the case, they'd have been after *Ramage*'s towed array, not your sonobuoys."

Daistrom fixed Bailey with a stare. "She's got a point."

"With all due respect, sir—we're not just a *reserve* command. We're a fully commissioned naval command, and one hundred percent of the navy's expertise in coastal surveillance and control. I know what we saw."

Daistrom straightened up from bending over the chart. He tossed the two-point dividers onto the plotting table. The tool hit the board and stuck point-down in the wood for a moment before toppling over with a metallic thud that sounded too loud in the enclosed space. "So you want me to believe that we're on the verge of World War III right here in the North Sea? Germany on the move to dominate the Continent again, and the first thing they go after is a coastal MIUWU unit?" He shook his head. "It doesn't make sense. The British are no slouches at ASW. If the Germans wanted to start something, they wouldn't have time to hunt down your sonobuoys and take them out, even assuming they had the capability to do so.''

"I agree—*unless* there was something up there they didn't want us to see. Like what hit *Brilliant*.''

She saw Daistrom start to answer, then stop. He glanced at Richardson, then at her, his eyes telling her he remembered the other incidents in the North Sea. Later.

"A healthy paranoia is the beginning of sound operational thought,'' Richardson answered. He turned to Bailey. "Something is not quite right out here. You can feel it, can't you? Your civilian occupation should give you some insight into this scenario.'' He frowned slightly at her look of surprise. "Please don't insult me with denials. We *do* have our own intelligence service, and they're quite competent in ferreting out information on our allies as well as the rest of the world.''

He knows about NSA. The policy is no confirmation—but denying it would be just as useless as he says. She kept her face professionally neutral and nodded. "I'm not sure that all my officers feel it yet, but I do. A couple of the senior enlisted men do. They were raised on the Cold War and Vietnam. It's like the hair on the back of your neck standing up, like being too near lightning. You can't see it, you can't smell it, but something in my gut knows.''

"Mine as well.'' He studied her for a moment. "Not to intrude on your country's security regulations, but I must ask: Do you know anything else that would explain this situation?''

"Such as?''

"Admiral, I hardly think Commander Bailey is withholding information from either of us,'' Daistrom said quickly. He looked at her for confirmation. "I mean, what *could* she know? We've seen all her acoustic data ourselves.''

The admiral smiled, a small, wintry movement of his mouth. "I suspect that we will have to cope with this before anyone else believes us. Be prepared, Captain. We may have to move very quickly, even without orders. Make sure you're ready and that your people remember the *Wasp*. She had no warning. We may have less.

"Now, if you'll be so good as to notify your flight deck, Captain. With *Audacious* out of action, I'll be shifting my flag to *Victory* instead."

Daistrom stood, made the telephone call from the phone next to his chair, then saw the admiral to the wardroom door. He watched the tall officer move off down the passageway, then turned back to his officers. "Quite a fellow, isn't he? Worries a lot." He walked back over to his chair and slumped down comfortably in it. "Wonder if there's anything to it."

"I'm not worried." Collins stood. "Captain—if you could excuse me? I need to relieve the TAO in combat."

Daistrom waved her off. He watched her leave, then said, "Smart lady. I suggest you listen to her, Bailey."

U-504

"Two contacts within range, *Kapitan*," Sonar reported. "Classify one as probable U.S. Burke-class destroyer, the other as a British frigate."

Merker felt the XO's eyes on him. At first he was tempted to ignore the scrutiny. Men learned their trade by studying their seniors, and it was only natural that the XO should watch carefully what his captain did. But there was something uncomfortably critical in the man's gaze, the slightest tinge of disdain backlighting the too-familiar eagerness to attack. Merker looked up slowly, felt their eyes lock together, excluding the rest of the crew, and waited until the XO looked away.

"The frigate," Merker said finally. "The British ship, not the American."

A flurry of course orders for intercept followed his decision. He watched the XO's face lighten and wondered whether some impulse to win the man over had influenced his decision. From a tactical standpoint, the frigate was just as dangerous as the destroyer. More importantly, his orders were absolutely clear: There were to be no attacks on American units, none. His superiors were taking no chances on drawing America into the conflict.

With the two ships this close together, he dared not take the shot. Attacking a British ship in the company of an American one might very well provide the provocation he was ordered to avoid at all costs.

"*Kapitan*, may I—"

"Make the approach, XO," he said. "For practice. We will not fire—not now." He studied Kraeken, wondering if the actual taste of killing would change him as it had changed Merker.

USS RAMAGE

"Richardson sounds like he knows what you do. In civilian life, I mean."

Bailey shrugged. She'd briefed Daistrom on her civilian occupation shortly after their first meeting, cautioning him that her exact position within NSA was classified. "Maybe. He mentioned that their intelligence service tracked allies. We do the same thing, so I wouldn't be that surprised if he knew. Doesn't mean I'm going to confirm it for him or tell anyone else on your ship."

"There're too many open secrets in the world, Bailey. I think your job's one of them." They were standing on the flight deck, staring out at the wake churning behind the ship and watching the admiral's helo fly east toward *Victory*. "Some of what he says makes sense, but the old bird's got a streak of paranoia a mile wide. And this whole European thing—these people have been fighting each other for centuries over events that happened a thousand years ago. You should understand that."

"Not much we can do about it. Look how long we stayed in Germany and in Eastern Europe. Didn't do a damned bit of good then, it wouldn't now."

"Well, then, you understand." He shook some more peanuts out of the brown paper bag and offered her a handful. "Boiled in salt water, the old-fashioned way."

She took the soggy mass and cracked open one with her teeth, tangy salt biting into her mouth. "Good. An old southern tradition, right?"

"Right." He smiled slightly. "In light of what we're talking about, appropriate, don't you think? Our traditions, theirs?" He pitched a handful of empty shells over the side. "You have to understand about Collins, by the way. She was one of the first women ordered to a destroyer. A good officer—hell, an excellent ops boss—but she's had to fight her way through the bullshit. Might make her a little arrogant sometimes."

"I hadn't noticed." She saw him chuckle at the lie.

The faint blat of the 1MC circuit reached them, almost lost in the noise of water churning up from the twin propellers and washing around the stern. He frowned. "You catch what they said?"

"No, sir, but it sounded like—" The announcement was repeated, louder and more urgent now, as the boatswain's mate evidently remembered to turn on the weather-deck speakers.

"Captain to the bridge!" Seconds later, the gonging call of general quarters began.

"Holy shit." Daistrom dropped the bag of peanuts and turned to run forward. He had time to take one step.

Ramage rocked violently to starboard. Her stern shot up fifteen feet, exposing the tip of the propeller blade.

The first motion threw Bailey against the jackstaff. Off-balance, she grabbed it reflexively, wrapping first her arms and then her legs around the hollow metal shaft. As the stern dropped away underneath her, the motion catapulted her upward, sliding up the jackstaff like some child's toy on a stick. The American flag standing out stiffly in the breeze flicked her in the face like a whip. She clung to the jackstaff, facing aft, suspended over the water.

A second later, she heard a scream. She focused on the sound, saw Daistrom still airborne, coming down toward the water in a steep arc. The ship's motion had acted like a catapult, flinging him off the deck.

The stern started on another upward arc. Daistrom fell past her, almost within arm's reach. She reached out blindly toward him, felt her fingers graze the back of his khaki shirt.

The steel arc of the propeller protruded from the water.

She followed his path downward, saw him hit the water just inches from it and disappear. The water boiling out behind the ship spouted red-streaked flumes in the wash of white water. She stared, unable to look away.

A minute later, the violent yaw and pitch had stopped enough for her to shimmy down the jackstaff. As her feet hit the steel deck, she looked around for the stern lookout. His sound-powered phones lay on the far side of the deck, but there was no trace of the man. She stumbled toward them and pulled the mouthpiece toward her.

II

---

4 MARCH 2002:
THE ENGLISH CHANNEL

USS RAMAGE

The sound-powered phone circuit was a babble of voices. Engineers reported flooding from damaged saltwater cooling pipes, serious but now under control. The shouted reports were barely audible over the background din of machinery and screams in the spaces. The starboard lookout kept reporting sightings of the submarine, although no one else in the area appeared to be able to see it. Combat tried desperately to break in with other orders and demands for information, to no avail. Someone, somewhere, was muttering quietly, "Oh, God, oh, God, oh, God," in a quiet litany of shock.

Lookouts stopped talking, and the engineers announced their decision to switch to the bitch box. Only the anonymous babbling voice continued, cutting in and overriding the conversation between the OOD and combat.

She interrupted. "Man overboard, starboard . . ." She stared back at the water, finally settling on the best patch of discoloration she could see. "Correction, port side. It's the captain!"

Abruptly, chatter on the net ceased. The surface plot voice came on, demanding range and bearing information. She kept her eyes fixed on the discolored patch aft of the ship, estimating distance and relative direction from the ship.

Ramage turned hard to port, a maneuver designed to

screen her deadly screws from anyone in the water. She grabbed for the jackstaff for balance.

Too late. For a moment she lost sight of Daistrom's body.

U-504

"It wasn't us," Kraeken said rapidly, his voice growing louder. "I swear—*Kapitan*, it was another submarine! Our orders—they must have changed."

"Dive the boat," Merker snapped.

"But we could take a shot. Finish her, perhaps." What Merker had come to think of as the killing blush crept up Kraeken's face. "I could—"

"No. My orders have not changed."

"At least let us send out a message verifying that, *Kapitan*. Surely in light of what has just occurred, you must consider the possibility that we may have missed a schedule change."

"Get us out of here." Merker deliberately turned his back on his XO, pretended to concentrate on the navigator's plot while waiting to see how far his subordinate would dare to challenge his authority.

Kraeken rapped out the orders, his voice cold with suppressed fury. Merker felt a moment of gratitude that the confrontation that was seemingly increasingly inevitable had once more been delayed.

He stared down at the plot as the submarine executed a standard dive and baffle clearing evolution. Kraeken, mechanical problems, and now a radical deviation from the schedule that had guided his every tactical decision for the past seven months.

Had another U-boat attacked? Had his orders indeed changed, as Kraeken had suggested?

No. It simply made no sense, not in light of the regular radio traffic the U-boat was receiving. Another U-boat had simply made the absolutely wrong decision, had failed to exercise that degree of decision-making that the General Staff expected. Another Kraeken on another boat somewhere, filled with eagerness to kill, ignoring the danger of attempting to take the British boat so close in company with the American one.

But which U-boat? According to the plot, *U-504* should be the only one within range of the two ships. Another misjudgment, perhaps a more fatal one—leaving an assigned patrol area.

The fog of war—just how many other mistakes would be made? And how many could Germany tolerate?

USS RAMAGE

"How bad is he hurt?" Bailey asked the corpsman.

The senior medical person on board shook his head. "Bad. We need to get him to a shore facility immediately."

She shook her head and stared at the XO. He was stretched out on the examining table in medical, unconscious. His head lolled to one side, the skin along the right side of his face blackened and burned.

"He came down to check on the flooding from the salt-water line. The break was near the sea chest, and it could have been a showstopper." The lieutenant commander crouching down next to the XO looked up at her. He wore blue coveralls and a red turtleneck faded to pink from repeated washings. Short-clipped gray hair, startling bright blue eyes with the red, bleary look of an engineer operating on too little sleep and too much coffee. "I told him it was under control, but he wanted to see himself. When we took the hit, he was right next to the pump. Oil sprayed out, and flash-ignited immediately. We pulled him out before it got any worse, shut down the pump, and had the fire out in a couple of minutes. I guess it wasn't soon enough for the XO."

"A concussion, at the very least," the corpsman said firmly. "Could be a skull fracture, too. That's why he needs to be airlifted ashore immediately."

She noticed the other officer looking at her curiously. "We haven't met. Mike Wentworth, chief engineer. I answer to CHENG fastest." He paused, touched the XO's head gently. Still looking down at Brubecker, he asked, "What's your date of rank?"

"Why?"

Finally he looked up. "It may not have occurred to you, but we have a problem here. Think about it. Both the captain and the exec are gone. Somebody's got to be in command. I know Collins and Kelso are junior to me, and they haven't completed command-at-sea qualifications. And I'm a limited-duty officer. I qualified OOD under way years ago, but I haven't stood a bridge watch in centuries. What about you?"

"Command-qualified on USS *Dixon* during my second cruise. But I can't—who's Kelso?"

"Weapons officer. You're from the MIUWU, right? You probably haven't had a chance to meet him yet." He shifted his gaze back to her. "That makes you the senior command-qualified line officer on board. You understand what that means?"

"No, it's not . . ." She stopped, took a deep breath. "Okay. For now, I've got it." She turned back to the corpsman. "Talk to the operations officer, tell ops to coordinate with the helo getting the XO off as soon as possible. If there are any questions, refer them to me." She turned back to the CHENG and studied him carefully. "I haven't been on a ship full-time in five years. I'm going to need some help. Let's start with the damage control situation. How bad is it?"

"Under control. Like I told the XO," he said, "there was a small leak. It's patched, holding well, and the fire was contained quickly. We're ready to answer all bells. And, for your information, I'm the senior watch officer."

"Very well. I'm going up to the bridge. I'd like all department heads to meet me up there immediately. As soon as I talk to Sixth Fleet, we'll decide what to do."

"Commander? A word of advice?"

"Go ahead."

"Not *we,* ma'am. *You'll* decide. Make that clear from the start."

She paused for a moment at the hatch. "Understood. But I doubt I'll be on board long enough for that to become an issue."

"It's always an issue, Commander. Always."

• • •

"Wrap up the exercise and get *Ramage* headed back to the States," the Sixth Fleet chief of staff's voice said over the command circuit. "She needs a depot-level up-check before she goes to Korea. We'll notify the Brits."

"How—I mean—"

"Look, lady, it's a brand-new ship with a good crew on it. You've told me there's no major damage, that you're the senior officer on board. Fine. Every spare officer I've got is on his way to Korea to augment the staff there. So you're it. The admiral will release a message later today confirming you as temporarily in command of *Ramage*."

"But . . ." She caught herself before she said it: *I'm just a reserve officer.*

"Navy regulations say the next senior officer succeeds to command. I know, I know, it's supposed to be an officer regularly attached to the ship. But you're the only one who's been to the command board, and there're some other people who think you'll do."

"What other people?"

He ignored the question. "You have any problems, call us. Now, if there's nothing else, we're a little busy right now. It may have escaped your attention, what with all the British accidents over there, but we've got a war going on." The circuit went dead.

She hung up the receiver. And just what the hell was she supposed to do *now*? Sixth Fleet's position was understandable, but still . . .

"Commander?" the surface plot petty officer said. "They're asking for you to come to the bridge. The lookout thinks she sees Captain Daistrom's body."

"There." The starboard lookout pointed down in the water about fifteen feet off the bow. "You see it?"

"Get the boat in the water," Bailey said harshly. The thought of what the boat crew would find was already making her ill.

Floating gently on the surface of the waves, rippling back and forth in the water, was an arm and part of a torso. And the remains of a khaki shirt.

• • •

Collins strode onto the bridge and glared at her. "We need to talk."

"I asked for all four of you. Where are the weapons officer, the chief engineer, and the supply officer?"

Collins shook her head. "You and me first, Bailey," she said. "On the bridge wing. Now."

"It's not convenient." Bailey turned back to the chart laid out on the navigator's table.

"Not conv—? What the hell do you mean?"

She kept her eyes fixed on the chart. "When I'm certain this ship is no longer in danger, there will be time to talk." She looked up, met Collins's gaze, and held it. "Until such time as released by competent authority, my first responsibility is to the safety of this ship."

"You're just a reservist," Collins snapped. "Tell me, Bailey, how long has it been since you've been at sea other than for a two-week fun cruise?"

Bailey straightened up and slammed her pencil down on the chart. "Naval regulations say nothing about reservists versus active duty. I'm the senior line officer on board and I've completed command-at-sea qualifications. I suggest you review Section 1079 of Navy regulations."

"We'll see about this," she snapped. "You aren't even *attached* to the ship. I'll be in combat."

Bailey let Collins get to the door leading off the bridge before she added, "And Sixth Fleet agrees with me."

Collins whirled back around to glare at her. "Did you tell them who you were? *What* you are?"

"As far as Sixth Fleet is concerned, I'm in temporary command until they get someone out here to relieve me. Now go find the weapons officer and chief engineer." She looked down at the chart, dismissing the other woman.

U-504

Merker took the pencil from Ehrlich's hand and sketched a light line on the chart from the northern tip of Britain to the end of Norway, pointedly ignoring the executive officer's questioning look. "This line of defense next," the U-boat captain said. Without looking at the XO, he continued, "We'll block the northern approaches first, since they're the most vulnerable. If necessary, we can interdict the English Channel by ourselves."

The navigator glanced up at him uncertainly. "They're not likely to come, are they? I saw the message traffic last night. The North Koreans have moved two battalions across the thirty-eighth parallel."

Merker nodded. "I don't expect a reinforcement of American ships immediately, but we need to plan against the worst-case scenario. We have enough British harbors mined that we have some control over their naval forces. But if the Americans are drawn into this before we control the North Sea completely, it could be disastrous. No, we'll change the plan by that much, and make sure we're ready for them if they come."

Finally he allowed himself to glance at his XO. Kraeken stared at the chart, refusing to look up.

He studied the man, wondering what mistake in the selection process had allowed Kraeken to progress this far along the path toward command. Whatever it had been, a relative highly placed in the General Staff, some political favor-currying in a prior tour, it was up to him to rectify it. An officer had to have complete command of himself before he could be entrusted with the lives of others. When they got back—if—he'd make sure the General Staff knew what had happened. There was no room for Kraeken in command.

He shifted his gaze back to the navigator. "Give me a course to the intercept point."

The navigator busied himself with parallel rulers and a compass, and a moment later looked up and said, "The shortest course is three-forty-seven true, *Kapitan*."

He saw Ehrlich's eyes flicker over to the XO uncertainly, then shift firmly back to Merker's own face. "Very well. Make it so."

12

---

5 MARCH 2002:
THE ENGLISH CHANNEL

USS *RAMAGE*

Bailey grabbed a couple of hours of sleep in her stateroom, just enough to chase most of the fog out of her brain. Now, seated in the wardroom with her third cup of thick coffee steaming between her hands, leaving her in command of *Ramage* seemed to her the most idiotic decision she'd ever heard.

Second most idiotic. Her own conduct just four hours earlier hadn't been much better.

"She's right, you know," CHENG said. "Even without Sixth Fleet's blessing, she had to do it."

Ops stared at her temporary commanding officer, challenge in her eyes. "That doesn't make it any better, hearing it from the corpsman. Didn't you think about telling the rest of us?"

Bailey shrugged. "I apologize for not adhering to the finer points of naval protocol. I'm sure you don't consider that more important than the XO's life."

Kelso spoke up unexpectedly. Thus far, he'd evinced a calm, almost uncaring acceptance of the change of circumstances. "It could have been worse than that, though," he said mildly. "The crew has to know who's in command at every second. If there'd been another attack . . ."

He had a point. Had there been another torpedo, to have the crew stalled because of an argument between two lieutenant commanders about who was in charge could have been fatal. She turned back to Collins. "There was probably a better way to do it," she admitted. She tried for a smile, but the ops officer's face remained angry. "I'll keep that in mind for next time."

Collins snorted. "That doesn't do us much good now, does it? The captain dead, the XO off the ship—hell, we've got no business being under way."

"Jesus, what the hell do you want?" Bailey exploded. "We don't have any choice. Every U.S. ship except *Ramage* is in Korea, waiting for the world to blow up over there. Sixth Fleet knows what our situation is, but I hope you'll forgive them if their attention is focused on getting that amphibious battle group out of the Med and over to Korea.

"And the rest of you—you'd better understand what the situation is. We may be in Sixth Fleet's op area, but what's happening on one destroyer doesn't make a damned bit of difference in the world today, and I'll be damned if this ship is going to do anything other than what she's supposed to do right now."

"And what the hell *is* going on over here?" Collins said. "Doesn't anyone except me find it a little strange that somebody in the North Sea is shooting torpedoes?"

CHENG finally spoke up. "They can't handle two conflicts at once." He stared down at his fingers, drumming a soft refrain on the starched white tablecloth. "We've planned it that way for years, but we all know it's a joke." He looked up, meeting her eyes. "The commander—captain is right," he concluded, using her correct title. No matter what the rank, the officer in command of a navy ship was always called "Captain." "The United States must pretend this isn't happening until they get Korea mopped up. Then they'll be over here. Until then, it's up to us to hold the line."

With the lines firmly drawn between the operations officer and the chief engineer, she turned to the weapons officer. "And where do you stand? I'm not asking for a vote of confidence. It's neither required nor desired. But I want to know where each of you are—whether I'm going to have your full cooperation, or whether we're going to refight this issue every time I give an order you don't like.''

Kelso's still, pale face bothered her. It was unreadable, the face of a man turned more inward than most. Dark eyes contrasted sharply with his pallor. Thin, dark hair was already creeping back from his forehead. She felt him make an effort, focus on her, and finally he spoke. ''You're in command, Captain. That's all I need to know.''

It was not an entirely satisfying answer, but under the circumstances she was prepared to accept it. Enthusiastic support would have been better—yes, that vote of confidence she said she didn't need. Still, the final count appeared to be two to one. ''Next issue: Which one of you is senior?''

''I am,'' Collins answered. ''Aside from CHENG.''

''Fine,'' she said. ''Then you're the acting executive officer, in addition to your other duties.''

Collins leaned back in her chair, her face only slightly less truculent than it had been when the meeting started. ''Oh, goodie, just what I wanted.''

''We need to head north,'' Bailey said, ignoring the tone of voice. ''I want to clear the area where this attack occurred, get up toward some more open water. The North Sea is too small for my taste.''

CHENG nodded. ''We're fine on fuel right now, even if I'm not entirely happy with the stuff we got from *Spessart*. We're good for about two weeks before we go dead in the water. I don't want to get that low, though—sludge fouls the system.''

''Fine.'' She turned back to her newly minted executive officer. ''You'll pass that on to the navigator.'' It wasn't a question.

Collins nodded. ''Okay. I suppose it's as good a place as any to be.'' She tapped her pencil on the northern tip of Britain. ''We might be able to arrange some refueling services, too. Maybe if they get one of the ports cleared, we can pull in there.''

There's another reason for being north of here, Bailey thought. *Whether they know it or not, that's my closest source of replacement officers if I need them.*

U-504

"They're coming after us," Kraeken said. "Perhaps attacking the American destroyer wasn't such a bad thing after all. How nice it would be to have her lying at the bottom of the ocean instead of hunting us."

Merker felt Kraeken's eyes slither off the distant point that he'd been staring at. "They're not. She's just turned north, that's all. Don't confuse coincidence with tactics. Her sonar is in search mode only, and there's no indication of targeting. Aside from the helo flight six hours ago, there's been no air activity, either."

"How hasty will it be if she shoots a torpedo at us?" the XO said, pitching his voice so that only Merker could hear him.

USS RAMAGE

USS *Weeks* darted back and forth in front of *Ramage,* aggressively executing her ASW search plan. The small frigate's commanding officer, a full commander, was only one year senior to Bailey. She'd had a long, private conversation with the loquacious man, and had taken a great deal of comfort from his strongly expressed convictions that she'd done the right thing. Even after Sixth Fleet's affirmations, it meant a good deal to hear it from one of her peers.

Ramage proceeded north at a stately ten knots, while *Weeks* crisscrossed back and forth in front of her, moving at higher speeds to reposition herself, then slowing to six knots to listen for any hint of the submarine. *Ramage*'s towed array was also deployed, and, she reflected, was a good deal more likely than *Weeks* to gain initial contact. Nevertheless, the frigate took her role as ASW screen seriously, and two sets of eyes poring over the intricate noise sources and signals in the water were better than one.

Not that either of them was likely to detect this particular boat. Even after reviewing the sonobuoy tapes as well as those she brought aboard from the MIUWU, sonar technicians could find no hint of the boat's approach prior to the torpedo attack.

"Approaching the line of demarcation," the quartermaster announced, interrupting her train of thought.

"Very well," Bailey acknowledged. The invisible line that marked the transition from one set of international rules of the road to another was a key navigational event in any transit.

She walked out on the bridge wing, still uneasy on the bridge of the destroyer. Had she been a captain who'd ascended to command by normal means, she would have taken a seat in the captain's chair, located on the starboard forward portion of the bridge. The chair was elevated three feet off the deck and covered in brown vinyl. A similar chair, located on the far port side of the bridge, was reserved for the executive officer. Neither chair was ever occupied by anyone else.

Her feet would have appreciated the rest. For the past twelve hours, she'd been on her feet almost continuously, pacing the hard steel deck and learning as much about the ship as quickly as she could. Too little sleep, the shock of Daistrom's death—to just sit down for a moment, rest her feet, maybe even shut her eyes, was a too-tempting possibility.

She shot a wistful glance back at the chair and then reached a decision. Not now, not just yet. All department heads, along with most of the crew, had acknowledged her authority over the ship with a mixture of apprehension and reluctant obedience. As hard as his death had hit her, how much more difficult it must be for his wardroom. Some symbols were just too sacred to take lightly. That included the captain's cabin, still filled with his gear and personal belongings, and the chair on the bridge.

"Captain," the OOD said, the title coming slowly to his lips. "*Weeks* is recommending a course change to two-eight-zero."

A delicately worded order, she thought ruefully, stepping back onto the bridge. *Weeks*'s CO was senior, but his sole operational task was to protect her ship. While she and *Weeks*'s CO had worked out their working relation in a private conference, she wasn't completely convinced that he was entirely comfortable with the disparities between their rank and experience. However, with his far more junior crew on the smaller ship, it would have been unreasonable for Sixth Fleet to pull him off the ship and assign him to the destroyer. All of his department heads were first tour, while at least she had the advantage of experienced officers to back her up. All in all, the current arrangement was the most effective use of manpower.

"Concur," she said crisply. She walked over to the navigation charts to check their position. In another two hours they would be completely out of Admiral Richardson's area of responsibility and no longer under the control of NATO Command.

Weeks changed course smartly just as she said the words. "In her wake, OOD," she ordered. "Let's look sharp."

The OOD shot her a cynical look, as though reminding her that he knew a good deal more about the maneuverability of the ship than she did.

U-504

Merker stared at the two ships through the periscope and swore quietly. The two American ships—with the North Sea packed full of NATO participants, what were the odds? The one country he wanted to avoid drawing into conflict seemed determined to go into harm's way at every opportunity.

The frigate's profile changed as he watched as she made a sharp turn to starboard, presenting him with a full-beam view. Behind her he could see the superstructure of the Aegis-class destroyer just topping the horizon. Too far, at least for now. He paused, considering his options.

The frigate was well within weapons range, and running an approach on the destroyer would take more time. He glanced up at the clock. According to the schedule, he should have already had the northern minefield laid. Much more delay, and he would be intruding into the assigned water space of another U-boat. The U-boats assigned to lay the secondary patterns were quiet, but they weren't equipped with the sophisticated noise cancellation on *U-504*. Some of them were even tied to the ancient cycle of battery operations and vulnerable snorkeling to recharge them. If either the frigate or the destroyer came too close to those water areas, they stood an excellent chance of detecting the older German submarines.

"Another five miles, and they'll pass over the first mine." Kraeken took the pencil out of Ehrlich's hand and sketched in the course the surface ships were on. "If either of them detonates a mine, it will alert the rest of the NATO ships." He shook his head. "Every ASW asset in NATO will be saturating the area. That can't happen until we've finished the transit plan."

"A torpedo shot is hardly a discreet way of discouraging them," Merker noted.

"But at least it wouldn't alert them to the minefields." Kraeken looked eager.

"No.

"I could target the lead ship," Kraeken continued. "One shot only, straight run, right across her bow." He looked over at the sonar technician to make sure he understood. "I don't want to sink her, just scare her off. Make her run south, clear the area, and buy us enough time for the other boats to finish laying their mines."

"You will make the approach." The words were out before Merker had a chance to consider them carefully, but it was what he would have done with any other officer who had botched an earlier attack so badly. "An approach—no more." He turned to sonar. "You understand, there will be no attack. Ensure that your weapons are on safe."

Kraeken nodded without comment, and stepped over to the periscope. He studied the scenario, then ran the periscope through 360 degrees to check for any other contacts. The monitor showed nothing except dark, blue water capped with whitecaps. He refocused the periscope on the two ships, then moved the crosshairs slightly ahead of the frigate.

"Lead her a bit more." Merker rested one hand over Kraeken's and watched the periscope monitor, then guided the center of the picture farther forward of the smaller ship.

The XO's hands were cold and stiff under his fingers. He felt Kraeken shift his hands toward the outer edges of the handles. The distance between the center point and the frigate widened slightly.

"A shame to waste a good forward bow shot," Kraeken said.

"More of a shame to waste an entire mission," Merker snapped.

USS WEEKS

"Jesus, what a screwed-up cruise," Weeks's captain remarked to the bridge in general. He was sitting in the captain's chair on the right-hand side of the bridge. He lifted his feet, then rested them on the ledge immediately under the window in front of him. "Between the Brits and Sixth Fleet, I don't know who's worse."

Approaching the line of demarcation, the need to be free of the North Sea and all the political bullshit involved with Operation Northern Lights suddenly seemed important to him. He motioned to the OOD, who had taken up station in that distance from the captain's chair that gave the OOD a clear view of everything on the bridge, a degree of privacy for the captain, and yet was well within earshot of anything he needed to hear. He moved promptly over to the captain's chair.

"Let's kick her in the ass," the captain said. "Show Ramage's CO what she's been missing in the weekend warrior game. Gimme twenty-eight knots." With that, he settled back in his chair and reached for his cup of coffee.

The captain's coffee cup had just reached his lips when the blare of the sonar warning alarm blasted through the bridge. His hand jerked, and a cascade of hot liquid soaked the front of his shirt.

"Torpedo, bearing zero-three-zero," the speaker blared. Without waiting for the captain's order, the OOD immediately snapped out a series of rudder orders for the same bearing. The bitch box reported that the TAO had ordered a torpedo shot down the reciprocal bearing.

The captain opened his mouth to speak, replayed the orders in his mind, then shut his mouth. The frigate was already approaching her maximum speed, which might give her enough time to get away. He jumped out of his chair and moved over to stand behind the OOD. Blood was pounding in the captain's head and adrenaline was screaming through his veins.

He heard the soft thunk of a torpedo leaving the tubes located along the side of the ship as *Weeks* fired down the approach bearing of the torpedo. A straight shot, one not necessarily designed to hit anything, but simply to shake their adversary and force him into maneuvering. Decoys were already trailing behind the ship, deployed immediately when the buzzer had sounded. For now there was nothing else the frigate could do.

"Tell *Ramage*," he ordered, suddenly realizing the one thing he hadn't heard the OOD do. "Never mind, I'll tell her myself." He picked up the tactical net receiver and started talking.

USS RAMAGE

Five miles behind *Weeks,* Bailey stared forward at the horizon in horror. The smaller ship was now completely through her turn and was beating feet balls to the walls toward them, presenting a full bow-on aspect.

The maneuver, what was the maneuver? She frowned, trying desperately to dredge up the operating characteristics of the Aegis-class destroyer and match them with a tactical memo she'd seen years earlier.

"What are you waiting for?" the ops officer snapped. Collins turned to the OOD, snarled at the junior lieutenant, and took the conn. *Ramage* cut sharply to starboard, and Bailey felt the deck shake under her feet as the powerful turbine jet engines that powered her ramped up quickly to maximum speed.

"Watch the tail!" ops shouted, ignoring her completely. "Ease your turn a bit—that's it, that's it." The bow of the frigate was now sliding off to port as *Ramage* began her own turn. Bailey stared up at the ship's speed indicator, watching the needle climb slowly up to thirty knots, quiver, then inch up an additional two knots. The acceleration was sufficient to sway her on her feet, and she grasped the arm of the captain's chair for support.

The ops officer walked over to her, grasped her arm hard just above the elbow, and gave her a shake. "You're in command, now," she said sharply. "And I'll see you in hell if you let this ship get hurt because of your incompetence. I may have to live with Sixth Fleet's decision, but the second you endanger the life of anyone on this ship, I'll relieve you."

USS WEEKS

Weeks's bow pitched up at a steep angle, then plunged into the next wave. Head-on to the seas at flank speed, she was taking green water over the weather decks. Ahead of her, the larger destroyer rode more easily, cutting through most waves instead of riding up on the crests and down into the troughs, as the frigate did.

"Five thousand yards," the ASW officer snapped. He stared at the active sonar screen, feet wide apart and braced against the ship's motion, his hand curled around a metal bar protruding from one of the equipment panels. "Come on, come on," he muttered, urging the old ship on.

All around him he could hear the pounding of feet as sailors beat their way to their general quarters stations. The torpedo behind them was traveling at thirty knots, and *Weeks* was barely holding her own at twenty-nine. Slowly, inexorably, the torpedo closed the distance, its seeker head now within range and driving out active sonar pulses that pinged against the frigate's hull. It was a matter of time, now, of the delicate geometry between two objects on the same course, one with limited endurance but greater speed and the other not quite as fast but able to run for hours—days, really—without refueling.

"Four thousand, five hundred yards," he chanted, watching the torpedo close the distance. At thirty knots, most torpedoes had a range of five nautical miles. It was possible, just barely, that *Weeks* could outrun the torpedo.

The sonar screen flickered. Green strobes flashed across

it from left to right, flaring into painful brilliance. The screen went black, the color broken only by the fading luminescence of the noise spokes on the screen. The compartment lights went out.

Emergency power kicked in, the wall-mounted, battery-powered lanterns on the ship shook suddenly, and her speed dropped noticeably. The ASW officer glanced at the speaker overhead and paled. An engineering casualty now, of all times, was the worst possible event. He started swearing, masking his increasing terror with anger.

U-504

"Clear the area—*now*." Merker darted across the control room to stand behind the sonarman. As Kraeken snapped out the orders to dive, Merker stared at the sonar screen.

Nothing. Yet there must be another submarine in the area, there must be. Two shots, aimed at targets in his vicinity. Two clear violations of their rules of engagement.

The sonarman cleared his throat. "No contacts, *Kapitan*." He pointed to an earlier spiral. "The torpedo—it came from the north. But I did not hold contact on the firing platform."

"I can see that." Merker turned back to his XO. "As soon as we're twenty miles away, get us to communications depth."

Sometime in the past week, the rules had evidently changed. The question was: Why had he not been told? Or were the last two attacks the actions of a renegade commander, one who'd chosen to ignore the General Staff's orders and somehow persuaded his officers and crew to support him? What sort of a man would do that? Could do that?

Merker felt a chill as he looked at Kraeken and found the answer to both questions staring back at him.

USS RAMAGE

"*Weeks* dropped the load," Collins said. She stared at Bailey as though making sure the reserve officer understood what that meant. "No power—no main propulsion."

"If they get it back on-line quickly enough, they've still got a chance," Bailey said. "Is there anything we can do?"

"No. Even if you wanted to try to decoy the torpedo away, we're too far from them. We could never make it back in time. She's got five minutes, maybe less, depending on how much speed she loses." Collins turned back to the OOD. "Maintain course and speed."

Bailey bit back a sharp reply. Clearly there was no other choice, but the decision should have been hers.

USS WEEKS

The torpedo hit *Weeks*'s thin hull at Frame 68, shearing aside the thin sheet metal and traveling through three bulkheads before it exploded. *Weeks*'s bulkheads and supports, built out of aluminum as a weight-saving measure, fused and melted in the resulting fire, as remnants of the torpedo's fuel ignited. Below the waterline, the interior of the ship was a fiery inferno.

Fire engulfed the chief's mess immediately, killing the corpsmen and chaplain, who were at their battle stations there. It spread aft and up, consuming the mess decks and flooding combat with smoke and toxic fumes.

Weeks's captain realized the impossibility of the situation almost immediately. Within two minutes, he had ordered the crew to abandon ship's stations. Those who were still capable of movement under their own power obeyed immediately, sensing the utter futility of attempting to contain the damage.

Seawater flooded into the forward half of the ship, yanking her bow down by twenty degrees. The oncoming waves quickly claimed possession of her forward weather decks, and ten minutes after the impact were lapping at the windows to the bridge.

The captain clung to the radar repeater on the bridge. "Get aft and get the rest of the crew into the lifeboats!" he shouted at the XO. "I'll check engineering."

"You can't get down there," the XO answered, already

heading toward the stern. "You heard the reports—Captain, they're all dead."

"Go!" The captain leaned forward to keep his balance and headed for the door leading off the bridge and to the ladder to the lower decks. "Stay as close as you can, but don't endanger them." He staggered toward the port hatch and shoved the deck log at the XO. "Take it."

"Captain, you can't—"

"You're wasting time, mister. Get moving." He retraced his steps, sliding and slipping over the debris littering the deck, and shoved open the nonwatertight door on the back bulkhead.

Immediately in front of him was the hatch leading into the combat section. It was ajar, the frame clearly too twisted to ever reseat it properly. He stuck his head in, shouted, then listened.

No answering cries, no groans, nothing. The deck notched down another few degrees, and he grabbed the twisted hatch frame to steady himself. The door swung forward, slamming into his forearm. He shoved the door back with his shoulder, stuck his head into combat, and surveyed the wreckage. Not as bad as it would be belowdecks, and there was a good chance that all the Combat watchstanders had made it out.

He let the hatch bang shut and started down the ladder to the lower decks. The tilted deck put each rung at an angle to his foot. He grasped both railings and slid down to the bottom on his palms.

On the 01 level, the damage was more evident. Smoke filled the passageway. The captain struggled over to the nearest EEBD dispenser, shoved three packets inside his shirt and two more in each jacket pocket, then headed for the down ladder. The ladder down was twisted away from its hard points, and he jumped the last two feet down.

He was on the mess decks. Water was already washing over the linoleum, eddying around the bolted-down tables and affixed fast-food restaurant-style plastic bucket chairs, carrying with it a tide of flotsam and debris. Two sailors lay in small, crumpled masses in the far corner, unmoving and oblivious to the rising water. He started toward them, then slipped and fell. His feet scrabbled for purchase under the water and skidded. He stayed down on hands and knees and half-crawled, half-swam toward them, shouting.

No movement. He finally reached them, yanked one toward him. The sailor rolled over, staring up at him with dull, silent eyes. Half of his face was burned down to stark white bone. The captain swore, reached for the other sailor, turned him over. Dead also.

The deck lurched again, harder this time. The milk dispenser groaned, tilted, and broke free from its shattered supports. It hit the deck and slid across the deck toward him.

The captain held up his hands as though to hold off the silver metal box. It slammed him against the bulkhead. His foot caught on a mess table stanchion, held him for a moment, and then snapped at midthigh. He stared down in horror at the jagged shaft of bone protruding through the khaki fabric. The sloshing water around it turned murky red.

Maybe I could—he rolled over onto his stomach, trying to keep his weight off his shattered leg. If he could make it back to the ladder, haul himself up to stand on his good leg, maybe pull himself onto the first rung, it might be possible to . . .

He shoved himself up into push-up position, then screamed. The injured leg flopped uselessly, banging exposed bone and torn flesh against the deck. His vision swam, dimmed, then steadied down to a red-hazed blankness. Sheer survival instinct made him put one hand in front of the other. One hand landed on a piece of debris and slipped, dropping his face down into the water. A filthy potion of seawater, fuel, and blood flooded his nostrils. He struggled blindly now, rational thought replaced by sheer panic and fear.

The ship tilted forward again, and the forward bulkhead became the new deck. The motion carried the captain and the bodies of the two dead sailors forward. He slammed into the bulkhead and lost consciousness.

Fifteen minutes after she'd been hit, *Weeks* nose-dived

into the North Sea, carrying with her ninety-eight crewmen and her captain.

USS RAMAGE

"You can't be serious. Look at her." Collins pointed at *Weeks*'s stern, now the only part of the ship still visible. "That's what happens when a ship gets torpedoed. You want to leave something that can do that running around loose in the ocean?"

"We're going back. The submarine that attacked her will be clearing the area," Bailey said. "Survival time is down to five minutes in this water, and the men in the lifeboats won't last much longer. You want me to sign their death warrants?"

"This is a *destroyer,* in case you've forgotten. *Ramage* has plenty of ways to deal with a submarine. Leave the search and rescue to the Brits while we nail the bastard that shot her. Jesus, Bailey! You *can't* let that submarine get away!"

Bailey stared at her coldly. "I don't need your concurrence. Just your obedience. Now get this ship prepared to take on the survivors. I'll be on the bridge."

Twenty minutes later, the last of *Weeks*'s crew was piled on the deck. The corpsmen had taken charge of triage, issuing severely injured down to the mess decks for further treatment, sending the walking wounded to the wardroom. Damage control technicians carried stretchers, shuttling between the wardroom and the crew's mess with bodies.

Bailey took a quick tour of the area, uneasily apprehensive about being too far away from combat or the bridge. The last time she'd been on the flight deck, Captain Daistrom had been lost. She shuddered, made herself take a brief tour among the wounded, and stopped for a word with the corpsman. He barely acknowledged her presence.

Duty satisfied, she returned to the combat section, ashamed of the relief she felt at being away from the wounded *Weeks* sailors. She called a hasty conference with the department heads and assembled them around the plotting table.

"Our first priority has to be to get that submarine." Collins tapped the location at which the torpedo attack had occurred, drawing her eyes to it. "If she can make even five knots undetected, we're well within her range now. We can't take any chance of letting her go."

"If we can find her," Kelso said. He gestured back toward sonar. "So far, from what I've heard, this is a ghost boat. The only way you can fix her location is by following the torpedo back."

Collins glared at him. "No submarine is completely undetectable. Sure, it might be tough on passive, but that much metal in the water has to return an active sonar signal. I say we blast the hell out of the water, focusing on maximum range, and take an aggressive approach to any contact we find."

"What if she finds us first?" CHENG asked. "You keep active sonar on, and you might as well put a homing beacon in the water. If she doesn't have us before then, she certainly will after that."

"Our only detection of this boat was from a passive sonobuoy in the MIUWU. And we were active when she attacked *Weeks.*" Bailey stared at the symbol that marked the torpedo shot. "We had no contact, no warning of any sort before the torpedo."

"It would've been at maximum range," ops argued. "Not surprising that we weren't holding contact. But we were out of her weapons envelope as well. You let me stay active, I'll have her before she's got a targeting solution on us."

Bailey straightened up, putting her hands at her waist and leaning back slightly to relieve the tension in her muscles. "You don't know for sure. This boat isn't just quiet, it's silent. If she made a run directly by the MIUWU sonobuoys and we didn't detect anything, then we're dealing with an entirely new level of technology. And the possibility of noise cancellation equipment can't be ruled out, either."

"So we run blind?" ops said. "Just wait for the submarine to take a shot at us, hope that we survive the damage, and then fire down that line of bearing?"

Bailey shook her head. "No, I don't mean that at all. But I think that we need different priorities for the ship." She looked over at Kelso. "Make sure your ASROCs are ready to go," she said, referring to the rocket-propelled torpedoes that were launched from the ship's missile launcher. "When will our helo be back?"

"Later today, probably," Collins said. "Why?"

"Two reasons. We'll need to transport the seriously wounded to England immediately, and I'll want to do some ASW surveillance with the helo as well. Set up a screen, at least make them run through a line of active buoys to get to us. If your theory is correct, we'll pick her up off DICASS before we pick her up off anything else."

"So which way do we head?" CHENG asked. He sketched out a line to the north lightly on the chart. "If they operate anything like our submarines, she's got an assigned area of water that's hers alone. As long as we're outside it, we're okay. And, based on where *Weeks* was hit, I'd say her area is to the north of us."

"I agree." Bailey studied the chart for a moment longer, then reached a decision. "We go south, at least until we can get this mess straightened out."

"And head back toward mined harbors and the earlier sinkings?" Collins shook her head, disagreeing. "Better that we get some deep water under our keel, give us some room to maneuver and improve the acoustic conditions. We have a better chance of finding her that way. And killing her."

"And a better chance of taking a torpedo up the ass ourselves. Somebody doesn't want us out of the North Sea. For now, until we can get guidance from higher authority, we're going to go along with that. Besides, the Sixth Fleet battle group should be outchopping the Med soon. That'll give us some other assets in the area, plus ASW helos."

A few minutes later, Kelso and CHENG left, leaving her alone with Collins, who looked at her for a moment, anger plain in her eyes. "Could we talk privately, Captain?" Her voice reflected deliberate formality and studied courtesy.

Bailey nodded. "In flag plot."

Collins led the way to the small, curtained room off the main combat center, intended to serve as a command center for an embarked admiral. After she had drawn the curtains shut, she turned to face the reserve officer. "You froze up there." It wasn't an accusation, more a statement of fact.

Bailey nodded. "And you covered for me. I appreciate that."

"I might not be there every time," Collins continued as though the other woman hadn't spoken. "And I'm getting questions from my junior officers about it. Too many people saw your reaction." Collins studied her for a moment. "With the wardroom, confidence that you won't get them killed is going to be ninety percent of the battle. They have to know that you'll do the right thing. *Know* that you'll fight this ship just as aggressively as Captain Daistrom would have." Her voice hitched slightly at the mention of his name. "I need to know that, too."

"You need to make your junior officers believe that," Bailey said finally. "When you took this job as department head, you assumed certain duties, ones that may not be too pleasant for you right now. I may be a reservist, but I do know one thing: You owe me your undivided loyalty. If you can't give me that, the solution isn't for me to step aside and let you take command." She watched Collins carefully, saw her words sink in. "And if you can't do that, let me know now."

Collins took a deep breath, and the years seemed to slip off her face. All at once, she appeared to be exactly what she was—a junior lieutenant commander caught in the middle of a tactical situation she neither understood completely nor wanted, one that put the ship at serious risk of harm. The silence grew uncomfortably long. "For what it's worth, I'll do my best. As long as I think you're not hazarding the crew or the ship unnecessarily." Her confidence seemed to return, and her voice grew stronger. "But it's not going to take many more instances like that torpedo attack to convince me that I must relieve you. Must, if I'm ever going to live with myself. And God help us if I don't do it in time."

FOUR HUNDRED FEET BELOW THE SURFACE

The mine rested unsteadily on a small hillock of mud and rusting oil cans. One of the world's most peculiar currents ran above it. Warm water streamed out of the Mediterranean and into the Atlantic Ocean in the upper levels of the Channel, while seawater still chilled by its voyage near the Arctic Circle flowed into the Mediterranean along the bottom of the Channel. The current, though not strong by most standards, was sufficient to set the mine teetering precariously where it lay. Its firing circuits, designed to work under heavy pressure and withstand the impact of being launched, were more disturbed by the gentle to-and-fro motion of the mine than they had been by their original launch. The edge of the circuit board rubbed against the side of its bracket, occasionally losing contact with the rest of the electronics. The main firing circuit, confused by the intermittent contact with its subsystems, began reading the rubbing as a signal.

Designed to operate in the heavy-traffic environment of the entrance to the Mediterranean, the mine was of a different sort. In addition to the depth and target size discriminators, it incorporated a counter. It kept track of the ships that met its firing criteria, disabled until that number reached a preset value. In this mine's case, the magic number was one hundred.

The current count, augmented by the faulty signals from the loose circuit board, stood at ninety-eight. It slowly clicked over to ninety-nine as the magnetic distortion circuit noted the passage overhead of another large vessel.

Ten minutes passed before another magnetic signature meeting the threshold criteria neared the mine. As it had every time before, the mine broke the signal strength down into its component parts, calculating the size of the vessel overhead as well as its draft. Deciding that the signal met both criteria, the counter clicked over one more number: one hundred.

Two seconds later, the torpedo shot out of its housing, headed for lucky number one hundred.

SS FREEDOM'S GLOW

On board *Freedom's Glow,* a Bahamian-registered dry tanker, three crew members stood watch on the bridge. An unusually large number for a merchant ship, but in the constrained waters around Gibraltar, it never hurt to have an extra set of eyes. Captain Karl Herring, master of the one-hundred-ton-gross-weight vessel, was a stickler for safety.

Now, on the bridge himself in addition to his three officers, he checked the manual navigation plot, took a quick visual bearing on Gibraltar, and nodded his satisfaction. The *Glow* might be an old ship, but she was a good ship. She'd seen most of the major ports in the world in the past twenty years and never been involved in a single safety incident. That, Captain Herring thought, said as much for the inherent luck of the vessel as it did for the merchant mariners who crewed her, an ever-changing mixture of nationalities who barely found a common language among them.

A few more minutes and they'd be free of the constrained waters. He looked forward to that time, when he could relax his vigilance on the bridge and head below for a well-deserved nap. Unloading their cargo of wheat had taken up too much of their time, much more than the company had estimated, and *Glow* was slightly behind schedule in leaving port. Still, he ought to be able to make up the time on the cross-Atlantic transit. His next port of call, New Orleans, teased enticingly at the edge of his thoughts.

The bottom-mine-launched torpedo covered the two hundred feet between the bottom of the sea floor and the merchant ship in seconds. It entered the ship just slightly to the right of the keel, buried itself deep in the empty hold, and exploded.

The lightly laden ship shuddered violently. Captain Herring, who was walking forward to take another visual sighting on Gibraltar, hit the edge of the pilothouse, dislocating his shoulder. His first thought was that somehow they'd gone off course, struck one of the obstructions nearer to land, or impacted a smaller vessel that had slipped unseen next to the ship. As damage control alarms and sirens lit off, he realized that was impossible.

The crew of *Glow* reacted quickly, sectioning off the ship into a honeycomb of watertight compartments. While the compartments were much larger than their counterparts on a warship, the compartmentalization did provide some measure of damage control. With the small crew on board, *Glow* could not have handled the damage otherwise.

The explosion punctured two fuel tanks, and raw diesel and waste oil poured into the water, flowing out ahead of the ship on the warm current leaving the Med. Damage control sprinklers activated, dousing the fires with a mixture of Halon and fire-fighting foam. The old steel bulkheads of the ship withstood the fierce fire in a way that *Weeks*'s never could. Except for a small fire-fighting party, the entire operation was mostly automated.

Captain Herring began broadcasting a mayday on the local harbor control channel while monitoring the progress of the automatic systems from a status board on the bridge.

"Captain, I've lost control of the rudder," one officer shouted, straining to be heard above the alarms popping off like popcorn. Herring nodded, already aware of that fact from the way the stern was beginning to drift in the current.

"After steering is blocked," he shouted back, listening to reports of the damage control team. "We'll need a tug to get under way again."

And not for very long then, he thought sadly. *Glow,* nearing the end of her service life, would probably be consigned to scrap by the company.

Had he known more about the warhead on the mine, Captain Herring might have been a good deal more concerned. Naturally, the damage to his ship shook him deeply, and his adrenaline was already pumping through his body.

A few minutes later, so was the deadly gas. He had barely thirty seconds to feel his terror reach new levels as he struggled to breathe before he died.

Even automated systems require some degree of human intervention. Absent that, with the crew gasping and struggling for breath, the automatic controls lost the ability to fight the fire effectively. Creeping up fuel lines and through ventilation shafts, the flames progressed through the ship, while seawater flooded into the empty compartments. Now, turned ninety degrees from her former course, *Glow* drifted, barely afloat, blocking the Strait of Gibraltar.

Twenty miles behind her, the Sixth Fleet amphibious task force heard *Glow's* cries for help, and dispatched two destroyers and a frigate at flank speed immediately. Fifteen minutes later, as they heard the captain's assessment of the damage cut off in midgasp, the three American warships reversed course and found an extra knot or two of speed each to rejoin the battle group. The entire Sixth Fleet steamed away from Gibraltar and back toward the relative safety of the center of the Mediterranean. The cluster of merchant ships and cruise liners in line behind them saw the American ships leave and reversed course as well. None of them wanted to discover firsthand whether there was any similarity between *Glow's* mishap and that of HMS *Audacious*.

13

---

6 MARCH 2002:
THE ENGLISH CHANNEL

USS *RAMAGE*

"Within two weeks," Collins said firmly. "With all the firepower they've got massed off the coast, marines will be on the beach in Korea before we hit our first liberty port. Three weeks, max."

"Might even be sooner," CHENG mused. "Pass the ketchup, please. If they can get Gibraltar cleared quickly, they'll have defense in depth under way to back them up. That's the key to a successful amphibious invasion—sustaining and resupplying forces." The other officers around the wardroom table chimed in with their estimation of when the American forces would send their amphibious forces ashore in Korea.

Since *Ramage* was still under his tactical command, Admiral Richardson had returned to the ship as soon as his duties had permitted. After offering his condolences to Bailey and the officers and crew of the ship for both Daistrom's death and the loss of *Weeks,* he'd retired to his quarters and elected to dine alone. He'd been oddly silent on the question of tactics. Bailey had chalked it up to shock. *Ramage* had reasons to be in turmoil and Admiral Richardson had even more, starting with the loss of HMS *Oberon.*

Just as well. Bailey thought he might have had some interesting thoughts to share with the younger officers on the reality of war.

Odd, though, that he'd had so little to say about Sixth

Fleet and her sudden ascension to command of *Ramage.*
Aside from brief condolences on the loss of Captain Daistrom and an offer to provide any assistance she might need,
he'd made no comment on it. The whole chain of events
would surely have been as unusual in the Royal Navy as
in hers.

Egocentric to think so, she supposed. She pushed her
plate away. Admiral Richardson had lost two warships and
a submarine in the past week. That surely wore on his mind
more than an unexpected change in commanding officers
on a foreign naval vessel. Daistrom had been friendly with
him, sure—but the men Richardson had lost on those three
ships had been closer.

The conversation around the table dwindled off. Bailey
carefully put her cloth napkin back in its ring. It was time
for some answers. Only one other person on board seemed
to understand what was happening around them.

"*Bugger* NATO politics," the admiral said without pre-
amble. He'd had her summoned to his quarters and then
suggested a walk out on the weather decks. Bailey suspected it had more to do with privacy than propriety or
after-meal exercise. "There's a reason I'm back on
Ramage, and it has nothing to do with how Sixth Fleet
chooses to employ his forces. Tell me what you know about
Tabun."

Bailey frowned. "The word sounds familiar, but I can't
place it. It sounds like an aftershave or a perfume."

The admiral grimaced. "You'll want to think about that
remark after I remind you what it is. Tabun was the last
type of gas used in the Nazi concentration camps during
World War II."

"Destroyed by the Allies after the camps were liberated.
Yes, I remember now."

"Not all of it was destroyed." The admiral paused, and
fixed Bailey with a cold glare.

Bailey felt a sinking feeling in her stomach. *We've
crossed the line from paranoia into serious psychosis.*

"Admiral, it couldn't have survived after all these
years," she said quietly. "Besides, the Allies went through

every bunker, over every inch of that soil. If there'd been a cache of Tabun, they would have found it.''

"Are there any secret hiding spaces on a ship?" the admiral countered. "Where you've found drugs, perhaps, or other contraband?"

Bailey frowned at the apparent change of subject. "Every ship has a million nooks and crannies. But I don't see—"

"Do you know how much more difficult it is to search miles and miles of land? Captain, you couldn't even cover every square inch of this ship, yet you accept as an article of faith that the Nazis were not capable of concealing a few canisters of gas within their own homeland?"

"But it would have degraded by now," Bailey insisted. "Broken down into whatever chemicals it was composed of, rotted into water and gas or something. . . ." Her voice trailed off as the admiral shook his head insistently in the negative.

"Not necessarily. That was one of the primary advantages of Tabun. It was extraordinarily stable—even required a small explosion to separate it into toxic compounds. Quiet frankly, it's not even that difficult to manufacture. None of the chemical and biological agents is."

"But what does Tabun have to do with this?"

"Four months ago, we received certain information that a stockpile of Tabun was being moved to a weapons bunker near Peenemünde. You must understand that I can't disclose sources—even assuming that I've been given the correct ones." His eyes squinted slightly, a sign that Bailey had come to realize signaled ironic amusement. "The paranoids trust no one."

"What kind of weapons are they using as delivery vehicles?"

"According to our sources, the Tabun is mounted in a break-free container in the ass of a torpedo casing, just forward of the propulsion. The warhead on the torpedo punches through the skin of the ship and provides the explosive force necessary to break the gas into its toxic constituent compounds. The Germans perfected the technology just at the end of World War II at their research facility at Peenemünde."

"How bad is this stuff?"

The admiral looked grim. "Deadly. Your gas masks won't stop it. The molecules are microns smaller than your best filters. And even if the masks worked, Tabun penetrates the skin instantly. One drop—less than a drop, actually—and your sailor is dead in moments. A torpedo could easily carry a payload sufficient to wipe out an aircraft carrier."

"But why torpedoes?" Bailey thought for a moment. "Never mind—the answer's obvious. First, we're not equipped with a truly effective torpedo counter. We have some decoys and our own speed, but nothing like an antiair missile or a close-in weapons system. And second, the weapon uses our own systems against us. One of the first things we do when we're anticipating a chemical or biological attack is to clam up and put positive pressure on the ship. No outside air gets in—we recirculate what's inside."

The admiral nodded. "And what about fire-fighting procedures? Once you have the conflagration under control, you pump air into the space to clear out the smoke. With a Tabun-laden torpedo, you'd simply be finishing the job the fire started.

"Think about the psychological effect that knowledge of such a weapon would have," he continued. "Chemical and biological weapons are weapons of terror. There's nothing gallant about dying from a missile, but imagine the morale of a crew facing a submarine—another weapon of terror—armed with chemical weapons. How do you begin to counter the fear?"

"You're sure our people know about this?" Bailey asked. "I've never even heard so much as a hint of it, and now you expect me to buy this whole story?"

"And you'd have been in a position to know, wouldn't you? Would you have told the fleet? Would they have been likely to tell you? Knowing that there is no effective countermeasure, knowing how your people would react? Would you have *wanted* to know?"

"Hell, *yes,* I'd want to know!" *But I wouldn't have told*

anyone else, had I been the one ashore. What good would it do? Would you risk ships attacking every unidentified submarine, perhaps killing one of our own? Would it have made you more cautious—too cautious, perhaps—in conducting ASW games? Some small part of her mind was in complete agreement with the admiral.

And how the hell does he know about NSA? She'd leave that little puzzle for later, along with the question of why Jim Atchinson, the director of operations, had cut her out of the loop on Tabun. As an area specialist, she had every right to know about it.

"Admiral." She reached out and caught the senior officer's elbow with one hand and braced herself for a blast of disapproval. To touch an admiral so, especially one as formal and stiff as Admiral Richardson—but no, all she saw in the older man's face was resigned weariness. "One more question. You mentioned biological weapons a bit earlier when you were talking about the effects of positive pressure spreading the Tabun around the ship. I assume that might be a risk as well."

"But that's not your question."

"No, sir, it isn't. We usually talk about bio and chem weapons as part of a triad. *Nuclear,* biological, and chemical, NBC for short. This weapons facility you mentioned— is it also equipped to handle nuclear warheads?"

The admiral shook his head ruefully. "Always dangerous to teach an officer to think."

"Are they manufacturing nuclear warheads for their torpedoes and antiship missiles?" Bailey asked insistently. "You've gone this far with it, Admiral—now finish it. If I have a right to know about the Tabun, then the same reasoning applies to the nuclear question as well, doesn't it?"

"Yes. To both questions."

"But how—"

He cut her off. "You *don't* have a right to know the details. Just read your own newspapers, watch CNN, as I do. As the Germans do, as well. Since the breakup of the Soviet Union, nuclear material has been smuggled across every border of every country. How many checkpoints have the capability to even detect it? And what sort of internal controls do you think exist in such places as Ukraine, Belarus, Bosnia? I could think of fifty ways myself to transport it into Germany, and I'm hardly an expert.''

Bailey was silent, considering the implications.

The admiral regarded her gravely. ''Your bothersome little NATO exercise has turned into something considerably more serious, hasn't it? Command at sea for you, years before you should have expected it, and the start of a particularly vicious conflict. Although very few in your country will believe it.''

''You're certain about this,'' Bailey said finally. ''And if you're right—''

''*Now* may we go inside? It's too bloody cold out here for an old man.''

''Jesus Christ. The Koreans or the Germans. What a fucking lousy set of alternatives.''

The admiral turned and walked back along the port side of the ship toward the hatching leading into the skin of the ship. As he worked the dogged lever that secured the hatch, he looked back at Bailey. ''We live here. None of *us* even has a choice.''

FOUR HUNDRED FEET BELOW THE SURFACE

The next minefield woke slowly, producing the mechanical equivalent of grumbling and complaining. The two-hundred-mine pattern, stretching east and west across the English Channel from Dover to Calais, had been one of the earliest ones laid during World War II. Almost forty percent of the mines failed to respond to their low-frequency wake-up call, the result of mechanical failures and years of operation alone.

Of the one hundred twenty mines activated, another forty experienced mechanical problems in either the firing circuits or the propulsion system of the torpedo. Some of them were able to report their status, while most simply failed to detect a problem.

Of the eighty mines remaining, most of the failures were planted in shallow water. Fishing nets dragging across their

positions, cable-laying ships that disturbed their sites were
the primary causes for mechanical difficulties, but age was
a contributing factor to all of them. Even so, the mines that
clustered around the deep-water channels of the English
Channel were enough.

After all, it would take only one.

U-504

"And that's the last of checkpoint." Kraeken double-
checked the line of figures on his clipboard, counting again
the X's and check marks. He looked across at Captain Merker. "Minelaying operations are completed." He smiled.
"I know what happens next."

Merker nodded. The rest of the wolf pack would be on
station within the next four hours. All of them—assuming
the submarine that had started executing the mission too
soon would follow the rest of the schedule. For a moment,
Merker's thoughts drifted. How much danger would the
rogue pose to the rest of them?

Not that it mattered just now. The wolf pack had just
one set of orders: "Find the British flagship. Wolf pack
leader gets first choice of targets."

14

USS RAMAGE

"Here comes HMS *Battleaxe*." Ensign Blackthorne pointed at the gray hull just climbing over the horizon. "Wonder if they'd swap us some ice cream for some beer?"

Bailey regarded him wryly. "I'm not going to approve any after-dinner planning meetings, you know. I remember the open bar they have on board."

He chuckled, the first upbeat sound she'd heard on the ship since Daistrom's death. "Was worth a try. I was hoping you might have forgotten about the Brits."

She felt the answering smile wilt on her face. *Like I've forgotten so much else, he means. Even the most junior officer on the ship knows it.*

Countertorpedo tactics had not been the extent of it. After a comprehensive tour of the ship, she had started to realize how much can change in a few years. The weapons systems, the data exchange systems—hell, even sonar had gear in it she'd never seen. She'd thought she'd at least recognize all of their equipment.

Realizing just how much she *didn't* know about the ship and her capabilities worried her. Maybe ops was right. Maybe she should have stepped quietly to the rear, let Collins take charge, and just joined the wardroom as another officer.

No. She shook her head, became aware that the ensign

was watching her curiously, and turned away from him. Even as outdated as she was on the modern technology, she understood submarines, submariners, and how they operated better than any other officer on the ship. *Ramage* was safer with her in command, at least until the rest of the navy could spare the time and attention to get someone more senior out here. Collins would have charged in the first time there'd been an attack, and *Ramage* would now be settling into the muck and trash that littered the bottom of the English Channel.

She turned back to the ensign. "Signal *Battleaxe* that we're ready to receive their helicopter." Her face softened slightly. "I'll be personally inspecting any suspicious boxes they're carrying."

U-504

The British destroyer filled the periscope. "Emergency dive—*now*." Merker slammed the handles up on the periscope and spun around toward sonar. "What the hell are you doing back there? Do you realize—" He stopped abruptly and grabbed for a handhold as the deck careened down, aware that his voice was climbing up out of control. The slaved monitor would have shown them what he'd seen: the destroyer bearing down on them, a figure perched on the bridge wing staring in the submarine's direction through binoculars.

Eighteen hours after the last mine was laid, *U-504* was lingering around the entrance to the British naval base, taking furtive peeks at the coastline to pinpoint her location. Better to wait until night to mine the narrow approach to the harbor, but there might not be time now.

Merker watched the figures click over on the depth gauge and swore quietly at the unknown staff officer who'd planned the operation. There should have been five submarines deployed, and the harbor should have been mined before the first ship was attacked. But no, that would compromise the operation, running the risk of having a mine activate before all of the *Northern Lights* battle group was inside the line of demarcation, trapped in the killing field of the North Sea.

The destroyer above them had been far enough away to perhaps have missed seeing them, and there was sufficient time to get back to depth before she got much closer. The emergency dive, he realized, had not really been necessary.

"Make your depth seventy-five meters," he said in a normal tone of voice. "Sonar, you hold contact now?"

"Yes, *Kapitan,*" the technician said quietly.

"Is the destroyer changing course?"

"No, sir," sonar replied. "Sir, the propeller—she just appeared. It wasn't there before, not on aural or passive." The man's eyes verged on pleading.

Merker bit back a sharp reply. If the destroyer were showing no signs of interest in them, then they'd probably not been detected. But why in the hell hadn't *they* known the ship was there? An advanced surface ship quieting system, something similar to the web of acoustic monitors, cables, and signal generators that filled the space between U-boat's inner and outer hulls? Or more equipment problems?

After eight months at sea, numerous machinery and equipment gremlins had been surfacing unexpectedly, always at the wrong time and where they could do the most damage. A transient voltage could have fried some critical part of the sonar system, an undetected surface duct interfered with the detection, an anomaly in the digital beamformer—the list went on, endlessly.

The sonar technician interrupted his train of thought. "Sir, the destroyer is coming left, slowing to eight knots. New course puts her on an intercept with our last period of periscope exposure."

Merker eased his grip on the overhead bar as the deck leveled off. Eighty men on *U-540* knew something had happened in Korea, although most of them knew little more than that the ship had fired a torpedo. Most of them had not even known exactly where they were.

"Steady at seventy-five meters," the OOD reported. "Orders, sir?"

Secrecy and stealth—his and the destroyer's.

What was it? Suddenly he made the connection. The destroyer was probably confident in her new quieting measures, whatever they might consist of. But if she were unexpectedly attacked—successfully—it would seriously undermine that confidence. It would also give rise to a new furor of paranoia over the possibility of mines. He wondered which would prove to be the more effective—the actual mining, or just the fear of it.

" 'He who wants to be victorious on the sea must always attack.' You recognize that, Herr Ehrlich?'' Merker asked.

"The U-boat Commander's Handbook, Kapitan.''

Merker nodded approval. ''Weapons systems have made some of the lessons in it obsolete, but the basic principles don't change. You must know it so well that you don't have to think. Now, take the conn. We'll see how much you've learned.'' Merker glanced at the digital clock. Every minute that passed put him that much farther behind schedule. Waiting for the destroyer to leave the area before *U-504* laid her mines would also put them behind schedule. ''Make the approach. Sonar, open doors and flood tube number eight.''

He saw the navigator eye him uncertainly. *Pay attention, young man,* he added silently. *You may not be given much warning before you have to do this by yourself. I wasn't.*

''Helicopter,'' sonar said. ''Classify it as an American SH-60.''

''One?''

''Yes, *Kapitan.* For now.''

Merker nodded and turned back to Ehrlich. Merher's voice was quiet, insistent. ''You understand, they carry two. If they start triangulating on you with active sonar, it will be that much more difficult to evade them. Quickly now— your plan.''

''The destroyer won't go active,'' Ehrlich said rapidly. ''They may still believe that their quieting measures are working—which they are—and that it was merely bad luck that caused us to surface in front of them. Worst case, from their point of view, is that we were holding contact on her and positioning for attack. Either way, the active sonar would be a beacon for a torpedo. She'll stay silent and use the helos.''

''Eight hundred meters,'' sonar warned. ''Sir, I'm barely

holding contact. She's still in passive-only mode."

"When do you shoot?" Merker said.

Ehrlich thought for just a second. "Now?"

"Do it. Hit her before the Americans can launch their other helo and you make clearing the area that much easier. You're well within range."

"Sonar, solution?" Ehrlich asked, his voice firmer.

"Locked in, sir. Tube eight flooded, torpedo armed. Tube seven flooded, torpedo in standby."

"Fire one, tube eight."

"Now evade," Merker snapped. "Don't wait for her to turn—you know she will. Do it *now*. Give the orders while you watch her maneuver." He put one hand on the back of the younger officer's head and twisted it toward the sonar console.

Ten seconds after the torpedo left the tube, the destroyer ramped up to max shaft horsepower and twisted away from the submarine. The lines blazed through on the passive sonar. Merker kept his hand on the man's neck, feeling the pulse throbbing under his fingertips and perspiration break out. The seconds stretched into minutes as the officer gave a crisp series of orders for evasive maneuvering, stumbling only when the hull sang with the first pulses of transmissions from the helicopter's sonar dome. Merker coached him quietly from behind, whispering in the man's ear. The shrill scream of the torpedo was clearly audible through the hull at first, then only from the speaker overhead.

The submarine twisted and porpoised through the water, shedding decoys and creating knuckles. The helo pings grew stronger, quicker, then suddenly faded as Ehrlich found the layer.

"Three minutes. Torpedo has acquired," sonar announced.

Only three minutes. It felt like at least fifteen, if not more.

USS RAMAGE

"Helo's ready to—CHRIST!" Blackthorne shouted. "What the FUCK is she—" The blare of the sonar warning buzzer drowned out his words.

"Hard starboard rudder, all ahead flank," Bailey snapped, darting over to the port bridge wing. "Stay clear of her, but get us the hell out of here!''

"Combat concurs," she heard Collins's voice say over the bitch box, maddeningly calm. "Recommend steady on course two-one-zero."

"Navigator concurs."

"Do it." She forced her voice to sound confident. "Stay at least one thousand yards from *Battleaxe* if you can. And set MOPP Condition 1."

"Bridge, combat. MOPP Condition 1 is for an immediate attack from NBC agents. Are you sure—"

Bailey toggled the switch down, cutting Collins off. "MOPP 1. No discussion." She turned to the BMOW. "Pass the word for Admiral Richardson, requesting his presence on the bridge." She stared aft and watched their wake widen behind them as they ran for their lives.

U-504

One hundred meters above them, one thousand meters to the north, the surface ship darted back and forth, frantically trying to confuse the torpedo. The speaker bleated with noise from both the submarine and the destroyer decoys.

"Ten seconds," Ehrlich whispered. He stared at the overhead as though it were transparent and he could see the ship. "Come on, you bastard, come on come on come on . . ." Merker saw his lips continue the quiet litany as his voice trailed off.

USS RAMAGE

Bailey concentrated, trying to understand the announcements coming over the 1MC. The BMOW's words were muffled by his gas mask, but she heard enough to tell her that the ship was now buttoned up, as safe from an NBC attack as modern technology could make it. Admiral Richardson had made it to the bridge as the last airtight hatch slammed shut.

"*Battleaxe* reports the torpedo is gaining on her, Captain,'' Blackthorne shouted, carefully enunciating and speaking slowly to make himself understood. ''Torpedo is five thousand yards directly astern of her, speed fifty knots.''

She nodded. ''Tell CHENG I need every knot he's got. If *Battleaxe* shakes it, that torpedo is going to be looking around for a new target. We're the next loudest noise source in the water.''

''Too far away now. Max range is five thousand yards on their sensors.''

She shook her head. Getting into a debate over the sensor engineering on late-model German torpedoes was hardly possible. Or necessary. Command had its advantages.

Richardson stood in the corner, staying out of the way, his eyes fixed on the SPA-35G radar repeater. His face was cold, immobile, as he watched the digital signal marking the torpedo gain on the British ship.

''It has *Battleaxe,*'' Collins said over the bitch box. Her voice was still as unnaturally calm as a NASA control operator. ''Three thousand yards. Estimated time to impact—two minutes.''

A little more that two minutes, one part of her brain noted dispassionately. At fifty knots, the torpedo traveled five thousand yards every three minutes. She stared aft, watching the silent battle unfold.

The British ship cut back and forth across her own wake and *Ramage*'s, trying desperately to confuse the weapon's guidance system. Wake homer? *Battleaxe* must think so, although the probability was that it might also have an acoustic seeker head option. Both—a problem. Tactics varied against the two different types of torpedo, with only one constant: Speed and distance vectors always played.

The contact, when it came, was almost anticlimactic. At first.

Battleaxe had just begun executing a hard turn to starboard when the water seemed to recede from around her bow, leaving parts of her dripping hull exposed to the air. Bailey could see the beginning of the graceful stem to which the sonar dome was attached. Then the dome itself came into view, the large, bulbous structure that had told the ship a torpedo was in her immediate future.

Richardson groaned, then slammed his hand down on the chart table.

The sea hadn't magically been repelled by the hull, she realized a second later. Instead, *Battleaxe*'s bow had heaved itself up out of its natural element. The sea geysered up around the ship, completely obscuring the weather decks, then angling out to spatter the ocean around the ship. *Battleaxe*'s bow dropped back down into the water, but the damage was evident now. The clean line from the bow to the stern along the weather decks was now broken. Deep structural damage, maybe even a broken keel. That suspicion was confirmed a moment later by the ship herself.

U-504

Ehrlich overestimated the time of impact by three seconds. The explosion blanked out the noise from all the decoys, immediately overloading the gain control on the tinny speaker.

"Yes!" The sonarman made a sharp motion with his hand to accompany the quiet cheer. Around the rest of the control center, men started breathing again, surprised to find themselves starved for oxygen.

USS RAMAGE

"Slow us down," she ordered. "I want to be able to hear."

"But Captain, we need to clear the area! The British— they'll be out soon enough to rescue the survivors. We're only twenty miles off the coast," Blackthorne objected.

Bailey wheeled on him. "Ten knots—*now*."

The young officer started to voice another objection, then stopped as the bitch box sounded off. "OOD, what the hell are you doing up there?" The words were clear, evidence that the ops officer had already taken off her gas mask.

"The captain—" Blackthorne began sullenly.

Bailey reached across him to slap the TALK button down. "We're returning to assist survivors. And provide any other assistance that our allies might need." She looked over at Richardson. "And get your gear back on. I want this ship buttoned up."

"But the—" Blackthorne tried one last time.

"That's an order. Make it happen—*now*." Suddenly she was damned sick of having to repeat every order, to insist on the instantaneous execution that she was certain Daistrom had demanded.

But you're not Daistrom. And this is his crew—not yours. And, she argued silently, *I didn't ask for them. But nobody gave me any choice—least of all that submarine on our ass.*

She felt the ship slow, glanced up at the heading indicator, and noted that they were coming about. For the moment, at least, a direct confrontation had been avoided.

But for how much longer?

U-504

"Nicely done," Merker said. It was not just a pleasantry—the officer *had* managed the approach and evasion with a skill that Merker had not known he possessed.

They learn by example, he thought. *Perhaps more than I think they do. I wonder what attacking the British diesel taught him?*

The *Leutnant dur See*'s face gave him no clues. It was flushed slightly. There was a certain joy that came with executing a tactical maneuver with particular precision, fulfilling the role that the ship had been built to carry out.

"Now get us to point Alpha, navigator. OOD, you have the conn. Ten knots, please, as soon as you have a course."

Ehrlich glanced at him and looked slightly disoriented. "Point Alpha, Herr Ehrlich," Merker repeated. Ehrlich's eyes cleared and he nodded. He stepped back behind his plotting table and ran out a bearing line to the spot marked on the chart, then read off a course to intercept it. "Twenty minutes, *Kapitan*," he concluded.

Merker nodded and took a moment to study the navigator's face, wondering if he could see there what he could not find in his own eyes.

USS RAMAGE

"Still nothing, Captain," Digger said. The dark circles were growing under his eyes, and his face had a drawn, haggard look to it. As bad as he'd looked the day before, it was worse now.

"Any possibilities?" Bailey asked. Richardson was still on the bridge, staring at the silent hulk of his ship.

He shook his head. "Not yet. I've tried just about everything I can think of to find a signal in this noise, but nothing. The torpedo, yeah, but that's a hell of a way to find out you've got a submarine on your ass."

She sighed. "And no luck detecting any mines with the sonar, either, I suppose?"

"It wasn't designed for it, you know. Those high-frequency sets that the minesweepers have, they can see small targets easy. We're lucky if we get a return off them at all, with the frequencies we use for active."

"I'm running a course analysis on the last incident again," Henning volunteered. "I've souped up the low-frequency resolution some. It may not work, but it's worth trying."

Standing in sonar, she could almost feel the desperate anxiety that was driving them. The submarine that had been haunting them was a personal enemy to each one of them.

And there was nothing she could do to help. Ashore, in the MIUWU van, she would have known exactly what orders to give, could have double-checked the sonar displays herself to make sure no tired set of eyes had missed anything critical. The equipment in the SQR-89 sonar suite was as recognizable yet unfamiliar as a strange hotel room. Individual peculiarities—where the thermostat was, how soft the bed might be, whether the faucet dripped at night—were their specialties, not hers.

"I'll be on the bridge," she said, after having looked intently at the passive sonar printouts. She turned to leave, then paused at the hatch leading back into the combat section. "And when you call the OOD to tell him I'm on my way up, ask him to have the department heads and the XO meet me there."

The guilty look from the sonar tech told her she'd just read his mind. She smiled slightly. A small triumph, but the first one here. If she stayed on board long enough, she'd be able to do it with every one of them, just as she could in her own unit.

U-504

"The condenser again, *Kapitan*." The engineering technician wiped the back of one grimy hand over his forehead and muttered a curse under his breath. "It needs a complete teardown. The seals, perhaps, or a small leak on the wet side. It has to be—with this temperature seawater, the condenser should be producing much more water."

Merker nodded and tried to ignore the sudden clenching of his gut. The delicate life support within the hull was so frail, he thought, studying the offending equipment. The sea could kill them in a million ways—or they could commit suicide by missing the first hints of a malfunction.

"What can you do while we're out here?" he asked, already knowing the answer.

"Not very much. I can drain it, crawl inside, and look for a leak. Replace some of the seals, but not all of them. We used some of the last spares during the last problem. It might improve the efficiency a bit, but the whole condenser needs shipyard-level maintenance." The sailor glanced up at him, then looked away.

Merker heard the unspoken question: *When are we going home?* Not an unreasonable one, under the circumstances. If it hadn't been for his tirade on duty and loyalty the day before, the sailor might have dared to ask the question outright.

"Soon enough, then," he said, answering the question while avoiding it completely. "Change out the seals, do what you can. We'll have those pigs from the shipyard trampling all over our boat far too soon, moaning and complaining and billing the navy overtime for fixing what should not have broken in the first place."

The sailor nodded and grimaced. No professional navy man liked having his spaces invaded by the shipyard civilians. "We will hide our coffee and our tools more carefully next time."

"Be glad that they don't come to our homes and we don't have to hide our women," Merker replied. He was rewarded with a chuckle from the sailor.

The sailor gave him a few more technical details and promised to let the chief engineer know if he discovered the cause of the problem. Merker clapped him on the shoulder and left him as he started to crawl back into the still-steaming condenser cavity.

Merker climbed two vertical ladders, then walked forward along the boat's main passageway to his cabin, answering greetings from sailors and officers and dealing with a few small matters requiring his attention. He reached his cabin moments later, and slid the plastic accordion-style door shut gratefully. He stretched out on the narrow bunk and stared blankly at the wall. If he stared at it long enough, he imagined he could see it start to pulse with the tiny variations in water pressure on the hull, always slightly concave. What would happen if it reached the end of its tensile strength? What would he have—about one second to stare at the torrent of water that would crush him immediately? Or would it start with a small crack, one that he could do nothing about except watch grow under the pressure of the water behind it?

What would you say now if you could see me, Admiral Braudel? Hating my crew, this submarine, the ocean—what would you say?

"She's turning north, increasing speed to—looks like twelve knots, *Kapitan*," the sonarman reported. "Bow onto us."

"Take us out, then," he ordered. "We'll pass on her port beam and fall in astern of her." He rubbed his chin reflectively, hearing the coarse stubble under his fingers. "Stay in position on her."

The conning officer acknowledged the orders and turned the direction into a series of rudder directions. The small submarine turned slowly, the motion barely discernible inside the ship.

"Range, seven thousand meters." The sonarman looked

up from his display, making sure the captain had heard him.
"We should be at CPA—closest point of approach—in five
minutes. CPA range, five thousand yards, bearing two-
seven-zero."

"Very well." Merker frowned. They'd slip quickly past
the surface ship, fall in behind them, and wait for a while
longer.

USS RAMAGE

As the department heads arrived, she beckoned them out
onto the bridge wing. It was a compromise between the
uneasy certainty that she needed to be immediately available and her desire to resolve some of their problems in
private. The latter wasn't going to be possible if her new
XO didn't keep her voice down.

*She can lose the chip on her shoulder and get used to
it. She's been XO as long as I've been in command.*

"Don't you think you owe us an explanation?" Collins
glanced at the other department heads for support, first
among equals but clearly uneasy with her position.

"What is it you don't understand about MOPP conditions?" Bailey asked. "Has the name changed since I was
last at sea?"

"Of course it hasn't! You saw how fast everyone got
into their gear. What concerns me is why you immediately
ordered MOPP conditions right after *Battleaxe* was hit.
There's something you're not telling us."

She heard the frustration mount in the ops officer's voice.
From Collins's point of view, her behavior must have
seemed dangerously erratic. First, freezing on the bridge
for the first attack, and then immediately calling for maximum NBC conditions after *Battleaxe* was hit. Although,
she thought wryly, not in the mood to appreciate the humor,
at least Collins couldn't accuse her of freezing up the second time.

And, one part of her mind insisted, she *does* have a right
to know. As her acting executive officer, she was responsible for the training and operation of the crew, a job her
former billet as operations officer had hardly prepared her

to fulfill. By not disclosing to Collins what Admiral Richardson had told her about the Tabun-laden mines, she degraded the XO's ability to help her.

A help she could use, especially now. Admiral Richardson's information was an increasingly heavy burden to bear alone. While she suspected—no, she was sure—that her superiors in Sixth Fleet knew about the chemical dangers in the North Sea, she had no clearance to release that data point to her subordinates.

"It was a normal operational precaution," Bailey said finally. She glanced at the other department heads, trying to gauge whether they believed her. "At least it was when I was last at sea. As I said, perhaps things have changed."

Collins shook her head angrily. "I'm not buying it. Your active-duty time wasn't that long ago, and MOPP conditions were never a normal part of general quarters then. Not MOPP Level 1. You know something, something we ought to, and you're not telling us. That, in my estimation, is just as dangerous as incompetence." Collins glared at her, daring her to contradict her.

"There is something to what she says," CHENG said uneasily. His fingers beat out a staccato rhythm on the highly polished wooden railing. "Why MOPP Level 1? Why not 4, as a precaution? Or even 3 would have been routine. But Level 1 immediately?" He shook his head. "I have to admit, Captain, I'm puzzled by that as well."

Puzzled, she thought, but not verging on insubordination and mutiny. She transferred her gaze to the weapons officer, who was, as always, peculiarly detached from the entire conversation. He stirred uneasily under her gaze, evidently aware that some comment was expected. She saw a flush creep up his neck and start to darken his high cheekbones.

Finally, when the silence grew uncomfortable, Kelso said, "I know we don't always have all the captain's information, and I know you've taken command under some unusual circumstances. In light of what happened to *Battleaxe,* is there anything I need to know to do my job? Anything I *must* know to keep the ship safe?"

And that, she thought, hit the issue squarely on the head. How much did they need to know? How much must she disclose to fulfill her duty to the ship, to rationalize the breach of confidence?

And what would the real effect of the information do? She considered that, aware that the three officers were carefully avoiding looking at her. After all, there was nothing they could do about the threat of chemical attack. She could easily circumvent any safety-of-ship issues by simply ordering them to set MOPP Level 1 any time they went to general quarters. She reached a decision.

"There's nothing you need to know." She raised one hand to forestall a sharp rebuttal from Collins. "In the future, however, we will set MOPP Level 1 at any sign of attack, as well as any time we go to general quarters. Is that clear?"

"There's one other thing," Collins said finally, the anger now tight in her voice. "I had a damage control team take a good look at *Battleaxe* after she was hit. You know the goggles that we have, the ones that reveal clouds of chemical attack substances. They reported strong indications of some nerve agent around *Battleaxe*. What I want to know is this: Did you knowingly let us go into an area where there was danger of chemical attack without telling us about it?"

"There is no requirement in naval regulations that you be aware of every specific danger in a theater. Nor that I brief you afterward on everything affecting my decisions as regards the ship," she answered.

CHENG cut in before Collins could respond. "Of course there's not. That's one of the prerogatives of command, ma'am," he said calmly. "However, since there's evidently information you can't tell us, yet"—she noted with gratitude his use of the word "can't"—"then I'd like to ask a couple of specific questions that will help me do my job better." He waited for permission to continue.

She nodded. "Within the limits of my orders, I'll answer what I can."

"Do you want to set Circle William every time we go to general quarters?" he asked first. Circle William was the battle condition in which all communication between the interior of the ship and the outside atmosphere, air and water included, was terminated. While it was not fail-safe, it did reduce the possibility that any outside contaminant would enter the ship, and included positive pressurization of the interior of the ship as well. It was one of the major NBC improvements of the Aegis-class destroyer over prior ships.

"Yes."

"If we are hit, or suffer some other casualty, do you wish to make any modification to our desmoking procedures? Currently, as soon as I have the fire under control, I intend to provide positive pressurization to the scene to clear smoke and fumes out of the area."

CHENG was verging uncomfortably close to the truth, although she suspected that all three officers had already concluded that there was a serious risk of NBC warfare. "Is the positive pressurization set to the exterior or the interior of the ship?"

"It depends." He studied her face carefully. "If you wish, I can make sure it's vented only to the outside."

"That would work. And please advise me if that's impractical in any situation."

"Finally, do you want the NBC suits broken out and easily available?"

She nodded.

Collins sighed heavily. "Well, even if you can't say anything, I think those answers pretty well answer my questions. And, as your executive officer," she added, "I might recommend that you give the rest of the crew a little information. Use the 1MC. Not only will it get the word out faster, but it also will give you a chance to give them some explanation for it. Otherwise, we're going to have a serious rumor control problem. These sailors aren't dumb—not by a long shot."

CHENG and the weapons officer nodded. Bailey stood, scraping her chair against the slick deck tiles. "I'll consider it. In the meantime, please make those changes to the standing orders immediately. I want to meet with you again in one hour in . . ." She'd almost said her cabin. Maybe, the thought occurred to her, it was time. If she expected them to obey her as their captain, it was time to start acting like it. "In the at-sea cabin," she concluded finally, aware that they'd all noticed the hesitation.

A good compromise, she decided. She'd move into the small combat living compartment reserved for the captain directly off the bridge—but not into the larger cabin one deck down. Besides, as far as she could tell now, there wasn't going to be time for her to relax anytime soon.

SIX HUNDRED FEET BELOW

The mine buried in the mud pulsed quietly as the American destroyer changed course and its magnetic signature faded away. It had almost decided to fire, since the new target had seemed to meet all of the parameters. However, before its capacitor had charged to full strength, the ship had turned away. It subsided into waiting, as it had for decades.

15

---

7 MARCH 2002:
THE ENGLISH CHANNEL

USS RAMAGE

Another few hours of sleep—Christ, that's all I need. An hour, even. Bailey rubbed one hand across her face, feeling rough skin under her fingertips. She'd tried to grab a couple of hours in the top rack in Collins's stateroom, only to be awakened every fifteen minutes with a question or spurious-contact report from Collins.

"We're detaching you from NATO operational control," the Sixth Fleet operations officer said. "With this latest incident, there's no doubt something's brewing over here. You may not be able to get out of the North Sea immediately, but you have to keep *Ramage* out of it. This isn't our fight—not now."

Bailey reached up to the circuit speaker and turned down the volume so the crew inside combat couldn't hear both sides of the conversation. "Admiral, the situation here is critical. We're bottled up in the North Sea by minefields and subs. The issue of our chain of command isn't going to make much difference tactically. If anything, we've got more in common with the Brits right now than we do with the rest of the U.S. forces." She turned her back on Collins, who was seated at the TAO console, to avoid watching her reaction.

A deep sigh over the circuit. "You may not understand it, but it matters. It's a question of national security. The United States *can't* handle another regional conflict right

now. NATO's just going to have to understand that. To
avoid getting drawn into this, we're moving you back under
U.S. command. Do what you can to stabilize the situation.
You've got an absolute right to take any necessary and
proportional action you feel necessary to protect the safety
of your ship and crew, but try to avoid direct confrontation
if you can. We'll get you out of there as soon as we can.
Encourage Richardson to shift his flag to one of the British
ships, if you can. We don't want to offend him, but we
damned sure don't want you in the middle of a shooting
war."

"Just exactly how am I supposed to stabilize the situation and not shoot anyone?"

"You want rudder orders?" The voice on the other end
of the circuit was harsh. "If I had anyone to relieve you, I
would. Until that time, start acting like a commanding officer."

"So where do we go now?" Collins asked. For once, it
sounded like a real question instead of a jibe.

The department heads were gathered around the surface
plot in combat, ringing the small-scale plot that showed
most of the North Sea. Admiral Richardson was in his quarters, dealing with the aftermath of both *Victory* and *Battleaxe*. Given her last conversation with Sixth Fleet, it had
seemed prudent not to include him in the discussion.

"North again. Patrolling back and forth along here,"
Bailey said, tracing a racetrack course on the chart.

"That's what Sixth Fleet said?"

"My orders are to do what we can to stabilize the situation. If we stay north, we're in a good position to break
out of the North Sea at the earliest opportunity. It'll get us
out of the area of the latest attacks, too." Bailey tried to
sound more confident than she felt.

"Whatever that means, in this scenario," Collins answered. "It's like trying to stabilize a riot."

"Or a war." The weapons officer had an oddly animated
tone in his voice.

"What do you mean by that?" she asked.

He shrugged. "It seems obvious to me. The *Lusitania*. That's what we're supposed to be."

"Now, just a minute—" Bailey began.

"America didn't enter World War I until she had something to rally popular support behind," the man continued, speaking rapidly, as though the pressure of his own thoughts was too much to contain any longer. "The public's not going to care about a few British ships or a European ferry. Hell, they've even written off *Weeks*." The bitterness in his voice rose with the volume. "But let a ship like *Ramage* take it in the ass, and Congress will have to do something. Won't they? Don't you see it?"

"Mister, I think that's enough," she said, struggling for a calm voice. "The United States isn't writing anyone off, least of all *Weeks*."

"Damn you!" He gestured wildly out at the ocean. "There's a submarine out there killing surface ships. You keep spouting this nonsense about orders, duty, the way the navy runs—doesn't that mean a damned thing to you? Are we supposed to sit here and calmly wait to die while the United States decides to get involved?"

She saw tears start in his eyes, and his face freeze into a mask of fear. "In my cabin. Now," she said sharply.

"No, I think we'd better settle this now," Collins disagreed. She glanced over at Kelso. "Maybe I would have put it differently, but he's got a point. We deserve to know what's going on."

A peculiar stillness settled over the bridge as the watch team listened to the officers argue. It was a horrified quiet, a reflexive response to the absolutely inappropriate behavior of both officers. Wardroom disagreements were settled in the wardroom, and every sailor on the ship knew that those arguments could be just as bloody as any fight on the mess decks. Still, even when the voices behind closed doors were clearly recognizable in the passageways, the custom gave the rest of the crew at least the opportunity to pretend they hadn't heard. And when the officers emerged from the wardroom, they presented a solidified, united front to the rest of the ship. That's the way it was—the way it *ought* to be.

Suddenly, the master chief boatswain's mate appeared at her elbow. Where had he been? Bailey wondered for a second, the thought overwhelmed by the unexpectedly warm rush of gratitude she felt.

The senior enlisted man on the ship regarded the officers gravely. Then, nodding at Bailey, he said, "I think you'd better take this belowdecks." The tone of his voice said he would brook no discussion of the matter. "That's what the captain said."

There was a small motion on the bridge as the boatswain's mate of the watch and the quartermaster walked quietly from their assigned stations to stand behind the chief. There were no threats, no audible counting of numbers, but it was clear that the two department heads were outnumbered.

Ops shot her compatriot an angry glance. "We'll be in the wardroom, ma'am," she said, a hard note of disrespect in her voice. "That is, if you ever need us for anything. It looks like you might not." She slammed off the bridge, dragging the muttering weapons officer behind her.

Bailey turned back to face the master chief, wondering if there was any one thing about the navy that she still understood. "Thank you," she said finally.

"Captain, the OOD has your orders. Now might be a good time for a cup of coffee down in the chiefs' mess."

"In just a minute, Master Chief," she said wearily. "I will come down for it, but I need to check something first. Sonar, is . . ." She shook her head, felt her brain rattle inside it, and wondered how much more she could take. "We haven't had much luck so far, but sooner or later we'll get something. And they're right, you know." She tried for a weak smile. "I'll be damned if I'll let them shoot my first command out from under me."

"Ship's not all that big," he mused. He walked over to the door leading into the passageway and held it open for her. "I 'spect if we dropped by sonar and told them where you were going to be, they might be able to find you pretty quick if they needed you. I'll let Chief Wilson know," he said, referring to the chief sonarman. "Just my recommendation, ma'am, but after what just happened, I think you need to stop by the chiefs' mess. It doesn't hurt to have some support.''

She started to object, to explain that she *couldn't* explain but that there was a reason for her to stay in sonar. Then she saw the look in the master chief's eyes. Concern, anger, and outrage—and fear, she realized. Fear for her, not *of* her.

''A cup of coffee sounds good. Especially after—''

He cut her off with a sharp nod toward the watchstanders on the bridge. ''After you, Captain.''

U-504

''Stay on her,'' Merker ordered. ''The American ship will lead us back to the rest of the British forces faster than anything else.''

The American ship—why had she turned back toward *Battleaxe*? All of his experience had taught him that other ships would scatter from a torpedo warning area, steadily increasing their distance from datum while using their long-range sensors and helicopters to delouse the area. Only when their captains were relatively certain that there was no more submarine threat in the area would they risk bringing their precious high-tech vessels back into the area.

Not that a delousing operation would have been effective against *U-504*. But still, the ship should have tried.

Instead, the American ship had immediately slowed and turned, heading right back toward the area of greatest potential danger. It didn't make sense.

Unless, he added, the American captain *knew* that Merker had orders not to attack the U.S. vessels. His superiors had insisted that Americans would leave him alone as long as there were no American casualties. Indeed, based on what he'd seen so far, even losing the frigate hadn't been sufficient to goad them into action. If it had, he would have been avoiding the U.S. ship immediately after the attack on the British destroyer. Or had guessed it, or was simply tak-

ing a chance. There was no way to be sure, but one thing
was certain.

It would be dangerous to depend on the American ship
being predictable. Or, more specifically, her captain.

16

---

7 MARCH 2002:
THE ENGLISH CHANNEL

USS *RAMAGE*

"You have serious problems with your officers. Dangerous, even. It's got to be stopped before it spreads to the rest of the crew," the master chief said bluntly. He held out a steaming ceramic mug.

Bailey took it, wrapped her fingers around it gratefully. The heat seeped into her body through her fingers, thawing out the cold rage bottled up inside. "Tell me something I don't know."

The master chief looked at her gravely. "From what I hear, you could tell us a lot *we* don't know."

She froze for a moment, considered denying it, then decided not to bother. From what she saw, the members of the chiefs' mess were unanimous in their desire to resolve the situation. And not a one had even hinted that the answer was for her to relinquish command.

"Ordinarily," the master chief continued, taking her silence as agreement, "your XO would solve these wardroom problems. But you're not going to get that from Lieutenant Commander Collins."

"I'm finding that out. I've got to have some officers I can trust, and at least one that's senior enough to keep the others in line."

"Then get them," the chief boatswain's mate said. "Get us five miles offshore and bring some of your own people on."

She stared at him. "How did you know? Damn." She shook her head. "And I thought I was being subtle about it."

The master chief smiled. "The officers are important—but not as important as they think. If you've got the mess behind you, we can make do. Let's go get your MIUWU wardroom. And if you've got any chiefs in the unit, bring them along."

"If we're going to be short on experienced officers," the yeoman chief petty officer said, "let's just go ahead and bring the whole unit. Might as well."

"Hell, bring the gear along, too," said the operations specialist chief. "We've got space back in the hangar or on the flight deck for it."

For the first time in days—in years, it felt like—she felt something lighten in her soul. To have the men and women she *knew* she could count on around her—well, until Sixth Fleet decided to relieve her, she'd take the initiative.

"Do it," she said. "Tell me what you need."

"You got it backward, Captain. Time you started getting it straight," the master chief said. "You tell *us* what you need. We'll do the rest."

Ten hours later, a British Sea Stallion helicopter was fighting gusting winds off the cliffs of Dover. The MIUWU van dangled underneath it, leading the helicopter around as though it were a bull with a ring through its nose as the wind beat against the van's army-green metal. A thousand yards off the coast, three more helicopters holding essential camp gear and the MIUWU personnel hovered, watching their lead slowly negotiate a peace treaty with the ground.

The van skidded ten feet before finally settling down in a slow oscillation below the helicopter. The helicopter veered away, headed for *Ramage*.

The other helicopters made their approaches, encountering considerably less difficulty in landing. Sailors poured into the hatches and up the aft cargo ramps, working with the RAF crews to load their gear onto the other helicopters.

•   •   •

"Where do you want us, skipper?" Lieutenant Boston gestured at the helicopter on the flight deck, the three others orbiting in a starboard pattern astern. "People or equipment first?"

"People," she said immediately. She tried not to let the relief show on her face. "It's always people first." *And until I got to Ramage, I didn't know how true that was.*

U-504

"How many helicopters?" Merker demanded.

The sonar technician slewed his cursor around the round screen to rest on a set of lines. "Three, maybe four. Transport, not ASW."

"I don't like it," Kraeken said immediately.

"You don't understand it," Merker corrected. "And, at this point, neither do I."

"There're only a couple of reasons to have that many helicopters out here. The fact that they're concentrating on the American ship means that we can no longer consider them neutral." The XO's voice rose in pitch and volume. He slammed his hand down on the metal railing that separated the center of the control room from the rest of the compartment. "We *must* take them now."

"No. You're not thinking clearly. First, we have no reason to believe that they're concentrating on the American ship. We're out of range of the British at this moment. You may remember that the only reason we're anywhere near this ship is that it's our guide back to the Limeys."

"But there's no evidence that they're going anywhere else, either."

"Still. The other fact is that the General Staff has not changed our orders. We've made every scheduled communications break—even if we'd missed a satellite download, they would know we'd missed the message and they'd retransmit."

"Unforeseen circumstances require initiative."

"And using a wolf pack effectively means sticking to the plan." Merker raised his voice, pitching it to reach every member of the crew within earshot. "Think about it.

If I were to exercise this initiative you keep bringing up and attack the American ship, Germany would risk bringing the United States into this theater immediately. In another two weeks, they'll be completely committed to the conflict in Korea. Then it'll be too late—we'll have this all mopped up and settled before they can withdraw, rearm, and redeploy to the other side of the world.''

"But this ship—"

"Poses no direct threat to us," Merker said sharply. "In my judgment. I'm explaining the theory behind this so that you can better carry out my orders."

And not to open the matter up for debate, he added silently. From the expressions he saw on the other men's faces, they agreed.

Merker watched Kraeken rein in his temper with a visible effort. "Thank you, *Kapitan,*" the XO said, forcing the words out. "I understand now."

And don't agree. But you won't win this argument, not in front of this crew.

"Increase our distance to ten thousand yards," Merker ordered, to drive the point home.

USS RAMAGE

"Any problems?" Bailey asked Lieutenant Boston, resisting the temptation to quiz him on the details of berthing and messing. The master chief had tactfully pointed out that if he had any problems, he'd let her know. And, seeing as she had more important concerns, he was certain the details wouldn't require her attention.

"Fine." He looked troubled. "But the wardroom—"

"Is in disarray," she finished. "Collins?"

"Yes, ma'am. But we'll work the problems out."

"If she doesn't fall in line soon, you'll relieve her as executive officer," she said bluntly. "Learn her job."

"Captain, I haven't been on a ship in five years."

"It's been longer for me. If you're not ready, get ready. Otherwise you might as well be still ashore."

He looked hurt for a moment, then determined. "Okay. I'll be ready."

•   •   •

"Where the hell did it go?" Carlisle pounded his fist on the table. Within fifteen minutes of arriving on *Ramage*, he'd found his counterparts and established his credentials as a former submarine sailor. So far, he'd found no reason to disagree with any of their conclusions about the previous detections. "I know it's detectable. We held it up North. Just for a few minutes, but enough."

Henning shoveled another forkful of chili mac into his mouth, then leaned back against the formed plastic chair. He chewed and looked thoughtful. "Might have been some strange ducting up there. You get those weird layers and currents just north of Scotland." He pointed at Carlisle's roll. "You going to eat that?" Without waiting for an answer, he reached over to take it.

"Mouth. You're all mouth," Digger said. He jabbed his own fork into his salad. "I don't know how you can eat that crap, anyway. You ought to weigh two hundred pounds, the way you eat."

Henning finally swallowed. "Tabasco sauce. That's the secret. Makes this stuff taste all right, and the spices burn off the calories. You ought to try it."

"Beats MREs," Carlisle said. "That's what we live on in the field."

"Yeah, I know." Digger stirred the mound of noodles, ground beef, and cheese on his plate, trying to convince himself that it was food. He pointed his fork at Carlisle, then said to Henning, "Good pair of ears on that boy. Came off subs. Give him a little time and he'll be as good as we are."

"As good now—if not better." Carlisle impaled a hollow noodle on his fork and brought it up to eye level. He shuddered. "If they didn't put all the crap on it, this would be okay. Pasta's good for you."

Digger sighed and dropped the fork. He stood up. "PB and J for me. I'll be right back." The ship kept a ready supply of peanut butter, jelly, and bread on the serving line for finicky eaters.

Two minutes later, he walked back over to the table, carrying a sandwich wrapped in paper napkins. "Let's go."

"You're not going to eat that?" Carlisle asked.

Digger smiled. "One of the things I miss about being in port—getting food to go. Come on, let's get back up there. Ain't nobody on this ship as hot as we are on that gear."

U-504

"Submarine," the sonarman said sharply. But quietly. Very quietly.

Merker whirled around to stare at him. "Where?"

The sonarman clamped his hands down over the headset to screen out the small noises in the compartment. He shut his eyes and frowned. "West," he said finally. "The bearing—I can't refine it."

"Classification?"

The technician kept his eyes closed. "It's long-range. A convergence zone detection, maybe. Not close, but moving fast. A few electrical sources, maybe—yes, there it is." He opened his eyes. "Probably a British Swiftsure-class submarine. I'm not certain, but that's my best guess. Whatever it is, it's coming toward us."

Merker glanced forward, running his gaze over the noise-suppression equipment indicator panel. All green. "She can't hear us," he decided. "She may be headed this way, but she's not after us."

"Helicopters, then a submarine," Kraeken said. "And we're in firing position."

"There's no proof the two events are related. My decision stands."

The XO put his hands on his hips and arranged his face in a pleasant expression. Something ugly lit his eyes. "As you say, *Kapitan*. It's *your* decision."

USS RAMAGE

"What the hell was she doing out here?" Carlisle said. Thirty minutes after she'd appeared, the Swiftsure quietly faded off all *Ramage*'s sensors.

"You think she's still there?" Henning asked.

Digger nodded. "I'd be out here if I were her. A U-boat

taking shots at your country's ships? Wouldn't you have been sorta interested in it? Back when you were on the boats?''

"Nope. Boomers," Carlisle said, using slang for a ballistic-missile submarine. "We heard somebody else around, we snuck out of town quietly. But I agree—it's a Swiftsure.''

Henning shrugged, less a negative than a gesture of frustration. "But what's the *point* of it? And why won't the Brits tell us what the hell their submarines are doing?''

Digger was silent for a moment, studying the sonar screen. He flipped the range scale knob counterclockwise, expanding the scale, then narrowed it back down to the five thousand yards immediately around *Ramage*. "Above my pay grade," he said finally. "This ain't an easy world to figure out these days. Back when it was just us and the Soviets, you *knew* who the bad guys were. Now, the bad guys are good, and the good guys are heading the other way. I don't know which side the Germans are on—hell, sometimes I'm not even sure which side *we're* on. We're in the middle more often that we're on a side, standing between asshole Bosnians and bigger-asshole Serbs, taking the hits while they fight about something that happened a million years ago. And the Koreans . . .''

"Putting a hole in *Wasp* ain't exactly what I'd call friendly fire." Henning frowned, and leaned over the plotting table. "Wait a second," he said.

"You got something?''

"Don't know. Let me look at a vernier." He changed one display channel to expand around the frequency that had caught his interest. "Take a hard look at bearing two-five-zero. Anything?''

Digger flipped back out to the larger range scale. "Nothing—wait, some clutter. It's not resolving well enough to be a contact, though.''

"These guys *ever* look like decent contacts? Anything else?''

Digger studied the scope more carefully. "Maybe something that looks the same on bearing one-eight-five," he said. "Not a hard contact, but some fuzz that drifts in and out. Based on what we've seen, I'd buy this as a German boat. You want to go to tracking mode?''

Henning shook his head. ''That'd tell them we're suspicious. Let's get the TAO back here first. Before we go advertising, we ought to clue her in.''

Digger flipped the toggle down on the bitch box and asked the TAO to step back into sonar. Moments later, Lieutenant Commander Collins was at their hatchway. Henning summarized their contacts, and showed her the frequency that had caught his interest. She studied the line on the passive array printout.

''Pretty iffy, isn't it?'' she asked.

Henning nodded. ''But considering how hard these boats are to detect, I wouldn't rule it out. This could be an air compressor or a pump of some sort. Just the sort of thing you'd expect to detect when they're running on battery.''

''You want to go active?'' she asked.

''I'm not sure it'd do any good. They've got something on the boats that makes them damned difficult to find when they want to hide,'' Digger said. ''You've seen that already. We hold contact on them for a while, solid contact, then they pull this vanishing act. The only thing going active would accomplish is telling them that we're having a hard time tracking them. We might pick them up, we might not.''

''Where is she?'' Collins asked.

Henning pointed to the chart covered with tracing paper that contained *Ramage*'s position. ''West of us, maybe ten miles,'' he said. ''And if Digger's other sea fuzz is one, it's to the northwest. Two subs, or one sub and some coherent noise. My bet's on subs.''

''I don't like this,'' Collins said immediately. ''We're only fifteen miles off the coast. It's going to be damned hard to run too far, especially if there're two of them boxing us in.''

''If they're after us,'' Henning pointed out. ''There's a whole shitload of Brit surface ships out here too, ma'am. They want to take a shot at someone, it's more likely to be them than us. Besides, it's going to be tough to take a shot at the Germans unless we know exactly where the British submarines are. From what we just saw, they're not telling us everything.''

"Do you want to depend on the Germans' ability to tell an American destroyer from a British one? Not me,'' she answered impatiently. "I'll brief Commander Bailey. In the meantime, stay passive. No active until I clear it with her, you understand?''

The sonarmen nodded. Collins left, pointedly dogging the door shut behind her. As the door lever snicked into place, Henning sighed. "Jesus. What're we supposed to do? Call the Psychic Friends Hotline?''

"Make that Psychotic Friends, and we'll give her the telephone number.'' Digger spun his chair to the left ninety degrees to face his shipmate. "I think we've got us a couple of submarines. What about you?''

"No doubt in my military mind.''

"Well, *hell*. What am I supposed to do, then? Wait until the Brits are all sunk and then come home?'' Bailey looked up at the overhead speaker, frustrated. Around her, the sailors and officers quit trying to pretend they weren't listening. "You *do* understand that we've got at least one German submarine within spitting distance of this ship, don't you? As well as a Swiftsure. And God alone knows what the French are doing.''

"If you're fired on, the peacetime rules of engagement allow you certain options. You know that,'' the voice on the speaker repeated. "Sixth Fleet has been briefed on the situation, and he agrees. There's no justification for modifying the current ROE, not for a NATO exercise. Your situation is no different than it's always been.''

"Except that someone's shooting at us. And our allies are involved in a war. Little details like that.'' Bailey felt her face flushing.

"There's been no declared war over there, Captain. If there were, we'd have pulled you out weeks ago.''

"And done what? Sent us over to Korea? Hell, I'm starting to doubt that *that's* even the right place to be.''

"*Ramage* is to avoid dragging the United States into this.

We sent you there as a signal of support to our allies, not as a combat unit.''

"You want to send a message, use Western Union. And as for *Ramage,* I'll be damned if I'll take the first shot from anyone." Lusitania. *If Weaps is right—*

"You want to be relieved of command?" a new voice broke in. "Because if you do, you better believe I'll do it."

Sixth Fleet himself. Aw, shit, I— "I didn't say that, Admiral. I said that your rules of engagement are placing my ship and my crew at risk without a well-defined objective or reason for doing so. I'm playing shepherd on a wolf pack, sir, and it's a damned uncomfortable role."

"Then don't do it. Look, Bailey, the last thing I need right now is another hot spot. You keep the Brits cool—as soon as we finish up with Korea, we'll come over and give them a hand if the Germans are still acting up. But until then, we're stretched too thin over there to start deploying anything to the Continent beyond what's there now."

"I got it. And in case anybody asks, maybe this NATO command of U.S. forces isn't such a bad idea. At least this admiral out here's got a hair on his ass. Anything else?"

"You don't have to like it, Bailey. Just do it." The circuit went dead.

An hour later, after she'd had time to contemplate just how thoroughly she'd fucked up with Sixth Fleet, Bailey broached the subject of *Ramage*'s role in the upcoming operations to Admiral Richardson.

"It's not that I'm reluctant to commit *Ramage* to a supporting role," she said carefully. "There are, however, some limits on where we can operate."

"Limits? What kind of limits?" Admiral Richardson asked sharply. "I thought you understood what was happening here."

"I do. Everyone else might not agree with you, but I do."

"Then do your part. That's all we ask."

"We will do our part—in the exercise."

"And the rest of this is our problem? Is that the gist of your position?"

"Not exactly. I don't think I've made it clear, Admiral. Forgive me—let me rephrase my comments. For all intents and purposes *other than exercise evolutions, Ramage* is under U.S. command."

"Are you requesting a change in your operational assignments?" The admiral's face had settled into impassive lines.

"No. I still think our towed array beats anything else in the water for finding submarines. Don't look at me like that, Admiral," she said. "It's not safe for us out here, either, you know. The Germans may just decide that the simplest solution is the oldest: Shoot them all and let God sort them out." Bailey shook her head wearily. "They may not think this is our fight—yet—but they're not the ones on the line."

"There might be consequences, you know. If you disobey a direct order—"

"I haven't yet." Bailey snorted. "They'll leave us here. If I screw up, they'll disown me."

"The French have a medal for that, you know. For disobeying a superior officer's orders when it turns out to be the right thing to do."

"If it comes down to that, I'll let you know. For now, everything we've got planned falls squarely within the peacetime rules of engagement."

"For now." Admiral Richardson regarded her solemnly for a few moments, then seemed to arrive at some decision. "Very well, we'll leave matters as they stand. *Ramage* takes point, as my infantry colleagues would say, patrolling out in front of the line of ships with tail wet. For exercise purposes alone, of course. We'll follow back some, say ten miles or so. Cut down on the noise levels for your chaps some."

"Absent any provocation—read 'attack' there, sir— we'll be counting on your forces to prosecute any contacts. The way I read my orders, I'm fully within my rights to pass information to you."

"Agreed."

•   •   •

U-504

Merker checked the message timetable, although there was no real need for him to do so. The dates and times were etched in his mind, beginning with the Korean mission. He folded the message slowly, the paper automatically falling into its well-worn creases, and slipped it back into his breast pocket. He could feel the few ounces drag down the fabric a bit, pooch out the pocket, even after so many months of being stowed there. Perhaps someday soon he would sport a faded outline of the folded message on his pocket, the way a can of snuff engraved its outline on a sailor's back pocket.

At 1600 today, according to the message, the second phase of the plan kicked off. Most of NATO's ships were deployed into thick gaggles and packs around the North Sea, concentrated in the middle and northern portions. With tensions already running high, German U-boats would begin a delicate game of luring the NATO ships south into the narrowing confines near the English Channel. With the ships concentrated in a smaller area hunting for submarines that disappeared at will, finding targets would be easy.

He walked back to sonar, noting that the tile floor seemed slicker than usual. The condenser, the dehumidifier—all around the boat, critical equipment seemed to be wavering on the edge of failure. The casualties were cascading, one malfunction compounding, then overloading a related system.

The sonar technician nodded politely. "The Swiftsure turned away. I lost contact fifteen minutes ago."

"Contacts?" Merker asked, already knowing exactly what the submarine was detecting.

"Two, Herr *Kapitan*. One north, one northwest. They are, I think, a British cruiser and an American destroyer. Past those two, some smaller ships fade in and out. Four others, perhaps."

"How certain are you? About the American, I mean?"

The man shrugged. "It isn't a positive identification, of course. Not without using the periscope. But the frequencies match and the turn count is consistent.''

"Of course." Why had he hoped for more? "We'll go in closer to take a look," he said, trying to sound casual and confident. He felt gratified when the sailor bobbed his head, disinterested.

Merker walked back to the control center, stepping carefully on the slick tiles, and ordered Ehrlich to give him a course to the second contact. The British one, he hoped, although any of the NATO ships—the bigger, the better—would do.

Except for one. He patted the message in his pocket. The American ships were still strictly off-limits—outside of Korea.

USS RAMAGE

"I don't understand the American aversion to mutton," Richardson remarked mildly. "After all, you eat veal. That *is* what this is supposed to be, isn't it?"

Bailey nodded. "The light-green color is a dead giveaway, isn't it?"

The British officer shuddered and reached for the brown jar in the middle of the table. "I believe I'm developing a taste for peanut butter and jelly." His hand had just touched the red plastic cover when the general quarters alarm sounded.

"Torpedo!" Digger screamed. "Oh, fuck, it's . . ." He hit the sonar warning buzzer, and rapidly relayed the bearing and range to the OOD and the TAO while initiating an active sonar search at the same time. In the middle of his spiel, he paused. "Down doppler." He looked up, and his eyes met Henning's. "It's headed away from us."

"I've got it here," Carlisle said, his fingers moving rapidly across the passive sonar printout. "Definite down doppler. Tell 'em." He gestured with his chin toward the bitch box.

"Headed away from us," Digger muttered. "Who's it after?"

"Does it matter? If someone's shooting, we're no safer than the next guy."

The three sonarmen watched the torpedo track south on their respective displays. The sheer terror all torpedo contacts immediately generate in any sailor's heart was replaced by relief coupled with no small measure of shame. Their good fortune was some other sonarman's threat. Although there was no assurance that the next shot wouldn't be aimed at *Ramage,* for the moment they were safe.

"The *Victory,*" Henning said. Digger nodded. The blip on both the active and passive sonar screens was headed directly for the British flagship.

The admiral had longer legs, but Bailey had a head start. She beat the British officer to the combat section by at least five steps. As she stepped into the darkened compartment, she heard voices in four different accents crowding onto the tactical circuit.

"*Ramage,* this is *Victory,*" a British voice said. Bailey recognized the voice of the TAO she'd spoken with before. She reached over and took the microphone from her own TAO before settling into her command chair. The admiral slid into one of the consoles forward of her.

"This is *Ramage,*" Bailey answered. "What is your status?"

"Not very good, I'm afraid. Bugger nailed us in the ass. Aft of the main engineering spaces, but we've got a small fire and flooding. The shaft's still turning, but we suspect it won't be for much longer. Should be able to stay afloat, though, unless we take another hit. We may need a tow back to port."

"Understood. Our helo is standing by. Do you require assistance at this time?"

"I think that—ah—" the voice choked off suddenly.

"*Victory? Victory,* this is *Ramage!*" Bailey shouted. "Damn it, answer me!" She turned to her TAO. "Call comms. Find out what the hell happened and get them back on the circuit!"

"Combat, radio. We were monitoring the circuit, sir. The

problem's not on our end," the communications officer said.

"Maybe damage from the torpedo?" Collins said. "I suggest we maneuver closer in to provide assistance, ma'am."

"No!" The word burst out of her mouth before she even thought about it. "No," she repeated. "Not until we know what caused the comm outage."

"But ma'am—"

"What part of 'no' don't you understand?"

Collins stiffened. "Understood, Captain. Shall we maintain present distance from the *Victory*?"

"Yes—no, move us out to ten thousand yards," she said. She rubbed her hands across her face. "Set MOPP Level 1."

"MOPP—aye, aye, Captain." Collins reached for the 1MC, concern and fear evident in her eyes.

Within moments, sailors were slamming gas masks down onto the tops of their heads, tightening the first straps. Combat echoed with the sounds of hatches slamming shut as the ship buttoned down. All connections with the outside air were shut, and the emergency washdown system was placed in immediate standby. Bailey's ears popped as the positive pressure was applied to the inside of the ship sufficient to keep any agent from leaking in from the outside.

A sailor handed Bailey her own MOPP combat gear and gave the admiral a spare set kept behind the plot for visitors. Bailey took out the mask and donned it, leaving it shoved onto the back of her head. The admiral took his without comment. His patrician face was gray and drawn.

This shit over who's in charge—the NATO commander or Sixth Fleet—doesn't make a damned bit of sense when someone's shooting at you. Bailey stared at the large-screen display in front of her. Sonar had entered a probable position for the attacking submarine, along with the position of the Swiftsure boat following it. She did a quick estimate: The submarine had been closer to *Ramage* than to *Victory* for most of its track. Looking at the relative positions between the units, it was clear that the submarine had made a point to circle around *Ramage* and attack *Victory,* firing the torpedo only when *Ramage* was well away from the danger bearings.

She jammed the flash-gear gloves down over her fingers, ramming them into the delicate webbing between. If *Victory* had indeed taken a hit from a Tabun-impregnated torpedo, the chain of command was the least of her worries.

"Does sonar still hold that submarine?" she snapped at the TAO.

"Yes, ma'am. Bearing, two hundred, range, fifteen thousand yards."

"Range, twenty thousand yards," Digger's calm voice said over the bitch box. "Down doppler." Bailey nodded. The submarine had turned away from them.

"You can't let her leave," Richardson said. The admiral stood and moved to stand in front of him, blocking her view of the screen. "I understand what your orders are, Captain, but you have just witnessed an act of war. There was no provocation, no *reason* for that submarine to fire on my ship. *Remember* what she was carrying." The admiral's face looked pinched. "*My God*—those men . . ." His voice broke off suddenly. Ten thousand yards away, British sailors lay dying, suffocating on a gas that should have been eliminated fifty years ago.

"The Swiftsure—she's right on her, Admiral." Her voice felt shaky, as though something had broken loose in her throat. "If we get in there, we'll just confuse the tactical picture for her. We can't—"

"You won't." Something that looked very much like disgust twisted at the corner of the senior officer's mouth.

"This isn't our fight," Bailey said finally. "TAO, get us out of here. I want twenty miles between us and any submarine."

"I'll require the use of your tactical circuits, madam. My helo will be here shortly to return me to a British *fighting* ship." The admiral turned away from her.

Bailey motioned to the TAO to assist the admiral. Then she turned away and walked back to sonar to avoid looking in her crew's eyes.

U-504

Merker wheeled around to stare at Sonar. The unmistakable
whine of a torpedo had cut through the control room like
a nightmare. "Where did it come from?"

The sonarman was pale and shaken. "I don't know. It
wasn't us."

"I *know* it wasn't us!" Merker took a deep breath and
deliberately lowered his voice. "Give me a bearing. A classification. Come on, now, it wasn't aimed at us. And it's
gone now."

"I—I—the bearing was one-seven-zero true. But it
couldn't be. *Kapitan,* that was a *German* torpedo—one of
ours. But the wolf pack . . ." The sonarman stopped, struggling to make sense.

"I think the answer is obvious," Kraeken said. "The
Americans—or the British, it doesn't make any difference
which—have either developed an operational deception capability with their noisemakers, or modified their own design to mimic ours. It couldn't be German—not according
to the war plans. Therefore, it must be theirs." The XO
nodded, clearly satisfied with his explanation. "Which
brings me to the next point. By launching this—device,
torpedo, whatever—they've committed a hostile act. Under
every convention of international law, we're allowed to re-
taliate."

"No." Merker started to point out the weaknesses in
Kraeken's explanation, then realized the man was too en-
thralled with his own analysis to listen. The fact that his
conclusion supported his incessant desire to attack, attack,
attack made debating the point a waste of time. "We know
it wasn't ours. There's no minefield planned for that area,
and we're under orders not to commence overt hostilities
yet."

"Then the General Staff changed the plan." Kraeken
was calm, unruffled, and convinced. "We may get word of
it during our next communications break." He pointed toward sonar. "In the meantime, we have an excellent target

angle on the American destroyer. I suggest we not waste the opportunity.''

Merker drew in a deep breath. ''If it is all the same to you, I prefer to wait for those orders.'' *And if it isn't, then too bad. I'm still in command here.*

17

7 MARCH 2002:
THE ENGLISH CHANNEL

USS RAMAGE

"An explanation, Captain. Now." Admiral Richardson was colder than Bailey had ever seen him before. "You held contact on the submarine that killed *Victory,* yet chose to do nothing. Four hundred and twenty men died. I believe I'm entitled to understand your reasoning."

"What would you have had me do? Take a shot at the submarine *before* it fired on *Victory*? On what grounds? Tell me just exactly what hostile intention or hostile act I observed that would have justified that? All we had was a weak contact that might or might not have been a submarine."

"Still, you could have—"

"When *were* you going to tell me about the Swiftsure, by the way? Would you have let me take an ASROC shot into the area without knowing exactly where she was?"

The admiral stiffened. "The Swiftsure is none of your concern."

"Cut the horseshit, Admiral. Until you start coming clean with me about the location of your forces, I'm not inclined to attack a piece of sea fuzz that may or may not have been a German submarine." She ran out of steam suddenly, appalled at her own tone of voice. "Besides, I doubt I could have prevented the attack. The contacts were at the edge of our detection envelopes."

"I am not referring to preventing the incident, Captain.

Victory herself was operating under the same restraints. However, your conduct afterward . . ." The admiral's voice broke off. "Were you afraid, Miss Bailey?" he asked quietly. "You went to *Battleaxe*'s assistance, even after I briefed you on the Tabun possibilities. But perhaps I misjudged what effect the information I gave you would have after you'd had a chance to consider it more thoroughly. I had thought the knowledge that Germany was capable of chemical attacks would have stiffened *your* backbone, if not that of your leaders."

"Are you accusing me of cowardice?"

"If you were British, I would have you shot."

"Get in line."

The admiral's expression changed slightly. It was no less frigid, but Bailey felt the arctic winds shift direction. "I see. It's like that, is it?"

"I don't know what the hell you're talking about," Bailey said sullenly.

"I think you do. You've gotten some very specific sailing directions from your superiors, haven't you? Ones that involved a considerable amount of arse-chewing sufficient to override your professional instincts. And that might involve your civilian career."

"I call it following orders. My civilian career's got nothing to do with what I do while I'm on active duty."

"Really? How odd. I suppose the U.S. Navy makes a practice of turning command of a destroyer over to an inexperienced officer?"

"These aren't normal times. You know what we're up against."

"Oh, I do, I do. And perhaps you're a better choice for the job than they know. Because the Jerusha Bailey I first met out here would not have let that submarine leave unmolested. Not with four hundred and twenty sailors dying particularly ugly deaths within shouting range."

"That was before I was in command. I'm going to remember that every day of my life, but I wouldn't change the decision now. Not under the circumstances," she said quietly. "If I could have done anything—"

"You couldn't then. You can now."

"*How?* They've tied my hands."

"Nonsense. Peacetime ROE permits a wide range of options that may not have occurred to you. Had I known of this, I would have made the necessary arrangement earlier."

Bailey shook her head. "*Ramage* is under your NATO command, Admiral, but we're here as exercise participants. Nothing more."

"Dammit all, woman, I'm not trying to give you orders. Do you think that I don't understand your position? With another officer in command, I would have simply terminated your participation and sent you home. But with you— well, you might consider that I'm doing you a favor."

"How so?"

The admiral regarded her somberly. "Do you really want to live with the memories you have now? It might not bother some—and if I've misjudged you entirely, you may be able to live with it yourself. On the other hand, there are ways that you can be of assistance to us now without violating your orders. Shall I show you how?"

"I was following orders, Admiral."

"Fifty years ago, a number of German officers offered that same rationale for their actions. At Nuremberg. Now describe for me the constraints under which you are required to operate."

Two hours later, Admiral Richardson's wrath was firmly focused on Sixth Fleet. To the north, HMS *Victory* drifted silent and unattended in the sea. After conferring with his superiors, Richardson reported that a specially equipped salvage crew had been dispatched in an oceangoing tug to take her under tow. Whether the contaminated ship would be taken into port or sunk in open ocean, and exactly when Britain should declare war, were the subjects of agonizing discussion ashore.

"Look where the incidents have occurred." The British officer used a red pencil to circle an area of ocean on the chart. "The North Sea, historically the location of some of the bloodiest battles in history. It's not a large body of water, not in open-ocean terms. Norway to the north, Germany and Denmark to the east, and Britain to the west and southwest. The northern line of demarcation is only three hundred and thirty miles, running from the southern tip of Norway to the northern tip of Britain. From the south, they'd have to sail up through the English Channel. But the pattern should suggest something to you.'' He laid his pencil down and stared at her, clearly waiting for an answer.

Bailey ran her finger over the chart, touching each of the red circles. ''A lot of water, sir. But if I wanted to isolate the North Sea, I'd lay minefields here.'' She pointed to the narrowest part of the English Channel. ''And from the tip of Britain to the tip of Norway.''

''And mine our harbors so we couldn't sortie. That would explain *Audacious,* wouldn't it? But it can work in our favor as well.''

''Because if we're trapped in here, we know where they're going to be. Coming at us, not waiting for us in open ocean.'' She looked up at him. ''Hell of a playpen.''

''But less difficult than having to hunt these bastards down in the open Atlantic. We kill them now, here, in the North Sea.''

''How are we going to kill submarines we can't even detect?''

''There's really only one way I can think of. These boats are detectable at two times—when they surface and when they are forced to transit at higher speeds. And you must remember, it appears to be key to the German plan that they be in place undetected, as a deterrent to any action we might contemplate on the Continent. Think of it, if you will, as a rodeo. Forty ships, lined up abreast, sweeping down from the north with all active sonars pinging. They'll move, I promise you.''

Bailey mentally sketched in the formation. ''Two hundred miles, forty ships. Do the math. If this works, we sweep them all south into the English Channel. Nasty water for detecting submarines. You'll have to close it to commercial traffic as well, which is going to be a major task.''

''Just as nasty to hide in for a submarine,'' the admiral pointed out. ''Commercial vessels will simply have to accept the closure. If we don't do a clean sweep, they'll suffer more in the long run. Many of them *do* remember the last world war, and their owners are not eager to repeat those losses. There will be some, I suppose, who insist on steaming into the channel, just as there were ships in the Persian Gulf during your Desert Storm affair. Can't be helped.''

''If they're willing to play sacrificial lamb, so be it. So what happens if we manage to herd them south? Who's covering that end of the channel?''

''Some more of your blokes. Our Nimrods will be the attacking platforms. When it comes to that. They don't even have to control the North Sea themselves,'' the admiral pointed out. ''Merely deny it to *us*. If word leaks out about *Victory* and the Tabun, there isn't a merchant master around who will risk the passage.'' He sighed. ''While the Admiralty keeps the lid on that one, Britain will not declare war. That buys us a little time, perhaps a little surprise advantage.''

Bailey stared down at the chart. There'd been no rebuke in the admiral's tone. There didn't have to be.

She shut her eyes for a moment, trying to clear her head. A mistake—the movie started again behind her closed lids. The torpedo moving through the water, silent, trailing streamers of deadly bubbling Tabun behind it in fluorescent orange and puce, penetrating *Victory*'s hull. The putrid cloud filling the engineering spaces, sailors dying clutching at machinery, dead before the rising water from the breach in the hull could reach them. Their faces—her mind drew tortured grimaces on the faces that gradually disappeared under the frigid seawater pouring into the spaces, their hair whipped in front of their faces by the torrent.

Then the gas drifting up to the top of the compartment, forced into the rest of the ship by the rising water and the ventilation systems, seeping into every compartment and slipping fetid tendrils down the mouths of every sailor, dropping them wherever they—

''Stop it.'' She felt someone shake her, and she opened her eyes. The admiral's hand was on her shoulder. She squinted, trying to see through the unexpected wetness in her eyes.

''I'm sorry. I—''

"You didn't do anything for them then. You can now. Madam, this will not be easy, but those dead men deserve your best efforts right now. Wallow in your self-pity and thousands more will join them."

Bailey nodded, not trusting her voice.

"Now." The admiral studied her for a few moments and then seemed to arrive at a decision. "I've taken chances with you before, Bailey. Shall I take another? Or is it better if I shield you from some of the nastier elements of our profession?"

That hurt. "I . . ." Bailey paused and cleared her throat. She took a sip of coffee and a deep breath. "Tell me everything I need to know, Admiral."

"Very well." The older man grimaced. "I'm uncertain how you will regard this little tidbit of information. You should know, however, that your government has not been entirely honest with you."

"Something more sensitive?" Bailey laughed harshly. "Don't see how that's possible, with all due respect."

"Another of the advantages of rank, madam. More sensitive information that will get both of us sent to jail for many years. We will be receiving some additional assistance from the Americans on the southern end."

Bailey smacked her hand down on the tablecloth. "If they're going to leave me in command, they can damned well tell me what's going on."

"Not under my cognizance, Captain. You might find out more of how this game is played when you put on your first star. Two American submarines will cover the English Channel to the south of that."

Bailey stared at him. "We're sending forces over here already? After they give me this big song-and-dance about staying out of it? If I'd known that, I might—"

"Irrelevant now. If I thought you'd needed to know, I would have told you sooner." The admiral rubbed his eyes with his knuckles for a second, looking oddly childlike. "I didn't think it would be so soon. One never does. No matter. The issue now is how it complicates our tactical picture. While I must appreciate the generosity of the assistance, it does raise some questions about our tactics."

"First problem: How do we avoid a blue-on-blue engagement?"

"Not impossible. Your submariners are quite definitive about which areas of the ocean they own and which ones will belong to the surface ships. No ship will go south of their position except *Ramage*."

"Which submarines?" Bailey asked.

"Unfortunately, I don't know the names. I do know that they've been taken off strategic patrols to join us here."

"Strategic—you mean these two boats are *boomers*? Ballistic-missile subs, not fast-attack?"

"Exactly. While it may not appear so, someone in Washington is quite concerned about this little scenario unfolding over here. Enough so that they've taken two submarines off nuclear deterrence patrol and assigned them to this area of the world."

"But a boomer—"

"Actually, when you consider her strong points, she's the natural choice. Quieter than your fast-attack boats, armed with torpedoes, and with a top-notch passive acoustics suite. If anyone can find those Germans boats, it will be your missile submarines."

"What about your Swiftsure boats and your *own* diesels?"

"The diesels are of limited use due to their battery limitations. They'll have to come up to snort too often. The Swiftsures will participate, of course, as will a few of our missile boats." The admiral's face looked grim. "They lost the other boat. The bastard that hit *Victory*. I wouldn't have thought it possible, but they did. At any rate, the arrangements are being worked out as we speak for water space management. This *will* work, I assure you."

"And if it doesn't?"

The admiral's face took on a hard sheen. "That option is not acceptable. Another very bloody conflict on land will touch every nation in the world. If politics prevent our leaders from confronting this threat openly, then we must do what we can."

"Regardless of orders."

"Not disobeying them, but working within what they

have not thought to forbid. You understand.''

Bailey nodded. ''I suggest we proceed with your plan, Admiral. Can we get all ships to send a representative over here tomorrow morning? We'll want to hold some sort of planning conference, make sure we're all on the same wavelength. Then—well, we'll see what happens. Admiral, you mentioned the United States becoming involved in two ways. Did you mean the two boomers?''

''No. One other bit of operational deception. You recall, as the Germans undoubtedly do, that America's entry into the last two wars made a critical difference in the outcome. The attack on *Weeks* will undoubtedly draw America into this conflict eventually, even if the attacks on British forces is insufficient to invoke their wrath. The Germans may attempt to avoid additional provocation. They would very much like for your forces to stay in Korea long enough for Germany to solidify her hold on the Continent. I've suggested certain measures that may make it extremely difficult for them to tell the difference between our ships and yours. Trying to avoid involvement with an American ship may be just the ticket to spooking them into running.''

''How?''

''You'll see soon enough. If you are so inclined, I suggest you add the following request to your nightly petitions to the Almighty.''

''Pray for victory?'' The unintended double entendre made her wince.

''For the ship, yes. And that both you and I are completely wrong about what has happened.''

U-504

Merker flipped the periscope to higher power and studied the V shape on the horizon. The American ship.

It struck him as ironic. Four months ago, in foreign waters, an American ship was the only acceptable target. Now, when he wanted anything *but* an American, he seemed to run into the bastards every time he surfaced. And an oddball at that, a captain who did the unexpected.

He watched a small speck separate from the blip barely

visible on the horizon and nodded. A helicopter. Routine
operations, or had they gotten lucky and detected the periscope just barely peeking above the waves? He touched his
talisman schedule and decided it didn't matter. His only
option—for now—was to evade.

"Down periscope," he ordered. "Make your depth one
hundred meters, come left to course two-three-zero."

"Sir, the ship bears—"

"I know where she is. She's just launched a helicopter,
and I intend to conduct evasive maneuvering. Another
time." He saw the puzzlement on the conning officer's
face, coupled with fear at the presence of an ASW helicopter and no small trace of relief that his captain was
breaking off the attack.

"If you hear the transducer hit the water, create a
knuckle and launch the decoys. This depth will work to our
advantage." He paused and consulted his chart. "We will
move south and wait for him to tire of this game, then
return to find a different target. You understand?"

The conning officer nodded and gave the necessary orders. Two minutes later, sonar reported that an active sonar
transducer had entered the water. The deck tilted sharply.
Merker reached for the overhead bar for balance.

18

8 MARCH 2002: THE ENGLISH CHANNEL

USS *RAMAGE*

It took a little longer than Collins had predicted, but eventually the last helicopter twisted away from *Ramage*. The officers from all the ships listened as Admiral Richardson briefed his plan. There were few questions from the haggard faces jammed into *Ramage*'s wardroom. They left as quickly as they'd arrived, doubled up in helos for quick trips back to their ships.

Moments after the ship secured from flight quarters, *Ramage* heeled sharply to port, came to flank speed, and headed for her position in the line of ships that now stretched from the tip of Britain to the end of Norway.

Twenty minutes later, the first pings probed the ocean depths.

U-504

"What the *hell* are they trying to do?" Merker shouted. He flinched from the sound of his own voice, the reflex to avoid noise too deeply ingrained to ignore. But the normal soft tones that sufficed on board the U-boat could not have been heard above the cacophony bombarding the thin hull separating the men from the ocean.

"At least ten ships, sir," sonar reported. "Maybe more."

Merker swore quietly, the habit of silence reasserting itself. The interior walls of the submarine, separated from the water by an outer hull and a layer of air, seemed to flex under the sheer volume of the sonar pings. He glanced up at the counterdetection panel. Indicator lights flickered madly as the signal generator tried to keep pace with the noise battering its sensors.

"Layer depth?" He pressed his hands to his temples as his head started to ache.

"One hundred twenty meters, sir," the conning officer reported.

"Get us below it—*now*. Sonar, refine bearings and classifications immediately."

"Aye, aye, sir," both the conning officer and the sonar supervisor replied.

The deck tilted forward as the submarine dove for the relative quiet of water beneath the layer. A few minutes later, the pressure from the sonar noise energy abated slightly. In the icy sea beneath the thermocline of the North Sea, pressure was the only factor affecting the speed of sound in the water. Much of the sonar energy bent away from the increase in velocity.

Not safe yet, but at least I can think. He watched the pressure gauge carefully. "Another twenty meters," he ordered.

The conning officer, he noted, had broken out in a light sweat. A few of the crew members looked ill. The noise from the sonar barrage still seemed to echo in the control room.

"Nasty stuff." Merker yawned, popping his ears in the process. "Works to our advantage, too."

The conning officer glanced over at him, then returned to examining the array of green lights across his board. Merker pointedly did not notice the flash of fear he'd seen in the man's face.

"With that many sonars operating in one area, of course, the odds of actually detecting a contact decrease dramatically. We've known that for fifty years. You understand why, I hope?" He finally looked at the conning officer directly and let the force of his gaze draw the man's attention to him.

"Herr Gilbert—give me one reason why," Merker ordered.

A trace of apprehension, then his face suddenly cleared. "More noise in the water—from whatever sources, *Kapitan*—increases the overall ambient noise in the sea. Discrete signals, such as those made by our machinery, are harder to detect."

"Entirely correct." Merker breathed a sigh of relief that the man had managed to regain his equilibrium. "Anyone else?"

"Interference," Ehrlich said suddenly. "When the transmitted frequencies of two different sonars are so close, the transducer may become confused between its own return and that of the other ship. False contacts, erroneous bearings—maybe even phase cancellation if the ships transmit at the right times."

Merker nodded his approval. "Another correct answer. There's one other answer, too, one of critical importance to us." He looked around the control room, wondering if they understood how he was manipulating them. First, the feigned calm. Now, realigning their view of their place in the world, changing their viewpoint from hunted prey to . . ."

"We know where they are," he said softly, his words now carrying over the faint beat of the multiple sonars. "There's only one absolute counter to an active sonar system."

He looked around the small compartment slowly, catching each man's eyes for the briefest second, instilling through that contact his own indomitable conviction that they were invulnerable—knowing it was a lie, but knowing even more that they must believe it to win.

"A torpedo," he said finally, and was rewarded with the beginnings of smiles on several faces. "It works every time."

USS RAMAGE

"*Jesus,*" Digger swore. "How the *hell* am I supposed to see *anything* in this soup?" His sonar screen was a mass of conflicting concentric circles and noise spokes. He toggled the bitch box on. "Combat, sonar—this ain't going to work, ma'am. I've got a hint of a contact off to the east, but I damned sure can't resolve it in this muck."

"Too much interference?" the tinny voice asked.

"That, and noise. We need to come up with a plan—the sooner, the better. All this is doing is blinding all of us while telling him where we are. Recommend we get everyone else to shut down long enough to let me figure out if I've got a contact. And I'd like to get the tail depth down below the layer. If his sonar tech's ears are hurting as much as mine, that's where he's at."

"Roger, go ahead. I'll talk to the admiral's staff."

"Could we turn north and get this possible contact on our beam?"

"Can do."

"Anything?" Digger asked Henning.

"Not yet. I wouldn't hold my breath, either. If he's on battery again—which is where I'd be, knowing so many ships were around—he's quiet. We want him to show up, we need to spook him into doing something noisy or going fast."

"And to do that, we have to find him." Digger sighed. "Lining up all these ships and killing fish sounds dandy on paper, but it just don't work. Let's rethink this before those bozos come up with another great plan for us."

"I liked my original idea best," Henning said mildly. "Helicopters shallow and tails deep."

"You got my vote, but we got overridden by the khakis. Maybe they'll rethink it now." Digger motioned to Carlisle, who was sitting on the back bench. "Jump in here and keep an eye out to the east," he said, swiveling the padded operator's seat away from the console and standing up. "I'll be on the bridge if you need me."

Henning watched the LPO leave sonar and slam the door behind him. "Want to lose some money?" he asked Carlisle.

"On what? The Chargers going to the Super Bowl again?"

"Nope. I've got a winning proposition for you. Five

bucks says we set flight quarters in the next fifteen minutes.''

''Fifteen minutes?'' Carlisle glanced up at the clock. ''I'll take your five, just because I happen to know that half the flight crew is sacked out right now. I'm saying it'll be more like twenty minutes.''

''You're on.''

Neither man had any doubt that the ship would soon launch its helo. Not with that expression on Digger's face. It was just a matter of when.

U-504

''You see?'' Merker asked. Sonar had just reported a sudden decrease in the number of surface ships dumping sound energy into the ocean. ''Already, they are starting to realize that their plan won't work. They'll go back to just two or three widely separated ships radiating, perhaps working with their helicopters. Now we have the advantage—we know how many of them there are and where they are.''

''*Kapitan*! One of the ships to the west has started a search turn. Range, twenty thousand meters; bearing, two-seven-zero.''

''Get the decoys ready,'' he ordered, studying the counterdetection console carefully. ''And reboot the counterdetection console—it's in a loop. The noise probably overloaded it.'' He kept his face carefully and blandly confident. ''Make your course two-seven-zero. It's time we taught the British a lesson in sonar etiquette.''

USS RAMAGE

''Five bucks,'' Henning said. ''Pay up.''

''And half goes into the sonar party fund,'' Digger said. ''You bet in my spaces, you ante up. Hell, I was damned near ready to pay *them* to launch that fucker.''

''So what's the plan?'' Carlisle asked as he dug four crumpled bills and some change out of his pocket.

''Just what I said. We stay below the layer with the tail and use the helo as our active pinger. There's enough difference between his freqs and the ships to knock out the mutual interference problem. Ops is talking to the other ships working out the plan, but since we've got the best tail, we'll probably be out in front.''

Digger looked over at Henning. A sudden change in the rhythm of the hard-copy printer caught his attention. ''Got something?''

''I don't know yet,'' the technician muttered. ''Be quiet, let me think.'' He shifted the center frequency of the display and started programming in different display characteristics. ''It's not a submarine, but—I don't know. Something funny just happened with the background noise and the multipathing interference patterns. I don't have any *mechanical* sources coming of it, just a change in the back-ground noise.''

''Got a bearing?''

''Not exactly. Like I said, it's not a noise source. Just that fuzz again off to the east. Southeast, east, somewhere in there.''

''Gut feeling and best guess,'' Digger demanded, resting his forefinger on the bitch box toggle.

''No classification—just a noise source anomaly. Best guess''—Henning shrugged helplessly—''I don't have one. Gut feeling, though, is that something's moving through the water and tinkering with the noise from the other ships reaching us. It looks like a black hole moving through the water, sucking up sound waves.''

''Not a bad description of what we've seen from the Germans.'' Digger relayed the information to the TAO, sounding a good deal more confident than Henning had. ''We got to start searching somewhere, and that part of the ocean is as good as any. Better, if you've got something a little hinky.''

Henning frowned. ''Hinky is hardly weapons-release criteria.''

''Not for us. Maybe for her, wherever she is. Let's go find out before she decides it's good enough for her.''

U-504

"Range, five thousand meters; bearing, two-eight-zero. Targeting solution," sonar reported. "*Kapitan*, the ship is still in active sonar mode."

"Classification?" Merker prompted.

The technician frowned. "A five-bladed warship—that's all I can tell."

American or British? Merker shifted uneasily and touched the message in his breast pocket again. Did it really matter? According to the timetable, this part of the North Sea would be declared a German bastion sometime in the next two days. One American warship and thirty-nine from British and European countries. The odds were with him.

Still, he had his orders.

"Launch three noisemakers on ten-minute delay, come right to course three-two-zero, and close her," he ordered. "Let's give her a taste of her own medicine. The distraction will allow us to get a closer look."

USS RAMAGE

"*Up* doppler! TAO, the contact has increased speed to twenty knots and is closing us!" Digger shouted. "He's— *oh, JESUS*!" Digger ripped the earphones off his head and let out a sharp yelp of pain. Simultaneously, Henning reached up to turn down the volume on the speaker.

All around them, the hull of the ship throbbed with acoustic energy. "Noisemakers," Digger said. "Loudest bastards I've *ever* heard! Combat, sonar—ma'am"—he glanced over at Henning's display and swore—"broad-spectrum noisemakers. We're blanked out completely. I can't even hear a torpedo in this mess! Recommend we snapshot a torpedo down the bearing *now*!"

"Cool it, Digger," Collins's voice said over tactical. "The helo's on top of him. No torpedo—yet. But this constitutes a hostile act, blanking out our sensors."

"What the hell *is* that?" Henning breathed.

Digger grimaced and rubbed at his ears.

"You okay?" Henning asked belatedly.

"Not yet. You hear what it's like just radiating in
through the hull. Try piping that straight into your ears."
Digger shook his head and winced again. "It hurts, man.
But not as bad as that bastard's going to be hurting in a
minute." He turned back to his weapons console.

U-504

"Any indication of what they're doing?" Merker shouted.
He'd walked back into sonar and had to raise his voice to
be heard over the noise radiating in through the thin skin
of the submarine.

The senior technician shook his head. "We're blind until
the decoys go dead."

"Not blind. Deaf, perhaps." Merker walked forward to
the control room again. "Periscope depth," he ordered. A
risky maneuver, perhaps, if the helicopter were still overhead.

The U-boat rose slowly from her safe depth. The conning
officer was particularly concerned that the ship not broach
and provide an excellent target.

"Up periscope," Merker ordered. He followed it up from
the deck and spun around, searching for the ship. The V
silhouette of a surface ship dead on to them slowly length-
ened into a rectangle as the ship turned toward the noisemakers.

The American. He slammed the handles up in frustration.
What were the odds? Never mind.

He ordered the periscope down and turned to the navigator's table to plan his next course. According to his orders, his attack position in the wolf pack was fifty miles to
the north. The decoys would last for another thirty minutes,
giving him plenty of time to move past the American ship.
He did a quick calculation and gave the new figures to the
conning officer, with orders to take the boat back down to
one hundred meters. He then relinquished the deck to his
OOD and stepped back to watch.

USS RAMAGE

"TAO, I can't see a thing in this mess," Digger shouted into the bitch box. "She was headed straight in on us when I lost her!"

Fifteen yards away, pacing back and forth in front of her elevated chair, Bailey swore quietly. Time, there was no time. This might not be America's war yet, but blanking out *Ramage*'s sensors damn well qualified as a hostile act, and the doctrine of self-defense clearly gave her the right to fire. No admiral, including Sixth Fleet, could make her take the first hit.

But how close was the submarine? At last contact, it'd been heading straight toward them. The range—was *Ramage* clear of the area?

"*Snoopy 1* has contact," the ASAC announced. "Active only—range to submarine, eight thousand yards. The pilot is requesting weapons free."

Eight thousand yards. Probably far enough away from datum. And each second I wait . . . She reached for the mike wired to the circuit with their helo.

"*Snoopy 1*, take with torpedoes," she said firmly over the net.

U-504

Merker stood by the periscope and feigned confidence. Around him, the crew had changed from a hunted pack into a feral crew focused on the next kill. Sonar pings from ships in the area were still audible, though as soft chimes against the hull rather than the killing blows that beat against the ship at shallower depths.

Do they know where we are?

Probably not, he decided. If the ships had detected the submarine, they would have shifted transmission modes to a higher frequency radiating down the bearing wedge instead of maintaining the omnidirectional transmissions of a general search pattern. Still, the American captain couldn't be discounted too quickly. Since the counterdetection gear had been down for almost five minutes, it was possible that—

The high, sharp ping cut through his equanimity like a blade. "Helicopter. SH-60—American," sonar reported unnecessarily, his voice three notes higher than normal. Merker felt the unnatural calm seep away like sea haze burned off by the morning sun.

A spread of surface ships blasting away in the water posed far less threat to a U-boat than a single ASW helicopter with a dipping sonar. And two helicopters working together— "How many?" he snapped.

"Just one." Merker heard the unspoken phrase that followed that: *for now*. One helicopter with a target would soon be joined by a flurry of others, dancing around the submarine, dropping buoys and lowering sonar domes along every avenue of escape. It was essential that they lose this one aircraft—*now*.

"Does he have us?"

"I think so. He couldn't miss us, as strong as that pulse was."

"All ahead flank." He let the speed build for a few moments until sonar warned him that the screws were starting to cavitate. "Hard left rudder." As soon as the submarine turned through ninety degrees, he'd shed the forward speed, launch decoys, and try to slip away quietly while the helicopter gnawed at the mass of air bubbles and false targets churning the ocean in their wake.

"Torpedo in the water!"

Merker swore. "Decoys—*now*! Make your depth two hundred meters!"

The next thirty seconds stretched into thirty years as he listened for the torpedo. Closer than the one they'd evaded so easily in the Yellow Sea, much closer. His ears felt strained and raw as he waited for the telltale pings from the torpedo seeker head—high-frequency, searching for the target. If it acquired the U-boat, they'd all have ten seconds or so to listen to it increase its sonar pulse rate to a frantic speed as its tiny electronic mind decided it had found its purpose in life. At that point, luck rather than tactics would determine whether they survived.

Merker put the submarine through another series of hard turns and speed changes, generating more illusory contacts to confuse the fragile electronics in the torpedo's nose. Lights flickered frantically across the counterdetection console as the electronics struggled to keep up with the barrage of sonar pulses. Finally, he played his last card.

"Make your depth three hundred meters. All stop," he ordered.

Pale-faced and shaken, the conning officer relayed the instructions without question. There really was nothing to discuss. Three hundred meters was approaching a dangerous depth for the submarine, still above her rated crush depth but deeper than they routinely liked to operate. To drift down to that depth on momentum alone and the bow planes, the propeller windmilling silently behind them at a few revolutions per minute, was to sacrifice their maneuverability. If *U-504* had to make a drastic maneuver to avoid the weapon, the boat would first have to overcome inertia. Depth had one saving grace: The submarine could go faster without cavitating.

The hull complained as the U-boat drifted deeper, slowing now with her propellers stilled. Pressure did odd things to metal, flexing and stressing it in ways that the boat's designers could never have fully anticipated. If the helicopter was operating in passive mode or had dropped passive sonobuoys, the sounds would confirm that they were virtually on top of the submarine.

No one spoke. Even the quiet whispers normally allowed during evasive maneuvering seemed too risky. He could feel the crew's confidence seep away, flushed out by the torpedo in the water.

Finally, sonar whispered, "It has acquired a noisemaker, *Kapitan*. Homing, homing—" The noise of the explosion slammed against the hull, needing no explanation. Seconds later, he heard the hard ping of the sonar dome rattle against the hull.

"They're farther away," sonar reported, his voice now steady and firm. "We've lost them."

For now.

"Give me a course back to intercept her," he ordered

quietly. "Four knots." What he'd told them before had been true—the surest way to deal with helicopters was to destroy their airfields, the surface ships they launched from. "Fucking British bastards."

"Sir—that wasn't a British torpedo. At least I don't think so," sonar said uncertainly.

"Why didn't you tell me that?"

"There wasn't time—sir, it happened so fast right after the helicopter started—"

"American?"

"I think so." Sonar quailed under Merker's glare, then said firmly, "Yes. American."

"And the helicopter? American as well?"

The man nodded.

Suddenly the attack looked like a less reasonable option. If the American destroyer were attacking, then normally he would have had every right to stalk it. But his orders were explicit: Avoid involving the American ship in the North Sea operation. He touched the timetable message for reassurance. But if the Americans were already attacking German submarines, something must have happened. Did Braudel really intend for him to avoid contact even if the Americans attacked? Did those orders still apply now that the unknown U-boat had attacked another American ship?

Merker grimaced. By failing to follow orders and torpedoing the small frigate, his colleague had botched the plan royally. Keeping the Americans out of it—giving them any excuse to avoid aiding the British—was a key part of controlling the sea approaches to Germany.

Another thought occurred to him: What if sonar was wrong? His sonarman had sounded uncertain until Merker pressed him. He glanced at the man who was staring fixedly at his screen. The technician was one of the few sailors retained by Germany from the East German Navy. Merker had detected an air of obsequiousness in his manner that was doubtless the result of years of Soviet training.

Or what if the *Americans* had been the ones to make a mistake? He couldn't discount the possibility, knowing the extensive independence and situational authority that American naval tradition reposed in its commanding officers. If the man hunting him above had exceeded the scope of his authority, had fired a torpedo—or had it fired from his helicopter, same thing—then someone would shortly be putting a stop to it. For America to enter this conflict when she was supposed to be preoccupied with matters in Korea would be military suicide.

Can I hunt the American ship now? Not now—not with a helo on top of me. Escape first, then consider it when you have time to think about something besides staying alive. I need to know whether they've joined the British before I do anything. He sighed, and was ashamed to find that the decision brought him a weak-kneed sense of relief.

"Break off the attack," he ordered. "Navigator, a course to safe water, please. Get us as far as we can get from them in the next two hours, assuming they continue their present course and speed, then come to communications depth."

"*Kapitan,*" Kraeken said insistently. His usual tone of arrogance had changed to almost pleading. "Surely you must attack now. They've *fired* on us."

Merker just shook his head. Minutes later, *U-504* was headed away from the still-pinging ships and toward relative safety. Once he was sure he was out of range of the active sonars, he'd be able to find out whether his orders had changed. Meanwhile, the crew would have a couple of hours of relative safety, stand down from battle stations, eat perhaps, stomachs finally able to accept food once they knew they were not seconds away from ugly deaths.

He was tired, bone-tired. He needed to eat, try to take a catnap, regroup internally, and prepare himself for the next attack. For a few minutes, the situation would be stable enough to permit him those luxuries.

Without warning, the phrase that kept popping into his mind repeated itself as an unwanted addition to the thought.

For now.

USS RAMAGE

"Evaluate it as a miss," the pilot said over the net. "Good solid contact, but that bastard's got some damned impressive noisemakers. They ran an excellent capture on the tor-

pedo.'' He sounded resigned and grim. ''If they've all got
that gear—''

"We'll see if we can give him a little less warning next
time," Bailey said crisply. ''An ASROC will be on top of
him before he can start that crap.''

"We've lost her now.''

She sighed. ''Come on in and rearm. We'll wait for the
next shot.''

19

---

8 MARCH 2002:
THE ENGLISH CHANNEL

U-504

Once they were safely clear of the helo, Merker retreated to his stateroom. Fatigue was building up, clogging his brain and draining away his ability to think clearly. He stopped by the galley first and picked up a cold sandwich, intending to eat in privacy. Food, a short nap—basic maintenance for the crew was as critical as for the machinery, and that included the captain.

He'd just stretched out on his narrow rack, felt the muscles and bones in his back and neck start to relax, when a gentle tap sounded at his door. He answered, sluggishly surprised that his voice sounded as though he'd just awakened.

"It's the antenna, *Kapitan*." The radioman tried to meet Merker's eyes, then dropped his gaze down to the floor. "The explosion, perhaps. It was so close . . ."

"You're certain?" Merker asked the question even though he knew it was futile. Of course the man was certain—he would not have come to him without exhausting every possibility.

"Yes, *Kapitan*. The coupling, probably."

Of course. It would be the one thing that cannot be repaired or replaced while the submarine was safely submerged. If they surfaced—he refused to follow that train of thought. Suicide if they were detected. At the very least, he'd be forced to surrender, evacuate his crewmen onto lifeboats, and allow a foreign prize crew on board. Not only defeat but disgrace as well.

Was that his fate? Had everything in the past eight months—no, his entire life—been driving him to this one moment when he would face this decision? Merker felt a crushing sense of inevitability, as though nothing he could have done or said at any point in his life would have avoided this one moment when he would be alone in the sea with the destroyer.

With the antenna out, he'd lost satellite communications with the General Command. There was no way to determine whether he could attack the American ship. It came down to—as it always did—one captain on scene making a decision. Merker reluctantly abandoned the nap he'd barely begun and returned to the control room.

"The American ship . . ." the navigator began uncertainly.

Merker shifted his attention back to the men around him. If he was uncertain, how much more so they must be. The battles with Kraeken, the mounting equipment casualties— all they had left to sustain them was the inherent belief of every submariner that they were invincible. Of all the things he could take from them, that would be the most tragic.

"The destroyer committed an act of war when her helo fired on us," he said firmly. "What she started, we'll finish. A few days earlier than we'd planned, perhaps, but it will be just that much sooner that we're back in port." He avoided looking at the XO. "The rest of the wolf pack will be here tomorrow—and we'll be eighty tons ahead of them in kill tonnage."

Ehrlich nodded and turned back to his chart. Merker stared at the sonar screen, watching the edges where the first traces of the American ship would eventually reappear. Unpredictable or not, the American captain had thrown down the gauntlet as clearly as if he'd signed a formal declaration of war.

It struck him as odd that his unpredictable adversary and he were about to do just what the statesmen in both their countries had tried to avoid: draw America back to Europe again.

• • •

Seven hours later, *U-504* quietly approached the line of ships arrayed across the horizon. With the counterdetection equipment working at peak performance, she was virtually undetectable. When sonar reported the first traces of active sonar pings, Merker brought the ship to port. The new course would take them back behind the line of ships, into their baffles, where the surface sonar would be less effective. At the very edge of the ships' detection envelopes he crept up toward the surface, stopping short of broaching.

A dangerous move, but necessary.

After sonar assured him that there was no traffic in the immediate area, he ordered the U-boat to periscope depth. He took the ship up cautiously, pausing every one hundred feet to listen, remembering the silent, undetectable American destroyer. Five minutes later, he took a quick scan of the horizon and started swearing.

"Down scope. Play it back," he ordered. Not that it would help. He was absolutely certain of what he'd just seen through the scope. Still, he watched the picture on the monitor shudder for a moment; then the quick scan replayed at a slower speed. He heard the conning officer take a sharp breath.

The hulls of the ships were barely visible through the sea fog and mist. The American destroyer was out in front, leading the pack of surface ships sweeping the ocean, more compelling proof that the Americans had actively joined the fight.

He felt a sense of relief, coupled with a feeling of anticipation. To take this rogue American on, the one that consistently did the unexpected—finally, he might find out what victory really felt like. Unlike Korea, this would be a fair fight between equally matched opponents.

USS RAMAGE

"Contact," Digger snapped. "Bearing, two-three-zero true; range, ten thousand yards. Active sonar only, TAO." He grease-penciled the lozenge-shaped blip on his screen, then glanced over at Henning. "Got anything?"

"Nothing. No surprise—a diesel on battery, we're not going to see much of anything."

"S'okay. Got him solid myself. Vector in one of the Brits for the kill. I'm handing him off to them now, now—*now*." He fed the target data into the combat section and dialed the air controller frequency into his right headphone to listen to the ASAC guide the helicopter to the contact. The British helos were serving as pouncer assets while Snoopy rearmed.

"Sonar, intell," a voice said on the circuit piped into his left ear. He toggled the transmit switch with his foot and answered.

"Message from SUBPAC. They're declaring a no-attack zone with the following coordinates." The intelligence specialist read off a series of latitudes and longitudes.

Digger looked up at the digital readout of his own ship's position. Not too far from—"Oh, shit," he said suddenly. "Intell, interrogative range and bearing to the box from *Ramage*?"

"I make it two-three-five true; range, three-nine-eight-five-zero yards."

Over the speaker, Digger could hear the *whop-whop* sound of a helicopter proceeding down the bearing *Ramage* was providing. His heart skipped, then resumed beating faster. The two positions were so close—was it possible? It couldn't be—*but if it were* . . . He shuddered.

"Carlisle," he said suddenly. "Get over here and take a look at this contact."

The MIUWU sonarman looked up from the acoustic publication he was studying. "Might be one of ours?" He moved quickly over to the passive console and looked over Henning's shoulder. "What's that?" He pointed at a narrow black line on the printout.

"Artifact," Henning said promptly. "Own ship—it's us. I've seen this source a couple of times in the past week." He shrugged. "Something grounded out in engineering. We'll track it down the next time we're on the acoustic range. It's got nothing to do with the active contact Digger's got."

"How certain are you?" Carlisle pressed.

Henning frowned. "What else could it—oh, shit."

"Talk to me," Digger demanded. "No games, unless you want to be the one responsible for a blue-on-blue engagement."

"I did two tours on boomers and that line looks damned familiar," Carlisle said decisively. "Get that helicopter off of it! *Now!*"

"You're certain? That boat's within weapons release range of us in about five mikes," Digger said. "Any chance there are two contacts in there, one good, one bad?"

Carlisle was pale. "Yes. This isn't our fight. Not with a friendly in the area." The dawning look of horror on his face convinced the senior *Ramage* sonarman.

"Plover one-zero-one, this is Ramage," Digger snapped. "Break off, break off. Friendly in area, friendly in area!"

"What?" A flurry of questions and objections flooded the circuit from the helicopter crew. "The hell you say!" The obscenity sounded almost charming in the clipped British accent.

"Get the fuck away from it, you fucking Brit," Digger screamed.

A pause. Then, "You needn't be so bleeding testy."

Digger saw his hands were shaking slightly. He curled his fingers around the arms of his chair and turned to Henning. "I just aborted an attack on a submarine. Tell me it's not about to kill us—just tell me."

A little color had returned to the man's face, but not much. "The electrical sources," he said quickly. "Down doppler on them, just as they reported the contact. It's not *Ramage*—it's someone else using the same sort of power sources. Oh, Jesus, I can't believe we almost—oh, *shit,* why don't they tell us where the hell they are?"

Digger sighed, still feeling shaky. "They're supposed to all be well south of here. Screening off the end of the pen. Not supposed to be *anywhere* around that we might shoot at them—God, one of these days I'm going to *kill* one of those bastards."

"Don't say that," Henning answered, looking just as stricken. "I think we almost did."

"She's hunting something," Carlisle said. "Look, two

slow turns in the past fifteen minutes.'' He pointed to the passive acoustic printout. ''Jesus, I can't believe we're holding her at this range.''

''Convergence zone detection. That happens—strange, long-range detections you'd never expect,'' Henning suggested.

Carlisle shook his head. ''She's not clearing her baffles. She did that a few minutes earlier—right here.'' He pointed to an earlier portion of the printout.

''Maybe she's doing it again—you know, trying to keep from establishing a predictable pattern.''

''Possible, I guess, but I don't think so. Look at *how* she turned. This wasn't to check her six, it was a search turn.''

''Why?'' Digger asked.

Carlisle studied the lines for a few moments, then dialed up additional display frequencies. He waited for the green waterfall of lines to build, then shook his head. ''I thought we might be able to see what'd caught her attention. A long shot, though. That submarine's acoustic gear is a hell of a lot more sensitive than our tail. I bet the sonarman on that boomer saw something that bothered him. Not enough to call a contact, but something he wanted to check out.''

''And if they find anything, we won't hear about it. That boomer's not going to come to communications depth just to make a contact report.''

''It's not like there's anything we could do about it. And as for hearing it—if she finds a German submarine, there's a damned good chance we'll hear something.'' Carlisle's face was grim. ''A torpedo makes a hell of a lot of noise. So does a sub breaking up.''

''She'll shoot?''

''I'd bet that's what her orders are. They don't pull those boats off nuclear deterrence patrol to play hide-and-seek. There's only one possible justification for bringing her down here, and that's to kill other submarines. A damned unlikely move, and one nobody's going to anticipate.''

''So unlikely that it'd be deniable,'' Digger said thoughtfully. ''You think?''

''Yep. As quiet as that Ohio-class boat is, I doubt there's anyone else that could detect her out here. No submarine, no proof unless someone who survives hears the torpedo in the water. For all the rest of the world would know, the German boat just had an accident or an engineering casualty.''

''*We'd* know.''

''Maybe. If we hear it.''

''Well.''

Bailey swore quietly but passionately. Of all the damned idiocy that she put up with from the submarine community, this was at the top of the list. Admiral Richardson had told her the boomer was in the area, but she'd assumed that it would respect the normal separation parameters that prevented mutual interference between friendly forces. To venture in so close to a battle group without a position report or any form of coordination exceeded all bounds of common sense. The sheer arrogance . . .

''They probably thought we couldn't detect her, Captain,'' Digger said, echoing her thoughts. His eyes were riveted on the sonar screen. The green blip they'd almost targeted was tracking away from them now.

''Fucking brilliant. What about active sonar? What about an ASROC? What about the chance of dragging our array across her hull? There were a million things that could have gone wrong.''

Digger nodded. ''It was too close this time. But at least we didn't take a shot at her.''

''We almost did. Or the Brits did—it wouldn't matter much *who* actually launched on her if we'd put one ballistic-missile boat at the bottom of the channel along with all her weapons,'' Bailey raged. ''It's not *your* fault,'' she added, finally noticing the still, shaken expression on the sonarmen's faces. ''Nothing we did. It's only because you paid attention that we even had a clue she was a friendly.''

''Carlisle did it, Captain,'' Digger said. ''What you said is right—on active sonar, all submarines look alike.''

''How far are we from them now?'' Bailey asked.

''Forty thousand yards and opening. Be better to get out of the area a little faster if we could, ma'am.''

Bailey studied the sonar contact and the fluorescent

screen-trace of previous detections trailing away behind it like the track a snail left behind it. Even taking into account *Ramage*'s own motion, the submarine was clearly maneuvering. "She's got something?"

"I'd say so. She's been circling for about ten minutes now. Sniffing out a trail."

"And we aren't seeing anything else in the area?"

Digger glanced at Carlisle, who shook his head. "Not on passive or active. If there's another submarine in the area, it's damned quiet and has the best antiechoic coating on its hull that I've ever seen. Look, sir, even our boomer isn't that good at hiding from active sonar. Funky layering in the water or some damned good counterdetection capabilities that soak up everything we hit her with. Whatever it is, we don't see what the boomer's hunting."

"The last thing we need is to be in the middle of a sub-on-sub attack approach," Bailey said. "Shooting blind, blue units in the area, and some invisible bastard submarine out there. All we could do would be to complicate the tactical picture for the boomer and get in the way of a stray torpedo."

A low mechanical rumble quickly crescendoed to a screaming whine. Carlisle bolted off of his stool, knocking it back against the onlookers.

"Torpedo," he snapped, although the pale faces clustered behind him had already given her the classification. "Sub-launched, one of ours. And there's the target!" He pointed to four lines that abruptly appeared on the sonar screen.

"TAO," she snapped, toggling down the bitch box transmit button, "get us the hell out of here."

The only sound in the van was the *scritch* of the sonar stylus across the paper, recording the innocuous black lines slowly building on the green screen above it. The lines wavered in frequency as both the submarine and the torpedo maneuvered. A noise spoke shot across the entire spectrum, briefly blanking every other sources, as the submarine fired a noisemaker. She saw a hard-up doppler followed by a down doppler, evidence that the new contact was maneuvering, attempting to create a knuckle of air bubbles in the sea. The American submarine signature faded from the display, its quiet noises masked by the fury of the battle between torpedo and target.

The torpedo scream abruptly ceased, followed immediately by a muffled thud and silence. She heard Carlisle gasp. Her eyes never left the screen. Five seconds later, a series of sharp noises lacerated the silence.

"Secondary explosions," Carlisle said in a hard monotone. "Cold water on hot engines, hull noises, and bubbles. She's breaking up."

"Who?"

Two faint lines reappeared on the sonar screen. Carlisle sighed. "Not the friendly. That's her." He pointed to the middle of the screen. "But whoever she was shooting at is dead."

U-504

"It was very faint, *Kapitan,* but I heard it clearly." The U-boat sonarman had lost all traces of his earlier uncertainty. "A sub-launched torpedo—an American one, by the frequency."

"How far away?" Merker pulled the worn paper diagram of the wolf-pack positions out of his breast pocket. The other U-boats should have been farther south, awaiting his signal to begin their deception operations.

"Ten thousand yards, maybe fifteen, to the south."

He traced out the lines dividing the attack zones. If one of the other boats had left her assigned area to make positive visual identification on a passing contact, it could have been that far north. He swore silently at the other *Kapitan.* The wolf-pack positions had been carefully planned to use *Northern Lights* as both a deception and a screen for German operations. "Did it hit?"

The sonarman shook his head. "I'm not certain. I thought I heard an explosion, but it was so far away. If there were breaking-up noises, I didn't hear them."

Merker digested the information. Sonar masking, the attack on *U-504* by the American helicopter, and now this.

How much more do you want? one part of his mind jeered.
Coward.

He reached a decision. "Very well." He turned to Ehrlich. "Give me a course to the nearest warship."

USS RAMAGE

"The boomer's turning south, Captain," Digger reported.
"Headed back into the submarine operating area at twenty
knots. If she continues on this course, she'll be in her designated water in two hours. The helo's already working a
new contact, and two Brit ships are about to put torpedoes
in the water."

"About time our sub got the hell out of the way. That
could have been *her* breaking up," Bailey said. "TAO,
let's take a quick look for survivors. I don't expect to find
any, but we'll look anyway. Can we get there without interfering with the other prosecutions?"

"Yes, Captain. We're twenty minutes away from datum,
and the Brits are working well to the south," the TAO said,
and then gave the bridge a course and speed to intercept
the location of the explosion.

Bailey leaned against the bulkhead and watched the sonar
technicians for a few moments. *I should be back in combat
proper,* she chided herself. Modern combat doctrine required the captain of a ship to orchestrate the complex sym-
phony of sensors and weapons from the nerve center of the
ship. Sonar was tied into all the shipboard and exterior
communications circuits, and she would be just as well informed from combat as she was standing in sonar.

There was something different about watching a battle
from sonar, though. Perhaps it was that their equipment
actually showed the sources coming from the target rather
than just the processed and enhanced bit of energy returning
from a radar pulse. The passive gear was particularly compelling, spelling out every frantic twist and turn of both the
hunter and the hunted.

All they knew was that the U.S. submarine had taken a
shot at something—a successful one, from the sounds of it.

Had the submarine captain decided on his own that the

rules of the game had changed? Or had he been ordered into play by higher authority? Just what had induced him to risk detection by conducting an attack on the other submarine? Surely Sixth Fleet would have told her if there had been a change in the rules of engagement.

Or maybe not. They hadn't even told her the boomer was in the area, so why should they brief her on its mission?

To prevent the very sort of blue-on-blue engagement that just happened. I should know—we have a right to know. There's been too damned much that I've not been told about. The loss of Oberon. The Tabun. What else? And will it get me killed?

Odd, too, that there'd been no counterattack, and not even a hint of the other submarine on the sonar. Damned poor training if the adversary couldn't get off a return shot in the three minutes they'd had between hearing the torpedo and taking a hit.

That thought struck her forcefully for a moment, and she paused before walking back into combat. Three minutes was more than enough time under most circumstances for a submarine to launch a torpedo down a reciprocal bearing—maybe even two or three. The submarine must have been at full readiness, based on what appeared to be the German force's intentions, yet there'd been not a single return shot. *Ramage* damned well could have done better.

The lack of return fire continued to bother her as she reentered combat. She crossed the room and reluctantly settled into the elevated cushioned chair designated for the CO. Admiral Richardson had ordered them to move toward the battle group and resume the back-and-forth patrol as point. She watched Collins give the necessary orders. The calm, confident voice made her own uncertainty all the more painful.

Five minutes later, *Ramage* gained contact on another U-boat to the south and vectored British helos in to prosecute. Another contact, then another popped onto the screen, all well south of the battle group. British ships swept in from the flanks to contain them and herd them south, as Admiral Richardson had planned. The large-screen display in com-

bat was soon cluttered with arcane symbology for submarine contacts, torpedo attacks, and confirmed kills.

The more she saw, the more Bailey's frustration grew.
Ramage was a hunting dog, pointing the way for someone
else to attack. There was little else she could do under the
circumstances. The United States was already verging on
entering a war they weren't ready to fight by sending the
ballistic-missiles submarines, silent and deniable, down to
cover the southern end of the English Channel. Absent any
indications of hostile activity directed at her own ship, all
Bailey could do was sit and wait.

"It's got to be the wolf pack, Captain," Carlisle said.
"South of us. There're too many detections for it to be
anything else. They've got a perfect excuse for being out
in force, too. *Northern Lights.*"

"Maybe," she said. "That's what I'd expect from the
Germans. They've done it that way in every war so far.
But why are they so far south? That's not normal—I'd
expect to see them stalking us, not lurking around down
south waiting for us. Not in constrained waters."

Carlisle leaned back in his chair and stretched. "I don't
know. Maybe the boomers just blew their cover."

She shook her head. "Maybe, but I don't think so. Something's wrong with this whole scenario, and I don't know
what."

"That was the whole point of forming up in a line abreast,
Captain," Admiral Richardson said. He leaned over the
chart and pointed at the southern portion of the North Sea.
"And it's worked. We've forced them to concentrate in a
smaller area of the water, turned their wolf-pack tactics
against them."

"But *why* are they there?"

He straightened up. The old Brit looked like he'd lost
ten years off his face. For the first time, she saw anger and
confidence return.

"Obviously they've made an error in their timing. Had
we not begun barrier operations as you suggested, they'd
have moved north and assembled their attack force. Then
it would have been our forces trapped down south, with the

wolf pack picking off strays at will." He looked across at her. "You've done well, madam. And now I believe *Ramage* may leave the clean-up action to indigenous forces."

Her sense of uneasiness grew. "Five days ago, when we were talking about their tardiness to scheduled evolutions, you told me that the Germans didn't normally make this sort of mistake. Nothing I've seen so far convinces me that you were wrong then."

"Except their tactical formation now." He regarded her warmly. "It's a fact of warfare, Captain, that even the most capable opposing force will occasionally go awry. The essence of a good offensive is to be prepared to take advantage of those times. This will be a textbook example of that principle in a few years, mark my words." He turned to his aide. "Execute Phase II of the plan. I want my ocean clear of these bastards in twenty-four hours."

The two ends of the NATO line of ships flanked inward, sweeping the German submarines toward the middle of the North Sea like a seine closing around tuna. Patrolling back and forth in the middle of the op area, Bailey watched British forces stream past her, southbound toward the wolf pack of German submarines that seemed to pop in and out of detection envelopes at will. British helicopters and Nimrods circled overhead, picking up locating data and then vectoring to the contacts still well south of the battle group.

The tactical net chattered with sharp, crisp reports of submarine contacts, the enthusiasm in the British voices barely contained by the veneer of professionalism. The mood in *Ramage*'s combat darkened as the British forces darted ahead of the only ship not actively chasing a submarine. To stay behind, serving as SAR and logistics support, ate at every one of the Americans.

U-504

The submarine continued south, moving silently toward the rest of the wolf pack safely screened behind a line of mines the other boats had laid across the English Channel. According to the plan, the other boats would now be arranging intermittent detections, luring the surface ships into the killing field with brief glimpses of periscopes and occasional acoustically detectable high-speed runs.

Kraeken paced back and forth in the control room, clearly at the end of his patience. A range of sonar pings reverberated off her hull, hard and crisp from nearby ships, softer, almost caressing from those more distant. Finally he smacked one fist into the palm of his other hand and turned to Merker.

"At least flood the tubes. *One* tube. For self-defense, if nothing else."

Merker ignored him.

"*Kapitan,* you *can't*—"

"I can. And if you ever have your own ship, you will understand. The *Kapitan* selects the targets—no one else. And I chose the American destroyer."

USS RAMAGE

"This is too easy," Bailey said. The orderly line of NATO warships was breaking up into small units as Admiral Richardson vectored assets onto the submarine detections scattered about the ocean to the south. "Every experience we've had with them has been a nightmare. Why are they so detectable all at once?"

"We've taken them by surprise," Admiral Richardson said. Fierce fire burned in his face. "Their last mistake was concentrating their wolf pack too early and too far south."

"Their last mistake?" Bailey stared at the radar scope. "Or ours?"

U-504

"There," Merker said finally. "It's him."

Kraeken looked relieved. "The American."

"A stern shot—I want him dead in the water, knowing he can't run."

HMS *TROIKAN*

Twenty miles to the south, the Danish corvette *Troikan* plowed through the seas, bow onto the waves. Her hull, a lighter, green-gray, was barely distinguishable from the seawater. Fifteen miles to the southeast, a British Lynx ASW helicopter had a German diesel pinned up against the coast. The helicopter darted back and forth across datum, her crew howling in frustration. The helicopter's torpedoes were preset for deeper water. In the shallow littoral region, they would impact the seabed before they had a chance to even acquire the target.

Troikan was glad to assist. Two technicians were struggling to maintain their footing on the starboard weather deck as they hastily reset the targeting depth on the corvette's surface tube-launched torpedoes. Another was aft, clutching a precarious handhold with one hand poised over the depth-charge firing circuits. Unlike the Americans, the Danish had maintained all the weapons that had been so effective during two world wars. Depth charges were cheaper than rocket-assisted torpedoes—and a hell of a lot more effective in shallow water.

The corvette's captain paced the bridge of his ship, barking out orders and keeping his binoculars trained toward the submarine. A British destroyer followed, carefully staying fifteen thousand yards astern and well clear of the corvette's torpedo envelope.

"No—no Nimrods," Admiral Richardson said. "Shallow water is the Danish forte. There are more than enough targets for everyone. Vector the aircraft south to establish the southernmost limits of the wolf pack's position and to pick off stragglers."

The Nimrod aircrew broke off their approach and shifted their orbit to the south, leaving the corvette free to take the submarine.

USS *RAMAGE*

"No." As she said the word, a sense of sureness lent strength to her voice. "No farther south. OOD, execute a starboard turn and head north along a reciprocal course."

"Running from the fight this time, Captain?" Collins asked softly. She was seated at the TAO console in front of her. She pointed at the tactical formation spreading out across the large-screen display. "That's your style, isn't it, ma'am? Wait for some other ship to take a hit, then go on in. Don't worry—we're not in any danger with that many ships screening us from the pack."

"Get us headed north—*now*."

Collins stared at her, hesitating a few seconds longer than courtesy would allow. Finally, she picked up the bitch box handset and relayed Bailey's orders to the bridge. She waited for an acknowledgment, then turned back to Bailey. "Do you know what you're doing?"

"I do." She pointed at the last known position of the submarine stalking them. "He doesn't."

HMS *TROIKAN*

"Active contact. Range, eight thousand yards; bearing, one-nine-eight true." The corvette's sonarman sounded excited.

"Very well," the captain said. He leaned against the bridge wing, bracing himself against the light steel wall topped with a wooden railing. The Lynx was in view now, moored to the ocean's surface by the line running from her acoustic equipment to the active sonar dome fifty feet deep. He trained his binoculars on the water below the helo, quartering it and scanning it for any trace of the submarine.

"She's running," the sonarman said suddenly. "Helo's vectoring to prosecute."

"Which way?"

"South. Speed up to fifteen knots. Passive contact now, too. Verifying turn count." The sonarman looked pleased. "No way she can get away. Five minutes to weapons release."

FOUR HUNDRED FEET BELOW THE SURFACE

The mine quivered. The first contact was too deep by far, and the targeting circuits immediately dismissed it as a contact. The second, however . . .

Speed, depth, and acoustics all matched. It ran a preliminary burst of energy through the fire control electronics. A confirmatory echo raced back through the circuits.

There were twenty mines in the area. This one had been laid just two days before by a U-boat, and it was moored to the bottom. Below it, unbeknownst to the wolf pack, the older mines listened for the acoustic signals that would match the primitive analog recognition circuitry. One by one, as the line of ships approached and the submarines prowled just south of the mines, they all armed.

HMS *TROIKAN*

"Weapons release criteria," the sonarman announced. "Leading lag geometry, all stations reporting ready."

"Very well. Fire one." The captain's binoculars were still glued to his face.

FOUR HUNDRED FEET BELOW THE SURFACE

Now. The mine expended one last burst of electrons, emptying its capacitor charge into the ignitions circuits.

HMS *TROIKAN*

A disturbance in the water in the lower portion of his field of vision caught the captain's attention. He started to refocus his binoculars, looking for the periscope he thought had caused it. The eyepieces slammed into his cheekbones. He had a few seconds to stare down at the water, start to try to puzzle out the cause of the violent surge in his stomach and why the ocean seemed to be directly in front of his face, approaching rapidly, before he hit the water.

The shock of ice water set in immediately. Within seconds, his fingers started to numb, his chest tightened. He flailed instinctively for a few moments before consciousness kicked in. Overboard—but how had he—? He started treading water, rotating in the ocean to find the ship. They'd notice, of course. How could they not? The starboard lookout had been standing right next to him, must have *seen* him go into the water.

The water around him shivered, vibrating in hard, sharp jolts. As he topped a wave, he caught sight of *Troikan,* her starboard quarter barely three hundred feet away. He started to swim, forcing blood and energy to pump through his already numbing body.

Why wasn't she turning? The first order in any man-overboard evolution was a hard turn in the direction of the man in the water. The maneuver kicked the deadly stern away from the swimmer and started the process of coming about to retrieve the man. He swam harder, more to fight off hypothermia than in any real hope of approaching the ship.

Something odd—he stopped his forward progress and treaded water for a moment, staring at his ship. She seemed larger than she should, with more freeboard. Why was the safety railing so far above the water? Was it just the perspective of looking up at her?

The ship grew larger as he stared. Then the black-painted lower section of her hull hove into view. The superstructure, modest by most navies' standards, seemed even farther away. He started swimming toward her again.

Four strokes later, his perspective shifted and he understood what he was seeing. *Troikan* was dead in the water and heeling badly to port. Tipping over—*capsizing*. By the time he puzzled it out, the ship's port beam was already awash.

From this close to the ship, he could see the sailors scrambling over the steeply tilted decks, crawling up lines that had once been flat on the forecastle, trying to reach the railing. He swam harder, breaststroking now and screaming.

Seconds after the mine-launched torpedo hit, *Troikan*'s main machinery spaces flashed into a fireball of diesel fuel and shattered machinery. The ship had been refitted two years ago with automatic engineering controls. Only two men, an engineer of the watch and a messenger, stood watch in the compartment. The first casualties, and perhaps the luckiest.

The torpedo penetrated the midsection of the ship, veering slightly aft as it cut easily through both thin aluminum compartment bulkheads and rigid steel strakes. It sheered the massive diesel engine off its shock-mounted supports, shoving it ahead like a battering ram.

The engineer and the messenger were bent over temperature logs, the senior man pointing out a small variation in readings to the younger, explaining the difference was within normal ranges but could indicate a problem if the temperature increased more than five degrees in the next hour. The messenger was nodding impatiently, eager to finish this set of rounds so he could sneak off into the pump room for a quick smoke before starting the next endless series of readings.

The noise shattered their world. The engineer, hardwired for action by years of training, had just enough time to stand up and reach for the engineering alarm panic button before the diesel engine smashed through the thick plastic observation window.

The messenger, still turning to find the source of the noise, was crushed immediately against the aft bulkhead. The diesel engine—or what remained of it—flattened his chest, neck, and head to a thin, clotty paste. It caught up the engineer as well, shoved him aft and to the right. The engine was rotating, turning ninety degrees from its original orientation to the deck, the blunt snout of the torpedo protruding through iron and steel, the engine folding back along the sides of it, less a battering ram now than a jagged sheath.

The geared oil pressure pump was one of the few components of the engine to survive the initial impact intact, but even it now started to warp. As the projectile crushed the messenger, the pump's casing finally cracked. The shaft snapped away from the gear, pivoted forward, and protruded ten inches in front of the main mass of metal.

The shaft caught the engineer two inches above his right nipple. It shoved through shirt, skin, and flesh, jittered off the sternum, then continued on through his lung, severing the man's spine before embedding itself in the bulkhead behind him.

By then, the diesel engine had almost completed its rotation and was now aligned with the ship's fore-and-aft axis. It shoved the engineer into the far corner of the small space, crushed his legs below midthigh, wrenched the gearshaft out of his chest with a sideways twisting motion, then continued its careening course aft, finally coming to rest with the remains of the torpedo in the aft gun magazine.

The engineer was still conscious. He slid down from the wall and crumpled into a heap and the intersection of what once had been the deck and the bulkhead. His legs pooled into useless puddles of torn tissue and bone fragments around him, arterial blood spurting out of the ragged stumps. He watched it for a second, too badly hurt and shocked to do more than stare at the graceful arc of red droplets the blood traced over the water.

Water. Not here—not so far below the waterline! It horrified him on a level that only another sailor accustomed to living in the bowels of a ship could understand. To drown *inside* the ship was a nightmare he'd fought off since his earliest days in the navy.

He struggled to stand, to crawl, to do anything to escape the water. It was rising now, damping down the pounding blood to a dark upwelling below its surface, soaking his pants, creeping up his shirt. And the pain—sweet Mary, mother of Jesus. Dark, too dark. The emergency lighting must have failed, and his terror increased. Water, dark, trapped paralyzed belowdecks. He prayed harder, knowing it was useless but hoping the God and His mother who had kept him safe for so many years at sea would grant him one final request.

Forty feet aft, the remains of the torpedo fuel, the fire started in the engine room, and the rounds of five-inch and fifty-caliber ammunition intersected. The explosion consumed them all, then flashed back through the missile's path through the ship. In his last moments, the engineer saw one last blast of light and felt the water vaporize around him.

The Danish captain saw the last lifeboat tumble awkwardly from the nearly vertical deck, deploy and inflate in the water, then rock back and forth hard as sailors clambered over its rounded sides. It was bright orange, covered with a thin canopy of plastic to cut the wind and give the sailors huddled inside an increased chance of surviving the northern temperatures.

He shouted, waved his arms, felt himself sinking and water washing over his face as his legs tried clumsily to obey the order to tread. It wasn't enough anymore to keep him afloat, not with the waterlogged bridge coat now dragging him down.

He held his breath, fighting down panic as he kicked out of the coat, leaving it submerged barely below the surface behind him. Lighter, easy to move through the water. But colder without the body-warmed layer of water the coat had held trapped against him.

A few minutes more. He could already feel the cold-induced peacefulness nibbling at the edges of his mind, urging him not to worry, to quit fighting, perhaps float on his back and grab a nap while he waited for rescue. Hypothermia, that peculiar form of serenity that presages death in the North Sea.

He fought, swinging his arms, beating back the water, moving forward a few feet along the crest of the waves, glimpsing the lifeboat, then slipping back into utter isolation and despair between the troughs. Harder and harder to keep it up when the deep black beckoned.

"Captain!"

He heard the cry, one part of his mind noting that it must be addressed to him. He was the captain, wasn't he? He had been at one time, at least. He thought so, although why it mattered at all was beyond understanding. He drifted, not realizing his face was already in the water, although reflex kept him from breathing it in. For now.

Air washed over his face. He gasped, too cold to do much more, too numb to feel the hands under his armpits hauling him aboard.

"Strip him. Quick, the blanket!" The senior sailor on board the lifeboat took charge. After twenty-two years of sailing these waters, he'd seen men suffering from less exposure die fast. "You two," he continued, pointing to the sailors shivering the least. "Strip, crawl in with him."

The two men started to protest by reflex, then understood. Wrapped in the heat-reflective survival blanket, silvery metallic on the inside and rescue orange on the outside, they might have a chance of warming their captain. They stripped down, settled on the damp deck of the lifeboat, one on either side of the captain, and pulled the non-absorbent blankets around them.

"It's too late," one sailor said. "Even if they pick us up soon, he's not going to come out of it. Look at him." He pointed at the captain, who was now unconscious and breathing in shallow, irregular gasps.

The senior sailor shook his head. "We have to try. He would, you know. If it were you."

"It was him that got us into this. Charging in ahead of every other ship. Serves him right."

The senior sailor grabbed him by the shoulder, shoved him across the lifeboat toward the flapped hatch. He pulled back one flap and pointed toward the horizon. "You think it would make any difference? First or last? *Look.*"

Scattered around the horizon, painfully bright against the clear, cruel night sky, the ships burned. Four were close aboard, their superstructures outlined in odd, ragged shapes by flames gouting from their hulls. Secondary explosions from machinery spewed arcs of light across the sky, the sounds reverberating in the silence. *Troikan* herself was a dull, blackened shape, only occasionally illuminated by the others, her own flames already extinguished by the water forcing its way down her passageways and up into the highest compartments. Farther away, the horizon glowed at odd intervals, occasionally lit in a flash as though by lightning from a distant storm.

"Count them," the senior sailor ordered. "Count, then tell me how much difference it made, damn you. *Count.*" He dug his fingers into the back of the other man's neck, forcing his head from side to side. From what he could see, almost half of them were burning hulks.

"Eighteen." The man felt his anger seep away. How many ships had there been in the line? Thirty? Forty?

He cupped his hands on either side of his face, shielding

his eyes from the nearest burning ship. His night vision returned. He searched the horizon again, this time looking for the others, the ships that might have escaped. They were there, dark, gray shapes against darker sky, scattered out of their orderly formation by a dozen captains' interpretations of where safety might lie. Some were launching helos, still at darken ship, the cone flashlights used by the flight deck crew for signaling visible even at a distance.

He felt an odd flash of kinship with the other sailors, with all of those trapped in thin bubbles as he and these men were. Like champagne it would be—black water bubbling, small, invisible orange bubbles carrying the men who'd sailed with impunity on the sea just hours, maybe minutes, before.

The senior sailor pulled him away from the gunwales and gave him one last shove to the other side of the raft.

20

8 MARCH 2002:
THE ENGLISH CHANNEL

U-504

Merker laid his hand against the speaker. "It's the American ship." By now he'd come to know the destroyer by the way its sound felt under his fingertips, the high whine of her turbines, the solid *thunk* of her bilge pumps.

U-504 loitered fifteen miles off the coast of Britain, lying almost motionless along the fifty-fathom curve, farther north than any other boat in the wolf pack. His orders were to stay well clear of the killing ground while his fellow U-boat sailors lured the British forces south.

In two days, when the battle was to be well under way, *U-504* was to enter the arena undetected, avoiding any contact with surface ships, and follow a precisely defined path from west to east. Admiral Braudel had been particularly insistent that the only reason to deviate from the coordinates he'd provided was to stay clear of surface ships. Even then, if evasive maneuvering was required, *U-504* would have to retrace her steps at the first opportunity. As during their initial mining of the British ports, there was no reason given for the orders.

The first sounds of torpedoes firing to the south had cut through his fugue. The sense of vulnerability that had haunted him since Korea fed on the sounds, growing to almost unbearable proportions. Yet still, somehow he managed to maintain the icy calm that soothed the crew. He looked around the control room, noting dispassionately the eagerness he still saw on their faces, wondering in a detached manner if any of them really understood what was happening. He certainly didn't, not with the radio out of commission.

The irony of his position struck him. Off the coast of Korea, he'd tried to preclude the United States from entering the European conflict by attacking one of their ships. Now, despite his best efforts, an American ship he *hadn't* been stalking had prosecuted him with a helo-launched torpedo. Cause and effect—was there ever any concrete relationship? The brilliant German military theorist, Clausewitz, had written about the fog of war, the insidious confusion that inevitably permeated war, rendering even the best plans and most precise operational orders confusing.

Listening to the sounds of the attacks to the southeast, he came to the conclusion that the events were inextricably linked. The surprise attack in Korea had been—well, less than optimum. Shooting at a ship that had no warning, no reason to believe that it was in danger, had denied him the opportunity to test his skill against another commander. The more he thought about it, the more sense it made, especially after six months at sea. The only way to purge himself of the demons—the shame—was to take the American ship up on the gauntlet it had thrown down. Once he met it fairly and defeated it, he would be free of the sickness eating at his soul.

The U-boat moved forward at bare steerageway. Merker studied the sonar screen, then looked into the eyes of the man operating it. "Classification?"

"I'm—I'm not certain," the sonarman admitted. "Three ships, all large. Combatants. But American or British?" He shrugged.

Merker swore quietly. For all the miracles it could work under the sea, sonar was not magic. It was still just a tool, dependent on medium and the sources that were radiating from their targets.

He motioned to the conning officer. "Get me close, quietly. If sonar is able to puzzle out one ship from another, we'll make a submerged approach. If the water doesn't co-operate, then I'll need a periscope sighting before we fire.''

"Herr *Kapitan*—does it matter so much which ship we shoot?'' Ehrlich, the navigator, looked slightly embarrassed and afraid of his own presumptuousness in asking the question.

Merker let his cold stare rest on the young man until the navigator dropped his gaze. ''You would just let them walk away from this? That they attacked us yesterday? Does your own skin—your own *honor*—mean so little to you?''

Ehrlich mumbled an apology. Merker glanced around the rest of the small compartment. ''The rest of you, understand this: No one fires a torpedo at this ship and lives to boast about it. *No one.*''

He saw them bob their heads in response, small movements as though they were afraid to risk drawing his attention to them, yet equally afraid of not answering when a response was required. Not that he could blame them. The conduct of the rogue U-boat, the loss of communications— all changed right answers to wrong, sound operational plans to straitjackets.

And honor. What could he tell them of that? He himself had attacked without warning both the American amphibious ship in Korea and the virtually defenseless Korean diesel submarine. It seemed peculiarly appropriate that he should now be the victim of the same sort of deception he'd created in Korea, the same fog of war that made winning at least as much an art as a science.

Merker turned away, unsure of whether he was more disgusted with Ehrlich and Kraeken or with himself.

USS RAMAGE

''And now what?'' Collins's voice was cold. ''We run in and rescue survivors? Or do you just want to turn tail and run? That about sums up your tactics, doesn't it? No danger of you ever firing a weapon in anger.''

Bailey stared out at the horror on the horizon. The nearest burning ship was fifteen miles astern, a grimy, orange smudge on the horizon growing dimmer every second. Every other time, she'd done what her conscious had dictated, turned back into the battle to fight, to rescue survivors. She'd seen the damage, the danger, watched the other ships finally give in to the sea. That close, the tragedy could be rationalized, the fears of personal safety subsumed in the urgent need for action.

For some reason, this was worse. The sheer scale of it, the distance that let her imagination fill in the details. A shudder ran up her back. Her mouth felt dry, an incongruent sensation of fear surrounded by so much water.

Bailey turned back forward, took a deep breath, and tried to steady herself. Lights tracking from west to east caught her eyes. The ship was far to the north, visible only because of the exceptional clarity of the night.

"Look." She pointed at the green starboard running light, the fore and aft masthead lights. The bearing drift, the movement of the ship from left to right, and the green light told her the ship was heading east.

At least one other ship had survived the massacre to the south. Safe water to the north, then. A plan started to form in her mind. "Call them. Let's get their helo up. Ours, too. We should be able to vector in rescue forces, maybe horsecollar the wounded out. What is it? British? Norwegian?" There might be a way after all to do what duty required without foolishly hazarding *Ramage*.

"Shit," she heard Collins say. "You stupid bitch, that's a ferry."

ENGLISH CHANNEL FERRY

The ferry plying the route between Dover and Calais had been in service for nearly fifteen years. By dint of careful maintenance, sturdy engineering, and periodic refurbishments, she remained an economical and useful vessel. And a profitable one, her captain thought, as he gazed across the choppy water toward Calais. Even with the Chunnel, which now ran under the sea floor between the United Kingdom and the Continent, hundreds of travelers elected to take the ferry instead. Despite the increasingly treacherous waters of the English Channel, commerce—and the ferry's owners—still required the ferry to operate.

He himself had never been through the Chunnel. Something about being trapped that far under the surface of the ocean, confined to a narrow wormhole route tunneling through the mud, was unsettling. No, more than unsettling, bloody unnatural.

He'd been master of this vessel for almost five years, and made hundreds if not thousands of runs across the narrow strip of water. Only twice had he felt seriously in danger, when rough seas had proved worse than predicted, but that was also part of being a sailor. Weather patterns and sea states were still more of an art in prediction than a science.

But today they'd been well on the mark. The ferry stabilizers easily smoothed out mild chop, a relief for the crew that would have had to clean up after seasick passengers had the seas been any worse.

The ferry trudged along east at a steady twelve knots, now only a half hour from her portage in Calais. Two hundred passengers aboard were just starting to realize they were nearing land, and there was the normal rustle and movement of the crowd as travelers grabbed a last cup of coffee, families searched for children yelling and playing over the two levels of the ferry, and other passengers started to gather up their belongings. There were several groups of holidayers, both returning and departing. The European passengers returning home sported bright red cheekbones and noses, evidence that they'd managed to find the few hours of bright sunshine allocated to Britain every year. The Brits going on holiday on the Continent were still pale and ghostly, clutching carryalls crammed full with travel brochures and sightseeing guides.

The captain leaned back in his chair, swished the coffee gently in his mug, and reflected on how lucky he was to have earned this particular billet. The runs were regular, the hours steady, and the pay excellent by Britain's depressed economy standards. In another five years, he decided, he might think about looking for a larger boat, but in the meanwhile shepherding travelers back and forth across the English Channel suited him just perfectly.

THREE HUNDRED FIFTY FEET BELOW THE SURFACE

Contact. The torpedo mine that had been dormant for so many decades detected a large vessel transiting overhead. The firing circuits went through their normal routine, evaluating size and depth, and determined it represented a viable target. The relays flipped, electrons surged, and— nothing. The mine did what its hardwiring demanded, and tried to initiate the active firing sequence again. Electricity looped and circled through the circuit, trying vainly to launch the torpedo.

Decades of being submerged in corrosive salt water had done their work. A tiny flaw in the resistant coating that covered the gap between torpedo and mine had corroded, and the torpedo's fuel had leaked into the ocean. The small residue that remained was contaminated with salt water and incapable of firing.

The mine settled into a futile loop of sequencing until its battery was depleted. It fell quiescent on the ocean floor, reverting to charging mode.

ENGLISH CHANNEL FERRY

"A bit choppier near the coast, what?" the captain remarked mildly to the first mate.

"That it is." The mate glanced over at the captain and shrugged. If the master wanted to chat, he'd chat, but most of his mind was fixed on the evening he planned on enjoying in France. Two years of daily journeying back and forth had yet to dull the anticipation of his layovers, when he could arrange them.

It had been a month since he'd spent the night in France, and he was looking forward to returning to a bar he'd discovered last time. The beer had been cold, a taste he'd acquired many years ago, to the disgust of his British compatriots—he missed the captain's next words, thinking about the seductive, dark-haired woman he'd met there last time. Now if only he could remember her name—he squinted, trying to remember. Claire? Was that it?

Again, a shrug, entirely too Gallic in nature to suit him naturally. Whatever. If she weren't there, doubtless there'd be another lass agreeable to keeping a sailor company. He heard the captain's voice pause and nodded agreeably, preoccupied with his own thoughts.

THREE HUNDRED FIFTY FEET BELOW THE SURFACE

One thousand yards closer to the coast, one of the eighty active mines lay waiting. Unlike its westward counterpart, its makers had ensured that the gap between torpedo and mine was securely sealed.

As the ferry approached, it made the same evaluation. It reached the decision that its inoperative brother had, but with different results.

When the ferry was two hundred yards away, the torpedo fired.

ENGLISH CHANNEL FERRY

In the first microsecond of the attack, the master of the ferry thought he'd hit a rogue wave, an unexpectedly rough swell in the mild chop. He braced himself, or started to, and turned toward the first mate.

Unlike the surface ships that had been hit before her, the ferry had no deep-draft keel to hold her in the water. The mine arced up, exploding under the starboard side of the ferry. The ungainly vessel rocked to port, hesitated, then capsized, exposing its shallow-draft keel to the air.

The five seconds it took the ferry to turtle was barely time for the passengers to start to panic. Seawater poured into the large, open ports on either side, filling the upper deck immediately. The sea raced up the stairwells, in the direction that had been down just moments before, quickly filling the lower level as well. The weight in the ferry's lower half, now precariously above the ferry's center of gravity, drove the entire structure underwater even farther.

Ten seconds after the torpedo hit, the master of the vessel found himself trying to swim through a debris-laden pilothouse. The water bubbled and churned, and he completely lost his bearings. Holding his last breath inside his lungs, frantically resisting the temptation to breathe, he tried to make it to the hatch. Disoriented, his strokes took him toward the middle of the pilothouse, a fact he realized only when he bumped into the large, old-fashioned wheel in the center of the deck.

The water was dark, so dark—or so he thought, as his vision faded. Deprived of oxygen, his brain began shutting down portions of his body, beginning with his higher consciousness and judgment. Still struggling reflexively toward the hatch on the other side of the pilothouse, his arms and legs moving spasmodically, the unconscious officer gulped in a deep lungful of seawater.

On the lower levels of the ferry, the passengers had a slightly better chance. Most of the passengers on the upper levels had already drowned, but a pocket of air trapped inside had enabled a couple of the lower-level passengers to gulp down a deep lungful of air and head for the open ports. Five of them made it out, struggling to the surface more by reflex than by reason, surfacing gasping and coughing. Still operating on survival instincts, most of them swam away from the sinking ferry, resisting the tugging suction.

Five minutes later, the last bit of the ferry vanished under the water. Three passengers were still alive, bobbing in the rough chop, surrounded by the floating bodies of those who'd almost made it. They grabbed frantically for debris nearby, finding bits of wood and flotsam to support their weight, and floated in stunned shock.

USS RAMAGE

"That's the last of them, Captain," the master chief said. He was at her side, watching from the bridge wing as the boat crew hauled the last of the ferry survivors up the accommodation ladder. So few. Too few. If they'd gotten there a few minutes earlier, perhaps—she pushed the thought away, unwilling to consider it. It might haunt her later, but for now there were more immediate problems demanding her attention. Like the sailors to the south.

"You'll get them some clothes, some food," she said, barely aware that she'd spoken. Of course they would, one part of her mind chided. She felt her mind fixing on that as something she could do, unlike the rest of the situation.

"Yes, ma'am," the master chief said, an oddly gentle tone in his voice. "We've got it under control." She felt his eyes search her face, then he looked out toward the sea again. "Most of it. The only problem is the officers."

She looked up, surprised. "I beg your pardon?" she said, intending to inject just enough ice in her voice to let him know he was out of line. He continued to stare out at the ocean.

"I'll say this once, then I'll shut up and leave you alone, Captain. Those few people—they're alive because of you. You focus on that, try not to think about the rest of it. There's nothing you could have done, anyway."

"Master Chief, I hardly think—"

He cut her off. "The other problems—the ones we talked about down in the mess—they're still there. Getting worse, too. You've got a lot of support on this ship, too, ma'am. More than you probably know about. The sailors down on the mess decks, they see how things are. And maybe some of us understand a little bit more about command than your department heads do."

She shook her head, unwilling to acknowledge understanding what he'd said. "Master Chief, I appreciate hearing your thoughts, but there aren't any major problems in the wardroom. None at all. The whole situation"—she groped for the right words—"has been difficult for them."

"You come back down and talk to us, ma'am. There's some things we'd like to talk over with you. When—if it's convenient." The master chief stood up straight, saluted, then turned sharply and walked away.

She remained on the bridge as the boat crew disassembled the ladder, wondering if he'd meant what she thought he'd meant. And if it mattered.

U-504

It was the American ship again. No need to even surface and verify it through the periscope. He'd become familiar with every burp and wiggle of her acoustic signature. The same one that was now screaming down the waterfall display, dominating both the upper and lower spectrums with auxiliaries and the myriad low-frequency rumblings of a ship that bears steerageway.

"Searching for survivors, I suppose," the executive officer remarked. Merker noted the bitterness in his tone without surprise. Survivors, survivors—the executive officer had read that particular portion of their orders and completely missed the big picture.

"Sooner or later, it would have happened," he remarked mildly, unwilling to disturb the fragile truce that had arisen between them. "It wasn't a mandate, just guidance. More important last week than this, I think."

"Orders are orders," the other man snapped back.

"It was a civilian ferry. It's not the same as a military vessel."

"They are the enemy."

Merker let it pass. That a minefield had been planted in the course of the ferry was just another example of critical shortfalls in his information. According to his briefing, the containment fields were to be laid well south of that route. It angered him, the unnecessary risk to his own ship, transiting through a German minefield that some other U-boat had just planted. He could have been told—should have been.

A few more days and it wouldn't matter. It could be resolved after the trap closed on the remaining NATO forces. He considered his next move.

"Where's the layer depth?" he asked the sonarman.

"Shallow today, sixty meters." The sonarman held up a batheothermograph trace, indicating the change in water temperature with depth.

"Very well. Make your depth seventy meters."

"Course, *Kapitan*?" the conning officer asked.

Merker turned to the navigator. "I want to move us aft

of the American ship, maintaining firing position. Stay ten thousand yards away, and notify me if she commences any maneuvers. Hold us within firing range.''

"Aye, aye, *Kapitan*," Ehrlich responded.

Ten minutes later, the submarine was in position. Merker watched the surface ship's acoustic signature fade on the sonar display as the submarine started a gentle turn away from her.

Sooner or later, when the General Staff was satisfied with the situation on the ground, the orders would come. Then it wouldn't matter whether the Americans were involved. Germany's position would be consolidated on the Continent, and there would be little short of a massive amphibious invasion they could do to stop it.

And when the orders came, Merker would be ready.

ONE HUNDRED FEET ABOVE THE SURFACE

The wooden partition of the ferry sank slowly. It had been part of the original hull, well above the waterline, and divided the galley area from the pilothouse. After years of baking under the radiant heat from the stove, it was as brittle and dry as a piece of balsam. Still, seawater weighted it down some, seeping in through the fibers and knotholes of the barely finished wood, the water reducing its buoyant mass until it reached neutral buoyancy two hundred feet below the surface of the water. While most of the debris either floated to the top or sank quickly to the bottom, a few other like structures lurked beneath the water, invisible and uncharted hazards.

U-504

A sharp thud echoed through the control room, an alien and dangerous sound in the close confines of the submarine. Merker felt the initial surge of raw panic, quickly tamped down by his iron determination. *Thud*. There, again, farther aft on the submarine. He looked over at the sonarman, who had gone pale sitting at his console.

"I thought it was a torpedo," the sonarman said shakily.

"They say you hear that sometimes, the first impact on the hull. An old tale . . ." He shook his head. "I should've known better. You'll never hear the one that gets you. Not up close, anyway."

"A bit of debris in the water," Merker said, relieved that his voice sounded calm and competent. "It hit the bow and bounced off the sail."

"We all heard it, *Kapitan,*" the executive officer said. He looked up at the overhead. "The question is, who else did?"

USS *RAMAGE*

"What the—" Henning broke off the sentence, looking down at the paper unrolling under his fingertips.

"I've got it, too," Digger said. He pointed at a sharp green blotch on the sonar screen. "Impact noise."

"From a submarine?" Bailey asked.

"Had to be," Digger said. "There's nothing out on that bearing. And that damned sure wasn't a biologic."

"But what—?"

"A transient of some sort. Maybe the periscope rattling in the tube as she changed depths. Maybe the cook dropping a pan of spaghetti. Hell, I don't know," he finished, shaking his head, a look of grim satisfaction on his face.

She stood at the sonar screen, where the fluorescent green mark was already starting to fade. "You bastard," she said softly. "I've got you now."

"Commander Bailey," she heard a voice behind her say loudly.

"Not now," she snapped, without looking away from the screen. "Digger, straight shot down that line of bearing. Two shots—now!"

"Belay that," the same voice ordered.

She wheeled around, instantly enraged, ready to rip the throat out of whoever had dared to interfere with the first shot she'd had in a week. "Fire now," she ordered again, staring at the figures in the doorway.

Collins was in front. She wore a black leather holster and had her hand resting conspicuously on a military-issue

.45 pistol. Five officers carrying shotguns and pistols stood behind her. She stepped into the center of the compartment. "Two days ago, you told me to reread navy regulations. I did." Collins stopped, her fury barely controlled. "Section 1088 of navy regulations allows a subordinate to relieve the commanding officer if the commanding officers conduct will 'seriously irretrievably prejudice public interest.' " She pronounced the words slowly and carefully. "Given the tactical scenario, failing to obey Sixth Fleet's orders and otherwise hazarding this ship fall into that category. Some people would even call running away from the enemy treason.

"Commander Bailey, I relieve you of command."

U-504

A second set of noises tore through the submarine with a vengeance, shattering Merker's already fragile nerves. This time the initial impact was followed by a long, slithering sound, as though a metallic snake were crawling down the hull.

The propellers. His thoughts focused on that, seeing the eighteen-foot-diameter screw turning, imagining the debris catching first on one bladetip, then curling around the propeller shaft. It became so real that any second he expected to hear the shrill squeal of the fouled shaft, hear the frantic reports coming up from engineering.

The silence that followed was excruciating as he waited for the next bit of debris or the first engineering casualty. Time seemed to have stopped inside the control room, as the crew held their breaths. Finally, as the XO turned to him, he found his voice.

"Reverse course," he ordered. A small tremor crept in at the edge of his voice. "Get us away from this area."

The conning officer complied, too shaken to do more than order a full right rudder without giving a new course. He saw the man glance at the ship's heading indicator, take a deep breath, and then wait for the arrow to circle around in the opposite direction.

Three minutes later they were headed away from the soupy ocean and straight toward the American destroyer.

USS RAMAGE

"This is mutiny." There was no question in her voice. She felt a vein throbbing in her temple and raised her voice. "You will leave this compartment immediately."

Collins shook her head. "Not this time." Pale, frightened—and determined, Bailey decided. It was obvious Collins knew the consequences of her act. Regardless of whether she was right or wrong, her naval career was over the moment they set foot back on land.

Bailey tried one last time. "We have contact." She pointed at the sonar screen. "This is the submarine, the one that shot *Puller, Victory,* and probably that ferry. The minefield to the south—it laid them. I'm certain of it." She drew a deep breath, hating the pleading note in her voice. "If we don't kill it now, there will be others. Maybe us."

Collins's eyes shifted to the display and dismissed it. "If you succeed. Two days ago, I would've agreed with you."

"And now?"

Collins's eyes left her face, sought out a corner of the compartment. "I don't know," she said finally. "But what you're doing isn't right."

"And what would you do instead? I have a right to know that. If you intend to try to relieve me, you should at least have the guts to tell me exactly what you would do instead."

The silence stretched out until it was deafening. Collins looked over at Kelso for support, then fingered the gun at her side. The weapons officer was seated at his console, pointedly oblivious to what was happening in the back of the compartment. "Not a one of these men has the balls. Whatever I decide, it will be for the good of the ship." Collins nodded toward the door. "Take her down to her stateroom."

Bailey regarded her levelly. "I don't need an armed escort. I'm leaving, but you will regret this. You *will* regret this."

U-504

"It wasn't a warship," the U-boat sonar technician insisted. "The speed, the engineering sounds ..." He shook his head insistently. "Whatever the mine hit, it wasn't military. Not ours, not theirs."

"Approach slowly, periscope depth," Merker ordered. He glanced at the chronometer, a sudden, sick feeling in his gut. Ten-thirty at night—could it be?

Memories flooded back to him. A woman—what had her name been? Silvia, that was it. He'd had three days off between engineering schools, the first holiday in five years of naval service. They'd taken the ferry to England, escaped Germany for a while. What had happened to her? Suddenly he regretted not knowing.

"Four hundred meters off below the minefield," the navigator announced.

Merker shook away the memories and stepped toward the periscope platform. "Up scope."

He followed it up, through the dark blackness six feet below the ocean's surface at night, through the frothy mixture at the boundary of ocean and air, and up one foot above the waves.

His first impression was that the last weather forecast they'd received had been correct. The seas were relatively calm for the English Channel, the night clear and starlit as it had been on his holiday so long ago. He swung the periscope through its arc, searching the surface for traces of debris. Dim bonfires lit the sky to the south.

Halfway through the circle he stopped, stepped away from the periscope, and slammed the handles up. Without waiting for orders, the conning officer brought the periscope down, not needing to ask why. They'd all seen what their *Kapitan* had seen reflected on the monitor in the corner of the compartment.

The child's head had been turned to one side, eyes half closed, a dull, vacant look to his face that no one could ever mistake for life. Under the full moonlight, his features had been plainly visible. Light hair, even soaking wet in the sea, and an impression of pale eyes. And the face—

white, already starting to pucker slightly from exposure to the seawater, floating on his belly over the gentle rise and fall of the waves.

The body had been no more than three meters from the periscope, and the magnification factor made it seem as though he were directly on top of the periscope. For a moment, as his gaze had swept across the face, a stray wavelet had lifted the child's hand slightly, as though he were going to reach out and grab the periscope mast.

Was it never going to be right? Victory at sea, a battle of wits between adversaries, the hunt, the kill. Submarines—his—skill against his opponent's, the ultimate test of a military man against the best his adversary could bring to bear against him. It should count for something, it *should*.

Instead, triumph was dead children floating on the ocean's surface. No glory, no sweet succor of success, just small bodies drifting in the current.

PART
3

THE FOG OF WAR

As a result of the element of surprise by which it is characterized, the submarine—apart from direct naval successes which it is sought to obtain by its use—exercises a great influence on the military and strategic position, because the enemy must everywhere reckon with its appearance and is influenced in a correspondingly high degree in his strategic decision and military operations (detours, defensive measures, safety patrols, zigzag course).

—THE U-BOAT COMMANDER'S HANDBOOK,
Section I.A.8

21

---

8 MARCH 2002:
THE ENGLISH CHANNEL

USS RAMAGE

Bailey stood in the middle of the two-person stateroom, trying to follow the action from the 1MC announcements. The last of the ferry survivors was on board, that much was clear. The roll of the ship in the sea increased, the fore-and-aft pitch decreased. The seas must be on the beam, then. They'd been heading directly into the waves when she'd been in sonar. South—Collins was taking the ship south.

She'd refused to acknowledge Collins's assumption of command of *Ramage*. An armed guard was now stationed outside her stateroom. Bailey had tried talking to him. The first-class petty officer was clearly unhappy with his duties—and not inclined to make a bad situation worse by disobeying Collins. She gave up. After all, what could she do simply by being out of her stateroom? Provide some warning, maybe. Point out any obvious tactical mistakes Collins was making. The odds were, the operations officer wouldn't listen to her anyway. Their basic agreement went far deeper than rudder orders.

She tried to pace, but the stateroom was large enough for only two steps along its length. Sitting down was out of the question, not with adrenaline and anger hammering through her blood. Lying down on the rack—she didn't even try.

Fifteen minutes after she'd been unceremoniously confined, she heard quiet voices outside her door, then a soft thud. She darted to the door, jerked it open. Lieutenant Commander Wentworth and two grimy engineering technicians stood in the passageway. The petty officer lay crumpled on the deck, his arms bound behind him with dull gray duct tape, another piece covering his mouth.

Five minutes later, they were inside the main engineering spaces. The hatches at either end were dogged down and crowbars were slid between the handles on the hatch and the bulkhead to prevent anyone from entering.

"Tell me I haven't just made a major mistake." Wentworth stared at her over a battered coffee mug.

She ignored the question. "What's Collins doing? Tell me now."

He appeared to consider insisting on an answer to his own question, then shrugged. "Okay, Captain. I'm in this up to my neck. They are, too." He gestured at the small cluster of engineers around him. "For their sake, you'd better be right."

She brushed away his concerns. "I'm taking full responsibility for it, for what it's worth. Later on—if there's a later. Answer my question."

"She's taking us south. Back toward the Brits. She thinks her sensors and weapons have been keeping the U-boats away from us, and she intends to kick some ass. Do you know why they haven't attacked yet?"

She nodded. "Not because they're scared of us, that's for sure. *Lusitania*. They're trying to avoid drawing the United States in too early, just as Kelso said. That, and they've been tied up luring the other ships south." She saw the doubt in his eyes. "I'm certain of it."

"So what? Collins does *this* for a living. Everything she's worked for for the past ten years, just so she can do the right thing in a situation just like this." Wentworth's voice was hard. "Why should I believe you?"

"You already do. Now tell me how we get control of this ship back."

•   •   •

After gathering up necessary tools and sailors, Wentworth led them aft, sticking to small belowdecks passageways, through long-unused but carefully maintained escape hatches. Ten minutes later, they were bolted into the after-steering compartment at the very stern of the ship.

Wentworth dropped down onto a bird's nest of line. "Most of the crew doesn't know what's going on. The topside technicians, sure, but not the rest of them. The chiefs suspect, but they're over their heads in this one. I think we can count on the master chief to handle them."

"My people?"

"She's got them under guard in the wardroom. That's a loyal bunch you've got there. Boston took a swing at her. She decked him. Right now, the people you can count on are mine." He glanced at his watch. "Any second now."

"What?"

The lights flickered, then went out. The hard pounding of the propeller shaft and blades immediately started spooling down. The compartment was eerily silent, lit only by the red emergency lights.

Wentworth motioned to two engineers. They placed their hands on the emergency aftersteering mechanism. "Which way do you want to go, Captain?" He pointed at the ship's course repeater over his head. "North?"

"Yes. Get us out of this area."

CHENG turned back to the men. "You heard the captain—north." They began turning the rudder by hand, straining against the pressure in the system. "A bit awkward, Captain, but it works. They should start noticing topside any second." He picked up a sound-powered phone set and plugged it into the receptacle. He started to slip it over his head. She reached out and caught his arm.

"No." She felt him resist, start to pull away from her. "It's my ship. And, for future reference, you are never to intentionally drop the load without my permission. Got it?"

He flinched slightly, then handed the headset to her. "Grateful little thing, aren't you?"

She took the phone and slipped the earphones over her head. "I'm not required to be grateful. I'm the captain."

He regarded her for a few moments, then nodded. "I thought I knew that."

Bailey held the headset away from her ears. Collins's angry shouts were clearly audible in the silent compartment. She let the other woman rave for a few moments, then interrupted her. "SILENCE on the circuit. You listen now or you listen at your court-martial. Make your choice."

"I don't listen to traitors."

"Or to the captain."

"You are *not* the captain of this ship. Daistrom was. And he would never have run from a fight—*never*. You'll never be what he was."

"Neither will you if you take this ship into the trap they've laid."

"Horseshit."

"Just listen to me for a minute. The longer we sit here dark and deaf, the better target we make." Bailey took a deep breath. How to convince the one person on board this ship who was convinced she was a coward. "It's a trap. Part of it's already sprung—count the fires you see on the horizon. You take us south and we end up part of it."

"That submarine can't—"

"Of course she can. Did you detect her before she shoved those green flares up your ass? During any one of the attacks on the Brits? No—and you won't this next time either."

When she finally answered, Collins's voice was sullen. "We'll go active this time. We'll find the boat."

"You *won't*. Think about what happened with the MIUWU. The active buoys didn't go off-line. The passive ones did. That ought to tell you that the submarine's not worried about active sonar countermeasures. Only passive. Jesus, woman, *think*."

"Prove it to me."

Bailey tried to hold her voice level and calm. Standing at opposite ends of the ship, separated by more than four hundred feet of honeycombed steel compartments, it was a standoff. Bailey held control of the electrical power and propulsion, with the help of Wentworth and his people.

Collins owned the weapons. Unless they found a middle ground, both groups would die.

"European wars are fought on the land—but they're won at sea. Germany's always known that—they proved it in two world wars. But there was no way Germany could have repeated her performance, not after decades as a divided, occupied country. Getting the production lines rolling, cranking out enough U-boats to control the sea, and preventing the United States from interfering—couldn't be done. Especially not with the rest of Europe watching their progress and getting worried about the new economic powerhouse they're becoming. It got worse after Germany started mass-producing diesel submarines for export. They couldn't have trained enough crews, built enough boats, to take on the rest of Europe and Russia that remembered the last time.

"But they had to have the sea. Remember, this is *Germany* we're talking about. There's no way she could have not made a power play. That'd go against everything we know about them. But what they *could* do instead was use a small number of U-boats to lay mines, then use the U-boats they *did* have to lure the rest of the riparian nations down into the mines. This whole *Northern Lights* scenario was perfect for them. It's the only way they could use the wolf pack with a limited number of submarines."

"All the more reason to go south and hunt subs. You're not persuading me, Bailey."

"Listen to me. Wolf packs operate together, each one knowing a small part of the plan. But in this scenario, somebody's got to have the big picture. There's one submarine out here that's commanding the whole pack. We take her out, we might make it out."

"I still don't see why—"

"*Ramage* is good, but she's not that good. We have to outthink them, not outweaponeer them. Look, what are the odds that the one boat with all the details is trapped down in the area south? Zero. Nil. We don't know what else they have planned, what the contingency measures are. Whoever's in charge isn't down there, though—no more than the command and control ship of a U.S. task force is in the

middle of the shooting. And, for what it's worth, I'm willing to bet that its the same boat that took out our sonobuoys. It's the only one talking to General Staff via
satellite.''

Wentworth was motioning to her frantically. He was
pressed up against the skin of the ship, his ear against the
hull. "Listen to this—I don't believe it."

"Wait one." She walked over to him, pulled one earpiece off. Collins was silent in the other. She pressed her
ear against the hull.

Ramage was quiet and dark. She shut her eyes. Against
the background noise of her own blood pounding through
her veins, she heard it. It was barely audible, but there was
no mistaking the sound. She looked at Wentworth, who
nodded. She pulled away from the hull.

"Collins," she said, "listen to me. Tell me if the lookouts are reporting any surface contacts anywhere near. Is
there *anything*—any contact at all?"

"Nothing," Collins said immediately. "Why?"

Bailey held out the sound-powered telephone to Wentworth. "Get the power back on. We'll settle this out in the
open."

"You think it's a submarine?" He rubbed one hand over
his face, digging his knuckles into his eyes.

"No. I'm certain it is. Unless we give her power and
weapons systems back immediately, no one's going to give
a damn about who's in command of this ship. Except the
morticians."

22

U-504

The U-boat reeked of sweat, stale food, and fear. Merker could taste it in the air. Despite Braudel's orders, it was quickly becoming impossible for him to avoid the battle raging to the south. The look in the crew's eyes coupled with his own guilt would soon drive him to action.

The crew. Captain Merker tried to feel the concern for their well-being that was his duty. Duty—that all-encompassing obligation that was supposed to bring meaning to life, that drove every good officer past the limits he imposed on himself. A captain was charged with the care and feeding—indeed, the very lives—that were entrusted to him. It was a sacred trust.

And one he would willingly put down. He felt an increasing resentment toward the eighty men who defined his very existence. Their fears, their oddities of personality and conduct—how was he to cope with their problems when all he could see was the face of the dead child? In the past eight months, he'd gone from being proud of the trust placed in him to bafflement to sullen resentment of the burden. Now, so close to being able to surrender the awesome responsibilities of command, all he could think of was how sweet it would be to no longer see the same faces every day, no longer have to maintain the pretense that he knew what he and the country he'd swore to serve were doing.

He might die soon, he realized suddenly. Not at sea, no,
but alone and by his own design. The past eight months
had taught him that there was little worth dying for—and
less worth living for. It would be a relief to finally abandon
that last pretense as well and seek out the quiet of the grave.

"Sir?"

Merker forced himself to focus on the voice. *U-504* had
barely started to follow the peculiar course laid out for her
when they'd detected the ship.

"What is it?" he said, aware of the rasp in his voice.
When was the last time he'd spoken? For a moment, remembering that simple fact seemed critically important.

"Five thousand meters from the ship, *Kapitan*," Kraeken
said.

"Surface," he said. "Let them see us. When I take her,
I want her to know who did it."

The XO moved closer and pitched his voice for Merker's
ears alone. "Are you insane?"

Merker examined the man's face carefully. Dark circles
ringed his eyes, and the skin looked gray and coarse. Stubble flecked the cheeks, more gray than brown. Still, of all
of them, Frederick Kraeken had changed the least in the
past eight months.

"Ehrlich, hand me your weapon." Merker heard the
words come out of his own mouth, and marveled that some
reflex of command still operated under the crushing blackness in his soul. He accepted the 9mm pistol from the navigator, checked to make sure it was loaded, then drew down
carefully on the XO. "The penalty for mutiny is a firing
squad."

Kraeken regarded him coldly, then turned and gave the
order to surface. "I'll see you in hell, *Kapitan*."

Too late, Merker thought, watching the figures silently
click off on the depth gauge. *I'm already there.*

USS *RAMAGE*

The general quarters alarm sounded as they undogged the
hatches to aftersteering. Two sailors ran into the compartment as they vacated it. In the flurry of activity, no one

stopped to challenge them or tried to stop her as she made her way back up to combat.

Collins was standing in front of the command chair, staring at the tactical display. Lights played across the surface as the computer regenerated the database and began coordinating the myriad sensor and weapons systems inputs into a single picture. The course repeater overhead confirmed Bailey's suspicions. *Ramage* was turning south.

"You almost got us killed." Collins sounded unexcited, almost bored. She pointed at the two sonar blips glowing on the screen. "Another five minutes and she'd have been within weapons range of us."

"She is already," Bailey answered. "The new German systems have a longer range than the fleet knows about."

"Nice if you civilian geniuses would share that information with the people who depend on it."

"Not my call. For what it's worth, I argued in favor of it."

Collins turned to the combat watch officer. "Torpedo ready?"

"Yes, ma'am." The chief avoided looking at either of the two women.

"Watch this," Collins said to Bailey. "I'm going to show you how we fight a war. Pay attention. You might learn something." She toggled the bitch box switch to sonar. "Go active. Get me a targeting solution."

"No. You go active and you'll just draw the U-boat in. I agree, we have to attack. But not like this."

"We'll see."

U-504

"Active sonar," the technician announced. "Classify it as a Burke-class destroyer in search mode."

The lights on the counterdetection panel flickered. The pointer on the acoustic analyzer darted up and down the scale, finally settling on one frequency. Another light came on, indicated the equipment had analyzed the incoming signal and had begun generating a signal exactly out of phase with it.

Merker nodded. "Get us in closer. This time I want to make sure we've got the right ship."

USS RAMAGE

"She'll come shallow now." Bailey tried to make the words sound more convincing than she felt. "Have the bridge watch the Furuno radar. It's a high-frequency radar and more likely to pick up a periscope than the SPS-10 or SPS-64. And get a watch team in the MIUWU van. She's got a high-frequency radar as well."

Collins shot her a withering look. "You're an instant expert now. A week ago, you wouldn't know where to look for the Furuno. It's down anyway. If there's something there, the -10 will pick it up."

"It won't. The resolution isn't sharp enough. Put power to the MIUWU van—there's a Furuno on it."

Collins turned to the CIC watch officer. "Have the master at arms escort two of her people aft. Get the Furuno up—nothing else. Don't let them near the radios." She turned back to Bailey. "No tricks. I swear to God, I'll have you shot if you endanger this ship."

Bailey clamped her hands down on the back of a chair, willing the tremors away. "Just do it. You'll see."

U-504

"Range and bearing?" Merker asked quietly. He felt a touch of his old arrogant self-confidence return as he reached a decision.

"Twenty thousand meters, bearing one-two-zero, *Kapitan*." The XO turned to face him and added, "Target angle zero-zero-zero—she's headed straight for us."

"Open the outer doors," Merker ordered. "Any indication she's maneuvering?"

Kraeken shook his head. "No, sir. She's doing twenty-two knots, headed south directly toward us. Her sonar just went active. At that range, she must have seen us."

"Good. Not much point in surfacing otherwise, is there?" Merker said calmly. He tapped the butt of the pistol in his palm.

Kraeken stepped closer and spoke in a quiet voice to Merker alone. "There are other targets—*better* targets. The

British ships to the south—we could be inside their defensive perimeter in minutes. By insisting on attacking the American, you put the entire mission at risk.''

Merker closed his eyes and let the weariness seep through him. A few more hours, a few more days—what did it really matter? "We're not paid to think about the dangers. We're paid to do our duty. A targeting solution, now.''

The XO stepped back and regarded his captain gravely. For a moment, fear warred with something else on his face. Finally he nodded abruptly and began issuing a stream of commands to the attack team. Moments later, he reported the targeting solution to the captain.

"If we proceed slightly north, we'll have a classic angle for a bow shot, *Kapitan.* Recommend we come to course one-zero-zero at five knots to close her.''

"Make it so.'' Merker was too tired to check the solution himself. His sense of fatalism deepened.

USS *RAMAGE*

"TAO, pop-up contact to the north. On the MIUWU Furuno.'' The OOD's voice cut through the silent, staring standoff between the two women. "Three thousand yards and closing.''

Collins looked away first. "You're certain?''

"I'm holding it—ma'am, it's gone now. It was there, though.'' Boston's voice was clearly audible over the speaker.

The silence in combat deepened. Finally Collins said, "Come right and get us back on the northbound course.'' She turned to Bailey. "I hope to God you know what the hell you're doing.'' She turned and stalked back over to her console, slipped her headset on.

Bailey nodded. *So do I.* She felt the tension in combat subside as twenty technicians, two chief petty officers, and three surface warfare officers simultaneously decided to pretend that the past two hours had never happened.

U-504

"Excellent," Merker said calmly. "This would have been suicide during the last war, when they still carried depth charges. Fortunately, they're too advanced for that now. Nothing that they carry in their current inventory will arm this close to their own ship."

He saw Ehrlich summon up a wavering smile of relief, and nodded. The officers and men knew the ring of truth when they heard it, no matter what doubts they'd had about the captain in the past two months.

He ran through the attack geometry in his mind, never taking his eyes off the sonar screen. Minimum arming distance for the Americans: eighteen hundred yards. Minimum for the U-boat: the captain's discretion. The advantage of having a wire-guided torpedo instead of a fire-and-forget weapon was about to prove decisive.

Time was the primary factor. As long as the submarine stayed close to the American ship, she would be safe from the other's torpedoes. But their haven would exist only as long as it took the ship to build to her maximum speed and outrun the submarine. Additionally, trying to pace the surface ship would quickly drain the batteries. *Two minutes,* he decided finally, and opened his eyes. That's how long he would have to attack, if that, before he once more was within the ship's weapons range.

He stared at the green blip now dominating the active sonar screen, and spared a glance at the passive printout. *Ramage*'s acoustic signature danced across the spectrum, the lines shifting to the right as she increased her speed.

USS RAMAGE

"The sooner we get the fuck out of the North Sea, the happier I'll be." Digger tossed his headphones on the table and leaned back in his chair. He stared at the sonar, letting his subconscious take over the watch.

"At least it ought to be an easy trip home," Henning commented. "Though you'd think they could have given us liberty."

"They sure would have been grateful. All those young ladies," Digger said reflectively. He stretched his arms back and yawned, one eye still open and watching the screen. "It would have been like after World War II."

Henning snorted. "You think with your dick. If they ever put women on submarines, all we have to do is lower you into the water and it'll point them out."

"And I suppose your idea of liberty is a lot more fulfilling. Old churches and dead kings. Yeah, man—some kind of fun, Henning. That Henster, he really knows how to party, they'd say. Not like poor ol' me, who—OW!"

Henning had snapped a set of parallel rulers out to full extension and smacked him on the side of the head.

"What the hell's that for?" Digger whined, rubbing his head.

"Teach you some manners. Jesus, Dig, you can be an ass."

"At least I'm not a pussy," Digger muttered. He contemplated retaliating but settled for complaining. Ragging Henning was just a hobby—Hen-man was usually pretty good about taking it, but even Digger had to admit that he'd gone a bit farther than usual this time.

"And at least I won't catch AIDS or some other permanent little souvenir of a good time," Henning retorted.

"Okay, okay, I—" Digger broke off his halfhearted apology as his eyes registered an anomaly on Henning's screen. "What the hell's that?" He pointed.

"What's wha—oh. Wait one." Henning's hands flitted over the frequency controls, expanding one section of the screen. "Aw, shit. Don't tell me there's another one out here."

"It's a German?" Digger said, already reaching for his headphones and the bitch box switch.

"Yeah. Fuck." Henning hit the sonar alarm switch while Digger called the TAO and briefed him. They received permission to go active. Seconds later, the haunting *ping* of the sonar transducer reverberated through the hull.

"Got him—just barely. Stronger than we got any of the others, though. Bearing, three-three-seven degrees; range, three thousand yards. Course—*up doppler*! Whatever she was doing before, she's turning toward us now. Turn count increasing, target angle zero-three-zero degrees.''

"Twenty-five hundred," Digger said. "She's still accelerating—*Christ,* she's going to be within minimum range before we can get the shot off."

"Concur," Henning added crisply. "I'm holding her main propulsion. TAO, she's making almost twenty knots. Too close for ASROC, recommend we take with torpedoes."

"I have a targeting solution." Digger switched circuits, checked on the technicians manning the torpedo stations, and then returned to the ASW circuit. "All stations ready," he added.

Bailey darted into the compartment and took a few seconds to evaluate both the passive and the active displays. "Range," she demanded.

"Two thousand yards, still closing," Digger said. "Captain, we need to—*shit, she's within minimums!* Combat, hold fire!"

Ramage was already heeling away from the submarine's bearing. Bailey braced herself against a plotting table as the ship accelerated quickly, the increase in speed steepening the turn.

As nimble as *Ramage* was, she was still subject to the laws of physics. Even a gas-turbine-powered ship takes time to overcome the enormous inertia of eighty thousand tons of steel. The submarine, now moving at twenty-five knots, quickly closed on her.

"Combat, she's at fifteen hundred yards and *still* gaining on us," Digger snapped.

"Lord," Henning breathed. "We shoot now, it's just as likely to come back on us as hit her."

U-504

"Now." Merker put all the force he could behind the word, as though his conviction would help spur the torpedoes on

their way. Seconds later, the submarine shivered as the weapons left the tube.

USS RAMAGE

"Torpedoes inbound!" Digger screamed. He looked around frantically for Henning, his other half, his shipmate.

U-504

Thirty seconds, perhaps. Merker watched the sonar technicians monitor the wire-guided umbilicals that connected the torpedoes to the submarine. They were, he realized, the most experienced men in the German Fleet. Between Korea and the hunt in the North Sea, no one had executed more live torpedo shots than the two men sitting before him.

Although that could have changed. During the attacks on the British Fleet, it was possible that some other ship had fired more. But still, *U-504* was the first. He took some comfort in the thought, knowing that if the torpedoes now in the water did not seriously damage the ship, the Americans now a thousand yards away would bring every asset they had to bear on the Germans. With *U-504* as their first target.

USS RAMAGE

Bailey grabbed for a stanchion for support. *Ramage* cut sharply to port, then back to starboard, trying to shake the torpedoes.

U-504

"I thought it would feel different," Ehrlich said, his voice pitched high and straining to remain steady. "Beginning the next world war." His voice quivered on the last word.

Merker glanced up sharply. *Beginning the next*—suddenly, he felt dizzy.

That was exactly what he'd just done. Despite his orders

to keep the Americans out of the conflict at sea, he'd just substituted his personal pride and anguish for any trace of sound operational judgment.

With fifteen seconds left until the torpedoes reached the American ship—*ten seconds, since the wires are cut five seconds before they reach the ship*—he came to a realization. Instead of relief and victory, as he'd anticipated, shooting at this American ship had not killed the demons inside him. Just as his own reaction had surprised him off the coast of Korea, so now he paused.

The face of the dead child framed in his periscope came back to him.

USS RAMAGE

"All hands brace for shock! Torpedo, starboard side!" Bailey ignored the 1MC warnings and lunged out of combat, headed for sonar.

U-504

"No. I can't—stop them. *Now.*" Merker grabbed the weapons officer by the shoulder and shook him, dispelling the hypnotic effect of the torpedoes tracking across the green screen. *"Self-destruct—NOW."*

The officer's hand reached out as though in slow motion and paused over the plastic-shielded red toggle switch. Merker shouted something unintelligible, knocked the man's hand aside, flipped up the cover, and palmed the two switches up.

Time stood still for a moment—a year. He could almost see and hear the electrons race silently down the wires trailing the torpedoes and enter the tiny seeker-head brain that controls the torpedoes' targeting function. The invisible electron bundle rested for a moment on the appropriate relay, then fell forward, its tiny weight triggering a response. He saw—*felt*—the relay flip over.

Time resumed its normal course. A red light popped on over each of the two torpedo status indicators. Two sonarmen ripped off their headphones in anticipation.

Seconds later, they all heard the blast. Eight hundred meters forward of the submarine, two hundred meters from the ship, the torpedoes detonated.

USS *RAMAGE*

"Gone," Digger breathed. "Oh, dear sweet Jesus, they're gone." He stared at his scope, almost unwilling but desperately eager to believe what it showed.

"Plenty of water to spare," Henning said. He shook his head. "Two hundred yards—what the hell happened?"

Digger shook his head. "Hell if I know. The decoys, maybe, bad engineering—who knows?"

"She's slowing," Henning reported, studying his screen. "You hear it?"

Digger nodded.

Ramage continued to accelerate, finally breaking free from the ocean clinging to her hull. The speed indicator in sonar edged up to thirty knots, then continued creeping upward. Henning watched it while Digger monitored the distance from the submarine.

Eighty seconds later, it was time. *Ramage* was two thousand yards away from the U-boat, the distance increasing every second.

Digger flipped up the protective cover over the firing switch, looked over at Henning again. A hard smile immobilized Digger's face. "My turn," he said. He flipped the switch up and armed the torpedoes.

"YOU ESS WA SHI." A ghostly, burbling voice issued out from the far bulkhead.

Digger started. "What the hell?"

"VEEEE SURREN," the speaker said. "NO SHOOO."

"On Gertrude?" Henning asked. "Holy—"

The voice repeated the message, odd poppings and garglings distorting it into something barely understandable as a human voice. By the second repetition, Bailey was entering sonar.

"Are you going to shoot or—"

"Captain," Digger interrupted. "The sub. She's calling us."

"She can call us from hell," Bailey snapped.

"No, sir. Captain, she just surrendered. Look," Henning said. He pointed at the printout, and Digger nodded in confirmation. "Hull noise. She's surfacing."

" 'U.S. warship—we surrender—no shoot.' That's what she said," Digger added. He paused for a moment and pressed one hand to his sound-powered telephone earpiece and listened. "Captain, starboard lookout reports a submarine mast—no, wait, the entire sail—surfacing on our starboard bow."

"Have your people stand by on the torpedoes," Bailey snapped. "Get combat to man the .50-calibers on both sides. She so much as twitches and we shoot, so help me God." With that, she strode out of sonar and headed for the bridge.

The submarine was a black swath on the water, laying six hundred yards off their bow. The conning officer had already taken off the flank knots, and *Ramage* was cutting a large, graceful arc around the U-boat, slowly closing her.

Bailey examined the submarine through her binoculars. Two figures had just emerged in the sail. She could see a third head pop up, struggling with a large light. "Stand by to receive flashing light," she said automatically.

Forty-five seconds later, a breathless signalman confirmed what Bailey had already deciphered from the submarine's signal. *U-504,* Captain Merker commanding, tendered her respects and wished to surrender.

Bailey took a deep breath. It was the wolf-pack commander. She was certain.

"Ramage!" the British voice snapped. "What the hell do you think you're doing?" Admiral Richardson's voice was pitched two tones lower that usual, a deadly monotone.

"You heard the Gertrude transmission," Bailey answered. "That submarine just surfaced and surrendered. I'm preparing to board her."

"After it became apparent that her torpedoes had mal-

functioned! Surely you're not going to stand for this?''

"I'm not sure exactly what happened to her torpedoes, Admiral,'' Bailey replied. ''That will be one of the first things I ask them.''

''Dammit, madam, if you don't know how to handle this, get your ship the hell out of the way! That submarine—or one just like it, I don't give a flying fuck which—*murdered* four hundred of my men.''

''I know that, Admiral.'' Bailey raised her binoculars again. ''She's lofted a white flag, sir.''

''For Christ's sake, Bailey—'' Richardson raged.

''Exactly,'' she said softly without punching the transmit button.

Thirty minutes later, the ocean area five hundred yards around *Ramage* became uncomfortably crowded. The U-boat was now hove-to alongside the destroyer, hastily improvised rubber bumpers holding her off of the ship's hull. Five hundred yards past her, HMS *Illustrious* loomed, her guns pointedly fixed in *Ramage*'s direction. Equidistant on *Ramage*'s port side, HMS *Gallant* sat waiting. The horizon was dotted with the upper masts of more British warships racing to the scene, and one new arrival was already taking station five hundred yards immediately in front of *Ramage*. Three British ASW helicopters crowded the airspace around the American ship.

Bailey stared down from the starboard bridge wing. Three men were now in the conning tower of the sub. One, judging by his age, was apparently an enlisted watchstander. The other two, both clad in dress uniforms, were officers.

The captain, Bailey concluded, studying the two.

Sixth Fleet had sounded puzzled at first, then seriously alarmed, at the turn of events. Fifteen minutes ago, they'd promised her an immediate answer on what to do with the German submarine. Fourteen minutes ago, the British warships had started closing in. Bailey lifted her binoculars and searched the bridge wing of *Illustrious*. The spare, rigid figure of Admiral Richardson stared back.

She swore silently, all the while holding a neutral expression on her face for the benefit of the men perched on the submarine below her. She tried not to stare overtly as she assessed them.

The German captain finally looked up and acknowledged the scrutiny. Bailey saw a puzzled expression on his face as his gaze flicked up and down the bridge railing. Finally, his eyes returned to her. An odd smile, then the German officer lifted one hand as though in greeting. Midway up, the gesture turned into a salute. Bailey straightened and returned the traditional military greeting sharply.

Hell with this, she decided suddenly. *Sixth Fleet's done nothing for us so far. Why the hell should I expect anything different now? They can say I'm in command, but I can't even depend on them to make that a reality. Collins is right about one thing: Command is something you take, not are given.* "Boats, get the ship rigged to receive these people."

"Aye, aye, sir," the man replied. It was not necessary— Bailey had already seen the chief boatswain's mate surrounded by a buzzing herd of deck apes rigging the gear the deck below.

"XO, go—no, never mind. I'll be on the weather decks. I imagine the captain and one or two of his men will come aboard. Appropriate honors, until I say otherwise."

"Aye, aye, Captain," Collins answered. The last ten minutes had leached all emotion out of her voice. Bailey pulled open the back door to the bridge, leaving Collins to puzzle out exactly what honors were required.

The captain of the U-boat climbed up the accommodation ladder first, stopping briefly before stepping aboard the ship. Four gongs rang out. He lifted one eyebrow, then tendered a salute to Bailey. She returned it, startling the German officer out of the world-weary equanimity that seemed his normal demeanor. As he stepped forward and his foot landed on the ship, a final gong signaling his arrival on board rang out.

"Good afternoon, Captain," Bailey said in German. The language she'd learned as an army brat, perfected at NSA, came automatically to her lips. "Do you speak English?"

"I speak some English—badly, but maybe enough," he

answered, his accent thick and harsh. "I am *Kapitan* Merker, commander of this *Unterseeboot*—submarine."

"Commander Jerusha Bailey, commanding officer of the USS *Ramage,* Captain. Pleased to have you aboard."

The submariner pointed at the British warships assembling off the destroyer's bow. "Maybe not? The British—they are not friends. Not now."

"Do you require any immediate assistance?" Bailey asked. "Any help—ship okay?" she amended, as the German's face clouded over. "Medical, food?" she added in German.

The German's face cleared. "No. We are fine, thank you." Even with a strong Teutonic accent, the man's speech was improving with every sentence, as though he'd once been fairly competent in English and now had just to dust off rusty skills.

"This situation—you understand, I am waiting for orders from my superiors. It is unprecedented, to say the least," Bailey said. "If it is convenient, we will take this discussion into my wardroom. Some coffee, perhaps?"

The German nodded once, sharply. "I understand. Coffee, thank you."

"Please follow me." Bailey led the way through a hatch and onto the second level. Merker followed her down the ladder and into the wardroom, carefully cleared of all personnel except the intelligence officer.

The intelligence officer poured coffee for both and politely offered sugar and cream. Merker's sharp, cynical look at the younger officer told Bailey he knew exactly *what,* if not *who,* the other man was. A silver plate of doughnuts and pastries left over from the morning meal rested on the sideboard, and Bailey reached for it. "I can offer you something more substantial, if you like."

"Maybe we wait and see what Sixth Fleet says." He pronounced the operational command's title carefully but accurately.

"I would like to ask you," Bailey began, pausing for a moment as the intelligence officer stiffened. *Fuck him,* she decided. *Maybe I'm not supposed to interrogate this fellow or whatever, but it was my ship he was shooting at. If anyone has the right to answers, it's me.* She pinned the younger officer with a glare and continued. "The torpedoes," she said, cutting to the heart of the matter. "What happened?"

"I . . ." the German started. He stopped and looked perplexed, as though the right words were momentarily escaping him. "I stop them," he settled for finally.

"Why?"

The German shrugged, the motion eloquent in its fatalism. "We are not at war with United States," he said carefully. "To shoot—not good." Something flashed across the man's face, a look of resignation, regret, and fear. "Not here."

"Not here? What do you mean?"

Merker told her. As the German talked, something seemed to break loose inside him. Although his words were still stilted and stumbling, Bailey had no doubt that she was hearing the truth.

Finally, Merker finished. Bailey took a deep breath and realized she'd almost been holding it. "I think—I think I will need to tell someone about this. Immediately," Bailey said. "One more question about your mines, the ones that were armed with torpedoes. Were they carrying nerve gas? Biological weapons or nuclear material?"

The technical words were evidently almost identical to their German counterparts. Bailey listened as Merker pronounced them slowly, puzzled. "Tabun? Of course not. If someone has told you this, they are . . . are . . . not true. We used bottom-moored contact mines, not torpedo warheads. Your analysis is wrong."

"You will excuse me for a few moments? And understand if I have you escorted for the moment?"

The German nodded as though it made no difference. Bailey reached for the ship's telephone, dialed the bridge, and asked the XO to send the master at arms and a senior officer to the wardroom. Five minutes later, she was striding aft with the intelligence officer.

The message was short, fewer than two screens on the WHISPER message traffic program. It summarized the surrender of the U-boat, Bailey's present tactical situation surrounded by the irate British warships, and ended with the startling conclusion that Germany was responsible for the attack on the USS *Wasp* and that data concerning German NBC capabilities should be viewed with skepticism.

Bailey punched the SEND menu entry, then leaned back in her hard-backed chair. *He's not lying. Maybe he doesn't know the truth, but he's not lying about what he does know. And if he's not, then Richardson is.*

23

---

8 MARCH 2002:
THE ENGLISH CHANNEL

USS *RAMAGE*

The situation continued through the night at a standstill as
Bailey waited for orders from Sixth Fleet. Merker remained
on board, his submarine loosely moored to the destroyer.
Ramage maneuvered slowly, carefully, to avoid damaging
the boat. The next morning, the tactical situation began
changing.

"The Swiftsure's back," Henning announced over the
bitch box. "Twenty knots."

"Not maneuvering?" Bailey shot a puzzled look at the
tactical display. "And what's she doing heading north
when there're still U-boats down there?"

"Steady on her course, Captain. It'll bring her within ten
thousand yards of us if she maintains it."

There was something off-kilter about the Swiftsure. First,
her course put her on an intercept with *Ramage,* and was
not the shortest course back to her home port. While Richardson had been markedly less than forthright about his
submarines' positions, at least he'd started informing her
when one would be transiting within weapons range.

Second, Captain Merker's insistence that the Germans
had no plans to use Tabun against the British or the Americans rang true, particularly after his damning confession
about Korea. There were too many questions and not
enough answers. If what the German said was true . . .

An ugly suspicion dawned. She debated briefly calling

Richardson and demanding an explanation for the Swift-sure, but decided against it. The old admiral was holding something back, of that she was sure. And until her supposed ally put his cards on the table, it never hurt to know a little bit more than her opponent.

"Get Petty Officer Digger up here. *Now.*"

"You understand, it's probably nothing." Bailey stared at Digger. "That British Swiftsure submarine has every reason in the world to be hauling ass out of here."

"Yes, ma'am."

"But you watch that boat. Run it as a practice drill, get a targeting solution on her the second you see her. And let me know when she's in weapons range."

Digger regarded his commanding officer gravely. "In our range, ma'am—or when we're in hers?"

"Guess we're not the only ones jumping through hoops," Carlisle said suddenly. "The other friendly is back—I mean, the one we *really* know is friendly."

"The U.S. boomer?" Lieutenant Boston asked.

Carlisle nodded. "She's in and out on our passive system, running about two miles behind the Brit. A lot quieter than the Swiftsure. I almost missed her myself."

"Wonder if the Swiftsure knows she's being followed?"

"Don't know. She's partially deaf, as fast as she's going. And that boat's quiet—oh, *man,* is she quiet! Don't know how the hell we ever got her in the first place before."

"Just good at it, I guess."

"But right now you're holding them, and they aren't holding you," Boston pointed out. "So what does that tell you?"

"That sometimes it's better to be lucky than good, Lieutenant. That's all."

"I'll let *Ramage* know she'd better put another plate on the table. She's getting more company than she expected."

The news that the U.S. submarine was hot on the heels of the Swiftsure decided Bailey. Before that, there'd been no tactical advantage to telling Admiral Richardson what she knew. Now, however, her options were rapidly increasing.

Communications took just a few moments to set up the private circuit she always used with Richardson. It took the TAO on the British ship longer to hunt down his admiral. Finally, the clipped voice answered.

Bailey took a deep breath. Whatever discussions were taking place in the Pentagon, in the embassy, and on Sixth Fleet staff, her problems were here and now. She couldn't wait, not with the Swiftsure inbound.

"And why the hell should I come over to *Ramage*?" Richardson demanded. "The only reason I'd do it is to get close enough to that bastard to shoot him myself."

"Admiral, please. There are matters we need to discuss. You remember the matters we were discussing out on the weather decks? About some old war material?"

"I remember. What's your point?" With her newly suspicious ears, Bailey heard a tinge of uncertainty in the admiral's voice.

"We've examined the contents of the U-boat rather thoroughly," she lied. "It appears your suspicions were correct. That puts quite a different light on this situation here, one that I think we should discuss face to face. Admiral, I have to apologize—it looks like we may be closer together on a decision on this than I thought."

A long silence. Then, "Very well. If you've finally come to your senses, expect me in thirty minutes."

Bailey broke the connection and slowly replaced the receiver.

Thirty minutes later, Admiral Richardson was sitting across the table from her in her cabin. New lines creased his face, furrowing the patrician brow and cutting funnels from the corner of his mouth to midchin. The older man's complexion had dulled from clear ivory to dirty gray.

"Out with it," Richardson said peremptorily. "If you have something on your mind, speak up." Despite the signs of age, his voice still bore the sharp note of command.

"I lied," Bailey said without hesitation. "Unfortunately, I have reason to believe that you understand that practice very well."

"I won't stand for—"

"Sit down, Admiral. You're the one who needs to start talking. First, you've got one minute to explain why a British submarine is headed toward my ship at flank speed. Second—and this can wait until you've broken off the submarine—you will explain to me why you lied about the Tabun." She watched the man's eyes dull. "Now, the Swiftsure."

The silence stretched into minutes. Finally, the admiral muttered something.

"What?" Bailey smacked her hand on the table.

"It was only an option," the admiral repeated wearily. His eyes refused to meet Bailey's, instead fixing on the boar's head mounted on the wall. "I wouldn't have used it, you know."

"*Used what?* Dammit, Admiral—no . . ." Bailey's voice trailed off. When she finally resumed speaking, her voice was hard. "You wouldn't have dared."

The admiral shook his head, still not looking up.

Bailey bolted to her feet. She reached over, grabbed the other man firmly by the elbow, and dragged him out of his chair. She slammed the admiral into the bulkhead. "We will walk to sonar now, you and I. You will get on Gertrude and call this whole thing off. How *dare* you even think about putting a torpedo into that submarine while she's tied up next to me. How *dare* you!"

"Oh, stop it." The admiral jerked his arms down. Bailey let him shake off her grip. "Haven't you learned anything at all? Tell me, please, exactly what you think torpedoing that U-boat would achieve. Or are you still the naive little woman playing naval officer I met four weeks ago?"

Bailey stepped back, suddenly cautious. *Lusitania.* She felt the blood drain from her face, then the hard flush of anger replace the pallor.

"It wouldn't do anything for Britain, would it?" she said slowly. "Sinking another German submarine, I mean. You've already several cluttering up the channel, and Germany has plenty more where they came from. Britain's still alone in the fight, along with a little help from the other NATO nations, and half your battle group is burning as we speak. You don't have a chance of winning, not with the odds like this. Unless . . .''

"Unless there were a reason for America to enter into the conflict immediately," the admiral finished. "Finally. Are you really so dense?"

"I guess I am. That, or naive, as you said. I thought the term 'allies' implied we weren't trying to kill each other, if nothing more." She paused, the inevitable conclusion finally dawning in her sleep-deprived brain. The blood drained out of her face. "My God—*Weeks*. You sunk *Weeks*." She stared at him, horrified.

"*Count the cost,*" the admiral snapped. "Each day that Germany is allowed to grow stronger, to solidify her position on the Continent will eventually mean ten thousand more troops dead taking it back from her. And was there any chance that we would get assistance from the United States? Of course not. Not unless there were some development so compelling, so horrifyingly directed at your country that your public would *demand* that you intervene. Look at World War I, World War II. Nothing mattered to you Yanks until your own ships started suffering. The Germans understood that—why the hell do you think they went to such lengths to *avoid* attacking your ship?"

"The only way you could capitalize on this situation was for an American ship to take a casualty, preferably one that came from a German submarine. So you were going to take a shot at *Ramage* from your Swiftsure, then blame it on the U-boat alongside. By the time the analysts figured it out, we'd be committed over here, and we'd never admit the truth," Bailey said. "As you told me before about the U.S. submarine—they're deniable." She stopped and waited for his response.

God, do I feel old. Older than this bastard. European wars, their way of thinking—you get fooled by thinking that they're like us. Two hundred years of separation, though, make for different militaries. It's like we said in the beginning—two peoples separated by a common language. But it's more than just the way we pronounce words, more than drinking coffee instead of tea.

"You have some code word to tell her to break off, I hope," Bailey said finally.

Richardson nodded. "The word is Destiny. For all the good it will do you. The authentication codes are back on the ship—I don't have them with me. And you can bet she's going to ask for them."

"Then you'll call the ship, tell them to do it." Bailey glanced at her watch. "Fifteen minutes until she gets within my ASROC range, Admiral. I will use them—don't doubt me on that."

"I don't know if they will obey. They'll assume I'm under duress here, you know."

"Do they know what the Swiftsure is doing?"

"The captain does—no one else."

"Then you'd better convince him—just like you convinced me last week. Come on." Bailey grabbed the man by his shoulders, spun him around, and shoved him out the door of her cabin.

An ensign standing in the passageway waiting to see Bailey watched curiously as his captain shoved the British admiral toward the ladder that led down to combat, then shrugged. The ways of senior officers were clearly beyond his understanding.

"I think he believes me," Richardson said wearily. "He sounded as though he did."

"He better. Is there anything else you need to tell him?"

"No. He either will or he won't." The admiral sat slumped in a chair in front of a console. On the big-screen display in front of her, the computer symbol for the British submarine continued its northerly track.

"Combat, sonar. Someone's talking on Gertrude— sounds like a Limey," Digger's voice said. The admiral grimaced.

"*Must* you people use that word?" he snapped, showing some signs of his earlier temperament.

Bailey ignored him and turned to the TAO. "Has the sub shown any signs of changing course or speed?"

The TAO complied. "No change, sir—ma'am, I mean," he reported.

"Come on." Bailey took Richardson by the arm and half-shoved him toward sonar. "You're not the only one who has a trump card." *A trump—why did that word come to mind?* she wondered. *Something about it—trump, trump, why? Ah.* She stopped, jerking the other man back. "The Tabun. That was a lie, too. You knew what our likely re-action would be to the very idea of chemical weapons based on Desert Storm."

Richardson sighed. "Like any good deception, it was partially true. For years we've had reports that there were stockpiles of Tabun left over, supposedly hidden away for a last defense of Germany during World War II. The an-ecdotes were never sufficiently supported by collateral ev-idence to convince us. The fissionable material—very close to being completely true. The United States has ignored the smuggling of the material out of Russia for years now. There's no doubt Germany has taken possession of at least part of Ukraine's stockpile. But the chemical weapons, par-ticularly on a weapon that might affect your own ship—now, that's a different story, isn't it?"

Bailey restrained the urge to strike the man. She settled for planting one hand on the man's chest and shoving hard enough to put the admiral off-balance. The older man stum-bled, then caught the side of the sonar hatch and steadied himself. "I was right when I said I ought to have you shot," Richardson said evenly.

"Being court-martialed for striking a senior officer is the least of my worries right now. Yours, too, in about thirty seconds. Get in there." Bailey motioned at sonar.

"Carry on," Bailey said as she entered, forestalling the reflexive leaps to their feet at the sight of the admiral. "Digger, is Gertrude up?"

"Far as I know, Captain. It was when we came on watch, and we just heard that Li—uh, British transmission."

"Good. Watch the admiral, son. He's not to touch any-thing or even move from that bench." Bailey pointed at the padded seat along the back wall. "If he does, coldcock him. On my orders, son."

The sonarman nodded, his eyes dark. Bailey had the dis-tinct feeling that Digger had been every bit as uneasy as she was about the Swiftsure now transiting toward them.

"Speak slowly, Captain," Henning reminded her as he handed her the Gertrude telephone.

Bailey nodded. She took a deep breath and thought out what she would say. She lifted the underwater telephone to her mouth.

"U.S. Naval Unit, this is USS *Ramage*," she said slowly.

"Naval unit—that's what we call our own submarines," Carlisle said.

"British unit you are trailing has demonstrated hostile intentions. Request you surface and clear the area. I intend to take the British Swiftsure submarine with ASROC in fifteen mikes. Over."

She repeated her message three times. There was no response.

"One more time," Bailey said.

The admiral appeared almost to be dozing. He had not moved since Bailey had directed him to the bench, and his eyes were drifting shut.

"Turn up the volume on the speaker," she said.

The noise hissed and popped as Carlisle complied. Suddenly the gentle wash of water sounds over the speaker gave way to a squeal, then the hard click of someone keying a microphone. The voice was sepulchrous and warbling as it multipathed through the water.

A ghostly voice said. "Authenticate," and followed the command with a series of figures taken from the crypto card of the day. A strong Mississippi accent added an extra syllable to the word.

Bailey breathed a sigh of relief.

Carlisle checked the small rectangle hanging in front of him and provided the correct response to the voice, then followed it with an authentication demand of his own. Finally he turned back to her. "Correct response by the submarine, ma'am. That's one of ours. And she's taking *Ramage* at her word and getting the hell out of Dodge. But first, her skipper wants to talk to you. In person."

•   •   •

Ten minutes, two hundred yards off *Ramage*'s port bow, a sleek black hull slowly slid up from the depths. While the lookout screamed bearing and range information into his sound-powered telephone, two figures appeared in the sail. One looked across at *Ramage* through binoculars while the other hastily ran a flag up the detachable yardarm.

An American flag.

Moments later, Captain Bailey and the sub CO were discussing options that couldn't be addressed on Gertrude. Not with the British forces listening in.

"As I said, you wouldn't have gotten involved for years," Richardson said tiredly. "A few improvisations on the truth, and we had a chance to stop this madness before it started again. Sixty-three years ago, it took America two years to come to our aid. It wouldn't have this time."

"*Victory,*" Bailey said suddenly. "You were willing to kill four hundred of your own men to make me believe the U-boats were carrying Tabun?"

"Perhaps, but it wasn't necessary. Once they were hit, they did a damned fine imitation of it. They were towed out of your view, then released to steam under their own power. There were casualties, yes—the torpedo *did* come from a German U-boat, that much was true. The tragedy wasn't a lie. An exaggeration would be more like it."

"Convenient for you," Bailey said.

The admiral finally met her eyes for the first time since admitting the truth about the Swiftsure. "I don't make history, madam. I just use it."

Five minutes after the U.S. submarine surfaced and the British warship monitored the conversation with the sub— the American boat had declined to give either her hull number or her name—the underwater telephone gurgled with transmissions again. This time the voice was British.

The Swiftsure reversed its course 180 degrees and slowed to a quiet, undetectable speed. As she faded off the sonar display, she was headed south toward the English Channel at a peaceful five knots.

U-504

The German radio operator clambered up from the submarine into the conning tower. He snapped his safety line onto the padeye, giving himself enough line to reach the malfunctioning antenna coupler. He paused for a moment, reveling in the fresh air and sunshine, something most of the crew didn't expect to see for another two months. They'd all appreciated the gushes of fresh air flooding the submarine from the outside, but actually being outside was a rare privilege.

He moved to the back of the conning tower to the metal casing that housed the faulty equipment and sat down cross-legged on the deck in front of it. He unscrewed two metal plates, setting them carefully down on the deck beside him and slipping the screws into his breast pocket, and stared into the exposed equipment cubbyhole.

The coupler looked intact. He sighed and reached for a multimeter, resigning himself to a couple of hours of tracing circuits and connections in an effort to isolate the problem. He paused as a gleam of new metal caught his attention, then bent over and looked up to examine the ceiling of the space carefully.

Tucked back into the far left-hand corner was a square metal shape. He frowned and reached out to touch it, then stopped himself with the reflexive caution of a technician accustomed to working with high voltages. A new filter maybe. Probably the source of the failure, since the standardized troubleshooting procedures hadn't pinpointed the problem. Typical of the shipyard, he thought, to install new equipment and not bother to tell them what it was. Or how to fix it.

He noticed a small switch on the side of the box. A reset button, perhaps. He weighed the advantage of finishing the job quickly against the disadvantage of having to return to the interior of the submarine. If it worked, he decided, there was no need to actually *tell* his supervisor immediately. He could try it, then spend a few more minutes relaxing in the thin sunshine before returning below.

He reached out and pushed the button. The multimeter

indicated that the current flow to the affected coupler was restored. He smiled, stood up, and leaned back against the sail to let the sun shine on his face.

FOUR HUNDRED FEET BELOW THE SURFACE

Ten miles away, the old German mine heard its wake-up call. Relays still untouched by the corrosive sea clicked over silently. The mechanism ran its self-check routines, decided it was still functional, and transmitted a GO signal. Then it tripped its magnetic sensors on-line and waited.

24

USS RAMAGE

"Now, *that's* odd," Henning said.

"What?" Digger asked.

"Look for yourself." He pointed out a fat blip on the passive screen. "Low-frequency signals—strong, close aboard. Ten-second transmission, a break, then ten more seconds at a different frequency."

"A sub?"

Henning studied the screen for a moment. "No. I remember where I've seen it before, though. Or something like it. There were some scientists from the Woods Hole Oceanographic Center doing tests on low-frequency, long-range transmissions. They had a seabed transmitter that put out a signal a lot like this. Strong, low-frequency, with a pattern of transmissions. They planted sonobuoys at long ranges to see how far away they could pick up the signals with different models. It was weird—the signal was so strong that the minor-lobe detections looked just like the main bearing. You can tell generally what direction it's coming from, but I never did figure out a way to isolate the bearing."

"So what's causing it?" Digger asked, his curiosity now piqued.

"Hell if I know, but it's about the least threatening signal we've seen in two months."

"You want to run toward it, try to isolate the bearing?"

"No, like I said—it's damned near impossible to get a refined direction on them. Too much noise in the water for our gear. If anything, I'd like to turn away from it so we decrease the noise. I think it might be to the east. See if the TAO will try putting it in our baffles. It might not make any difference, but it's worth finding out."

"Okay." Digger picked up the mike and called the TAO.

THREE HUNDRED EIGHTY-TWO FEET BELOW THE SURFACE

Ever since it had heard the unique two-tone acoustic signal that enabled its firing circuits, the mine had been ready. Since then, a number of ships had passed over it, each one contributing magnetic flux to charge the battery without ever coming close enough to trigger a reaction. Until now.

The mine felt two gentle tugs of metal masses impinge its rudimentary magnetic sensing circuits. It paused, considering whether either signal was strong enough to warrant activating the warhead. The stronger signal began diminishing almost immediately, but the second one held steady. It waited.

USS *RAMAGE*

"TAO said to wait," Digger said, replacing the mike in its bracket. "We just stared a turn into the wind to launch the helo. Maybe after that we can try a few turns."

Henning glanced up at the course indicator repeater on the bulkhead. "Fine with me. I'm not getting anything right now anyway. The transmitter may be on a long-interval schedule."

"Well, it's not like it's going to be a high priority anyway." Digger smiled. "Nice to have something radiating we don't have to worry about for a change, isn't it?"

Bailey escorted Admiral Richardson to the flight deck. The British officer paused at the edge of the hangar, then turned to look at his escort. Disdain flickered across his face as he eyed the two sailors carrying sidearms.

"That wasn't necessary, you know," the admiral said.

"I decide what's necessary from here on out, sir," Bailey said. "First on my list is getting you off my ship."

The admiral started to hold out his hand, then thought better of it. "You might understand someday, Bailey. If you spend enough time in this part of the world."

Bailey regarded him coldly. "As you said, we're two peoples separated by a common language. Your definition of the word 'ally' doesn't match ours."

The admiral nodded abruptly, turned, and walked out to the helo. Bailey watched it rev up, lift awkwardly off the deck, and veer off. HMS *Victory,* returned to active service now that her part in the deception was revealed, was clearly visible on the horizon to the west. She saw the British ship turn toward *Ramage* as it hunted for the right relative wind for flight operations.

Bailey watched the helicopter circle the British warship lazily, waiting for the destroyer to steady up. *Victory* finally settled on a course parallel to *Ramage*'s, and the helicopter began its cautious approach. The British ship was aft of *Ramage,* showing her port quarter. The helicopter disappeared behind her, its final landing approach obscured by the superstructure. Bailey stood staring at the other ship, waiting for her to make a turn that would open up the distance between the two ships.

THREE HUNDRED EIGHTY-TWO FEET BELOW THE SURFACE

Another one. The mine quivered as the details of a new magnetic signature coursed through the circuit. Close, growing stronger by the minute, but still below the preset firing threshold.

Now. The firing circuit clicked closed and sent out a small electrical signal to the barnacle-encrusted canister. Two seconds later, a small explosive charge broke the metal container loose from the muck. Compressed air surged into two bladders, creating positive buoyancy. The entire apparatus arrowed up to the surface.

The pressure of the water on the canister decreased as it neared the surface. Finally, the thin metal shell was no longer able to contain its contents. It exploded outward in a spray of shrapnel that did no damage to the relatively calm seas.

The gas contained inside it was another matter altogether.

USS RAMAGE

Victory finally started a smart turn away from *Ramage*. Bailey watched her port come into view and waited for her to steady on her new course.

Suddenly a red haze thickened the surface of the water around *Victory*. She stared at it for a moment, puzzled, then felt her guts clench into a hard, cold ball. She darted out onto the flight deck, grabbed the first sailor she could reach wearing a headset, and screamed out an order to get inside the ship. The sailor turned pale and ran, relaying the order over the flight deck circuit.

The TAO, monitoring the flight deck circuit inside combat, grabbed the 1MC. Seconds later, hatches slammed shut and the gentle wheeze of the ship's ventilation system stopped as the ship set general quarters.

Ramage's deck heeled sharply as she leaned into a hard turn to starboard. One of the padded doughnuts between the U-boat and *Ramage* slipped out of place, and the bow of the submarine slammed into the side of the ship, scraping paint and creasing the metal in a five-foot streak.

U-504

U-504's radio operator had no warning. The collision catapulted him out of the conning tower and over the side. He swung out away from the U-boat to the maximum length of his tether, only ten feet above the waves at the end of his arc. The line held. On the return arc, his head hit the submarine's hull, killing him instantly. As the two ships continued their turn, his body dangled lifelessly above the waves.

USS *RAMAGE*

"Zoom in on the British ship," Bailey ordered.

The TAO nodded and carefully moved the joystick that controlled the camera focused on the flight deck. The depression angle decreased and *Ramage*'s wake came into view, followed shortly by the blur of the British ship. The TAO tweaked the focus knob, and the lines of the ship sharpened.

Bailey could see five sailors sprawled awkwardly on *Victory*'s forecastle. Another body hung lifelessly over the safety line. The bridge looked deserted. The only movement on the ship was the relentless rotation of the radar.

Combat was silent, as quiet as she'd ever heard it. Every operator not immediately occupied with his or her scope turned to watch the small monitor that displayed the aft camera's picture. Bailey could feel the horror working its way among them, read it in the pale faces and shell-shocked eyes of the sailors.

"Her bridge wing hatches are shut," she said out loud. "There's a good chance she was far enough away and responded quickly enough to save most of them." She wondered for a moment whether *Victory* had as effective a positive pressure system as *Ramage*. Without that, it was only a matter of time until the deadly molecules of Tabun seeped in through tiny cracks and gapped seals.

"Sir, *Victory* is coming back around. She's—she looks like her rudder is set at a constant angle, sir," the surface plot radar operator said quietly.

"Assuming a constant turning radius, what's the closest point of approach?"

"Twenty miles, if we maintain current course and speed," the man answered.

Bailey nodded. It should be enough. It had to be.

Suddenly, metal clanged against the starboard side of the ship. Bailey swore quietly as she remembered the submarine cinched to their flank. "Do we still have communications with them?" she asked the TAO.

"The sound-powered line we ran down to them is inoperative," the TAO answered after a moment. "They might have severed it dogging down their hatch.''

"Try them on IAD—International Air Distress," Bailey
ordered.

Moments later, she heard Merker's distinctive voice
against a background of noise and other voices yelling. Ignoring the commotion, Bailey summarized the situation for
the submarine captain, emphasizing the possible danger
from a gas warhead in the mine's torpedo.

"Cut us loose," the German officer demanded.

"I can't. Not without sending men outside. I'm not willing to risk that yet, not until we know for sure that there
aren't more of these—devices—in the area. Do you have
any damage?''

Static filled the airwaves for a few moments. Finally,
Merker's voice came back. "Not serious. A small leak from
the collision. Controllable at this depth, but not good for
submerging.'' Bailey heard the man sigh heavily. "It seems
we are tied together for a while. Warn us of any turns,
Kapitan. We will use our rudder, try to minimize the damage next time.''

"At the present time, my only intention is to put as much
distance between this ship and *Victory* as I can, but we will
advise you if we intend to maneuver.'' Bailey suddenly
became aware of a figure shifting impatiently from side to
side in front of her.

"What is our current distance from *Victory*?" Merker
asked.

Bailey focused on the sonarman standing in front of her.
Digger looked worried. "What is it, Petty Officer Digger?"

"Captain, that chemical attack on the Brits—I think I
know what caused it.''

U-504

Merker waited for an answer for a few minutes, then hung
up the mike. The lack of response did not bode well for
keeping the submarine tethered to the destroyer. He swore
quietly for a moment, then reached a decision.

"Assemble a damage control team with axes," he ordered. "If the Americans won't cut us loose, we'll have to do it ourselves."

"Sir, the gas—" Kraeken said.

"Is twenty miles behind us and growing farther each second." Merker touched his pocket gently. The blurred outline of his sidearm was visible. "There's no danger."

Kraeken nodded, his eyes on the gun. He turned away and began barking orders to the enlisted men.

USS RAMAGE

"This was some sort of signal, you say?" Bailey asked.

"Had to be," Henning answered. "The timing was too coincidental. Captain, we've been steaming around these waters for a couple of months. If there'd been an acoustic exercise, we ought to have heard it before now."

"From whom? How?"

"The only thing I can tell you, sir, is that it was close aboard. Real close." Henning looked pointedly at the starboard bulkhead.

U-504

The team of men and cutting tools assembled below the short ladder leading up into the conning tower. Merker ignored the fear on their faces and quickly explained what they were to do. The most senior man acknowledged the orders quietly, then turned and began barking directions at the others.

USS RAMAGE

"They were working in the conning tower when we saw it," the OOD answered. "There was one sailor up there. He kept ducking down out of view, so I assume there are some equipment access panels near the deck."

"What happened to him?" Bailey asked.

The OOD pointed at the rope still stretched tautly from the padeye to the edge of the sail. It shifted back and forth,

fraying against the metal, clearly still supporting the body
it was intended to protect.

"*Kapitan* Merker—dammit, Merker, answer me!" Bailey
stared at the mike, frustrated. There was no reply.

U-504

The first man paused just below the hatch to the conning
tower and looked back down. "Ignore them," the submarine *captain* directed. He reached up to turn off the speaker.

USS RAMAGE

"Okay, *Kapitan,* I know you hear me. If you won't answer,
at least listen. Just before *Victory* was attacked, you had a
man working up in the conning tower. We have reason to
believe that he may have been working on a radio circuit
or a transmitter. My sonar detected two low-frequency
bursts three minutes before the cloud appeared on the surface. It's probable that the transmission armed whatever it
was that hit *Victory. Kapitan,* I don't think you knew about
this, but if it was your ship, we have to do something about
it before you set off any other devices. Do you copy?"
     Bailey waited for an answer.

U-504

Kapitan Merker paused at the mention of the man in the
conning tower, his hand inches from the speaker knob. The
antenna coupler—was it possible? He shook his head, remembering the flood of engineers and technicians who had
been working on every corner of the boat during her three
days in port, remembering the two men he'd seen in the
conning tower. What had they been doing up there? He
realized now that he'd never gotten an answer to that question.
     With his men poised on the ladder, he considered his
options. The man had been working on the gear, that much
was true. If Bailey was telling the truth about the sonar

transmissions, then it was possible that there was some equipment installed on his boat that Merker didn't know about.

More than possible, he decided. Considering the timing of the attack, it was probable. Without knowing how the devices were triggered, he had no way of stopping further attacks. And if the warship he was tied up to became incapacitated, the destroyer could very well batter the much smaller submarine into shreds before the submarine could free itself from the nest of lines binding it to the ship. Moreover, every risk he'd taken—surfacing in front of the ship to draw it in for the attack, disabling the torpedoes, even the attack on the *Wasp*—would have been completely in vain. If an American warship steamed into a cloud of Tabun, the United States would join in on the war against Germany immediately. As hard-pressed as they might be to maintain both the Korean front and the European one, eventually the massive military-industrial complex would gear up enough to support both theaters. After that, it would merely be a matter of time.

He remembered the look on Ehrlich's face as he'd talked about starting the next world war. This time, Merker decided, a German wouldn't be the one to do it.

USS RAMAGE

Bailey slammed the mike down. "He's not answering. Dammit, what—"

Suddenly a signal broke through the static. "Captain Bailey, we will discuss this possibility."

Ten minutes later, the two captains arrived at a plan that suited them. Merker would go ahead with his plan to send his men into the sail, with one change. Leading the party would be his most experienced electronics technician and his senior radio operator. A duplicate team from *Ramage* would be lowered down to join them, armed with electronics test gear and axes. If the two teams found nothing out of the ordinary in the sail equipment compartment, the *Ramage* sailors would return to the ship and sever the lines

tying it to their ship. Should they not do so, the Germans
would cut the lines from their end.

"I hope to God this works," Collins said quietly.

"Me, too, XO," Bailey answered. "If the activating
mechanism's not on that U-boat, then the North Sea is just
one big booby trap."

U-504

The two teams were crammed into the conning tower
within the hour, each figure clad in protective gear and a
mask. One German peered into the access panel while another hauled the line attached to the radio operator up. He
pulled the dead man into the sail, his motions peculiarly
gentle and respectful even in the bulky chemical protection
gear. Bailey saw the body sink out of view, presumably
passed down into the sub.

The German inspecting the gear motioned abruptly to
one of the Americans, pointed at the access panel, and ges-
ticulated. The American sailor crouched down beside him.
The two communicated by gestures and shouts, and appeared to arrive at some agreement. The American fished
a screwdriver out of his pocket and handed it to the
German. Moments later, the German stood, holding a shiny
square metal box in his hands.

The four technicians shook hands with each other, and
the Americans started clambering awkwardly back up the
cargo net to the ship. As they reached the top and turned
to wave, the German held up the screwdriver and waved
it. The American sailor who'd loaned it to him motioned
him to keep it.

USS RAMAGE

"We think that was it, Captain." Digger was still clad in
the bulky chem suit, although he'd removed the suffocating
hood. His hair was damp with sweat and plastered to his
head.

"You could communicate with each other well enough?"
Bailey asked.

"He made it clear that that box he hauled out wasn't supposed to be there. From what I saw of it, it looked like a signal generator. Feed it in series with their normal communications setup, set it to trigger on a particular day or when they reach a certain point in the ocean, and that submarine could have been an electronic carrier pigeon. If their passive gear doesn't do as well in the low frequencies as ours does, they'd never even know they were transmitting. Hell, you do it right and you can use the whole outer submarine hull as an antenna—transmit a real low-frequency signal with one that long."

"How are we going to know for sure, though?" the XO asked. "If that wasn't what triggered those mines, then we could still be headed for one right now."

"I think we'll give them a few hours to take a look at it," Bailey said. "After all, they're bound to know their gear better than we do. We'll stay buttoned up for now, though. No point in taking any chances."

"Captain," the TAO broke in, "we're getting indications that the Germans are transmitting on their high-frequency circuits."

"Not talking to mines," Digger said quickly. "Nothing but a low-frequency signal is going to penetrate very far underwater. Must be a communications circuit."

Bailey nodded. "Is it encrypted?"

"Yes, sir," the TAO said.

"I'd expect that," she said finally. "The question now is, just who are they talking to? That's almost as important as what they're saying."

U-504

"What do you mean?" Merker demanded. With the unknown box removed from the circuit, his command frequencies worked again. On the other end of this particular stream of electrons was Admiral Braudel's chief of staff.

"Since when am I required to provide explanations to go with your orders?" the man answered sharply. "Just do as you're told. Reinstall the equipment and conduct a slow-speed transit between the following coordinates.'' He followed the statement with a series of latitudes and longitudes. Merker wrote the coordinates, repeated them back, then signed off.

As Merker hung the mike up, he became aware of the focused intensity of the men's faces around him. He considered ignoring the questions evident in their faces, then decided they deserved better. He took a deep breath.

''I will not be the next German to offer the excuse that I was just following orders,'' he said quietly. ''War is one thing—this is another.''

He picked up the mike to call *Ramage*.

PART
4

THE ENEMY OF
MY ENEMY

War is not merely a political act, but also a political instrument, a continuation of political relations, a carrying out of the same by other means.

—KARL VON CLAUSEWITZ (1780–1831),
On War (1833)

25

U-504

"No." Kraeken's voice was harsh. "No more."

Merker turned and looked at his second-in-command. The XO was holding a small pistol. Not, one part of his mind noted dispassionately, standard issue from the small-arms locker. He must have brought it on board in his personal effects.

Kraeken took a step closer. "Put it down." Then he turned to Ehrlich. "Give me a course to put us on the forward bow of the ship."

Merker didn't move. The microphone felt solid, reassuring in his hand. Less powerful than the weapon his XO was brandishing—perhaps. So far it'd done more to change the course of this conflict than any amount of armament.

"Put it *down*, I said." There was a hint of something frantic, some emotion or force not entirely under control in the man's voice.

"They put you on this boat—*my* ship—to spy on me. Admiral Braudel," Merker said, his voice calm and certain. He shook his head ruefully. "I would have thought he trusted me. After Korea, if not before."

"He was right not to." The pistol stayed pointed at Merker, unwavering. "Korea—easy enough to take shots at an American ship and pretend to be a Korean diesel submarine. It wasn't like you actually tried to do what you're paid to do—kill it."

"Those were my orders. To approach, to fire for effect, not to destroy."

"And you wouldn't have." The XO sneered. "We've all seen what you do in actual combat, *Kapitan.*" The last word dripped with contempt. "You run, you give warning shots, and then you make friends with your enemy. Very impressive. I'm sure Admiral Braudel will think so."

"You think you'll have the opportunity to tell him?" Merker raised his free hand slowly and pointed at the pistol. "Fire that in here and you'll die with us."

"Not if I hit you with the first shot."

USS *RAMAGE*

"What the *hell* is he doing?" Bailey muttered. The U-boat headed directly for *Victory.* "What *can* he do? Sink a ship that's already dead?"

But he couldn't know that, she realized. He might suspect, after hearing the torpedo's whine over his own sonar, as well as the explosion, but he couldn't be certain. And, from their brief conversation on board *Ramage,* she knew that the U-boat was not capable of monitoring the Gertrude circuit.

"Maybe we shouldn't have let him go," Lieutenant Boston said hesitantly.

She looked up at him sharply. "We made a deal and we stuck with it. Besides, Merker's played straight with us so far."

The men and women in combat were quiet. Confusion showed on several faces, while other technicians stayed focused on their screens and displays, dealing with the sudden reverses in foe and friend by simply concentrating on the tasks immediately at hand. The ops officer was across the room, watching *Victory* recede on the radarscope, continuously checking the British ship's apparently random course changes.

"TAO, sonar," the combat circuit said suddenly. "The U-boat's moving forward on an intercept course. Getting indications of a depth change, too. She's diving and—Captain," the voice took on a new urgency. "The noise-suppression equipment. She's reactivated it. Lost contact, ma'am.''

Lieutenant Boston sucked in a hard breath. "Captain, I suggest we get the helo airborne immediately. If the good *Kapitan* has changed his mind about stopping this war before it gets out of hand, we're going to be first on his list.''

She nodded, not trusting her voice. How badly had she fouled up this time?

U-504

"You!" the XO said sharply. "If you don't want to stand trial with the *Kapitan,* you'll obey your orders *now.*"

"No," Merker ordered. "Maintain course and speed."

Ehrlich looked pale. His eyes flitted between Merker and the XO, unable to settle on one or the other just as he seemed unable to make up his mind whom to obey.

Still facing Merker, the XO edged sideways to cross the three feet separating him from the navigator. He grabbed the younger man's arm and jerked him toward him. "Odd that a traitor is able to inspire some semblance of loyalty in his crew still." He turned his face to partially face Ehrlich. "You know that's what he is, don't you? By failing to follow orders during time of war, he's committing treason. And if you follow him now, you'll share his fate at the court-martial. And in front of the firing squad."

Merker saw Ehrlich move behind the XO. The captain took a step forward to distract the XO. The man's attention immediately snapped back toward him, and he stepped away from the navigator. "One way or another, you'll get them all killed, won't you? Either by the American destroyer or by a jury. Surely you can't—"

Over the XO's shoulder, he saw Ehrlich dart forward, holding a pair of scissors. He felt a flash of real fear, an insane impulse to turn loose of the other man and try to save himself. He saw the young navigator paused for a second, then plunge the scissors down into Kraeken's back.

Kraeken's scream cut off his sentence. He staggered forward, the gun now pointing at the deck, and flailed franti-

cally at his back with his free hand, reaching for something
and turning in a circle as he did so.

Merker darted forward at the first note and locked a forearm around the XO's neck. He jerked upward, lifting the
smaller man's feet off the deck and pulling him toward him
into a tight embrace.

Hard metal protruded from Kraken's back and dug into
Merker's chest. Merker grabbed the XO's gun hand with
his free one and pointed it down at the deck, struggling to
wrench the pistol away from the man. He writhed and
thrashed, trying to break the captain's grip. Merker shifted
his grip, clamping his arms down around the XO's arms
and holding them pinned in front of the other man's body.
He could feel the XO trying to work his gun hand back to
get the muzzle pointed toward him, and tightened his grip
until his muscles and tendons turned to long lines of fire.

Two other men were grappling with them now. *Which
side—whom do they believe?* Merker held on.

A deafening explosion, sudden numbness in his right leg.
Merker struggled to hold himself and the XO up.

There was no pain, just a quickly mounting sense of loss
of control, of a hot seeping across his thigh followed by
weakness. The noise—he couldn't tell whether the explosion had temporarily deafened him or whether one of the
quiet, insistent buzzers on the submarine had gone off, but
the white noise grew louder, gradually blanking out his vision along with his consciousness. His last thought as he
felt the XO's body slip away from his was relief that the
sea outside hadn't gotten him in the end.

USS RAMAGE

"We're on top of him," *Ramage*'s helo pilot reported
tersely. "Though why you people think he's so hard to
track is a mystery. This bastard's as loud as a NASCAR
Chevy."

"He is *now*," Digger replied. "Five minutes ago, it was
a different story."

"Requesting weapons free?" the pilot said, his voice
changing to a more formal tone. "I have attack criteria."

"You say the boat's loud?" Bailey asked suddenly. "How loud?"

"Real loud. If he's got all that high-tech noise-suppression and countering gear you claim he has, he's not using it. Equipment casualty maybe." The pilot sounded annoyed. "Listen, can we take him or not?"

"No." The word was out of her mouth before she'd realized she'd decided. "Maintain contact and firing solution but don't do anything aggressive."

"Okay." The pilot sounded dubious.

Lieutenant Boston turned to her. "Based on—"

"Call it a gut feeling. But every time we've seen that boat, we haven't. That makes sense, doesn't it? But you get the drift."

"You mean when she wants to be undetectable, she is, right?" Boston asked. He nodded.

"Exactly. Nothing lost—there's no indication she's ready to launch, and we've got contact on her again. Let's see what Merker's up to."

"You trust him that much?" Boston asked.

She looked at him thoughtfully. "I wouldn't call it trust. Let's say 'respect.' "

U-504

"*Kapitan,*" the voice said gently. He could hear it finally, barely audible beneath the buzz of the white noise. Merker groaned, tried to remember why it was so urgent that he pay attention to the voice. It was, he knew. There was something he had to do.

The XO. Consciousness flooded back cold and clear. He opened his eyes, squinted. Ehrlich's pale, worried face came into focus.

"You've been shot in the leg," the younger man said, the expression on his face belying the calm, confident words. "It missed the bone—I think. The medic administered some morphine for the pain but assures me you're not in danger."

"What—" His voice failed. He tried again.

"The XO is in medical. And in restraints," Ehrlich said.

"The ship is surfaced, approaching the American ship."
The unnatural lines on his young face deepened. "We're
damaged—the bullet had enough energy after it passed
through your leg to penetrate the hull. The leak is controllable, but not for long. It hit a plate that must have already
been overstressed by the near-miss. The gap between the
seams is increasing."

"Emergency destruction," Merker managed to say, relieved to find that he was regaining control of his voice.
He concentrated, trying to think despite the morphine haze
that crowded his head.

"I ordered it fifteen minutes ago." Ehrlich glanced up
at the overhead as a peculiarly sickening creak resonated
throughout the boat. "*Kapitan,* we're going to have to consider abandoning the boat. It won't be long now. Unless . . ."

Unless you order us to go down with the ship. Merker
grimaced, tried to prop himself up on his elbows. His arms
felt oddly limp and weak. Ehrlich barked a short command
at two other sailors, who linked their arms behind his back
and helped lift him to a sitting position. Ehrlich was squatted down to his right, one of the other enlisted sailors to
his left.

So young. For a moment, looking at them, he remembered the dead child bumping up against his periscope.
How old had that boy been? Ehrlich was closer to the
child's age than to Merker's in chronological terms, but the
past few hours had aged him beyond his years.

Merker cleared his throat. "Finish what we can, then
abandon ship. Call the Americans, tell them what we are
doing." He tried for a smile. "Better them than the British."

Ehrlich nodded. "Another twenty minutes, then. I'll start
evacuating the nonessential personnel immediately. And the
wounded."

"The XO. Not me. I will leave last."

USS RAMAGE

U-504 roiled uneasily in the light seas five hundred yards off *Ramage*'s port bow. Black smoke poured out of the sail and the aft escape hatch. It bubbled up raw and pungent from the surface of the ocean, escaping from some rent in the hull below the waterline.

Conducting sea-air rescue was clearly permitted by the peacetime rules of engagement, and freed the British forces to continue the hunt.

"Our helo reports it's finished searching the area—no other survivors," the OOD said.

"Very well," Bailey answered automatically. Her own binoculars were glued to her face as she scanned the ocean. She sighed and lowered her binoculars.

"Captain, the master at arms reports that two of the prisoners have serious injuries. The corpsman recommends we arrange for transport to shore."

"They're not prisoners, mister. We're not at war here. All we've done is rescue survivors at sea, something required of any seaman. Understand?" Bailey cringed slightly as she listened to her own words. The tone might carry conviction, but she was damned if she knew how she managed it. The last thing she needed right now was to have to come up with a rationale for holding *survivors* under armed guard.

"Yes, sir." The OOD's face was impassive. "The survivors."

26

---

9 MARCH 2002:
THE ENGLISH CHANNEL

USS *RAMAGE*

"You call this stabilizing the situation?" Sixth Fleet's voice was cold.

She stared thoughtfully at the speaker, trying to picture the man at the other end. The last picture she'd seen showed brilliant blue eyes peering out from shaggy brows, a jowly face. A sheepdog, soulfully staring at the camera.

But what was behind that? She tried to remember where he'd been before he commanded Sixth Fleet, whether anyone had ever talked about working for him. A politician—or a warrior? Would he be more worried about medals or men?

Nothing. He was just an admiral.

"I'm not sure how many options we—I had, sir," she said. "At least we're not pinned down in the minefield like the Brits are."

A sigh. "I know that. Believe me, I know it. And, for what it's worth, you did a good job tactically. But the situation's getting out of control."

"The Brits probably think so." She glanced at the tactical screen in the forward part of the compartment. The twenty NATO ships trapped inside the two lines of mines had organized themselves into a line formation and were slowing steaming in circles inside their ocean cage. "If those mines have counters on them, they're playing Pop

Goes the Weasel in there. When the music stops, it's going to be ugly.''

Silence. Finally, ''I heard you were a smart-ass.''

''From whom? My commodore? I doubt it.'' Across the room, Lieutenant Boston made a sound that might have been a choked-back laugh or a gasp.

''No. Someone else.''

''Ah.'' She waggled one finger at the speaker. ''Admiral, have you been talking to my civilian employers?''

''Not on this circuit, Bailey,'' the admiral said wearily. ''How many times do I have to explain that to you? But I understand a few things now.''

''Like why *Ramage* isn't sunk? That sort of thing?''

''No. Like why I was pressured into leaving you in command when the reasonable course of action would have been to airlift out an experienced *officer* to relieve you. I should never have . . .'' His voice stopped abruptly and then resumed in a colder, more formal tone. ''Commander Bailey, you will prepare to receive a helo tomorrow at fifteen hundred.''

''Why?''

''Because I'm going to do what I should have done five days ago—relieve you. Commander Brubecker has recovered sufficiently to return to the ship. Don't count on a fancy ceremony. The helo will be on your deck long enough to let him off and take you on. Be on it, Commander.'' The circuit went dead.

She slammed the receiver down in its cradle and turned to face the combat crew. Shock, outrage—whether over the relief or her disrespect to Sixth Fleet—and disbelief warred on their faces.

Collins slowly took off her headset and laid it on the desk in front of her. She pushed back her chair to the length of the bungee cord that held it bound to the desk, let it clatter onto the deck, and walked over slowly to stand beside Bailey. The silence in combat grew uncomfortable.

''I owe you an apology,'' Collins said finally.

Bailey shook her head wearily. ''None of that matters now. You did what you thought was right. For the record, your actions have been entirely correct. Not that my as-

sessment of your performance matters. You heard the
boss—I'm getting relieved tomorrow.''

Collins brushed aside the comments with one hand. ''I'm
sorry, Captain. I don't understand what you're talking
about.'' She turned slowly around, looking every sailor and
officer in the eyes. Evidently satisfied with what she saw,
she nodded, and looked back at Bailey. ''I'm talking about
the communications outage we just experienced. As the operations officer, that would be one of my responsibilities. I
can assure you, I'll have a word with the ensign immediately.''

''Nice try, but it won't work, XO,'' Bailey said.

Collins took a step closer to her. ''What won't? Trying
to stop this war? Or just keeping our people alive? Seems
to me, you've managed to do both.''

Bailey straightened up, looked her in the eyes. ''I can't
disobey a direct order from *Sixth Fleet*. And neither can
you.''

Collins shrugged. ''I didn't know the subtleties of naval
courtesy mattered so much to you. Seems to me the first
priority ought to be keeping this ship and the people in her
alive.''

''But . . .'' Bailey stopped and considered the matter.
Collins had a point.

The helo hovered along the port side, barely higher than
the radar mast. From close range, the bobbles and jinks as
it encountered turbulent airflow around the ship were obvious.

She stepped out onto the port bridge wing. The pilot in
the right-hand seat, his copilot in the left, and a passenger
in the back.

The door slid back, exposing the rear seats. Commander
Brubecker leaned forward, bound to his seat by a flight
harness, his right hand holding on to something out of view,
his left gesticulating. His mouth moved open in an angry
manner, but no words reached her.

She shook her head and pointed at her ear. The speakers
on the bridge and in combat played British pop music, with
the exception of International Air Distress and Military Air

Distress. Collins and the others would have enough to answer for later without putting them in the spot of disobeying direct orders again. Sixth Fleet, an unreachable entity, was one thing. But to make them face their former XO in person was another. Lieutenant Boston had the deck, and MIUWU sailors manned all positions in combat and on the bridge. It was bad enough that they had to be involved, but, she hoped, slightly more understandable at court-martial.

"What're our winds?" she asked Lieutenant Boston.

"True tailwind right now. According to the pubs, we're well outside of the landing envelope. Any mistake and he'll smash straight into the ship. I don't think he's going to want to take that chance."

She looked back up at the helicopter. "Depends on how bad he wants down on the deck, I suppose."

Ten minutes later, they saw how bad. The helo wheeled away from the ship, circled, and approached the stern. It approached the flight deck sideways, carefully crabbing up the wake toward the small helo landing area. Brubecker was poised at the hatch with a harness strapped around him. A line coming off the front of it led to a winch anchored to the top of the doorway.

Boston shuddered. "I've done that before. No, thanks."

She looked aft somberly. "You know those tactical signals you screwed up in Korea last year during the training exercise?"

He looked at her in confusion. "Those were—"

"Zigzag patterns, if I remember correctly." She pursed her lips. "Your performance was entirely inadequate. I've been negligent, letting so long pass without requiring some remedial training."

"Zigzag? No, it was . . ." He caught on. "You're right. In fact, Captain, I've been studying the tactical maneuvering manual, and I'd like to give you a brief demonstration."

"A lengthy one would be better. Proceed."

Ramage cut sharply back and forth through the ocean, sometimes heading directly into the wind but more often abeam of the seas. Aft, Brubecker swayed pendulumlike at the end of his tether, thirty feet above the ocean, fifty feet below the helo.

Twice, the Seahawk made a tentative charge toward the destroyer, once bringing Brubecker over the deck for a few moments. She had a moment of sheer dread, wondering if the former XO had the balls to simply release his harness catch and try to drop to the deck. Or worse, into the ocean near *Ramage*. Whatever her disagreements with Sixth Fleet, they didn't extend to leaving Brubecker in the ocean and steaming away.

Fortunately, Brubecker didn't appear to believe it. She heard one brief scream of anger and pain as the helo jerked back from the pitching deck. The apex of Brubecker's arc had brought him within twenty feet of the surface search radar.

After an hour of chasing the ship's flight deck around, the helo gave up. Brubecker was quickly winched back inside, and the helo banked away toward Britain.

"Now that that's over with, I need to talk to Merker. Get the gig in the water."

"How bad is your ship?" Bailey asked. "She looks like she's riding badly." The U-boat was a hundred yards off *Ramage*'s bow . . .

"We can fix it. We need some supplies, some tools. Your people help." His voice sounded drawn and tired.

"Good. How long?"

"Four hours, I think. Maybe not so much."

"We can do this," she said.

"There is no choice. Let me show you the plans."

"Look at the pattern," he said. He unrolled the chart he'd brought with him and pointed to a series of black X marks. "These are the mines I laid."

"And the red marks?"

"The—events. Some with no explanation." He touched the points in order. "The ferry, *Victory*, the others. Even if a few mines had broken loose from their moorings, the"— he searched for the word—"'set and drift would not account for these attacks. No, there is another minefield. The gas one."

She shook her head, frustrated. "But when were they planted?"

"Not hard. Any submarine can lay mines. But these, with gas—I think not new. Old, very old. Maybe from the last war."

"I still don't believe that."

"Yes. At Staff College, I remember some rumor about it. Hitler's last defense against the Allied invasion. He did not plan right. If the mines are sleeping, I think the transmitter we found in my conning tower would wake them."

"Assuming you're right, what then? We don't even know where they are, much less how to disarm them. Without the codes, we can't deactivate them. And I'm damned sure not going to turn this destroyer into a minesweeper." She repressed a shiver, thinking of the deadly gas seeping through the ship, killing her people.

"The last question is easier." He cleared his throat and stared down at the deck. "There are some things my ship can do easier than yours. This evolutions—I have done it before."

"Disarming mines? When?"

"Not mines." He looked up. "But give a good place to start looking, I can find small metal objects in the sea. Like sonobuoys."

"Like—oh." She remembered the sonobuoys that had gone dead so unaccountably. Was it only the week before? "That was your sub?"

He nodded. "And, I think this is not more difficult." He pointed back at the chart. "I think I know what spacing the mines are set at. *Were* set at," he amended, tasting the verb carefully and looking for her reaction. "They are buried on the seafloor. My ship—we have equipment."

"What do you—"

He shook his head, cutting her off. "Some questions I don't answer now." He glanced around the small flag plot office. "So I don't lie later. For the same reason we stay in this room and do not go into the rest of your combat."

They'd worked out the security aspects of their strange partnership carefully, both understanding that there were going to be too many explanations required afterward. And

there would be an afterward—neither of them was foolish
enough to believe that *Ramage* could continue to avoid a
change in commanding officers nor that Merker would de-
fect to the United States. But, for the moment, their worlds
were comprised solely of their ships and the men and
women on them. Later—well, that was later.

"He'd better get the idea soon," she said, watching the
helo. "There's not much time left."

Boston shot her a worried look. "Two miles until I've
got to be back on a steady course, Captain. Do you want
to come around, clear the area a bit?"

She shook her head. "Not a chance. We give them anything like decent winds, they'll horsecollar Brubecker
down. We need the tailwind."

Boston stared ahead at the water. "Then he better leave
soon. Otherwise we're going to have a hell of a problem
negotiating that minefield."

She turned to the BMOW. "Set general quarters, along
with Circle William. Prepare for NBC attack."

The submarine plowed through the water five hundred
yards ahead of the destroyer, barely surfaced with most of
her weather decks awash. Merker was clearly distinguishable in the conning tower, even with the binoculars obscuring most of his face. His bearing, the movements of
the others around him, gave him away.

Her own binoculars were etching red circles around her
eyes. Along with everyone else on the bridge, her eyes were
fixed on the seas ahead, searching for the one small sign
that might save their lives.

Finally, she forced herself to lower the binoculars. The
mines, if they were still in place, would be seated on the
seabed, not bobbing on the ocean like surface contact
mines. If Merker's theory was correct, that would be the
only way they could have survived the decades since the
last war. Despite the compelling logic, she found herself
unable to look away from the water ahead.

"Two thousand yards," the navigator announced. She
saw him sneak in a quick scan of the water ahead, then

force his eyes back down to the chart. Of all the watch-standers, he alone was binocularless.

She reached for the microphone. "*Kapitan* Merker, do you read me?"

"Yes. We are preparing to submerge to communications depth. There is too much noise surfaced. Sonar requests it."

"A radio check at your earliest convenience," she said.

The figures disappeared from the conning tower, Merker leaving last. Two minutes later, the sea washed over the stern deck, crept forward foaming around the conning tower, then covered the forward weather deck. The conning tower slid down into the sea quickly, disappearing in a furiously foaming wash. Only a slim mast remained above the surface, spewing up a rooster tail behind it.

"God, I hope they aren't lying to us," Carlisle said softly.

She raised her binoculars back to her face. "They aren't. Let's leave it at that, shall we?"

"I guess we have to." He sighed, the sound borne more from frustration than worry. "It's not like we have a choice."

U-504

The old torpedoman frowned. "With all respect, *Kapitan,* I do not understand the question." He patted the mine affectionately. "Two thousand meters. That's what they prefer."

Merker squatted down on the steel grate deck next to the sailor and inspected the weapon. The dull gray shell housing the explosive charge was spotless, and fresh grease was smeared neatly over every seam in a precise pattern. "Exactly according to the manual, I see."

"Of course. How else would it be?"

Merker looked at him. "You keep your publications current, I know. It must take some time, entering the changes that the weapons facility orders."

"It does, sir." The torpedoman whipped out a clean, lint-free cloth and rubbed the weapon housing gently, chasing down an imperfection invisible to Merker's eyes. "But most of the changes are small—important, of course. But small.''

''What was it like after the war?'' Merker probed gently. ''I know, you were not there. But you must have heard stories from your instructors. As I did from mine.'' *And I pray that your teachers were more accurate than mine,* he added silently.

''Oh, of course.'' The sailor settled back on his haunches and rested one hand on his mine. ''Very primitive weapons when I started out in submarines. Good for their time, but nothing like this.''

''Less range, for one thing, I would guess.''

The torpedoman nodded vigorously. ''Of course. I remember Klaber—he was in U-boats during the war, not much as a teacher but a hell of a sailor. He used to tell us how hard it was in the old days, how many mines they had to lay just to cover one square mile of ocean. The weapons themselves were much smaller, of course. You could carry more. And much less reactive. The torpedomen pitched their pallets on them, hung hammocks from the ends—you could do almost anything you wanted with them. Much less reliable, though. That was one reason for using so many of them.''

''What kind of spacing did they use for them? Back then, I mean.'' Merker held his breath. He could see the memories chasing themselves across the older man's face.

''About two hundred meters, I believe.'' The torpedoman thought for a moment, then shook his head. ''I can't be sure, *Kapitan*. It's been so long since I talked to Klaber.'' His face brightened for a moment. ''The stories he could tell. I remember one time he was on patrol—''

Merker stood, and felt a faint twinge of guilt at the look of disappointment on the other man's face. ''We'll continue this very soon,'' he said, his voice unusually gentle. ''I'm looking forward to hearing more of Klaber's stories. They're important.''

In more ways than one, he thought, as he turned to walk back forward to the control room. In more ways than one.

27

9 MARCH 2002:
THE ENGLISH CHANNEL

USS RAMAGE

"Steady as she goes," Lieutenant Boston ordered. The helmsman swung his wheel through 180 degrees, shifting the rudder to check *Ramage*'s arc through the water. Boston turned to Bailey. "One thousand yards, Captain."

She nodded. Somewhere up ahead, the U-boat was already cutting its way through the treacherous fields of mines. She stared out at the ocean ahead, looking for the first of the bobbing communications buoys that would mark the safe channel.

"Captain?" the quartermaster asked. "What spacing will you want on the ships as they leave the area?"

"One thousand yards. No," she said, thinking of the rate at which the deadly gas would drift between the ships, "let's make that two thousand yards. Close enough to maintain a good column formation, but far enough apart to avoid mutual interference."

Mutual interference. A suitable euphemism for the devastation that would overtake the remaining ships should the maneuver fail.

U-504

"Make your depth seventy meters," Merker ordered. He stared at the noise-suppression panel, now dark and silent. With the equipment secured, the American ships should have no difficulty tracking them through the minefield. Tracking them, and following them to safety.

"Contact," sonar announced. He turned to look at the screen. Two thousand yards ahead, bearing slightly to the right of their course. On the active sonar screen, the first mine was a faint speckle of phosphorescence, barely brighter than the noise surrounding it.

"Come right, steer course two-nine-zero."

The quiet litany of order and reply, acknowledgment and report, followed immediately. The voices were calm, with no indication that what they were about to attempt was potentially catastrophic. He surveyed the crew members, surprised at the quiet pride he now felt in them. After the events of the past week, to be able to continue so professionally following the mutiny of Kraeken, steadied him.

"Contact bears zero-zero-zero relative; range, one thousand yards."

"Three knots." He glanced over at the conning officer and nodded. "Deploy the mechanical arm."

A low mechanical growl filled the control room. Noisy, too noisy, and probably easily detectable by the American ship above. One part of his mind noted that for future discussions with the technical experts attached to the General Staff. Another wondered if he'd ever be given the opportunity to explain anything. No matter. Nothing mattered now, except preventing a war that neither side wanted.

USS RAMAGE

She paced the bridge uneasily, wishing there was some justification for moving aft into sonar instead of staying there. There wasn't—at least none that she could justify to herself, although no one on the bridge now would be likely to question her.

The operations specialist manning the sound-powered headphones said, "Sonar reports winch noises."

It might be mitigating evidence, she decided. If the court-martial convened—*when* the court-martial convened. She grimaced. What were the odds that it would make any difference? None, if it didn't work.

"Captain, I think you'd better come back here," Lieutenant Commander Collins's voice blared over the bitch box.

She took two quick steps forward, and toggled down the transmit button. "What's wrong?"

"It's the Brits. The two contacts off of us have increased speed and are closing at twenty knots. If they maintain course and speed, they should intercept us in eight minutes."

She swore quietly. They had no room to maneuver, none at all. The slightest deviation from course might take them in range of one of the ancient mines. Even with Merker's best guess on the location of the mines, neither ship could be certain that they would avoid them anyway. But maneuvering to avoid the British ships would complicate the tactical scenario past any safety margins he'd built in.

"I'll be right back." She wheeled and headed aft, pausing at the hatch leading off the bridge. "Maintain course and speed. Notify me if any communications buoys are sighted."

"Aye, aye, Captain," Lieutenant Boston said, not taking his eyes off the ocean in front of him.

U-504

"Thirty meters," sonar reported. "Recommend one knot."

"One knot," Merker said. This last reduction in speed would take them to bare steerageway, just enough forward speed to maintain control of the submarine's depth. In front of the boat, the two metal arms of the shears had already deployed, extending forward of the ship by twenty meters. Each arm was a thin, titanium strut fifteen meters long. When deployed, they formed a straight line of metal positioned forward of the ship.

A few minutes later, sonar reported, "Contact," indicating that the wire line tethering the mine to the seabed had rasped across the sensing range of the shears.

Merker bit his lip. How certain was he that the minefield he'd laid just days before was the only barrier to getting the ships out of the area? Wasn't it possible that one of the ancient gas mines still lay below, buried in the muck of decades of ocean ooze? After all, the submarine was safe from that minefield, since they were targeted only at surface ships. It had to be—the fragile truce with the Americans would be immediately shattered if it weren't. There was no point in worrying about it. This was their only opportunity to avoid the conflict that neither side wanted.

"Execute," he ordered. He drummed his fingers uneasily on the metal railing surrounding the periscope shaft.

USS *RAMAGE*

"Your approach on my ship constitutes a hostile act," Admiral Richardson said. His voice was thin and scratchy over the tactical net.

"At three knots?" Bailey shook her head. "You can't be serious. We've done nothing threatening."

"Except close to within weapons range of my remaining ships. I believe an excellent case can be made for the possibility that you are preparing to attack with Harpoon missiles. At least I believe any board of inquiry will find it that way."

"We're allies," she said harshly. "I know the word seems to mean something different to you, but I would expect you to know what it means to me. Just because you have no hesitation at violating that trust, you should not assume the same of me."

"*Ramage* is no longer under my command, as you made abundantly clear not so long ago." The British officer's voice was even more clipped and distant than normal. "You will immediately reverse your course and prepare to be boarded. Britain, if not the United States, is at war. Your conduct indicates you have no longer chosen to remain neutral. Based on a request from Sixth Fleet, I have been ordered by my superiors to take you into custody for immediate transport to your own authorities. The charge, as you may suspect, is mutiny."

U-504

A low metal grinding sound rumbled through the U-boat as the blades of the shears slowly closed. Serrated edges curved inward, designed to prevent the cable from sliding off the tips. Merker watched the angle indicator decrease as the blades slowly approached each other. The rasping sound deepened as the blades closed, and the light tinkle of a trapped cable was clearly audible over the loudspeaker.

"Sixteen seconds," Ehrlich announced. Merker nodded. The cable tethering the mine to that part of the ocean was far thicker than the light line that had connected the sono-buoys to their small antenna transmitters. While the shears were designed for just this sort of work, the operational tests had been far from satisfactory.

"Five seconds." Ehrlich's voice was calm and soothing.

Moments later, the thin metallic rasp changed to a harsh squeal. Merker could see it as clearly as though he were in the water ahead of the submarine, the giant blades closing, the thick wire line caught between sharp edges. The motor driving the blades whined, and the noise vibrated through-out the control room. Titanium was biting deeply into the wire, the motor shoving the blades together. Finally there was a loud, sharp clang as the blades slammed together.

Had they cut it? There was no way to be certain, not without communicating with *Ramage* to see if she'd no-ticed the mine floating to the surface. It was possible that the cable was still caught and kinked between the blades, the mine tether with its deadly cargo now clamped firmly to the submarine. If that was the case, any additional for-ward speed would drive the mine down, bringing it level with the submarine. The only option at this point was to come to communications depth and talk to *Ramage*. At least that way, the submarine would hoist the ballast off the bottom of the ocean and let the mine float to the surface, whether or not it was tethered now to the U-boat instead of the seabed. As he and Bailey had discussed, the Amer-ican ship would then attempt to detonate the mine with .50-caliber machine guns. He shuddered at the thought of bullets piercing the water so close around his boat.

"Communications depth," he ordered.

USS RAMAGE

"Captain! The OOD reports visual contact on a mine, bearing one-six-zero relative, range one thousand yards," Collins said.

"The U-boat?" she asked.

Collins shook her head. "No communications yet."

She looked back up at the speaker slaved to the tactical circuit. There was a chance—not a good one—that Richardson might believe her. "Admiral," she began, "I think we need to talk."

U-504

"Communications depth," the OOD announced. He glanced back at Merker, waiting for further orders.

Merker picked up the handset to the small marine-band radio. "*Ramage,* this is *Geist*—pardon, Ghost," he said, giving the translation. "Do you see it?"

USS RAMAGE

Still holding the handset to the tactical circuit, she grabbed the bridge-to-bridge radio. "Yes! It's on the surface. Stand by for surface action."

"Five minutes while I clear the area, please." Merker's voice contained a clearly audible note of relief.

"Clear the area, but stay at communications depth. We seem to have a problem." She turned back to the other handset. "Admiral, your lookout should be able to tell you that a mine has just floated to the surface. Do you have it?"

"We see it. And if you're trying to threaten me—"

"It was the U-boat," she said rapidly. "The U-boat captain is severing the mine cables as we speak. It's the only way to get your ships out of the containment area, Admiral.

You and I both know that neither of us has the minesweeping resources to clear this area quickly.''

The circuit was silent. Would he believe her, she wondered, or was that too much to expect after her last lie?

"Still closing," Collins reported. "Intercept by British forces in three minutes."

"Admiral, you must listen to me," she pleaded. "You've already lost eighteen ships. Do you want to lose the rest of your fleet? This is the only way. My God, man, you've got to believe me."

"As I believed you the last time?"

U-504

Merker listened to the conversation between the Americans and the British officer, his heart sinking. "Prepare to submerge."

USS RAMAGE

"Admiral"—she took a deep breath—"you should understand my position. We're in so much trouble right now that not much is going to make a difference either way. Not to me. The only thing I care about at this point is stopping this war before it starts. And you should, too."

"We had thought to do that, before you interfered."

"I'm placing *Ramage* under your command," she said, speaking as the idea occurred to her. She heard sharp gasps around combat. "Admiral, I request you come aboard and accept my surrender."

She picked up the bridge-to-bridge circuit. "*Ghost,* are you there?"

"Yes."

"If you're monitoring tactical, then you know what's happened. *Kapitan,* our only chance is to convince the British not to attack. My intention is to brief Admiral Richardson completely on the situation, and to trust his judgment in sorting out fact from politics. However, I cannot expect you to hazard your vessel as well. Therefore, please be advised that this vessel is now under the command of Brit-

ish forces and will follow Admiral Richardson's orders."
She took a deep breath. "For what it's worth, *Kapitan*, you
have my respect. And my gratitude."

"Understood." The circuit fell silent.

28

---

9 MARCH 2002:
THE ENGLISH CHANNEL

USS RAMAGE

"*Ramage,* this is Sixth Fleet." She stared up at the speaker that had been silent for so long. She recognized the voice.

"This is *Ramage,*" she acknowledged.

"Normally, I wouldn't bother explaining my orders, but since you show a marked tendency to disregard those with which you do not agree, I will make an exception in this case." The voice paused.

"I'm listening," she said.

"We've just discovered the wreckage of a Korean Romeo-class submarine in the Yellow Sea. Recovery assets are being deployed as we speak, but preliminary indications are that this is not the boat that took a shot at *Wasp.*"

"So you've got a sunken submarine. We have a few more out here than that."

"You will allow me to finish without any other editorial comments," the voice snapped. "Since the Koreans are claiming that we began this conflict by sinking their submarine, we took a close look at the damage to the boat. Not only was it out of range of *Puller* when the attack on *Wasp* occurred, but the damage is not consistent with an American weapon. Furthermore, it's exactly where your German captain said it would be. Therefore, at least for the time being, we're inclined to believe him. We've ordered all our assets to back off two hundred miles off the Korean coast, and we're trying to prevent this from happening."

"Great. Just great. I guess we can expect some help over here in about three months, then," she said, without keying the microphone.

"Based on those assumptions, we are transferring operational control of *Ramage* back to the on-scene British commander. As of this moment, you are an operational part of his force. Subject to Admiral Richardson's requirements, your first priority will be to prosecute the submarine responsible for this atrocity. It's important not only for the safety of our allies but also to convince the North Koreans that we're sincere."

"Do you know what that U-boat is doing right now?"

"I've seen your message. The fact remains that that commander is responsible for starting a major regional conflict on the other side of the world. For once, try to act like the commanding officer of a warship. You follow orders, lady—not pursue your own agenda."

"My own—what's that supposed to mean?"

"I think you know. Your work at NSA is centered around improving U.S.-German relationships, isn't it? There have been some thoughts around here that you may have gone native."

"I'm trying to prevent a war, here," she said. "I thought that was the whole purpose of the military."

"War is simply the continuation of politics by other means."

She hung up the handset, wondering just why Sixth Fleet was quoting the German military genius Clausewitz to justify his orders.

U-504

"Small-arms fire," the sonarman announced. "And active contact on the next mine."

Merker nodded. "It might make some noise, but we're too deep for it to bother us. Give me a vector to the next one."

USS RAMAGE

"You are still holding contact on the submarine?" Admiral Richardson asked.

She nodded, not willing to trust her voice. It was too much, all of it. The responsibility she'd neither sought nor wanted, the sudden escalation from peacetime exercises to all-out war, and the problems she still faced on the ship.

"You will reinitiate LINK procedures immediately. In the next two minutes, I expect to see every bit of your targeting and locating data being transmitted to every British ship in the area. Is that clear?"

"Yes, sir." She was tired, so tired. It took every bit of energy she had left to nod at the TAO, asking him to comply with the admiral's order. A small buzz of noise arose from Tracker Alley as the operations specialists synchronized their data link with that of the British ships.

Two minutes later, it was done. Radar and sonar contacts from the British ships popped into being on her display, and she knew that their data were similarly being transmitted to them. The symbol designating the German U-boat in front of them seemed brighter than the others.

"Captain? What about the .50-caliber crews?" Collins asked.

She turned toward the other woman, aware that her movements felt slow, as though she were moving underwater. "Have them destroy any mines we detect on the surface," she said finally. "No matter how screwed up the rest of this situation is, we all want those out of the area."

"About the data link with the British," Collins said. "I think I might have an idea about that."

Thirty minutes later, the first British cruiser steamed out of its holding pen through the safe channel cut by the U-boat, followed shortly thereafter by another ten frigates and destroyers. They broke off to the left and right as they exited the narrow channel out of the minefield, streaming past her to guide on the British ship behind her. Two hours later, the last one was free. Only the slower German submarines remained inside the killing zone.

"Now what?" Bailey asked, staring at the large-screen display.

She was seated in the captain's chair, slightly elevated above the deck. Sometime in the past hour, an operations specialist had pressed a cup of coffee into her hand. Beside her on the deck were the remains of a cold sandwich.

"Captain?" Worry tinged Collins's voice.

She raised one hand and pointed at the screen. "It's fairly obvious, isn't it? It's a reversal—they've merely changed positions. While the minefield might not be a barrier to a submarine, they're still conveniently clumped in one relatively small area of the ocean. The faster surface ships will fan out, form a line, and sweep in toward the minefield. They've got them trapped in there."

"We still have targeting data on Merker's boat," the ASWO said. "He's just now reentering the edge of our weapons envelope." He looked up at her questioningly.

"You heard our orders," she said harshly.

"No." Richardson turned on her. "We're taking the first shot at her."

HMS *BREVARD*

HMS *Brevard* approached the submarine at a silent, almost undetectable eight knots. Her advanced sound masker system streamed a sheet of bubbles between her hull and the ocean, greatly reducing the radiated noise from internal machinery. The shrouded propeller reduced her wake and propeller noise to a bare background rumble.

Her towed array streamed behind her, soaking up the small noises in the ocean, beam forming and amplifying them into discrete frequencies. After twelve hours trapped inside a minefield, her crew was nervous, exhausted, and running solely on adrenaline. Still, the opportunity to make the first kill on the submarine that had pinned them down gave them a burst of energy.

"Targeting solution," the sonarman announced, his

voice drained but buoyed up by the last remnants of his anger.

"Very well," her captain said. "Weapons free."

On the forward missile launcher, a warning Klaxon sounded. Down in engineering, exterior vents were secured to prevent toxic fumes from the missile's propellant from reentering the ship. The final preparations for launch took just moments.

The ASROC shot off the missile rail, obscuring the weather decks with thick clouds of toxic white fumes. Inside the bridge, the captain watched it, marveling at how something so massive could stay aloft yet seem to travel so slowly. The antiair missiles the ship carried, larger in length and diameter, were barely visible just seconds after they fired, yet this missile-mounted torpedo seemed to hang in the air for almost ten seconds before disappearing from view.

Its eventual target was ten miles away, still running shallow around the perimeter of the minefield. The targeting data from the American ship were solid—at least they seemed to be. He wondered for a moment just how reliable they were.

USS RAMAGE

Bailey walked back into Tracker Alley and rested her hands on the back of the track supervisor's chair. "How good is the lock?" she asked.

He shook his head. "As close as I could get it, Captain. There are a few gridlock problems, though. I wouldn't be surprised if our targeting data are a little bit off." He glanced up at her for reassurance.

"By how much?"

"Maybe fifteen hundred yards. Something like that."

She touched him lightly on the shoulder. "That's enough."

U-504

"Torpedo!" The word was barely out of the sonarman's mouth before they all heard it, the whining, chilling sound

of a small propeller turning at high speed. The first delicate
whisper of the active sonar head stroked the hull.

"Energize all counterdetection circuits," Merker said.
Why had he left them in standby? One part of his mind
grieved at the necessity, while another was fiercely and sav-
agely exultant that he'd taken that precaution. Even the best
of partnerships occasionally fell apart unexpectedly. Like
the British-American one. Like *Ramage* and the U-boat.

He watched the screen mounted just above eye level
flicker into life, a cascade of yellow and red lights chasing
each other across the panel until each one blinked into a
bright, steady green. There was a collective sigh in the control room as each man felt his cloak of invisibility descend
around him.

"It might not be enough," Ehrlich said. His hand was
frozen around a pencil, poised to make some small mark
on his chart. "It almost wasn't before."

"I know," Merker said softly. He turned back to the
control room. "It worked well last time. Noisemakers,
now."

"Range, two thousand yards, bearing constant." The
sonarman's voice was climbing up in the spectrum.

"Wait for it. Not too soon, or it won't work," Merker
said.

A few moments later, soft thuds echoed through the submarine as the decoys fired. "Now!"

This was how it should be, this almost psychic link between captain and crew. The OOD gave the orders, putting
the ship into a sharp turn and steep dive, creating the
knuckle and diving down for the safety of the layer. No
more detailed instructions had been necessary. If they'd had
more time, what a crew it could have been.

The noise of the torpedo's propeller wavered, then faded.
He heard Ehrlich take a deep breath. He started to relax,
then stopped. It was still too close, too close to relax anything.

He turned to sonar. "Put it on the speaker." The small
metal box above his head sprang to life. Just background
noises, the cold wash of sea against metal hull, the faint

traces of biological sounds in the background. No high-pitched pings, no—wait.

The sonarman heard it before he could decide. "Reacquired. Captain, it might be the noisemaker. It's not maintaining depth. It's sinking along with us."

Merker swore silently. "Eighteen knots. Increase down bubble to ten degrees." That might do it, might enable them to clear the area sufficiently to avoid the torpedo. It was a risk, since the noise generated might cancel out the silencing measures they had available, but it was one he would have to take.

"Closing now," the sonarman said.

"Another knuckle. Eject a noisemaker into the center." Merker felt his stomach tighten, an ill feeling sweep through him.

He grabbed for the overhead railing as the submarine swept through an arc, generating another distraction for the homing torpedo. "Close, too close."

USS RAMAGE

"He's taken the shot." Carlisle looked up at her, his face pale. "Solid contact."

"Give me range readouts every ten seconds." On the large-screen display, the tiny symbol for a torpedo popped into being.

U-504

"Sound the collision alarm." Merker held his voice calm and steady. The soft, barely audible gonging sounded in the ship.

USS RAMAGE

"One thousand yards."

"Get the .50-caliber teams inside," she ordered. "If we have to take evasive action, I don't want them out on the weather decks."

U-504

"*Kapitan*, it has us." The submariner's voice had lost its earlier trace of hysteria and now sounded blank and emotionless. "Range, seven hundred meters."

Merker picked up the handset. "All hands brace for collision."

USS RAMAGE

"Two hundred yards. Captain, he's not gonna make it." Carlisle stood, and reached out to turn down the volume of the speaker on the sonar circuit.

"Leave it on high," she ordered harshly. "If we're going to be part of this, we have to face it all. Every bit of it."

U-504

Given a choice between a loud, attractively large contact and a silent volume of sea just the size of a U-boat, the torpedo did what it was built to do. It slammed into the mass of air bubbles comprising the knuckles and headlong into the noisemaker. The impact was sufficient to detonate the explosive warhead.

The noise hit the U-boat first, followed shortly thereafter by the concussion. This time the explosion was broadside to them. The submarine rolled violently to port, rotating on her axis by almost ninety degrees. Men, paper, and chairs slammed across the deck, smashing into the port bulkhead. Merker's feet slid out from under him, and he dangled, suspended by his hands for a few moments. He thought he could almost feel his palms bleed, as they had in Korea when they'd surfaced to take the final approach on the *Wasp*.

The patched rivets sprang loose, and small streams of water shot into the control room at odd angles. All hands sprang for patches and repair kits except for the men actually at the controls. Even the sonarmen grabbed damage control kits and tried to fight off the invading sea.

The submarine shuddered suddenly, and a long, ominous

groan shook her hull. It was serious this time, then, not the minor leaks and warping they'd experienced last time. A better shot? Perhaps, but it might simply be that the hull had been stressed beyond all reasonable expectations. He listened to the cold flow of information and damage reports and wondered how much longer they had to live.

29

---

9 MARCH 2002:
THE ENGLISH CHANNEL

U-504

The planesman hung from his seat by the seat belt around his waist and his iron grip on the control yoke. Merker could hear him swearing, invoking alternating pleas to God for assistance and obscenities as he tried to fight the U-boat back to an even keel.

The angle indicator located forward on the bulkhead indicated thirty degrees of port list. It felt like more, as it normally did on a stable and level submarine deck.

Finally, the submarine began responding. Hydraulics wheezed and complained as fluid seeped out of the lines, joining the cascade of seawater on the deck, its pungent odor a dark grace note to the salty tang.

"Port ballast tanks are flooded, *Kapitan*," the OOD said. "Trying to compensate, but there may be a tank breach."

"Trim the boat, then compensate with planes," Merker said, noting the officer had already started to do just that. "How much damage to engineering?"

"A flash fire and a hydraulic leak, but they've got it under control. It couldn't have lasted more than a few seconds."

But long enough for the acrid smell of burning to begin to infiltrate the air system, Merker noted. He could smell it now, the thing of which nightmares are made for submariners. Fire amid so much water—the most deadly adversary. But had the torpedo not found the noisemaker the more attractive target, even this chance for survival would not exist.

"I've got her," the planesman announced, relief evident in his voice. "They've rerouted to auxiliary hydraulic lines. She's starting to respond."

A few minutes later, the tilt on the deck decreased to five degrees. Uncomfortable, noticeable, but bearable. Merker released his death grip on the overhead stanchion, transferring his hands to the rail surrounding the periscope shaft. They should have been bleeding—felt like they were—just as they had four months before.

He took a deep breath. "Who was it?"

"British," the sonarman responded. "An ASROC—the run time was too short for it to be anything else."

"Are you holding contact?"

The sonarman nodded. "I think so. It's barely there, but I have a trace of her on passive. If it's not the American."

"And you're sure the torpedo was British?"

He nodded again. "Fairly certain. Besides, the American ship is within minimums for an ASROC shot. If it had been her, she would have had to take an over-the-side torpedo shot."

"Well." Merker considered the options, vaguely relieved that it was not the American ship. "Range of bearing to contact."

"Bearing, zero-one-zero; range, ten thousand meters. Bearing constant—she's closing us at twenty-two knots, *Kapitan*."

Merker turned to the OOD. "Make your course zero-one-zero."

Ehrlich spoke for the first time since the attack. "Intercept in twelve minutes, *Kapitan,* allowing some additional time for our turn."

Merker nodded. "Find her."

Half an hour earlier, he'd been convinced that it was possible to avoid this war. Now, fifty meters below the ocean's surface, the sea held at bay only by the battered, leaking hull around him, he knew it wasn't.

USS RAMAGE

"She's turning," Carlisle said. He pointed at the shifting lines on his screen. "And noisier than hell. The Brits may have missed her, but they hit something close enough to do her some serious damage."

Bailey studied the tactical display. "He must know that the Brits have taken a shot," she decided. Merker was no fool, and that was the only reasonable tactical conclusion. Still, what if he took the attack as evidence that the Americans had changed sides? They had, on orders from Sixth Fleet, but he had no way of knowing that.

And what were her options? To disobey Sixth Fleet once again? To let the submarine run past her, try to make the approach on the British ship, and attack? Or intervene, take a shot at Merker as he passed abeam of her?

No. Regardless of what Sixth Fleet said, this wasn't their fight. Then it came down to a question of which was the more treacherous ally. From her point of view, it would be the Brits. Not only had Admiral Richardson lied to her, but he had also threatened the safety of her ship. Merker, on the other hand, while he had taken a torpedo shot at them, had at least taken a step toward peace by executing a destruct command. In the end, for her, it boiled down to a simple question: Which one of her allies was more likely to kill her?

"Put us on an intercept course toward the British ship. We'll stand by to assist survivors." The question of from which nation was still up in the air.

U-504

"The forward torpedo doors won't open." The weapons officer shrugged, a fatalistic gesture that conveyed more than his words. "The stress on the hull, damage to the control circuits—I can't tell at this point. We're trouble-shooting, but . . ."

"But you don't think you'll find the problem," Merker

finished. "Or if you do, it's going to be beyond the onboard repair capabilities."

The weapons officer nodded. "The stern tubes seem to be still operable, but the two remaining torpedoes are stored forward. I may be able to shift them out, but it's going to take some time. Even assuming there's sufficient hull integrity to have prevented the forward tubes from flooding. If not, opening the tube to extract the torpedo could scuttle us."

Merker nodded. "The tubes-flooded indicator is shot?" It figured.

"As I said, we could try it."

Merker shook his head. "No." He hesitated for a moment, contemplating the next move.

U-504 was fatally injured. Without weapons, and with limited maneuverability, there was little danger she could pose to the British task force. Still, there was one option left. He felt despair and anguish seep away as he made his decision, replaced by an oddly peaceful calm. "Prepare to abandon ship."

The weapons officer looked startled. Merker heard a small movement behind him, from Ehrlich. "Kapitan, we can still return to port. I think I can guarantee you that much," the weapons officer said.

Merker shook his head. "I won't risk this crew anymore. Even if we could get her back to the shipyard, there's no chance they could repair her. You know that. The hull is too warped."

And if this boat is going to die—and her captain along with it—let it be doing what they were both built and bred to do. Not torn apart by welding torches and court-martials, but fighting at sea.

"Prepare to abandon ship," he repeated.

The weapons officer nodded slowly. "I'll assemble the crew. Surface?"

"Shallow," Merker said. He noted the startled look that passed across the weapons officer's face as the implications of the statement started to sink in.

"*Kapitan,* you can't—"

"I can," Merker said harshly.

USS RAMAGE

"Reverse your course," Admiral Richardson ordered. "Clear the area immediately."

"I'm maneuvering to avoid a submarine," Bailey said carefully. "Admiral, I understand I'm under your operational control, but my overriding duty is to the safety of my ship."

"Dammit, Bailey, stay out of this."

"I am staying out of it, Admiral." *In more ways than one,* she added silently. *In more ways than one.*

U-504

The remnants of the U-boat crew crowded the control room, clustering around the base of the ladder leading to the conning tower. They trailed down the central passageway like ants, the able-bodied assisting the wounded. Merker had insisted that those who had died fighting the fire be left where they had fallen. After all, it was only fitting that their final resting place be near the boat they'd tried to protect.

"Ready to proceed with abandon ship," the weapons officer said. "*Kapitan,* request permission to remain aboard?"

"Denied." Merker saw fear, frustration, and guilt chase each other across the other man's face. He softened his tone. "Someone needs to take charge of the crew. It'll have to be you."

"I would prefer to remain aboard," the weapons officer said.

Merker shook his head. "I won't allow you to do that. Your duty is to these men, not to me."

"You're going to ram her, aren't you?" Ehrlich said suddenly. "*Kapitan,* you can't do that alone."

"I can."

"No. You'll need help. You can't manage both the helm

and the plane controls at the same time." Ehrlich shook his head. "As your second-in-command, I require that you allow me to assist you."

Merker turned back to the weapons officer. "At this depth, you'll only have about ten meters of water above you. The survival hoods are capable of handling that easily." He gestured at the two packages two of the sailors were carrying. "As soon as you get on the surface, inflate the lifeboats. Get as much of the crew in them as you can. Some of them may have to hang off the sides, but it won't be for long."

The weapons officer took a deep breath and tried one more time. "*Kapitan*, I—"

"Go." Merker pointed at the ladder. "The men don't have much time."

"Range to the British ship, two thousand meters," Ehrlich said. "*Kapitan*, they need to leave now."

The weapons officer finally capitulated. He grabbed the nearest sailor by the shoulder and shoved him toward the ladder. "Go. Remember the procedures. Breathe out continually to prevent your lungs from exploding on the way up."

The sailor needed no more encouragement. He scrambled up the ladder, pausing to undog the interior pressure lock, then clambered up the side. Five of his crew members followed him, then another five. Once the sea lock was full, they dogged the lower hatch shut below them.

The sound of water rushing into the lockout compartment was clearly audible in the control room. The remaining men stood uneasily. Ten minutes later, they repeated the procedure, again and again, until the entire crew except Ehrlich and Merker had evacuated the submarine. And the dead.

"You remember how to handle the deck controls?" Merker asked, for something to say.

Ehrlich nodded. "It hasn't been that long."

"Very well, then." Merker took his seat before the planesman's controls and belted himself in. Ehrlich moved away from his plotting table and took the opposite station, handling the deck controls. "I should tell you that I—"

"Orders, *Kapitan*?" Ehrlich interrupted. Merker noted

the slight quaver in the other man's voice. Regardless of
how bravely he'd acted, he was still a young man.

"Keep us at this depth," he said. "The ship draws only
twenty-eight meters of water, at most."

"Will it work?"

"I don't know," Merker started to answer. Then he realized that he owed this young officer one final lie. "I'm
certain of it," he said calmly.

USS RAMAGE

"Clear the area or I'll kill you." The admiral's voice left
no doubt in her mind that he'd do exactly that.

"You've tried that before. It didn't work then." She
glanced back at the tactical screen and saw the U-boat closing on the admiral's ship. "What makes you think it would
now?"

The U-boat was only five hundred yards away from the
British boat now, closing on her at a loud, ear-shattering
ten knots. How he managed to maintain neutral buoyancy
and yet guide the submarine toward the boat, she'd never
understand. The British ship was on a reciprocal bearing at
twenty knots.

The rooster tail behind the submarine's periscope was
clearly visible from this distance. She saw a streak of oil
churning in its wake, giving the white water a sickly gleam-
ing tinge. Large-caliber machine guns chattered across the
distance separating them, evidence that the British officers
had decided that the submarine was too shallow for a torpedo shot. Two helicopters buzzed around futilely.

"Targeting mode," one of the operations specialists announced suddenly. He turned to her.

"Captain, they've got their fire control radar lit off.
We're illuminated," the electronics warfare technician said.

"CIWS in full automatic," she ordered.

"Ahead of you, Captain," Collins said. She pointed to
the two firing keys already locked into position on the
close-in weapons systems panel. "For all the good it will
do us."

"It just has to work as advertised," she snapped. "Just once."

"Port lookout reports missile launch from the British ship," Collins said rapidly. "Harpoon—Captain, suggest we maneuver to bow-on to the missile."

"Ten degrees off bow-on," she said. "As small a profile as we can manage without masking the CIWS and the guns."

"Five-inch gun tracking now. They have a lock. Fire one—fire two," Collins reported. The heavy thud of aft guns shook the ship. Ten seconds later, Collins said, "Evaluate as misses."

"It's up to CIWS now." She studied the screen as the symbol for a missile popped into being. "Hard right rudder."

"Fifteen seconds," the operations specialist said. "Ten seconds. Nine, eight . . ."

The sudden chatter of CIWS activating sounded like a machine gun. Shooting two thousand rounds a second of depleted uranium pellets, the self-contained radar tracking and targeting system detected the incoming missile, evaluated its parameters and speed as matching threat profile, and spat out a steady stream of bullets at it, automatically tracking its own trajectory and self-correcting onto target. But at this range, even if it managed a direct hit on the incoming massive antiship missile, the rain of fiery debris would cause significant damage.

"Got it!" A brief cheer echoed around combat. Five seconds later, the first chunks of debris and melting metal pelted *Ramage*'s superstructure.

"We're hit aft!" Collins shouted. "The flight deck— Captain, damage control team eight deploying."

"Captain, missile away from the British ship. It's another—damn!"

"What is it?"

"It's not another Harpoon, Captain. I don't know what— I've lost contact." Collins looked worried.

The electronics warfare panel started chattering an alarm. "Tomahawk," the technician shouted. "Jesus, they've gone for land attack."

"At us?" She realized how idiotic the question sounded the moment she asked it.

"No," Collins said, as though the question hadn't been ridiculous. "Whatever it was, it's headed for the mainland. To Germany."

U-504

The British ship was now too close to provide any discrete target on the sonar. Sonar energy reflected back from the massive metallic hull blanked the U-boat's display, minor lobing into odd shots of noise spokes off the main bearing. It filled the screen, shimmering and wavering with an eerie phosphorescence, as if it were the only light left in the control room. Above him, the counterdetection equipment panel was black and silent. Other indicators spanning the control room were the same, with the exception of a few glaring lights that still screamed of fatal malfunctions within vital systems.

Merker kept his eyes riveted on the course heading indicator. They could almost navigate by sound alone, as the steady thump of the cruiser's propeller beat through the hull. Just a few more seconds. It was surreal, too large a moment to comprehend. Even if he wanted to, at this late moment, there was no way to stop the forty-five hundred tons of U-boat hurtling through the ocean at the thin hull of the British boat.

At the last moment, he stood up from the controls. He walked over to Ehrlich's station, barely able to keep his footing on the tilting deck. He touched the younger man on the arm, drew him up, and drew him into a close embrace.

USS RAMAGE

"Tomahawk. What warhead are they using on the ships?" she demanded. "Conventional or—"

Collins looked pale. "They've had nuclear capabilities almost as long as we have." Her voice was soft with horror. "Would they use it against Germany?"

Bailey thought back to the last war games NSA had modeled on the Continent. The results had indicated that without the U.S. deterrent presence there, the island nation of Britain would tend to use tactical nuclear weapons at an early point in the conflict. Too many generations of English, Scottish, and Irish soldiers had battered themselves bloody in the shallow waters of the European coast for Britain to replay an invasion scenario. The next time, it was generally agreed, Great Britain would make sure that the end result was a foregone conclusion.

"Yes." She felt the shaking start in the knees, move up her body, and extend to her fingers. It was more than cold, or exhaustion. The sheer horror of what they were witnessing had finally sunk in. "If they've got them, they will use them."

U-504

Merker had miscalculated slightly. The U-boat's bow moved forward under the bow of the British ship. Instead of ramming into the area just aft of the sonar dome, the British ship cut across the midsection of the U-boat. The results, if not tactically what he had intended, were the same.

The sonar dome snapped off first, leaving a gaping, six-foot-wide entry for the seawater. The hatch at the end of the compartment was secured, holding the salt water temporarily at bay. In the next few seconds, it would make no difference.

The bow of the ship followed shortly, slicing through the part of the U-boat the sonar dome had already crumpled. The U-boat's hull, a titanium alloy, had a tensile strength slightly greater than that of the aluminum and steel mixture used in the lower portions of the keel. The plating sheared off, with the strakes and keel member resisting only slightly longer. The keel speared through the U-boat like a fork, leading the way for the rest of the mass of the ship.

Despite the U-boat's greater structural strength, it was no contest. Eighty thousand tons of warship versus forty-five hundred tons of U-boat. As every sailor knew, tonnage counts.

As the cruiser's bow dissected the U-boat, the forward half of the smaller ship rolled to starboard, turning the bulkhead into the deck. Merker and Ehrlich were thrown across the compartment, smashing into the equipment-studded wall.

The noise was ungodly. Everything prior to that point, including the scrape of the wooden debris across their hull when the United States had first detected them, paled into insignificance. This was not damage, it was death. Merker screamed, one arm still thrown around Ehrlich. The other man's head lolled at an unnatural angle, and blood trickled from a corner of his mouth. Ehrlich's eyes stared at the overhead, empty and unseeing.

Merker fought for consciousness, dimly aware of some survival instinct insisting that he do something, anything. Pain was a distant sensation, perceived more as a dull, throbbing background, uncannily similar to the beat of the propeller they'd heard just moments before. He tried to focus, tried to see, but the black haze shot with red creeping around the edges of his vision blanked out most of the scene. He screamed one last time, an angry, defiant protest, before he lost consciousness.

The back hatch of the compartment quivered, holding for a few moments against the flood of seawater beating against it, before it gave up. It collapsed, tearing away part of the bulkhead, and three thousand pounds of seawater per second flooded into the control room. Before it reached the two men, both were dead.

USS RAMAGE

"He rammed her." Carlisle looked over at her, as though making sure she'd heard. "It had to be. There were no weapons in the water, just this ungodly . . ." He pointed at the speaker overhead.

"Captain. The starboard lookout reports two lifeboats in

the water. They're not from the British ship. Do you think—''

She cut him off. "Get us alongside them."

U-504

The U-boat's weapons officer hauled the last sailor into the brilliant fluorescent orange lifeboat. Twenty men per boat, with a few others dangling off the edges still in the sea-water. Sharks, hypothermia—his mind automatically ran through a litany of dangers.

A movement off to his right caught his attention. A red light, then a green one popped into view, hazy and indistinct in the fog and sea spray. A ship. Could it see them? Was it prepared to render assistance, or would the chatter of machine guns finishing off the attack, seeking vengeance, be the last sound he heard?

He glanced down at his shattered arm, bones protruding through the dark blue, wet fabric of his uniform, and decided it didn't matter.

USS RAMAGE

"There they are." The port lookout pointed at the raft.

"Small boats in the water." She watched as the ship's motor whale boat swung out over the ocean and dropped gently on the surface of the sea, the five crew members hanging above it from the ropes and monkey knots. "Get them aboard, then we'll decide what to do."

U-504

The Americans. The weapons officer watched the small boat approach. They might survive long enough to face an international war crimes trial after all. For a moment, he wondered if that were preferable.

USS RAMAGE

"Captain." The port lookout touched her on the arm to catch her attention. "They're asking for you back in combat immediately."

She tore her eyes away from the scene below, with the five U.S. crew members gently hoisting German sailors out of the lifeboats. She turned to the OOD. "Keep them under guard. In the wardroom." This time there was no need to debrief her prisoners. The acoustic evidence of what had happened was all too clear.

Seconds later, she was striding into combat. "What?"

Collins pointed at the large-screen display. "You need to see this." The missile symbol on the display had veered away from its steady north-northeast course and was heading due north.

"When did it change course?" she asked.

"Just after the explosion. I think the U-boat rammed the British ship before the seeker head on the Tomahawk took over guidance. With the ship out of commission, the missile wandered off-course. If it's anything like ours, it should initiate self-destruct twenty seconds after it loses command guidance."

"Ah." She pointed at the radarscope. A bright blast of light lit up the area formerly occupied by the missile symbol. "No more Tomahawk."

"As soon as the last survivor is on board, get us headed north at flank speed. I want to be out of the North Sea before both sides start shooting at us."

"TAO," the weapons specialist said suddenly. "Unidentified air contact from the south. Range, fifty miles; altitude, twenty thousand feet—no, ten thousand feet . . ." The technician turned away from his console and stared at them both, his face pale. "Speed in excess of Mach two. Captain, it's a Tomahawk land attack cruise missile. An *American* one."

"What the . . ." Suddenly she remembered what lay just south of the minefield. Not more German U-boats intent on the destruction of the British fleet, nor British warships equally determined to wipe the last U-boat from the face of the earth. American units—American ballistic-missile submarines. "Course?"

"Germany," the technician said simply. "It's headed to Germany. And I don't think this one's going to miss."

"*Ramage,* this is Sixth Fleet. How copy?" The voice sounded tired.

She picked up the mike. "You bastards."

"We may be, but we're *American* bastards. You seem to understand the difference."

"Oh, I do. I do. I'm not so sure the American public is going to."

"Commander, I'll excuse your rudeness on the grounds that you're inexperienced and overstressed. Now listen very carefully. It's crucial that you understand what just happened.

"We've just finished minesweeping the Strait of Gibraltar. Within the next twenty-four hours, an American battle group will be joining you in the North Sea. Since the British have fired a nuclear warhead at Germany, it's essential that we stop this conflict before it escalates. For your information, the United States will be issuing a carefully worded statement condemning the use of tactical nuclear weapons while announcing our support for our NATO allies."

"The British launched . . ." she stopped, suddenly seeing the entire picture. "Just tell me one thing: Did you know that they were going to launch a nuclear warhead at Germany? Or were you planning on having our boomer launch one anyway, and then letting the British take the blame? That's the whole point of submarines, isn't it? That they're deniable."

"I don't know what you're talking about." The circuit fell silent.

Twenty-four hours later, the battle group slipped into the data net, took control of the track symbology, and began quietly rearranging history.

30

10 MARCH 2002

USS *RAMAGE*

"They're going to get away with it." Boston handed her a yellow roll of news messages.

She took them and skimmed through the traffic. The world community, convinced that Britain had used nuclear weapons on Germany, was appalled. Pressure was brought from all corners onto both nations to end the conflict immediately. The North Koreans, quietly convinced at the highest levels that the United States had actually initiated the attack, withdrew back across the border, still rattling spears and threatening immediate invasion for public consumption, but in reality resigned to a continuing stalemate with their southern half. She handed the messages back to him without comment.

"What do we do?" Boston asked. His face was lined and tired, older than it had been when they'd left San Diego on the C-141 transport. "*We* know what happened."

She studied him for a moment, wondering what answer she could give him. It would have been easier if she'd been able to decide exactly what to do herself. Finally she shook her head. "We need to buy some time. This situation—it's more than any of us bargained for. All of us have some decisions to make, and they're not things that should be decided quickly." She reached a decision then and turned to Collins. "Secure all communications circuits except for one. I'm going to talk to Sixth Fleet, then we'll take that one down as well. Talk to the navigator and get us headed out of here. We're going home.''

Ramage headed north. She watched the minesweepers criss-cross in front of her, following carefully in their wake. Bailey brought up one circuit long enough to coordinate sweeping a clear channel out of the North Sea. The subsequent evolution was coordinated almost by telepathy. She ignored the insistent demands on their distress circuit as well as requests for information via the unclassified bridge-to-bridge circuits. *Ramage* followed silently in the mine-sweepers' wake.

The battle group stayed south, still occupied with hunting down the few German submarines that hadn't surfaced to surrender. From what she could tell, they would be finished within a few days. With the wolf-pack commander dead, the German General Staff was backpedaling furiously, claiming a group of dissident navy officers had single-handedly deployed the submarines, activated the ancient minefield, and started the conflict because of their own political views. The World Bank, concerned over the possible damage that would result from a German collapse, pressured the rest of the world into accepting the bold-faced lies.

Finally, the last sliver of land disappeared from the horizon. Ahead was the Atlantic Ocean, two weeks of relative peace and quiet as they crossed the Atlantic, en route to Norfolk. That would be enough time, she decided. Time to decide how to answer the charges that were certain to face her, and time to prepare the crew for what would happen.

Sixth Fleet had made some tentative request that she receive a senior officer on board. Just before *Ramage* turned west toward the United States, she brought up the circuit again, briefly, to politely decline.

24 MARCH 2002:
VACAPES OPERATING AREA

Two weeks later, fifteen miles off the coast of Virginia, Bailey secured the radars and climbed up to the highest point on the superstructure. She took out her cellular telephone and dialed a familiar number.

"A small reception committee," Bailey commented, surveying the few people gathered on the pier to greet the ship. "We're too crazy for them to let dependents on the pier, I suppose."

Lieutenant Boston tried to smile. "I guess we'll know soon enough. None of them is armed—as far as I can tell. Your people here?" He glanced over at her.

She nodded. Although she hadn't explained to any of them what she'd planned, she suspected Boston would guess. And Collins. The other woman had spent two days consumed by a dark, almost suicidal depression, then emerged one day her normal, aggressive self. Collins hadn't discussed her mood—or her decision—with anyone, but Bailey suspected that it would be the same as her own.

The gangway was moved quickly against the ship, far more expeditiously than she'd ever seen the maneuver executed before. Within five minutes of bringing the ship alongside, the first harsh rasp of metal against the deck of the ship indicated they were once again connected to the outside world.

She was standing on the quarterdeck, waiting. A small bag containing most of her personal gear was in her hand. At the bottom of the gangplank, a mixed group of civilians and military personnel milled around uncertainly, as if deciding who would board the ship first. Finally, a familiar figure detached itself from the crowd and climbed up the rickety metal steps.

The quarterdeck watch looked at her uncertainly. "Ma'am?"

She tried to smile. "It's okay. I know him."

The tall, lean figure paused at the end of the gangway,

waiting permission to come aboard. "Hello, Captain."

She turned to the quarterdeck watch. "Log Mr. Jim At-chinson, of the National Security Agency, on board."

The man nodded, and stepped down the last step to the deck. "I think we should talk."

Forty minutes later, she was trying to decide whether to laugh or cry. "You can't be serious?" she said incredu-lously.

"I'm afraid I am." He shot her a rueful look. "Calling the newspaper right before you pulled in—I have to tell you, that didn't make it any easier to sell. I had to call in some serious favors to get the story killed. Fortunately, the editor is an old friend of mine."

"You shouldn't have. One way or the other, it'll come out."

"At the right time, maybe. Maybe not. It can't come from you. Not without your facing court-martial charges for disclosing classified information." He paused for a mo-ment, then added as an afterthought, "You'd lose your job at NSA, too. If that happened."

She stared at the deck. "You think that matters to me now? If you do, then there's damned little you understand about me at all."

"I understood you better than you know before you left," he answered. "Why do you think they left you in command out there? Because you're a reserve commander? Not likely." He shook his head. "We knew it was start-ing—we knew about the Tabun, too, just as Richardson suspected. The only way to keep the situation under control was to use the assets we had in position."

"Me."

"You. We didn't plan for you to be there—not like that, at least—but it worked out for the best. Listen, this is the only way out of this, Jer. For what my advice is worth to you, I suggest you go along with it. Terry Intanglio can't bail you out of this one."

"What about the rest of the crew? And my officers?"

"Same provisions apply. As of twenty minutes ago, you're all certified naval heroes."

She shook her head. "I'm not sure how that follows from disobeying orders."

He handed her a sheet of paper. "A presidential pardon can do just about anything. Although, for the record, I don't think your future in the naval reserves is too bright."

"So what happens now?"

"Just what I said before." He glanced at his watch. "You have about one hour to get into dress blues. A change-of-command ceremony—I'll be presenting the medal for the president—and then you head back to San Diego. That is, if you agree to keep your mouth shut about this."

She looked around the wardroom, studying the plaques along the wall. Carved along the bottom of the different ships' insignia were old naval adages. Words about strength, courage, and victory. "The French have a medal for it, you know."

"For what?"

"For disobeying orders. When it's the right thing to do."

NORFOLK, VIRGINIA

Four hours later, she stepped into the CNN studio. "I think I have a story you ought to know about."

THE NORTH SEA

Another signal. The mine's sensitive acoustic receivers thrummed, breaking it immediately into its constituent parts. It didn't take long—this time, instead of the complicated waveform of radiated noise from a ship, the sound was a simple, pure tone.

Another frequency followed. Preset relays clicked over, responding to the command. At the base of the torpedo, a small circuit switched off. It was now just another chunk of metal buried in mud.